Small towns are notorious for secrets ... but what if you bring your secrets with you?

Amy Adams arrives in Northpoint, Wisconsin on a Greyhound bus. Small towns are well known for not taking to strangers, but THIS stranger decides to stay.

Amy has a look around and to her, it 'feels' like home. She rents a cabin in the woods outside of town and proceeds to look for a place to open a store. Renting to own from one of the locals, she soon finds herself making friends and making waves. She won't discuss where she is from and has nothing to say about her past.

People are extremely curious. This Southern Belle has them talking.

Abby Shipman, the Chief of Police in this neck of the woods, is intrigued by the decidedly mysterious and straight redheaded whirlwind that has blown into town. It's strange that she won't talk about her past, and she is certainly uncomfortable around Abby ... or is it cops in general?

A K'Anne Meinel novel

Also by K'Anne Meinel:

Novels in Paperback:

SHIPS *CompanionSHIP, FriendSHIP,*
RelationSHIP
Long Distance Romance
Children of Another Mother
Erotica
The Claim
Bikini's Are Dangerous
The Complete Series
Germanic
Malice Masterpieces 1
The First Five Books
Represented
Timed Romance
Malice Masterpieces 2
Books Six through Ten
The Journey Home
Out at the Inn
Shorts

Anthology Volume 1
Lawyered
Malice Masterpieces 3
Books Eleven through Fifteen
Blown Away
Blown Away
The Alternate Cover
Small Town Angel
Pirated Love
Doctored
Veil of Silence
Malice Masterpieces 4
Books Sixteen through Twenty
The Outsider
Pirated Heart
Vetted
Recombinant Love

Novellas in Paperback:

Mysterious Malice (Book 1)
Meticulous Malice (Book 2)
Mistaken Malice (Book 3)
Malicious Malice (Book 4)
Masterful Malice (Book 5)
Matrimonial Malice (Book 6)
Mourning Malice (Book 7)
Murderous Malice (Book 8)
Mental Malice (Book 9)
Menacing Malice (Book 10)
Minor Malice (Book 11)
Morally Malice (Book 12)
Morose Malice (Book 13)

Melancholy Malice (Book 14)
Mad Malice (Book 15)
Macabre Malice (Book 16)
Marinating Malice (Book 17)
Macerating Malice (Book 18)
Minacious Malice (Book 19)
Meddlesome Malice (Book 20)
Meandering Malice (Book 21)
Vaquera Safica (Spanish)
Surfista Safica (Spanish)
ケーアンヌ・マイネル (Japanese)
Maniacal Malice (Book 22)

Pocket Paperbacks:

Mysterious Malice (Book 1)
Sapphic Surfer
Sapphic Cowgirl
Meticulous Malice (Book 2)
Mistaken Malice (Book 3)
Malicious Malice (Book 4)
Masterful Malice (Book 5)
Matrimonial Malice (Book 6)
Mourning Malice (Book 7)
Murderous Malice (Book 8)

Mental Malice (Book 9)
Menacing Malice (Book 10)
Minor Malice (Book 11)
Morally Malice (Book 12)
Morose Malice (Book 13)
Melancholy Malice (Book 14)
Mad Malice (Book 15)
Macabre Malice (Book 16)
Marinating Malice (Book 17)

In E-Book Format:
Short Stories

Fantasy
Wet & Wet Again
Family Night
Quickie ~ Against the Car
Quickie ~ Against the Wall
Quickie ~ Over the Couch
Mile High Club
Quickie ~ Under the Pier
Heel or Heal
Kiss
Family Night 2
Beach Dreams
Internet Dreamers

Snoggered
The Rockhound
Stolen
Agitated
Love of my LIFE
Quickie in an Elevator,
GOING DOWN?
Into the Garden
The Book Case
The Other Women
Menage a WHAT?

Novellas

Bikini's are Dangerous
Kept
Ghostly Love
Bikini's are Dangerous 2
On the Parkway
Stable Affair
Sapphic Surfer
Bikini's are Dangerous 3
Bikini's are Dangerous 4
Bikini's are Dangerous 5
Mysterious Malice (Book 1)
Meticulous Malice (Book 2)
Mistaken Malice (Book 3)
Malicious Malice (Book 4)
Masterful Malice (Book 5)
Matrimonial Malice (Book 6)
Mourning Malice (Book 7)
Murderous Malice (Book 8)
Sapphic Cowgirl
Sapphic Cowboi

Mental Malice (Book 9)
Menacing Malice (Book 10)
Charming Thief
~Snake Island~
Charming Thief
~Diamonds are a Girls Best Friend~
Minor Malice (Book 11)
Morally Malice (Book 12)
Morose Malice (Book 13)
Melancholy Malice (Book 14)
Mad Malice (Book 15)
Macabre Malice (Book 16)
Marinating Malice (Book 17)
Macerating Malice (Book 18)
Minacious Malice (Book 19)
Sayyida
Meddlesome Malice (Book 20)
Meandering Malice (Book 21)
Maniacal Malice (Book 22)

E-Book Novels

SHIPS *CompanionSHIP, FriendSHIP,*
RelationSHIP
Erotica Volume 1
Long Distance Romance
Bikini's Are Dangerous
The Complete Series
Malice Masterpieces
The First Five Books
To Love a Shooting Star
Children of Another Mother
Germanic
Blown Away
Blown Away
The Alternate Cover

The Claim
Represented
Timed Romance
Malice Masterpieces 2
Books Six through Ten
The Journey Home
Out at the Inn
Anthology Volume 1
Lawyered
Malice Masterpieces 3
Books Eleven through Fifteen
Small Town Angel
Pirated Love
Doctored

Veil of Silence

E-Book Novels Continued
Malice Masterpieces 4
Books Sixteen through Twenty
The Outsider
Pirated Heart
Vetted
Recombinant Love

Videos

Biography of Books	Sapphic Cowboi
Ships	Timed Romance
Sapphic Surfer	Readings (SHIPS)
Ghostly Love	Doctored
Long Distance Romance	Veil of Silence
Germanic	She's Coming (The Outsider short)
Sensual Sapphic	It's Coming (The Outsider short)
Sapphic Cowgirl	The Outsider
Couples	Vetted
Lie Next To Me	

Dedicated to anyone who
thinks I'm writing about them.
I am.

K'A. M.

K'ANNE MEINEL

SMALL TOWN

ANGEL

ISBN-13: 978-0692528785
ISBN-10: 0692528784

2nd edition copyright © February 2018 by K'Anne Meinel
Copyright © September 2015 by K'Anne Meinel

K'Anne Meinel is available for comments at KAnneMeinel@aim.com as well as on Facebook @ http://www.facebook.com/K.Anne.Meinel.Fan.Page, Google + @ https://plus.google.com/u/2/+KAnneMeinel, LinkedIn @ https://www.linkedin.com/in/k-anne-meinel-a026385a, or her blog @ http://kannemeinel.wordpress.com/ or on Twitter @ https://twitter.com/KAnneMeinel, or on her website @ www.kannemeinel.com if you would like to follow her to find out about stories and book's releases.

www.shadoepublishing.com

ShadoePublishing@gmail.com

Shadoe Publishing is a United States of America company

Cover by: K'Anne Meinel @ Shadoe Publishing

SMALL TOWN ANGEL

PUBLISHER'S NOTE

This is a work of fiction. Names, characters, places, and incidents are the product of the author's imagination or are used fictitiously, and any resemblance to actual persons, living or dead, business establishments, events, or locales is entirely coincidental.

The publisher does not have any control over and does not assume any responsibility for author or third-party Web sites or their content.

CHAPTER ONE

As the bus pulled into Port Washington, she wondered if she should get off at this stop or go further up the coast. The bus *was* pretty crowded, having taken on a lot of passengers in Milwaukee, but Amy decided to wait it out, see where it went. She knew the end of the line for this particular section of her journey would be Green Bay but she was searching. Searching for something. Anything. She wasn't sure what, but her instincts told her to sit down and bear with the fates, to put up with the smelly, obese woman who had gotten on the bus back in Milwaukee and overflowed her seat and into Amy's seat. It seemed as if the woman hadn't washed herself in days. *And eaten garlic right before she got on the transport*, Amy grinned to herself. Still, she was polite to the woman. She probably had no idea that she smelled or that she even was taking up part of Amy's seat on the cramped bus. Amy was willing to put up with it. Something kept her in her seat and not just the fact that she was packed in like a sardine.

She watched as more passengers got on and off in Port Washington. The large, noisy bus took off once again and headed up the Eastern coast of Wisconsin toward The Thumb, the appendage-like shape of land that stuck out into the large inland sea, Lake Michigan. They headed into Door County, and the towns got smaller. These smaller towns enchanted her as they pulled in and out of them, dropping off and picking up other passengers. She didn't mind the constant start and stop; it was fascinating to people-watch, to see the different sights, and the changing fall leaves. Occasionally they pulled into a town where she caught glimpses of Lake Michigan. All her life the lake had been nothing more than a feature on a map and now she was *actually* seeing it.

Slowly the bus emptied as more people got off rather than on it. At Sturgeon Bay, they crossed a bridge that separated the 'mainland' from an island on the appendage. They continued north on Hwy 57 through places like Whitefish Bay, Bailey's Harbor, and Moonlight Bay. Later she would become familiar with Egg Harbor, Sister Bay, and other such intriguing and unique names. It was at Northpoint that her inner voice said to get off the bus. Her ticket was paid in full for Green Bay but something told her to get up, get out, and the driver obliged her. It wasn't his lookout where his passengers disembarked, and he helped her get her large bag out from under the bus. Northpoint was his 'turnaround' point anyway. The northern most point on The Thumb where he would turn the bus and go south once again on Hwy 42 this time and hit those little towns that relied on this service. He watched as she hitched her large backpack and managed to pull along behind her the large bag he had just pulled out from the luggage compartment. Fortunately, it was on wheels and had an extendable handle. He wondered if she carried a cast iron kitchen sink in the thing since it was so heavy. He shook his head as he began to pack the couple of bags his new passengers handed him and forgot about her.

Amy headed for a sign she had seen from the bus; the Duck and Swan Inn was charming looking. She knew since it was a bed and breakfast that it would be expensive, but she was tired, and she was cranky. After sleeping several days in various bus seats, she needed a good night's sleep as well as a nice hot bath. She rubbed her arms from the coolness of the evening as she looked around wondering if this was it; this was her last destination. Would this be her new home?

"May I help you?" a pleasant faced woman answered her ringing of the small discreet bell on the counter at the front of the home she had walked into. She had hesitated to just walk in to the inn, but an equally discrete sign had invited her in, and she hoped it was okay.

"Hello, I'm Amy Adams, and I was hopin' you had a room?" she asked with a pleasant smile, returning the one the woman was giving her.

"Oh, you timed it right. It's the end of the season, and we have a few open now during the week. Good thing you didn't come this weekend or there would be nothing in town available; would you like one with a fireplace?" she asked.

"Oh, a fireplace sounds lovely," Amy enthused.

"And how many nights?" she asked as she pushed a registration card across the small counter.

Amy filled it out quickly, and with neat handwriting, the woman noted. "A couple of nights?" Amy asked hopefully.

"That will be fine, but we do need the room for the weekend as we are full up," she replied as she read the details Amy had filled in. "I'll need payment up front and a picture I.D?"

Amy was ready for her and handed over both a credit card and a driver's license, which the lady took and processed efficiently. "I'm Sarah Katzenburger, and me and my husband own this house," she introduced herself as the credit card went through the little pin pad and printed out a receipt for Amy to sign.

"It's a lovely house," Amy commented as she looked around at the homey touches and antique look of the saltbox house. From the outside it was weathered, probably from the storms that must occur due to the lake.

"Well, breakfast is from six to nine a.m. and I can arrange a lunch or dinner at any of our fine restaurants around town if you are interested," she said brightly as she reached for an antique key and handed it with a receipt to Amy. She eyed her guest trying to figure out what a woman alone and with a southern accent would be doing this far north at this time of year.

"That sounds fine," Amy answered and ignored the inquiring look. She knew most people wouldn't ask too many personal questions until they felt more comfortable with a stranger, and she hid behind that for now. Tomorrow might be another day, and the woman curious, "I'll need to find someplace tonight to eat dinner," she commented with a broad hint.

"Well, the burgers over at Chuckies' are fantastic, but he also does a full meal of steak and veggies," she added when Amy first wrinkled her nose at 'burgers.' Grease didn't appeal after a long journey with only bus stop food to tide her over, but a full meal would sit just right.

"That sounds good, um where is it?" Amy asked.

She listened as Mrs. Katzenburger gave her a brief layout of the town and where Chuckies' was in location to the inn. Thanking her hostess, she climbed the stairs to the room that was inscribed on the key and found to her delight not only did it have a fireplace but the wood already laid. She put down her heavy suitcase and looked with delight at the private bathroom. She was looking forward to that deep claw footed tub as she quickly washed up, ran a comb through her thick red hair and lightly freshened her makeup. Looking in the mirror, she examined her detested freckles that had mostly faded along with her summer tan. She had smooth skin otherwise, brilliant green eyes, a fine narrow nose, and luscious 'kissable' lips. She thought her eyes were her best feature, while her eyebrows delicately outlined them along with the double set of eyelashes that made it easy for her not to wear mascara. Most redheads had light brown or red brows and lashes, but not her. Amy's were dark and clearly outlined her features. Though she had been teased over it her entire life, she liked the way she looked. One more run through with the comb and her hair was neat once again, and she headed out of the delightful room she found herself in, locking it behind her and pocketing the key.

Sarah watched as the new guest headed out for the evening and wondered about her once again. She seemed pleasant enough but a southerner, which was going to create a bit of gossip in this touristy town.

Amy found Chuckie's easily enough and was pleased at the selection on the menu written above the bar. She ordered a steak, home fries, a salad, and a Corona and asked if she could sit in a booth. The bartender assured her she could and that the entire meal would be brought to her when it was done. He had frowned when she said she wanted it well done, but her pretty smile with the hint of a dimple charmed him. She took her beer and headed for an out of the way spot where she could watch the restaurant/bar and read the newspaper she had purchased.

Amy started with the want ads and continued on through the 'for sale' ones, trying to get a feel for the area. It covered all up and down the coast, and the towns were all unfamiliar to her. She made a mental note to purchase a map of Door County tomorrow when she was well rested.

"Who's that?" a tall dark headed woman asked as she sat on a stool at the bar. The bartender didn't ask her what she wanted as he poured a beer from the tap and slid it down to her where she expertly caught it in her hand and took a sip.

"Tourist," he grunted, as he wiped the moisture from the well-polished bar.

She nodded as she glanced curiously at the woman from the reflection of the mirror and then quickly averted her eyes to the other patrons of the bar, classifying them by "tourist" or "townie" in moments. Her eyes were drawn back to the redhead though as the light above her booth hit the strands of her hair most becomingly. She could appreciate a good-looking woman, but when the woman either felt herself being observed or just looked up from her newspaper, the brunette hastily concentrated back on her draft.

"Eats?" the bartender asked and at her nod he wrote up a tag for the kitchen and picked up the tray that the redhead had ordered and gave it to one of the waitresses.

"This looks delicious!" Amy enthused as the waitress laid it out for her. It smelled heavenly, and her mouth was watering. She cut a few slices of the steak, delicately put down her knife, and picked up her fork to eat them along with the fries. She reached across the table and applied ketchup to her plate so she could dip. She carefully cut up her salad so she could eat convenient mouthfuls of it. Her left hand repeatedly returned to her lap where she had delicately put her napkin. She unconsciously showed off her manners and breeding to the establishment and anyone watching her.

Amy really enjoyed this first sit-down meal she had in days and when the waitress returned she ordered a second bottle of beer, relaxing over the newspaper, reading it from front to back. She glanced up occasionally to look at the other patrons and noticed one or two observing her as well, but her eyes glanced over them and kept going.

She felt delightfully full as she handed over her credit card and waited for the waitress to return with the slip to be signed. She had no problem leaving a twenty percent tip as she filled in the blanks, kept her copy, stowing it and the extra copy of the bill in her wallet. As she got up she carefully folded the newspaper back, tucked it under her arm, and headed out of the restaurant watched by a few people including the brunette who was eating her dinner at the bar.

CHAPTER TWO

"Hello, I'm lookin' for a realtor?" Amy asked the next morning as she presented herself at one of the local offices from the newspaper she had read the evening before. She felt much better after a good night's sleep and an excellent breakfast made by Mrs. Katzenburger. She had met Mr. Katzenburger and a few of her other guests and chatted amiably with them. She implied she was on vacation but found out a lot more about them than they did about her despite their well-meaning questions and inquiries. She eagerly went out into the early fall weather with the sun shining brightly and realized she would have to get some fall clothes as it was a lot colder this far north than she was used to. The lovely fall leaves were changing on the trees around the town. It was rather picturesque.

"Well you've found one!" The older woman told Amy with a smile.

Amy returned the smile as she looked around the well-lit office. Almost all of the small office was taken up by windows that allowed a two-sided view of the marina and the lake. It was light, airy, and perfect to show off the many pictures hanging on the walls over the windows and around them of properties for sale or already sold by this office. "I'm lookin' for a year-round rental, possibly lease to own," she told the woman, eyeing her nametag quickly. Lenora.

Lenora smiled at the possibility of a sale over just a rental and introduced herself quickly and efficiently. "What exactly do you want in a home—a stand-alone, a condo, a fixer upper? Will your husband be joining you? do you have children?" Her voice grew excitedly as she talked.

A brief shadow crossed Amy's eyes, but it was gone in a flash. Lenora didn't notice.

"No, this is just for myself so one or two bedrooms would be fine." Amy hoped her voice sounded natural. "I don't know about a fixer upper but what do you have?"

"Well we have—" Lenora started to speak.

"Oh, I should tell you I'm thinkin' of lookin' into any businesses that may be for sale here in town as I'm thinkin' of stayin'," Amy interrupted quickly.

Lenora thought she had died and gone to heaven but still she was cautious. Many tourists *thought* they would like to stay in one of the many little towns located in this area of the state, but they never stayed. It was all grandiose dreams and 'what ifs' and never came to anything, except maybe a huge waste of her efforts and time. She began to show the potential client the rentals she had on file, but she also surreptitiously noted the woman was well dressed in slacks and a nice blouse with an expensive faux leather jacket that completed the outfit becomingly. Her red hair was a little much and Lenora briefly thought it must be dyed to look that exact color especially with the dark eyebrows and lashes. She did however speak slowly and precisely in her southern drawl which bespoke nice manners and a certain flair. It impressed Lenora who began to discuss the businesses located in the town, both for the tourist trade and for the locals. Most shopped in the larger towns for groceries or even trekked down to Green Bay for the major things. Their town was a jumping off point to the islands that were out on the lake. The ferry, and the fishing trips that were a major income for their little town.

Amy was intrigued. It had started as a small fishing village and grown to accommodate the tourists and still retained its homey charm. It wasn't large and yet enough people came through here to make it worth the locals while to maintain the tourists' interests.

Lenora showed her a couple of houses, driving her in and around the town as she chattered away. Finally, Amy found one she liked. An old hunting cabin that needed some work but was private, discrete, and secluded. The closest neighbor was a mile up the road. The price was low even for a rental. but she knew that was because of its location than anything else. She carefully noted as Lenora showed her around how far it was from the town and determined it was a nice walk although with winter not that far off she would have to obtain a vehicle of some sort.

After reading the papers closely, Amy signed the papers to rent with the contingency to make an offer at any time up to a year from the date of the rental. Then Lenora began to show her some of the empty buildings in town as well as established businesses giving her a little gossip at the same time.

"This one has been owned by the same family for nearly a hundred years, and I know the current owner has no interest in maintaining it anymore," Lenora confessed as they went into a little market store with a few fishing reels on the one wall and a little bit of everything. A house was attached to the store with a police cruiser in the drive. Amy could already see the store was under-utilized and had shrunk from its former glory days, very little of the actual space was used. She could see potential though. It had a wraparound porch that went around the entire building except for the one side against the neighboring house, and one side was out over the marina where a gas pump stood on a dock.

"Hi Lenora, how's tricks?" a little girl of about six or seven asked from behind the counter. Amy blinked in surprise and tried not to laugh.

"Heather, that's not polite," Lenora hissed reproachfully. "You are to call me Mrs. Watson and not by my first name without permission."

"You call me by *my* first name," the girl returned sulkily. It was obvious her mode of address had been a repeat of something an adult had said at one point.

"Where is your …" Lenora hesitated before continuing, "Mother?" she asked cautiously.

"She's around here somewhere," the little girl replied saucily. She wasn't kept down very long by Lenora's tone and looked around the place as though to make her mother appear magically.

"Why aren't you in school today?" Lenora fired at the little girl.

Amy watched amused as the little girl handled the prickly realtor effortlessly. "Parent teacher conferences," she said distractedly as she called out, "MOM!" making the two adults cringe at the ear-splitting yell that came from the small girl.

"Yeah?" a voice answered from a back room and soon they all saw a brunette swagger into view; it was obvious she had been working on something as she was disheveled and looked like she had just gotten up. Amy was amused as she recognized her as one of the patrons from the bar of last night and wondered if she had been drinking today.

"Abby, I have someone here interested in your business," Lenora began in her best salesmanship voice. She didn't see the startled look on either of the other women's faces. Amy because she wasn't ready to just jump into it like that, and Abby because she hadn't expected to be approached like this.

"Who says I'm ready to sell it?" Abby asked, and the tone was similar to her daughter's sulky one.

"C'mon Abby, you know it's gone downhill since your grandparents passed on, and you don't have the time for it anymore," Lenora responded not in the least intimidated by her tone.

"Maybe, but who says I wanna sell it?" Abby asked again.

"Abigail Shipman, you know you yourself said it not so long ago. Now I have this nice lady who is looking at possible investments here in town, so are you interested or not in the possibility of someone taking it over?" Lenora asked hotly, sick of being toyed with, first by her impertinent daughter and now the mother.

Abby grinned as she shared an amused glance with Amy. "Maybe I am, maybe I ain't," she returned.

Lenora exhaled loudly through her nose at this news and crossed her arms in annoyance. "Well, we won't waste your time then," she said as she gestured to Amy that they should leave.

Amy found herself being ushered out and glanced back amused into the brunette's laughing brown eyes and nodded her goodbyes as Lenora puffed up like a wet chicken. The rest of their morning she showed her empty buildings, and while there were possibilities, most of the 'plans' she had were vague re-creations of what already existed in the town. Amy thanked her for her time, picked up the keys to her rental, and returned to the inn.

Sitting down she made a list of things she was going to need at her new house and knew she only had about forty-eight hours to accomplish them. She only had the room for another night and couldn't stay longer because of the tourists. With that in mind, she caught the bus before it left town that afternoon using up her ticket that had been paid until Green Bay to head there. She got to see the inland side of The Thumb. Faintly across the water she could see land but not the towns until they got to Green Bay. She got directions and took a cab to the car centers. She knew what she would need in an area that got a lot of snow and what would be necessary to survive up here. The salesmen were like any and her southern accent charmed them all. She knew as a woman alone shopping for a car that she was at a disadvantage, but she continued on until she came across a SUV she liked. It got good gas mileage, had a four-wheel drive, and was only *slightly* used with low mileage so that she got a discount off the newer models. She didn't believe the story that an older couple had traded in the vehicle as it was 'too much' for them, but she did like the four-door vehicle with plenty of cargo area in the back. She signed on all the necessary lines and took out a *small* loan to establish herself in this area; fortunately it was still early enough in the day that her bank account in the south checked out, and they knew she was good for it. Driving off the lot she felt powerful as she headed for the nearest home stores.

She bought paint for the cabin, an inflatable mattress, and a hunters sleeping bag until the sheets and pillows and cases she also bought could be used. She went to a restaurant and ate as she continued her lists and then hit the stores once again. She was really pleased with the selection and for the first time heard about a place called Appleton and the Fox River Mall that had outlet stores. Hearing it was an additional hour south, she decided to concentrate on where she was at for now. In short order she arranged for a beds and mattresses for her humble home as well as a living room set and a television. She got some of the basics, and with all this piled in the back of her new SUV, she headed back up the coast hoping she wouldn't get lost. It was a fairly straight forward ride, yet confusing to her in the dark as she was unfamiliar with the area. Strangely, once she got across the bridge in Sturgeon Bay, she had a feeling that she was heading 'home.' She was relieved once she hit Northpoint and found the Duck and Swan. Parking on the street, she went inside for a well-deserved rest after her full day; she was grateful that her hosts had obviously been in to clean the room and lay down new wood that took only a moment to light. She went to sleep with the screen in front of the fireplace dreamily watching the flames and wondering about her future here in Northpoint.

The next morning, she checked out of the Duck and Swan and thanked Mrs. Katzenburger for her hospitality. She mentioned she had rented a place outside of town and relieved her host's curiosity as she mentioned the location.

"Oh, that place, it's been empty for years. You are going to want to have the heating and vents checked; it gets pretty cold up here," her eyes knitted together. "I can recommend a handyman if you want," she offered.

Amy took her up on her offer. The best people came by recommendation, and she knew if her new friends recommended them they would probably recommend the best.

"Oh, you bought a truck?" was the next question-like comment.

Mr. Katzenburger chimed in on that, "I'm not so sure about them foreign jobs. I personally stick to the adage, buy American."

Amy listened respectfully, but as it was the first vehicle she had ever purchased herself, she was going to stick with it; she was proud of it and that she could afford it. While her hosts had their own opinions, she wasn't going to let them upset her with their comments. As she put the heavy bag containing all her clothes in the back seat, she was pleased she still had so much room in the SUV. It all belonged to her though; it was all *hers* and hers alone. She pulled up in front of her cabin and looked around at the tall trees, the deep layer of years of accumulation below them, and breathed in the silence. This was hers. Rented perhaps, but hers. The pride bubbled inside her while she began to unload her belongings.

She swept out the small cabin first, noting the thick logs and wondering if it would be warm enough to get her through the winter. She had no idea if it would, and the wood next to the cabin in a neatly stacked pile didn't look like nearly enough. She didn't see any other way to heat the small cabin, and thoughtfully sweeping every nook and cranny from the ceiling to the floor, she eliminated dust and debris from years of having no one in the cabin. She raised a bit of dust herself by her efforts and opened all the windows noting how cool it was as she worked. Finally, she felt it was clean enough to haul out the soaps and conditioners she had bought for her wood floors and walls. She started in the kitchen and began scrubbing the walls first and then floors, astonished at the amount of dirty water she soon had in the bucket she used. Throwing it outside beyond the porch, she stretched her back, realizing the time as the sun was starting to set. She would have to leave some of the house cleaning for another day if she wanted it to warm up.

She closed the windows and started a fire in the fireplace only to have the smoke start to choke her out. She tried the flue, but that didn't seem to work well, and she wondered if the chimney had something in it. She shrugged; it was too late in the day for her to do anything about it really, so she brought her sleeping bag and blew up her mattress. She realized she needed to get the electricity turned on in the cabin and get a phone. She made numerous lists as she realized how unprepared she really was.

Washing up with cold water, she checked and found an electric water heater in a closet in the kitchen, so she knew she would eventually have hot water. Having no idea how to turn on the electricity, she shivered from the cold water and rolled down her sleeves and put on a sweater to hide her dirty shirt and headed back into town. She tried another restaurant. This one was a little finer than Chuckie's, and she felt self-conscious in her jeans until she saw other patrons wearing the same.

"Table for one?" the greeter asked her, and she nodded as she was shown to a table near the marina side with a wooden sidewalk separating the window from the actual dock. It was very lovely and picturesque, and she was startled out of her reverie when asked for her order. She had to admit she hadn't looked at her menu and soon ordered the stuffed pork chops, green beans, and applesauce along with a cold glass of milk. She smiled as she realized milk wasn't that sophisticated, but it sounded so good with the rest of the meal she couldn't resist.

She looked out at the marina again and noted that she was in a great place to people watch, she could see and watch the other patrons in the reflections on the windows. She wanted to cringe and hide when she saw that brunette that Lenora had introduced to her earlier in the day. What was her name? Abby or something? She could see she was better dressed than the jeans and t-shirt she had worn earlier, in fact, she seemed to be dressed up, but not for going out or anything, just better. She glanced back out the window and began to mentally categorize what she needed to do to make her cabin habitable for winter.

"Mind if I join you?" Amy looked up startled at the voice; she had been lost in thought looking out at the lights in the harbor. She was more startled to realize it was the rude brunette. "I promise I won't bite..." she smiled and then added softly, so softly that Amy thought she hadn't heard her correctly, "hard."

Amy couldn't think of a single reason to refuse her, and perhaps they had just gotten off on the wrong foot, or maybe it was Lenora. She didn't know how to extricate herself from this awkward situation, so she gestured to the second chair and watched as the woman pulled it out and sat down.

"I'm Abigail Shipman," the brunette said holding out her hand to be shook.

Manners drilled into her from birth had Amy reaching across the table taking the hand that was offered. "Amy..." A slight hesitation and then, "Adams."

Abby smiled noting the hesitation but not saying anything as she firmly shook the woman's hand and then said, "Hello Amy Adams, welcome to Northpoint."

"Thank you," Amy said quietly as her hand was released, and she returned it back to her lap.

"What in the world is a woman from the south doing in so cold a climate?" Abby asked with a grin showing she meant no harm with the question.

"Can I get you anything Abby?" their server was at their table.

"I'll have what she's having," Abby said playfully.

The server grinned in return. "Even the milk?" he asked.

"Milk?" Abby asked alarmed and then shook her head. "Actually, that's probably a good thing; just add chocolate to mine if you would."

"Chocolate milk then with pork chops, green beans and apple sauce?" he repeated back with a smirk.

"Green beans?" she asked and the concern in her voice could be heard.

"The pork chops are stuffed otherwise I'd suggest potatoes," he was laughing at her and showed it.

"I'll take those potatoes, mashed, maybe with a bit of garlic," she laughed back at him as he wrote down her order.

"Will do, have it up in a jiffy, Chief," he said with cheerful good humor.

Abby laughed to herself, and Amy watched amused. "You don't like milk?" she asked.

"I like it; it doesn't like me. Lactose intolerance," she said pointing her thumb at herself before continuing, "But apparently chocolate milk is okay, something about the lactate being negated by the cocoa bean," she explained.

Amy nodded, it made sense. She was fortunate that she had never experienced it herself, but she knew people who had, and it wasn't pleasant.

"So why Northpoint?" Abby returned to her earlier question.

Amy shrugged, "Somethin' told me that I should check it out; you've got to admit that Door County is beautiful."

"The bajillion tourists we get here every season attest to that, but unless you are ready for snow and a lot of it, you are in for a shocker."

Their server brought them two small plates, a pile of butter squares and a basket of warm sliced bread, putting it down between them with a smile as he turned to head to another table to take their order.

Amy reached for the bread; she was starving, but her hand collided with Abby's, and they exchanged an awkward little laugh as they tugged from both ends, the bread hadn't been sliced through. They both soon had a slice and used the butter to smooth over the surface of each of their slices, the butter melting almost immediately with the heat generated from the warm bread.

"I'm hopin' I'll make it," Amy said with confidence she wasn't feeling.

"Well, that cabin you rented is going to need some work," Abby said as she leaned back and bit into her bread.

"How do you know…?" Amy began only to be cut off with a wave of Abby's hand.

"Small town, you don't think Lenora would keep that to herself, do you?" Abby's eyes twinkled as her perfect white teeth bit into the bread again.

Amy laughed at her own naiveté; of course, Lenora would tell all she knew about her. Despite spending many hours together looking at places and discussing things, Amy had told her relatively little about herself. It had frustrated the older woman to no end. Besides, renting a place that had no takers for a couple of years would be a feather in her real estate cap. "Well, I suppose not," she conceded gracefully. Her own mouth watered at the delicious bread she was eating.

"You gonna heat it with wood?" Abby asked knowingly.

Amy nodded and then asked, "You know anyone I can buy some good hardwood from?"

"Hardwood?" Abby asked feigning that she didn't understand.

"Hardwood's burn cleaner, and I don't want to gum up the chimney," she drawled, her southern accent sounding very becoming to the brunette's ears. "I'd like a few cords of wood if I could get them, and I need a chimney cleaner," she added.

Abby smiled; this wasn't some wilting wallflower from the south but some steel magnolia she had heard tell about. She obviously knew she would need wood and a lot of it from what she was saying. Good, she hated when people were ill-equipped to move into the area and got themselves in trouble. "Well for hardwoods I'd contact Jacob Meyers, he's in the book and has cords he will deliver."

"How many do you think I should buy?" Amy asked as she finished her first piece of bread and unashamedly reached for another.

"You have to figure at least one cord of wood for every month of winter and then some," Abby told her as she too reached for another piece so she would get her fair share. The redhead knew how to eat!

"How many months of winter do y'all get up here?" she drawled.

Abby grinned, a slight wrinkling of her nose and around her mouth showing she appreciated the question. "Depends, but it's in the air, so I would suggest you give Jacob a call and see about having him deliver that wood for you. He has others, so you don't want to wait. As for cleaning out your chimney, I'm sure Jacob can recommend someone; the last one that I knew that did it regularly moved away."

"Got sick of the snow?" Amy asked with a grin as she finished her second piece and reached for her third and final.

Abby gave Amy a dubious look. "There was probably not enough business for him, and I'm sure he didn't work too hard." She told her as she grabbed the last piece, the heel of the bread, before Amy could gobble it up.

They chatted back and forth getting to know each other through their delicious meal. Amy wasn't surprised that the woman asked more questions than she answered, but she was prepared for those questions anyway. She wasn't prepared for the next one though.

"You still interested in my store?" Abby asked.

Amy eyed her slightly. "I thought you weren't interested in sellin' it?" She asked as she enjoyed the flavor of the apple sauce; it was an excellent accompaniment to her stuffed pork chops and green beans.

"I might be to the right person; Lenora is right, but don't tell her I said so. I'm not interested in running it, and it's almost like every other store in town. It's been going downhill since Gramps and Grandma passed on. They were the draw anyway." She shrugged.

"Was it your grandparent's place?" she asked, genuinely interested with a gleam in her green eye.

Abby nodded. "Yes, once they were gone I just simply had no time, but we live next door so it was convenient, and I didn't want it just gone. It's time though."

"If it's not too much to ask, what about your siblings or parents, wouldn't they be interested?"

"It's not a secret. I never got along with my parents; they live across the bay in Oconto."

"Ocont what?" Amy asked, grinning unrepentantly at mashing up the name.

Abby snickered at her butchered attempt of the Indian name. "Oconto, it's a town on the mainland. They live there, I live *here*, and we are all fine with that. Besides Gramps left it to me to take care of Grams, and I did until she passed too. I love it here, and my children were born and raised here."

"Children? I met your daughter," she mentioned as she delicately wiped her mouth.

"Heather?" and at Amy's nod she continued with a prideful grin, "Yeah she's something, but Bailey is a bit of a handful; he's ten now and full of pre-teen mouth and angst."

Amy giggled as she was supposed to, and Abby's eyes were drawn to her.

"Do you have children or a husband?" Abby asked noting the faint white line that time hadn't erased from her left hand.

Amy didn't hesitate even a moment as she shook her head. "No, I'm a widow, and we were never blessed with children."

"Oh, I'm sorry to hear that; you're young to be widowed," she observed.

Amy nodded her thanks but didn't say anything as she looked down at her plate concentrating on her food. The two girls sat in silence for some time as they gobbled their food down. Amy enjoyed the flavor of her applesauce, occasionally dipping her pork chop into it when she was sure Abby wasn't looking.

"I didn't mean to bring up bad memories." Abby began to say as she pushed her plate away from her.

"Did you ladies want desert?" their server asked as he took their finished plates away.

"I'll have carrot cake if you have it?" Amy said shyly, thankful for the subject change.

"We do," he assured her before turning to Abby. "And for you Chief?" he asked with a saucy little grin.

"I'll have some chocolate cake with chocolate frosting if Lance baked it, but if Tasha did, I'll have carrot cake instead," she told him, smirking at the grin he gave her.

He nodded as he toted their used dishes away.

"Small town, I guess everyone knows everyone else, eh?" Amy asked hoping to avert the brunette's apology and forget what they had been talking about.

"Yes, it's a blessing and a curse. The tourists make it all interesting though," Abby told her, and while she had noted the change of subject, she didn't bring it up again. "What would you do with the store if I let you have it?" she asked instead.

Amy had seen the other stores in town and noted what they lacked. Touristy items were fine and they were well supplied in the other stores. She herself would carry…some. But she wanted a little more than that and began to discuss it with Abby who proved to be a good listener and nodded as they ate their carrot cakes, which apparently Tasha had baked today.

"Wow, it sounds like you know what you are talking about," Abby said as she finished the last morsel of her cake and the delicious icing.

Amy nodded. "My parents had a small fishin' place on the Gulf when I was growing up," she confided and then blushed

"You didn't want to work there?" Abby asked, noting the blush on the redhead's face.

"They passed away. The bank and my brother sold it before I could say yes or no," she told Abby and looked away.

"I'm sorry for your loss." Abby found herself apologizing again and for some reason it irritated her.

Amy looked up straight into those soft velvety brown eyes. She had been more forthcoming with this woman, and she didn't know why. "They were old; they had me and my brother late in life, but in the end it didn't matter, as neither the bank nor my brother got the proceeds after my grandmother's lawyer stepped up. It all went into a trust." She grinned ruefully and shrugged at life's intricacies.

"You seem to have had a lot of loss in your life," Abby commented as she finished her chocolate milk. It left a cute little moustache on her upper lip.

Amy resisted the urge to blot at the brunette's upper lip, as she pantomimed it for her dinner companion to make her aware of it without embarrassing her and then watched amused as she wiped her lips clean like a child would with the back of her hand.

"It's just...life. It doesn't always play fair."

Abby had to admit that was certainly true.

"Would you ladies like anything else?" Their server came up with separate bills, which he handed to each of them.

"I'm good," Abby answered as she glanced down at her check.

"It was delicious," Amy said courteously.

"Why don't I get this?" Abby asked her, reaching for Amy's check.

Amy looked up startled at the offer. "Why would you do that?"

Abby seemed surprised that she would question her offer. "Why not? We spoke about business; I could write this off." She grinned at the idea.

Amy shook her head. "Thank you, but no, perhaps another time, and if you are serious about sellin' me your store, perhaps we could do this again?" she offered, hoping to couch her refusal.

"Why don't you come by the store again tomorrow? I'll be...around. We could discuss terms that would be agreeable to both of us. I like your ideas, and I think you'd be successful at it. I'd like someone to succeed at it; God knows I have no interest."

Amy nodded as she slipped a twenty-dollar bill into her hand from her purse. They rose from where they were seated and headed to the cashier together. "I'd like that; perhaps we could have Lenora draw up some of the papers so she doesn't feel left out?" she suggested.

"You've already got her number, don't you?" Abby said astutely, as she watched Amy pay her bill and then catching Mike the server's arm as he walked past, she handed him a five-dollar bill.

"Thank you, ma'am," he said blushingly. Most people left the tips on the table, but he kinda liked the opportunity to thank her personally.

They walked out into the brisk early fall night, and Amy pulled her jacket closer. The air was so clear you could almost drink it, and she breathed deeply in appreciation of it.

"You look like a hound dog smelling the air like that," Abby teased as they walked along.

"Could be worse things that I look like. Daddy had a good pair of coon dogs," she answered with a laugh as she pressed the button on her key ring and unlocked the door to her new SUV.

"This is yours?" Abby asked in surprise. Her car was parked alongside. She noted that the vehicle still had the dealer plates on it. If it wasn't brand new, it was only recently old;it was a Mazda CX-5 and looked sharp. She gazed at it enviously.

Amy nodded proudly. "Yes, I bought it yesterday. I knew I'd need a good sturdy vehicle for the winters up here and to get in and out of the cabin I rented."

"It got four-wheel drive?" she asked as she nearly drooled over the modern SUV.

Amy nodded again. "Yep and all sorts of gadgets I'm gonna have to get used to."

Abby nodded wondering how much the SUV had cost her and smiled ruefully. A new SUV was far in the future for her and her children. In the meantime, she had her cruiser. She watched as Amy got into the SUV, and it smoothly started for her. "Hey, you might want to get a remote starter for it," she suggested to her new friend.

"Already got it thanks," Amy said with a grin. "I'll see you tomorrow." She waved as she closed the door and slowly backed out of the stall. She didn't notice that Abby was getting in the cruiser that had been parked next to her own SUV.

CHAPTER THREE

Amy spent a very cold night in her cabin. Without the fire and the electricity, it was rather spooky. She slept in fleece sweats and wore socks and was grateful for the foresight of purchasing the thick, warm sleeping bag. The blow-up mattress also made things comfortable, but it was noisy as she tossed and turned. More than once Amy heard strange noises from outside, though she knew it could be a number of things: leaves rustling in the wind or branches scraping. She had been thinking about rodents scurrying inside the walls when exhaustion finally hit her. She woke up shivering, snuggled deep in the sleeping bag. The air felt frigid, and she could feel the cold trying to seep into the sleeping bag from the air mattress. There was no thought of getting out of bed into that cold. She was already not happy with her new abode. Camping out was way over rated if this was what it was going to be like. She finally got herself out of "bed" and got going if only to get the blood flowing and to pee. She moved quickly to get dressed, to warm herself, and get herself out to the warmth of her SUV running quietly in the driveway, which she started fifteen minutes before she even got outside. Thank God for the remote starter! She watched it warming up as she brushed her teeth and then her hair, using different brushes of course.

When she first slid into the warmth of the SUV along with the fleece lined jacket, gloves, and hat, she sat there for a moment to let the heat seep into her bones. She couldn't remember ever being this cold before and wondered at her decision to settle here. It wasn't even winter yet, and here she was frozen to the bone.

Well, sitting here wasn't going to get her heat on, her chimney cleared, or her house cleaned. She put the SUV into drive and drove into town. After a small breakfast at yet another little touristy café, and a meeting with Abby that got them a tentative agreement, which they sent over to a delighted Lenora, she spent most of her day running around from pillar to post trying to find the electric company, the phone company, even a cell company, as well as tracking down one Jacob Meyers, who not only took her order for six cords of wood gladly, but agreed to check out her chimney for her.

The mess that Jacob made 'cleaning' out her chimney meant she should never have bothered to sweep out the cabin in the first place. He cleaned out birds' nests and other debris that had accumulated in the chimney, and that along with the soot meant her cleaning in the cabin would have to be repeated. Watching him clean the chimney, it occurred to her it was not a job she would have relished or wished on any other human being. She could only hope his delivery of the cords of wood would be a little neater.

The cleaning signified another aspect of her isolation though. She was going to have to add to the list one of those 'thingies' to shed rain and keep out the birds and any other animals that decided to use her chimney as an entranceway to the cabin. The old one had apparently rusted out, and Jacob removed this along with all the other debris. Amy was just glad it was all gone. She was also glad when Jacob too was gone to go get the first cord of wood she had ordered; he had explained he would deliver them all as soon as possible and stack them along the side of the cabin where she already had a partial cord. Six cords though would soon take up more than that area, and he recommended stacking them along the back too. Not knowing the significance of that, she agreed.

Having that first fire that drew out the smoke through the now cleared chimney was heartening. It quickly warmed up the cabin, which delighted and surprised her at its efficiency. She wondered if she had ordered too much wood. After all, how much was a cord of wood really going to take up? She found out as she cleaned up the cabin once again, the soot seemed to have gone everywhere, and she again found herself scrubbing and washing down the woods. She watched as Jacob and a 'helper' who he introduced as his brother Jonathan, both of who eyed her appreciatively as they stacked the wood. One cord seemed like more than enough for winter, but she would soon realize how much six cords took up in the area around the cabin as they delivered cord after cord and stacked them neatly.

When the phone company finally showed up to turn on her phones and then the electric company to turn on her electric, she finally felt settled; it took a couple of days, but the cabin shined as she scrubbed and cleaned and fussed. She had discovered in her scrubbing down of the cabin that the floor in the kitchen contained a trap door to a small basement, something that Lenora had failed to notice or mention. She also discovered that the floor was rotting above this death trap, and she spent hours poking and prodding and determining how much wood she would need to replace it. Checking her agreement once again, she saw any and all improvements were the area of the tenant, which meant her landlord wouldn't be fixing it any time soon. Well, if she bought this place, it would be to her benefit to fix these things. She added to her notes on her endless lists.

She finally got around to checking out the garage that was behind the cabin. It was big enough for her SUV, which when she tried to fit it inside, she found it took up almost the entire side of the small garage. There was room for a second small vehicle, but she was glad she hadn't bought a bigger SUV, or it would have overwhelmed the small garage. She swept out the dirt floored garage only to find a concrete slab well below what she thought was simply a dirt floor. It took her hours to shovel out the accumulated years of dirt and debris that people had left on the garage floor, making it a dirt floor until she found the whole slab. She supposed other tenants had thought it was dirt too and had never really cleaned as thoroughly as she. She found herself wiping down the walls as she had inside but not washing them as she had polished those in the house. She couldn't reach all the spider and cob webs in the upper portions and added a garden hose to her endless lists of supplies to pick up in the 'big' city.

The delivery of her bed and mattress as well as her living room set delighted her. She hadn't wanted to miss these, and it gave the cabin a homey look. She delighted in deflating the air mattress, folding it neatly away and rolling up her sleeping bag as she made the bed with the sheets she had purchased that first day. She realized she didn't have a comforter or any blankets and had to unroll her sleeping bag again, unzip it and spread it as a quilt across the queen sized four poster bed. So much for progress, she smiled ruefully.

She was grateful for the electricity though. After cleaning so much, she was able to take a hot shower in her small bathroom that was between the two bedrooms. She had hung her few clothes in the closet of the 'master' bedroom, and now with her bed in it, it felt cozy. The fireplace really put out a lot of heat and warmed the cabin nicely. Her first night spent in her bed felt luxurious even though the inflatable had been comfortable if a bit noisy. She still heard noises at night and wondered if she had 'roommates' that were better left alone and unseen.

She was planning on going back down to Green Bay and perhaps on to the Fox River Mall in Appleton that she had heard of. One day as she sat in her living area on her new couch making her lists and checking them a second time, someone knocked on her cabin door. She was surprised as she hadn't been expecting anyone.

"Why Lenora, this is a surprise," she said as she welcomed the realtor in.

"I brought the agreement over as soon as I finished drafting it. I didn't want to give Abby a chance to…" she stopped talking as she looked around the now swept and polished cabin as she walked in. She could see all the hard work Amy had put into the building. It was a far cry from the hunting cabin she had rented the woman originally. She could see she had wiped down, possibly washed the walls as well as the wood floors. Even the stones on the fireplace seemed polished. White paint around the stones made them stand out in contrast to the river rock. With the burning wood of the logs, it looked warm and cozy. She had a small dining room set to one side, and with the couch set, it looked lived in and habitable. She could see the four-poster bed neatly made up, except for a sleeping bag spread out on it through the doorway. The other bedroom door was closed. "Why this looks very nice," she said approvingly.

"Sit down, sit down. I'd offer you coffee, but I don't drink it, and I've not got a refrigerator yet," Amy said with a welcome. She suspected the realtor was just being nosy, but she didn't mind as she wanted to be thought of as a good tenant.

"Oh, that's okay. I'm glad you are settling in; you are very efficient, aren't you?" she said with a delighted smile as though she had picked Amy herself for the job.

Amy smiled as she gestured at the papers Lenora had with her. She read through them thoroughly much to the realtor's annoyance, but she found a few errors from what Abby and she had agreed to and tagged them with post-it notes that Lenora reluctantly handed her so it could be corrected. It took longer to read through it all because Lenora obviously wanted to chat, and Amy insisted on reading it through. "I'm so glad you are taking over that run-down store; Abby really has no time for it," Lenora confided after she was finished perusing the contract.

SMALL TOWN ANGEL

"Well, I'm going to make it my home here, and Abby's store will give me a purpose," Amy told her with a smile. She had heard the annoyance in Lenora's voice and wondered at it. She wasn't about to ask the reasons why though.

They soon concluded their business, and as Amy was ready to go out on her own errands, she followed the realtor outside with her purse, keys, and endless lists. Lenora watched as she carefully locked the door behind her and then watched as Jacob Meyers and his brother drove into the yard with another truck full of wood.

"That's an awful lot of wood," she commented curiously, but she had known the only heat source in the house was the fireplace.

"Yes, Jacob and his brother are still deliverin' all I ordered," Amy told her without elaborating.

When Amy was obviously not going to comment further or appease any more of Lenora's curiosity, she waved to the two men unloading the wood, and Amy watched as she drove away.

"Hi Amy!" the two men waved as they neatly stacked the wood in the back of the cabin. The side had been filled by only a couple cords, and now they were stacking it along the back.

She waved in return as she headed out to the garage to get her SUV. People sure got an early start on their work around here if Lenora and Jacob were any indication. It was still early in the morning; she'd had a bowl of cold cereal but was looking forward to getting a refrigerator in the cabin as well as a stove and other appliances so she could cook at home instead of going out once or twice a day. While it was nice to eat out, it was expensive, and she saw a lot more tourists than her fellow people from town, although she was learning the places where the townies hung out.

She thought about her chosen place to live as she drove south to Green Bay. She was loving how remote and homey it was. The trees and the lake were beautiful, and she even loved the crisp fall-like air as she sniffed eagerly at the smell of wood smoke and other fall smells. She was excitedly anticipating putting the store together and wondered how Abby would feel about the changes she was going to enact once their contracts were in order.

"Oh yeah, I guess I forgot to tell you about that clause," Abby said as Lenora showed her the changes Amy had indicated on the contracts. She was deliberately re-reading the contract slow as she knew it would annoy the realtor. It was a land-contract and would allow Amy to buy the store and building over time. Lenora wouldn't get her 'commission' until she did buy it, but she would get one as she was handling the contract. It annoyed her as she wanted her monies now,

- 25 -

but she could at least gloat about the sale 'she' had enacted. It was still a feather in her cap even if she didn't get paid for it right away. Abby suspected she just wanted to annoy her in some way and didn't really care. Amy seemed nice and knowledgeable, and while she was a study in contrasts, she really thought her ideas for the store were sound and would fit in well in their little town. She wondered about her, of course, as any new additions to their town would engender curiosity, but there was a lot that the redhead didn't say, and Abby respected her privacy.

"You should see how she cleaned up that cabin; it shines now!" Lenora enthused as Abby read through the notes Amy had made.

"She seems to be a go-getter. I'm sure she will be a welcomed addition to the town," Abby said absentmindedly as she read over some of the legalese.

Lenora's eyes narrowed slightly, wondering at Abby's seeming lack of interest in their new resident but then shrugged it off as Abby initialed the changes and handed back the contract for Lenora to finish making it up. "Do you think she will begin on the store right away?" Lenora asked. The two women had excluded her from their negotiations, but at least they had done the 'right' thing by including her in the paperwork; after all, she had been the one that introduced them. It was only 'right' that she gets her commission.

Abby shrugged. She knew it would annoy Lenora that she wasn't more forthcoming with the information that she and Amy had discussed, but she wasn't about to gossip or carry tales. Lenora, however, would. She was certainly aware that Lenora didn't approve of her or her lifestyle, but it was none of the busybody's business. She smiled politely as Lenora promised to have the contract done for her signatures that afternoon. She watched absentmindedly as the woman drove away, even though it would have been just as quick to walk in the small town.

CHAPTER FOUR

Amy spent the entire exhausting day in and out of stores. She found the selection at the Fox River Mall to be astounding and overwhelming sometimes, but she got dishes at outlet prices as well as other necessities. She put the back seat down in the SUV to give herself more cargo room and filled it well. She bought more furniture and appliances, but some of it was going to have to be delivered. She found that 'extra' few miles into Door County caused her to pay more for her deliveries, much to her annoyance, but she bargained with her charming southern accent with the different stores to reduce it as much as possible.

She ate alone at some of the chain restaurants, looking around as she people watched. No one paid her any mind unless she opened up her mouth and her accent came out. She looked like anyone else, busy shopping in the area. Glancing at her lists, she checked off dozens of things she had already picked up, ordered, or arranged for delivery on. She still had a lot of shopping to do, and it was with reluctance after her late dinner that she headed back up north when the stores began to close. While she hadn't dallied in the stores, she still shopped thriftily and enjoyed seeing the selections. Tomorrow or the next day she would confine her shopping to Green Bay, if she had the energy. She was exhausted as she drove the long drive up The Thumb.

She enjoyed the Sirius Satellite Radio that was installed in her SUV; she could listen to all-country or all-eighties music if she so desired and programmed in a few of her favorite stations. It came free with her purchase for six months, so she was going to enjoy it while it was free. She wasn't sure about paying for radio music. Since it was dark, she concentrated on her driving instead of looking out at the 'view', but she did note the occasional sign advertising antiques and other sights to see. It made her think about the store she would be opening and the many things she would have to find and do for it yet. She wasn't surprised to find a note on her screen door of the cabin from Lenora asking that she stop in tomorrow to sign the final contracts. She smiled that things were coming together. She started up the fire that had gone out in her absence to warm up the cabin while she slowly emptied the SUV of all her purchases, stacking boxes in the appropriate rooms. It was late by the time she got everything in the house and locked up her SUV as a matter of habit. She knew people probably left their cars unlocked and even the keys in the ignition in this area, but she was hoping she would never be that lax.

The next morning after a long hot shower, she began to open and put away the many things she had purchased. Carefully she hung scenic pictures of various artists around the cabin, including a couple of Robert Kincaid that reminded her of this area; she pulled back the couch and laid down a rug she had bought and then carefully pulled it back onto the rug. It made the room even homier and warm. She unpacked and washed dishes, glasses, and cutlery until she had her shelves and drawers full. She had found a dollar store that had every gadget for her kitchen. All hers!

Later as she started to burn the boxes, she thought about going into town and signing the lease. She knew the fact that if she wasn't on Lenora's doorstep first thing she would be annoyed, but she had other things to finish before she did that. She was finishing up when a knock sounded on the front door. Opening it, she smiled welcomingly at Jacob's flushed face.

"Hi, I wanted to show you we delivered the last of the six cords and here is your bill," he said with a smile as he blushed.

"Oh, let me grab my checkbook, and I'll write you a check, you wanna come in?" she asked as she welcomed him into her little cabin.

He looked around curious and was impressed to see what she had done to the cabin in the time she had been here. He had known it was basic, but he couldn't remember it ever being this clean, even when hunters he had known had stayed here.

SMALL TOWN ANGEL

Amy sat down at her small kitchen table and took her checkbook out and looked at the bill for the wood. It was high and included the chimney cleaning, but she consoled herself that she wouldn't have to buy oil or coal all winter long and having the fireplace was warm and homey. It was really quite romantic and efficient. Handing him the check, she smiled as she watched him admire a painting she had hung that contained a couple of Labrador Retrievers, one black, one yellow, in a canoe holding the oars in their laughing mouths.

"That's funny," he said pointing at the painting with his thumb as he accepted her check. He was well pleased that she had paid in full with no argument. Some of the vacationers up here tended to try to stiff him for his hard work. He realized though that she wasn't just vacationing up here if she was putting in that much wood; she was staying. He'd heard about the store, so maybe she was staying for good. She was an attractive woman, and while he was married, he knew there were a few bachelors that would come calling.

"I like it. I'd love to have a lab myself," she commented.

"Really?" he asked as he turned to look at her again in surprise.

"Yes, I'd love to canoe too, but I suppose it's too late in the season?"

"Not at all, but you have to dress appropriately. The water is still warm from summer, but it's getting cold quickly. I know someone who has a late litter of labs if you are interested?" he asked.

Her eyes lit up at the thought, and then she thought about all the work she had to do with the store and around the cabin yet. Thinking it over quickly, she nodded enthusiastically. A dog would be a companion and help her keep the loneliness away.

"I'll give him your phone number if you want?" he asked.

"I'd like that. Here, I'll get you the number; it's new, so I don't know it yet," she told him as she went to the kitchen table again and grabbed a pad of paper she had near the phone she had plugged in just last night. It had her new phone number on it, and she quickly copied it down for him. "Tell him I'm looking for a big male, and maybe I should ask what colors there are?"

"Well, I saw them a few weeks ago, and it seemed he had three different colors in the litter. They should be about ready to go from the mother. I'll have Stephan call you with the details and how much he is asking, and you two can work out the rest," he said with a smile at her enthusiasm. He liked how her eyes had lit up at the thought of a puppy.

"Thank you so much, I'd like that!" she said in reply as she escorted him to the door.

"Have a nice day!" he said with a swipe to a non-existent cap he should be wearing in the cold fall weather.

She watched thoughtfully as he left in his truck. She was surprised she hadn't heard it when he drove up, but she had been lost in thought, and she must have learned to ignore such sounds long ago.

CHAPTER FIVE

Going into town, she waved at some of the few people she recognized. She liked how friendly the people had been to her, but she realized she was already making friends and being recognized by them in return. She was sure she was the subject of conversation for many people. She didn't mind as they didn't really know her other than she was from the south. She hadn't told too much about herself other than she was a 'widow.'

"Oh, I thought you'd be here hours ago," Lenora lightly chastised her.

Amy almost said something about Lenora saying anything to her but thought better of it. The woman probably didn't have a lot of business in this area and the monies she would earn if and when Amy bought the cabin, and the business would earn her a decent commission. She smiled as she said, "Oh, I had a few things to finish." She read through the contract one more time to be sure everything she had noted was now in it.

Lenora tried not to show her impatience over her client's perusal of the contract. It wasn't like she hadn't known her job or how to draft it, but between Abby and Amy, her patience over this was wearing thin. Everything was finally in order though, and she breathed a sigh of relief when Amy finally signed below Abby's own untidy scrawl.

Amy noted the signature and wondered at it while her own neat signature was added to the document as well as her initials at various points. She was, for better or worse, now in a contract with the brunette to possibly buy the store, and in the meantime, it was up to her to maintain and develop it. She cheerfully wrote out her deposit, which Lenora just as cheerfully accepted.

Thanking Lenora, who promised her a copy of the contract later that day, she left and looked around the small town. The cracker box houses mixed with Victorians and single-family homes as well as weekend get-a-ways were quaint and beautiful. Today it was overcast and a bit drab, but she felt fine, really fine. She started up the SUV and headed for the little cable company office that served this area to arrange for service not only for her cabin, but also her new store eventually. The hassle of it and the unhappy employees in the office all made her wonder. She had experienced that with the electric company, the phone company, the cell phone company, and even the post office workers. There was no post office in town, and she had had to go down to the next larger town to arrange mail delivery. All of it made her wonder how the people in this little town had coped with poor service like that for so long.

Amy was on the roof installing her screen and watershed when she saw a police cruiser pull into her driveway. Her heart palpitated until she saw Abby's frame uncoil from the driver's seat and get out of the car.

"Hi there," Amy called to alert her guest of her location.

Abby looked up surprised to see the southern belle on the roof of the cabin. She watched as the redhead easily finished up her project before heading over to the edge and just as easily climbed down the overhanging logs. No child could have been prouder at the ease in which she climbed down them. Her answering smile of welcome was pulled out reluctantly as Amy walked over pulling off her gloves. "Protecting your chimney?" she asked as she looked up at the shiny new watershed.

"Yeah, you wouldn't believe the mess that was in the chimney that Jacob pulled out; I ended up having to clean the whole cabin again!" she laughed, showing even white teeth against her pale skin.

"Oh, I would believe it, worse is when the varmints get into the cabins and cause damage." She reached back in the vehicle and pulled out the copies of Amy's contract. "I saved Lenora a trip out here since I was heading this way anyway," she told her as a way to explain her presence here in the cabin yard.

"Oh, thank you," she said in genuine appreciation as she took the copies.

"You sure you want to start all those plans you were telling me about?" Abby grinned at her enthusiasm. It lit up the redhead's green eyes like nothing else.

Amy smiled at her, teasing. "I can't wait!" she told her.

"Well as of the first of next month it's all yours," she said in reply.

"Will you miss it?" Amy asked concernedly.

Abby shook her head. "I think Heather will miss it more, but if you don't mind her occasionally dropping in, she is looking forward to seeing the changes you are going to make."

"I don't mind at all; I like children. I hope to meet your son someday too. Will he miss the store?"

Abby shrugged. "Who knows, boys are…different."

"Who watches them when you go to work?"

Abby glanced at Amy to see if she was serious, but she obviously was as she seemed genuinely interested. She apparently didn't know the gossip, which surprised her as they both knew Lenora. "My mother-in-law lives with me and takes care of them when she can keep track of them in between her soaps."

Amy laughed ruefully. "Yeah, those soap operas can be addictive."

Abby had called them 'soaps' for so long it was funny to hear them called the old-fashioned phrase of 'soap opera.' With the southern accent, it was charming.

Just then the cable company pulled into the yard behind Abby.

"Oops, looks like you have company; I should go," Abby said reluctantly. She enjoyed talking to the redhead and hoped they would be friends.

"You don't have to go, do you?" Amy asked equally as reluctant. She too enjoyed talking to Abby but didn't want to impose on her.

"Well, I do have rounds to make, but I'm sure I'll see you around. Besides, I know Craig is probably anxious to get on with his work." Her thumb pointed back at the curly blonde man getting out of the cable van.

"Craig?" Amy asked confused and then realized in a small town like this everyone knew everyone else. "Oh yeah, I need internet and cable. I bought a television but couldn't see anything!" she exclaimed.

"Yeah, we went digital up here a while back, and the reception never was that great except for one or two of the stations out of Green Bay."

"Well, I'm going to need the internet to find some of the things I need for the store. Do you know or can you recommend someone to help with the remodel?" she asked before Abby could leave.

"Yes, I have a couple of names I can give you if you stop by the store," Abby told her as she got into her vehicle.

"I'll do that, and I want Craig to install high speed internet into the store too if that's okay with you?" she quickly asked.

"Sure, anything you need, let me know. Call the store or here," she fished in a pocket for a pad of paper and quickly wrote down a couple of numbers. "That's my cell and that's the house if you need anything. Just give me a heads up on any work or deliveries so I can tell Bonnie that they are coming."

"Bonnie?" Amy asked hesitantly as she accepted the piece of paper.

"My mother-in-law," Abby answered with a wry little grin.

"Oh, yeah, of course, thank you!" she said backing away as Abby started up the car and drove towards the garage slightly so she could back out next to the cable van.

"I coulda moved it," Craig called from where he walked up next to Amy, but Abby waved at them both as she left.

Craig turned to present himself to Amy. "Hi, you called for cable and internet?" he asked pleasantly.

Amy showed him where she wanted them, and he told her she was going to need a modem or a router. She was ahead of him there as she had also purchased a lap top, and anticipating the need, had purchased an all in one, which she had him hook the high-speed internet up to. As the cabin had never before been wired for cable or internet, it took him a while to get them both into the house, and he ran the cables into the basement and up through a relatively small hole in the corner to keep it discrete. She had cable in both bedrooms and the living room by the time he was finished. With the router, it could go anywhere in the cabin, probably even out to the garage if she wanted to use the internet on her new laptop.

Not wanting to bother him while he worked, she instead played with her new cell phone. She hadn't had time to program it before, but she knew so few numbers that she quickly had Abby's in it as well as Lenora's and the few others she had accumulated since she came to town. It startled her when her house phone rang as she certainly hadn't been expecting a phone call. "Hello?" she asked cautiously.

"Hi, is this Amy?" a cheerful male voice answered her hesitant greeting.

"Yes, this is Amy," she responded, wondering who was calling her.

"This is Stephan," he answered and waited. At her silence over his announcement, he added, "I have Labs for sale?" he added.

"Oh, hello, sorry I didn't remember the name that Jacob told me!" she said, feeling apologetic at not recognizing the name.

"That's okay," he accepted graciously. "Still interested in a pup?" he asked.

"Yes, yes I am, how old are they?" she asked as she sat down on her couch.

"They are twelve weeks," he told her and then went on to tell her about the unexpected litter. They hadn't even known their bitch was in heat. They suspected the neighbor's male lab was the father, but as they didn't know who really was the parent, he wouldn't be able to supply papers, and the pups were reasonably priced, even though his hunting bitch was papered and a champion. The reason they were so old was because it was the wrong time of year, and he hadn't wanted to take them to the pound where they might be put down.

Amy didn't care about papers but wanted to see the pups, so she made arrangements to go see them, and he gave her directions to his place. She would leave as soon as Craig the cable guy installed her service.

"Well, there you go; you are all set up," he told her a while later as she signed for his services. As an independent contractor for the main cable company, he needed the signature to get paid.

"I'm going to need high speed internet in the store I'm opening in town, do I call you or the cable company to come out?" she asked.

He whipped out a card and said, "Call me when you're ready, and I'll hook you up." He smiled charmingly at the double entendre.

She laughed at his wit and thanked him for his time. She waved as he packed up his van and left. Smiling, she stored the card's numbers in her new phone and then filed the card on the kitchen table before locking up and heading out in her SUV.

CHAPTER SIX

The directions that Stephan had given her went right through town and then south into an area she hadn't seen before, but it was pretty in the late afternoon light. She pulled into a yard with a house that had to have been built in the seventies from the architecture. It reminded her of something out of the TV series 'The Brady Bunch', but she didn't have a lot of time to look at it as a pack of Labrador Retrievers came running towards her SUV. She stood there as they thoroughly sniffed her and determined she wasn't a threat, their tails wagging madly as she looked on in delight at the different dogs. There seemed to be three adults and at least six pups. One of the younger pups after sniffing her, sat back and watched its siblings. Its eyes were an oddly human blue against its almost white coat. She wondered if it was an albino, and she had heard that albino pets were frequently blind or deaf, but this one saw her all right as it watched both her and its litter mates as they vied for her attention. She was trying to pet them as quickly as she could.

"Hi there, I see you've met the pack," a voice called, and she looked up into the grey eyes of a lumberjack.

She smiled in return. "Hello, I'm Amy," she held out her hand to be shaken.

"I thought I heard a southern accent," he commented as he shook it. "I'm Stephan."

"Yes, I just moved here," she said in reply, not giving out any further information.

"Well, these are the troops," he said, putting his hands out wide at the mass of dog hood. "They were unexpected, but they are a happy bunch," he told her.

She smiled as she knelt to their level only to be immediately overwhelmed by the pups. The adults were much better as they enthusiastically greeted her again, and she tried to pet them.

"Careful there, if they get you down, you're gonna be licked to death," he laughed.

Amy quickly stood up again getting her face out of range as she tried and failed to pet the many dogs, having to satisfy herself and them with a pet across each of the noble heads. Her eyes kept going back to the nearly white pup with the unusual blue eyes. "Is that one a male?" she asked pointing to it.

"That's Toby, and yes, he is," Stephan answered as he looked at the lone dog.

Amy went over to him where he stood apart from his over active siblings; he greeted her gratefully and enthusiastically, but the other pups had followed and were soon swarming him and her as she tried to pet the lone pup. She watched as they easily fell into rough dog play and soon were rolling and mock growling, Toby included. She smiled at their puppy antics. It didn't take her long to decide, and she wrote out a check to Stephan for the pup. He gave her a leash and a collar for the pup, told her they had already been house trained, and gave her a bagful of food for the night when she confessed she didn't have any.

"Well, I raised them on Iams like I would have any of our pure-bred litters, but you will have to decide what to feed him," he informed her as he helped her get the gangly pup into the SUV. "They've had their first shots, and I've got a certificate here I can give you," he said as he fished out a sheaf of papers. Toby wasn't sure he liked going somewhere without his siblings who were looking and trying to climb into the front seat with him. "Get down there," Stephan told them as he kneed them off the step and quickly closed the door after handing her Toby's shot certificate.

"Thank you so much," Amy told him as she waited for him to walk away with the others before backing carefully out of the driveway.

Toby looked around, but the idea of car ride must have appealed to him, and he didn't realize yet that he was leaving his parents and siblings.

Amy drove back towards the cabin and spent the evening getting to know her pup. He was house trained and told her a couple of times he had to go out. She thought it was more to smell around the cabin than because he wanted to pee. At the rate he was going though, every tree in the yard would soon be marked by his scent. She laughed at him as he dashed after leaves and anything that blew in the yard. She could tell he was looking for something, and she felt bad realizing it was probably his littermates.

He finally settled down after she fed him a bowl full of kibble, and she left the water dish down beside it. As she powered up her laptop, he tried to join her on the couch, but she had seen how big his mother and the other adult labs had been, and she pushed him to the floor beside her repeatedly until he gave up.

He whimpered when she attempted to close the bedroom door on his sorrowful face, so she let him sleep on the floor next to her bed. He tried to climb into it a few times, but again, like the couch, that was going to be a no go. Finally, exhausted, he fell into an uneasy sleep next to the bed with her hand dangling down to pet him.

The first order of business the next morning was to get him set up, and she took him with her after he pooped and peed in the yard. She headed south to the largest pet food store she knew of after Googling it. She got him a bed for the living room, one for the bedroom, a stainless-steel set of bowls, chew toys, and a large bag of puppy kibble as he was still a growing boy. She also got a soft brush and comb set. Labs didn't need the same type of grooming that other breeds did, so she knew she would be brushing to remove hair that would cling everywhere, but she didn't mind; she had counted on that in her new housemate.

It wasn't soon enough for the chew toys as she found one of her shoes chewed up and yelled at the pup with the now mangled shoe dangling from her hand, and the pup cowering in abject apology over it. She hoped that would be the extent of the necessary discipline as she felt terrible for yelling at him. He had to learn that her shoes were out of bounds as were the towels, socks, and other things he attempted to turn into chew toys. He learned slowly but surely as she took them away from him. Her encouragement of the designated dog toys taught him right from wrong, but still he tried her patience as any fur kid would.

K'ANNE MEINEL

CHAPTER SEVEN

The appliances and other furniture she had ordered arrived and were soon installed. She took Toby with her and kept him in the back of the SUV by a clever bar system that didn't allow the gangly teenager to climb over the back seat but forced him to stay in the very back. She gave him a doggie blanket and a chew toy to keep him occupied as she ran into the store to shop for human groceries for the cabin. She felt this need to stock up and planned to take a trip to Green Bay soon to the nearest Sam's Club as they didn't have a Costco in this state. He did pretty well in the car by himself, but she could tell he didn't like it despite the coolness with the windows rolled slightly down. He simply didn't like to be alone. She didn't know how she was going to break him of that as there would be times and places he couldn't go.

She met with a couple of contractors that Abby had recommended, and then had Abby watch amused as she explained what she wanted for the store. She had drawn it out, but her sketches either didn't make sense to these people or she was a really poor designer. She hoped it wasn't going to be a problem, but she was getting frustrated until a third contractor actually caught onto the theme she was working with and agreed to give her a quote.

Amy spent a lot of time on her laptop sending for catalogs and quotes for supplies for the store. The contract she had with Abby began officially at the beginning of the next month, which she was assured was a slow month for tourists after the fall leaves had all fallen and before they got snow or snowmobilers. The thought of snow that deep worried her.

"I don't know how I'm going to plow out my driveway," she confided to Abby as she watched the contractor measuring things for the displays that she was having him build.

"Maybe you could hire someone to come plow you out or maybe buy yourself a plow for your SUV?" she teased.

Amy laughed as she was expected to, but the idea did have merit, and she began checking out the ads in the newspaper. She decided against putting an after-market plow on her SUV as what she read up on-line indicated it could do more damage to the truck than it was worth. She did get another idea that she looked into on one of her many trips around the various towns and cities in Door County to check out her competition. She saw an ATV dealer, and she went in to inquire about a used ATV, but few if any dealers took trade-ins; she was advised to check the paper in spring if she really wanted a used one. They did, however, have 'end of year' deals on the new ATV's, and she bought herself a Yamaha Grizzly with a big basket on the front in front of the windshield, two packs on the back, and an extra seat that she could already envision Toby sitting in as she plowed. They showed her how to attach and reattach the plow, and after she mastered that, she paid for it all, and they registered the machine for her. They showed her how to drive it as she practiced around and around in the parking lot of the dealer. They also talked her into a small trailer to pull it behind her SUV, and until it was ensconced in her garage, she didn't feel like it was truly hers.

She was truly on a waiting game as she waited for the contract on the store to start, so she used it wisely as she decorated and made the cabin even homier. She taught herself to replace the damaged wood floor in the kitchen. Then she took it a step further and put down a 'floating' floor of laminate wood, which looked just as nice as the real thing. With the slight up level from the living room, she put a riser between the two rooms, and it flowed beautifully. She put a new ring in the floor for the basement where she stored the extra supplies she was accumulating for winter.

In the time she waited to take possession of her new store and before the contractor would begin, she went through endless catalogs using post-it notes to mark the pages of merchandise she didn't see her competitors having and equipment she wanted to order. She had budgeted exactly how much she was willing to spend on each item as well as if she purchased the store, even the cabin, and was pleased with how things were coming together.

It wasn't until Abby actually handed her the keys, locked the door between the store and her house, and she dead bolted it, that Amy really felt it was her place. She began to box up the remaining merchandise in the store. She had help in the form of Abby, her daughter Heather, Bonnie, and even Bailey, Abby's son she had finally met. They willingly helped her, which surprised and delighted her, but she sensed part of the appeal was the pup she brought with her everywhere.

Abby had been surprised to see the pup glued to Amy's side as she walked it through town. She had been a witness to Lenora finding out but had been impressed when Amy pointed out to the snooty woman that nothing in the contract for the cabin stated that pets weren't allowed. Lenora had been left gasping like a fish out of water at Amy's audacity of being firmly put in her place in regards to their 'business' relationship.

The pup was well behaved for the most part, mischievous occasionally; as they packed up the store, it soon had a bed in the store of its own. After packing away all the goods, the contractor came in and tore the store apart and still managed to retain the flavor of Abby's grandparents' old store. In fact, they enhanced the old store. It was revived as things got repainted, sanded, and brought up to code. Abby saw Amy occasionally as she was at her store every day. The boardwalk and dock around the store all got sanded and coated to restore and preserve it; any dry rot was fixed and dealt with. Occasionally, Amy had questions for Abby or Bonnie about their past suppliers, but all business had been halted while the store was restored. Amy had the outside done first since time was limited with winter coming on. The place was taped off to discourage tourists and townies alike from getting on the newly restored boardwalk or using the dockage as she wasn't up to selling gasoline. She had the tanks inspected and a certificate issued that showed the viability so she could sell gasoline at the dock in the spring or in winter with the snowmobilers.

As she watched the store come together, she checked out all the local utilities, sometimes traveling to other towns and villages to find their offices as she had when she had her electricity and other things turned on to check out franchise opportunities. Her store would be able to accept payments or make arrangements to have things such as that turned on instead of people having to travel all over as she had, from cable to electric, gas to phone, and even cell phones. She asked about putting a small franchise office into the store, making it a good-old fashioned full-service general merchandise store. She was as thrilled and amazed as they were at her asking, and while it took some time with some of them to actually get a 'yes', she slowly but surely got her replies. The only one that gave her a hard time was the U.S. Postal Service, but she knew that they wanted these small satellite franchises, and her putting in a bank of postal boxes in her store wall meant they would do that for her after she attended classes and was properly trained like the other utilities. She even hooked up with UPS and FedEx who had contracts with the postal service. She would personally be authorized to accept all that, and she even applied to be a notary. All this training would take weeks, months even, for some of the services. If she stuck with it, the store would be a great help to those, especially newcomers or elderly customers, who didn't want to travel all over for these services.

"Oh, look at that," she said delighted as the contractor put the finishing touches on the counter on one side of the store. She was thrilled with the colors she had chosen with him. It was all so warm and homey and nostalgic.

"You have an intruder," he told her as he finished up that day, and she swept up after him trying to help out and keep her puppy out of his way.

"What do you mean?" she asked alarmed.

"Look here," he showed her one of the backrooms that contained his contractor supplies, and they found small footprints in the sawdust that coated nearly everything in the store. They seemingly disappeared though, and that confused them both.

"What the heck?" she drawled out and scratched her head. "How often have you seen this?" she asked concerned.

"Nearly every day, but today I had proof they are playing around with my stuff, and I wanted you to know," he showed her where whoever it was had touched some of the tools.

This really concerned her, as anyone who got hurt might fall under her insurance, and she didn't want her rates raised. Furthermore, the size of the prints indicated a child. The only children she knew of were Abby's, and she didn't want to upset her new friend who had been so supportive. Still, the only one who had ever had keys to the store had been Abby and her family. The next day, she changed all the locks, including the one on the door between the store and house next door where Abby lived with her mother-in-law and children. She had never seen a husband nor had she ever asked about him. She felt her own secrets were safe from not inquiring too much.

"Hey Abby?" she called a few days later after she had changed the locks. She had also installed a chain across the connecting door and still they found the prints in the sawdust. She had seen Abby getting out of her car, she assumed after work. She was carrying a black sports bag that looked heavy, but her muscular arms seemed to carry it no problem.

"Hi, how goes the remodel?" she smiled in response, shading her eyes from the glare off the water from the setting sun.

"It's going good, um," now confronting Abby and telling her about the prints made her feel uncomfortable.

"Something wrong? Terry unable to handle the job?" she asked concerned.

"No, no, Terry is doing a terrific job, right on schedule. In fact, we are ahead of schedule, just waiting on a few people and the equipment we ordered," she told her. "It's just that...."

"What?" Abby asked, getting a little bit impatient.

"There seems to be a daily intruder in the place," Amy blurted out.

"An intruder?" Abby asked in concern. A brunette eyebrow, perfectly and naturally sculptured, rose in question.

Amy nodded as she looked into the velvety brown eyes of her friend. "Yes, we keep finding things touched and played with, and the shoes' prints in the sawdust indicate it's a child." She waited.

At the word 'child' Abby cocked her head in dejection. "Do you know which one?" she asked

Amy shook her head but indicated that Abby could come into the store and see for herself. She placed her bag inside the door and hitched up her slacks and followed Amy back to the storeroom where not one, but two sets of shoes were now visible. "What the heck?" Amy said in alarm. These two sets appeared out of nowhere and disappeared the same way, but she didn't understand where they had come from in the first place.

"I thought you said, 'a child?'" Abby asked as she examined the evidence.

Amy nodded. "I did, but this second set I hadn't seen before today."

"That's an adult shoe," Abby pointed out.

"But it's a sports shoe, all the guys, myself included wear work boots," Amy said showing off her foot with its stylish female work boot. Just then, the puppy started yapping and scrambling towards the other storage room where the supplies for the store were stored. The two women followed instantly and found Heather fending off the tongue of Toby.

"Heather! How in the world did you get in here?" Amy asked as she looked around. She had checked the whole store before locking up and seeing Abby. She had been about to grab Toby and leave for the day when she saw Abby and hailed her in.

The young girl looked terrified, not only to be caught by her mother, but the new owner of the store. She had been over a few times to watch as the men remodeling the store had brought in machinery and other things as they worked. Amy had asked her to stay out, but she had been so curious she had been coming over daily to see what new surprises the store held for her. Even Bailey had joined her earlier, but she had forgotten a doll she had left and came back for it when she thought Amy had left for the day.

"Heather, Miss Adams asked you a question," Abby said to her daughter. "Aren't you going to answer her?"

"I came in through the secret panel," the little girl lisped; she was shaking in her shoes, and just then a panel moved as Bailey hissed, "Heather, hurry up, Mom's home!"

Abby swooped down and pulled the panel aside and grabbed her son by the hair, pulling him through the hole the panel created.

"Ow, Ow, OW!" the boy yelled.

"What are you two doing in this store?" Abby stormed angrily. "Don't you know that's trespassing?" Then she thought for a moment as her son stood upright and began to rub his head where the hair pulling had occurred. "Where does this panel open up to?" she asked, but neither of the children answered her as they were too afraid of her anger. She knelt down and poked her head through and looked around into her own house. This was in her back room that butted up to the store but down a hall from the doorway they had locked. "For crying out loud," she said exasperatedly as she pulled the panel shut, effectively blocking the children from escaping back into the house. She stood up and turned to an amused Amy who was looking on and shaking her head.

"I am so sorry Amy; I had no idea this panel existed, and I should have, but I'll have the children pay for any damages."

Amy shrugged. "There is no damage, but we better make sure that we seal that so we have no more surprise visits."

Abby nodded as she turned to the two children who hung their heads. "You know better than to go onto other people's property. What do you have to say for yourselves?" she said in a steely voice.

"Sorry," both of the children said as they looked down at their shoes.

Amy tried not to laugh, but the twitching in her mouth belied that. Fortunately, neither of the children saw it.

"Come on you two, out, through the front door!" Abby roared as Bailey made a gesture like he was going back through the panel. Both children turned from the cramped store room and headed out into the main store. "I'm really sorry Amy; I had no idea that either of them was doing this. Bonnie was supposed to be watching them while I was at work."

"No harm no foul, at least we didn't have to get the police involved," Amy said cheerfully and was startled at the odd look that Abby gave her.

"Yes, that," she said in return as she ushered the two children out. "They will be punished I assure you," she said as she closed the front door that had been changed from the old single door to a double French door look.

Amy hoped that Abby wouldn't be too harsh on the children. The puppy returned, and she realized Toby had run when Abby raised her voice; she wondered where he had gotten to, and then she shrugged. She looked around and found a sheet of laminate she knew was extra and wouldn't be missed, so she propped it up against the wall in the storage room and pushed the boxes stored there against it so the children couldn't get back in. It was a temporary fix, but for now it would work.

CHAPTER EIGHT

With all the training and traveling she had to do to find things for the store, the rest of fall passed quite quickly. Winter didn't catch her unprepared though. The frequent trips to the bigger towns and then the city meant that she could stock up, and she took advantage of it to buy flats of canned vegetables, which she placed in her basement. She had managed to assemble some plastic shelves down there; she had chosen plastic because basements were frequently damp, and she didn't want them to rust. This gave her plenty of space to stack her supplies. Toby yapped at the scurryings now that he was older, and she wondered if she had rodents moving in for winter.

She saw Abby from time to time as she went to and from the store as the work progressed. Terry had expressed his delight in having work this late in the season as snow plowing was another of the many jobs the contractor did to help make ends meet. By having her remodel to do, he and his crew had an unexpected bonus of work before Christmas. He assured her that he and his crew would be done right after New Year's, and that would allow her ample time to open for the spring rush of tourists who came up to use the snowmobile trails and go ice fishing or cross-country skiing. To Amy, that sounded so far off.

Amy discovered that Wisconsinites had a wonderful tradition of Friday night fish fry's, and she soon found herself welcomed as a regular at Chuckie's as she sampled cod, haddock, trout, and other fish that was deep fried and served hot. She found herself making friends and was delighted when they allowed her to bring Toby in as the season turned colder. He learned to make himself as small as he could and to hide under her chair to avoid anyone treading on his paws or tail. He wasn't an only dog to this family affair and soon made friends with other townies who brought their pets to this socialization. Amy loved it as she got to know her neighbors, and they tried to get to know her. The southerner was notoriously quiet about her own history though. The rumor was that she was a widow and had moved far away from her past, but no one knew that much about her. They knew about the cabin and the store, but other than that, her past was a blank. Amy deliberately avoided personal questions and adroitly changed the subject whenever anyone asked questions she didn't care to answer.

"Why is that cruiser always parked in Abby's driveway?" she asked after being there for a couple of months. The work on the store was slowing down for Christmas, and their first light snowfall had fallen. She was talking to a few friends she had made at Chuckie's as she sipped a beer and waited on her beer battered fish.

"You don't know?" Kerry asked in surprise.

Amy shook her head wondering what she had missed. The cruiser looked like a cop car, but she had never seen lights on it; it just gave her a bad vibe every time she saw it. The thought that Abby drove an identical car too hadn't occurred to her. Maybe Abby's husband was a cop?

Just then Abby came into the bar with her children and mother-in-law, Bonnie. People greeted her as they did in a small community where everyone knew everyone else. Even some of the out-of-towners, the tourists, some of whom had been coming to this community for years were frequently greeted like this. It made Amy feel she belonged here as she watched the family welcomed. They were soon seated at a booth, and the server took their order as Abby came up to the bar and greeted some of the patrons.

"Not working tonight, Abby?" Kerry asked her with a grin, remembering the question Amy had asked her a few minutes before.

"No, not tonight Kerry." She looked up at the bartender. "Two root beers, two drafts please," she called, and he nodded to show he had heard her.

"No patrol?" Kerry persisted with a grin and looked at Amy who was wondering what her friend was talking about.

"No, no patrol, not tonight," she answered and frowned at the grin. She saw Amy sitting there with some of the regulars and smiled. "Hi Amy, here for the fish fry?"

"Yes, thank you, it's one of the best."

"Yes, it is, Chuckie's recipe must have been in his grandmother's grandmother's family; we always came here," she chuckled at her own joke.

"Abby, Amy was just asking about you," Kerry teased.

Abby glanced at Kerry before looking at Amy again inquiringly. "You were? What'd you want to know?" she asked.

Amy felt put on the spot and glared at Kerry who was grinning unrepentantly. "She wanted to know why there is always a patrol car in your driveway." She laughed.

Amy looked apologetically at Abby for having asked about her like that. She tried to explain; "I thought perhaps your husband drove it…" she began, but stopped when Kerry spewed the beer she had just taken a drink of. She turned in alarm as the spray hit her arm and leg. "Kerry! What in the world?"

Abby called to the bartender, "Bar rag!" and was thrown one, which she adroitly caught and handed to Amy who delicately blotted at her arm and leg cleaning up the sprayed beer. "No, it is not my *husband's*," she spat the last word. Amy looked up to see some sort of defiance in the brunette's eyes as she continued, "I'm the local police, and I need the patrol car for work," she explained.

"Oh, I'm sorry, I didn't realize," Amy sputtered, stiffening at the information. Only Abby realized it as she watched the pretty redhead turn red in the face.

"Furthermore, I never had a *husband*," she spat out that word again as she watched the redhead closely. Almost challengingly.

"I'm sorry, you introduced Bonnie as your mother-in-law?" she asked, now thoroughly confused and wondering how she had made such a mistake.

Abby nodded and continued, "Bonnie is my mother-in-law; she was my wife's *mother*." She watched as Amy became aware of what she was saying…exactly.

Amy's green eyes opened wide at the information of what Abby was implying. She tried to hide her shock but had been unsuccessful. Kerry was laughing openly now. Amy flushed in embarrassment over the mistake she had made and the assumptions. No wonder the children didn't look any bit like this brunette. She had assumed that they took after Abby's husband and now realized the enormity of her mistake.

Abby smiled suddenly as she watched Amy squirm. "It's okay, not everyone gets that around here either." She gathered the four mugs the bartender had put down and headed back to her table. She only threw one regretful glance at Amy before she sat down with her family.

"That was probably one of the funniest things I've seen in a long time," Kerry wheezed.

Amy looked at her friend and wondered how she hadn't seen how mean Kerry could be. That was really an awkward situation, and she hadn't made it any easier. Not only had Amy been embarrassed but so had Abby. She had never suspected that the woman was a cop or that she was a lesbian. She felt very bad at how that had made her feel, much less how Abby must feel explaining it to her.

"Bob, could I get that order to go?" she asked the bartender who nodded.

"Go—you have to go?" Kerry asked in alarm. She hadn't enjoyed herself more in a long time.

"Yes, I remembered some research I needed to do for the store. I have to get home to my computer and catalogs," Abby said to her in her pearliest southern tones. She had been raised to be a lady; she wouldn't strike out at this rude woman who had laughed at her expense.

"Can't that wait? It's Friday night, and you have the whole weekend," Kerry tried to be reasonable, but Amy wouldn't be turned from her plans, and she took her fish fry home with her.

Amy was shaking when she got home. She felt somehow betrayed as she thought over the evening and her new-found friends. She felt like Abby had lied by omission, but at the same time she had never actually asked what she did for a living. It felt...odd. She had gone into a land-contract with the local police officer and didn't even know it. The fact that Abby was also a lesbian didn't even faze her. It was the fact that she was a cop that had her reeling.

She heated up her now cold fish fry in the new microwave oven she had installed in the kitchen and ate a lonely dinner for one with Toby trying hard not to beg. She looked over at him and asked, "You aren't begging, are you Toby?" and then nearly laughed as he looked determinedly away. He was so smart and such a great companion that she had loved their months together as she taught and trained him to be the perfect roommate. His early chewing's had ruined more than one pair of shoes and other things, but she kept him well supplied with many things that he could use his puppy teeth on, and he learned to behave.

Going to bed that night, she heard the rustlings that meant she had some housemates she didn't desire, and she wondered about getting a cat. Then she wondered if she was taking on too much with the cabin, the store, and starting this new life. If she left tomorrow, packed up her

SUV and the dog and left, she would lose so much. Not just the material things, but the friends she had made. She had already crossed Kerry off her ever-growing list of friends.

She cried into her pillow that night, and Toby tried once again to get on the four-poster bed and comfort her. It was her concern over the dog, or so she told herself, that slowly quieted her tears.

CHAPTER NINE

The village was picturesque as the town got together and decorated. They put up large oversized candy canes and strung lights. Tourists still came despite the cold that took one's breath away. Amy bought herself a snowsuit, and the jacket was worn all winter long as she went out to her training and stopped in at the store for deliveries, progress reports, and to gaze about at the store that was coming together. Terry and his men really took pride in their work and had really understood the concept of what Amy wanted to put together and had more than surpassed it.

Amy didn't do it on purpose, but she managed to avoid Abby as Christmas approached. She bought her fur kid a surplus of toys, which he ripped open gleefully from under the tree she had purchased and put up. His tail knocked more than one ornament off the tree she had decorated. He seemed to know that most of the presents under the tree were for him, and when she allowed him to 'open' them on Christmas Eve, he tore into them like any child would. It wasn't until each one of them had been opened and the few she had bought for herself were opened that he went back to the toys and sat down with them to gnaw and play with them. Amy carefully gathered up the torn packages and wrapping paper and put it into the fireplace where it flared up as she sat on her couch drinking a local red wine and gazed at the little tree and remembered past Christmases.

She had baked cookies and taken them to Terry and his men in gaily wrapped little packages. She left a small hamper on Lenora's doorstep with a card and a larger one on Abby's. She had more cookies than she could possibly eat as she gazed around her cozy little cabin and watched the snow fall outside with only the lights of the Christmas tree on. She must have dozed off because suddenly Toby was barking and someone was knocking on her front door.

"Hello?" she called as she went to open the sturdy door. She had replaced the screen door with a weather door so she had a second door to open, but she could see through this one and saw to her astonishment a bundled-up Abby, Heather, and an obviously reluctant Bailey standing on her porch. "Come in, come in," she said as she opened the doors.

"Merry Christmas," she heard both Abby and Heather murmur through their wraps as they came in. Bailey didn't say a word as he came in, and she closed the doors behind him.

"Merry Christmas, why this is a surprise," she said as she began to help Heather off with her wraps and watched as Bailey and Abby began to take off theirs.

"I hope you don't mind; I knew you would be alone this Christmas, and Heather thought we should bring you a present."

"You did?" she said surprised as she took the last of Heather's wraps away from the child and hung them over the end of the couch.

Heather nodded as she held out an obviously child wrapped present to the redhead.

"Do I have to wait until Christmas day or may I open it now?" she asked the child.

"Well, I think you should open it now," Abby said with a grin as she removed the last of her outdoor clothes and plopped them over her daughters on the couch where Amy had laid them. Bailey followed suit. He also sat on the couch and pet the eager puppy who was greeting him effusively, trying to bring him one his new toys but turning away teasingly when Bailey reached for it.

Amy smiled at Abby and looked down at the little girl waiting for an answer from her. "I think you should open it now," she repeated shyly.

Amy opened it and found a picture of the store; it must have been from the 1800's as it was in black and white and looked so old. She gazed at it a moment before she beamed down at the child and said, "Why, this is wonderful; where in the world did you find it?" she asked excitedly.

"We were going through old trunks of my grandparents and came across the pictures; there are others, but that's the best," Abby explained.

"Why, this is fantastic. I know exactly where I'm going to hang it too!" she exclaimed in delight.

Heather smiled, and it was obvious she could barely contain herself as she danced in place.

"I wanted to thank you for the hamper; that was really sweet, and totally unnecessary," Abby told her as she looked at the genuine enjoyment over the picture.

"Oh, that's okay, you are most welcome; I hope you enjoyed all the little treats," Amy smiled in response as she picked up the picture and put it over the mantel above the fireplace. She stood back to enjoy it and then put the wrappings aside to burn later when her guests were gone. It would have been rude in her mind to burn them in front of her guests.

"I did, what little I got of them; this glutton here ate all the cookies," Abby said affectionately as she rubbed Bailey's hair.

"Stop," he protested, annoyed as he tried to play with the dog. He started to blush.

Abby laughed at him as Amy smiled at the family picture. "Well, I have more if you are interested?" She could tell her guests were interested as three heads came up in response to her question. She walked into the kitchen and flicked on a light. She went into a cupboard and removed a large plate piled high with cookies and brought out the entire plate for her guests to pick and choose.

"Only one for you, Bailey!" Abby warned in a joking manner as he reached for one, but no one was fooled; she meant it.

"So, how have you been?" Amy asked as she took a seat on the matching chair to her couch set and watched the children pick over the cookies. When he thought Abby wasn't looking, Bailey snatched a second cookie.

"Just the usual, lots of people don't know how to drive in the snow, so I go out on calls like that a lot," Abby said as she munched around a cookie shaped like a Christmas tree. "How's the store coming along? Since you put up the papers on all the windows, no one can see in," she teased.

Amy laughed; she had known that doing that would engender more curiosity, and that would be good for the store. "Well, Terry and his crew are almost done, then it's up to me to hire some staff and get the store in shape for its grand openin'."

"Do you know when that will be?" Abby asked, genuinely interested as she helped herself to another cookie.

The children were soon playing with the delighted puppy who showed them all his new toys one by one. They rolled them across the floor and tossed them before Abby could stop them, nearly knocking the Christmas tree over. Amidst all the chaos created by the children and the pet, the two adults managed to carry on a civil conversation as Amy told her what she had been up to.

"That's smart, bringing all that into the store; no one had thought of doing that before. I wondered when Ben McCormick said they would be closing his office what he meant."

"Who is Ben McCormick?" Amy asked, concerned.

"He ran the phone store down in Egg Harbor; they must be transferring the business up to your store then."

"Oh no, I meant to create jobs not take his away!" Amy said troubled.

"No, no, he was retired and was glad to hear they would be closing it; he hadn't wanted to work there anymore for years, but they didn't listen to him; now he can truly retire," Abby reassured her.

"Whew, that's good! I'll be able to take payments over the phone too, that way they are setting everything up for me."

"That's going to be very convenient," Abby told her as they continued their delightful conversation. Before she knew it, they had been there two hours. She thanked her host as they got dressed to go back out into the winter's night. The puppy was panting delightedly as the children had worn him out. Amy pressed more cookies on her guests as she saw them out and wished them a Merry Christmas. She looked out and waved as they got into the patrol car, and she saw how deep the snow was getting.

Amy thought over their conversations in the coming days. She had really enjoyed getting to know Abby better, and other new friends dropped by over the holidays. She didn't feel alone, and she kept a plateful of cookies and hot cocoa ready for her visitors. She went with a couple to the local Lutheran Church for New Year's. Having been brought up Southern Baptist, it didn't feel the same, even though it was a pleasant experience.

CHAPTER TEN

Amy got to use her ATV for the first time the next day as she plowed out her driveway. It wasn't as deep as she had hoped; the tall pine trees hid a lot of snow in their branches. She scared Toby the first time she started it up, but with a little coaxing and showing him the perch just for him, she was able to get him back on the machine. Moving scared him again, but the young pup was game, and she was soon trying out her blade and trying to remember what the salesman had taught her so long ago. She had fun, and the dog seemed to enjoy himself from the back of the machine as she slowly removed all the snow from her driveway and even the walk up to her front door. She was reluctant to put away the machine with all the fun she was having, but there would always be another day. She had heard of those who went on ATV trails even in winter and made a note to ask someone about that next Friday at Chuckie's.

Amy had the time of her life riding on the ATV trails with others from town once she found out about it. The ups and downs of the trail, the speed, and the snow whipping at them was exciting. She couldn't always take Toby as it got too cold. She herself had bought a snowmobile outfit right down to the goggles and a balaclava and was really quite warm as she joined the others on this adventure. Still others went out on the snowmobile trails, and she thought about getting one of those as well but instead just enjoyed her new friends and rode along on theirs when she could.

CHAPTER ELEVEN

Amy was looking out over the lake as she bit her lip thoughtfully. She had just come out from the store where she was setting up things for the final touches and had come outside for a breath of fresh air. Some of the chemicals that the guys were using to put in things in her store gave her a headache, and she needed to breathe the cool, fresh, air.

"Good Morning," Abby greeted her; she had seen her from her own kitchen window and came outside before going out on her patrol. Her front living room had been converted to the local field office, and while vague promises had been made to actually turn one of the buildings in town into the police station, it had never happened in the few years she had been an officer up here. The county found it too convenient to just pay her a stipend to use her own home. There wasn't enough crime in the area to make it worth their while to do a whole remodel of an actual building.

Amy turned from her thoughtful meanderings with a smile and dimples that took Abby's breath away, that and the cold weather that had moved into the area. "Good Morning, how are you Abby?"

"Middling," she grunted as she took a sip of the coffee she had brought with her out onto the deck.

Amy grinned at the surly tone, knowing it was affected for her benefit. Abby tried to come across as this curmudgeon, but everyone knew what a pleasant woman she really was.

"This place coming along?" Abby inclined her head to the store where she could hear the guys putting something together with loud bangs, a few cuss words, and lots of noise.

Amy nodded enthusiastically. "It should be done right on schedule," she lost her smile as she answered though.

"What's wrong then?" Abby asked seeing it.

"Well, I have to go out of town for a convention; I have to find things in person to buy for the store," she said as Toby walked out of the ajar door to see where she was, wagging his tail happily as he greeted Abby. Toby had never met a stranger.

"So, what is the problem? Terry will continue the work whether you are here or not? Gonna miss the rides on the trails?" she grinned teasingly. She'd heard about those trips and in fact went out on a couple of the snowmobile rides herself but had missed the ATV ones or the ones that Amy went on with others.

"No, I am sure Terry is perfectly capable of finishin' without me being here," she drawled with a grin as Toby insinuated his head under Abby's gloved hand. She tucked her own hands under her arms to keep them warm in the cold winter's wind coming off the lake; she glanced at the drifts, some of the shadows causing them to look blue. "It's just that I don't know what to do with Toby, and I hate the idea of him being in a cage at the vets." She looked at her dog with such adoring affection. She had found a vet shortly after getting him and made sure his shots were on time and keeping him healthy. She had gotten his license and a microchip registered to her at the same time. It made her realize that perhaps some of the licenses in town could be obtained through her store as well, and she had looked into it. Dealing with the county or state was a whole lot different than dealing with the different businesses she had already contracted with.

"So why don't you let me keep him?" Abby offered generously.

"Oh, I wouldn't want to bother you," her accent made it sound so pretty. "I couldn't impose," she said doubtfully.

"It wouldn't be a bother; the kids would love it," she rubbed under the dog's ears who lifted his head appreciatively. "They've been after me for a while to get a dog; this might determine if we ever get one."

"But how would your mother-in-law feel?" she asked knowingly. She had heard the gossip of Bonnie trying to get custody of the kids who were her grandchildren, but that Abby had been left sole custody of her wife's children. It had caused a lot of gossip and hard feelings after her wife's death.

Abby shrugged knowingly. "She'll have to live with it, won't she? Just like everything else." She was very well aware that Amy probably had heard some of the gossip. No one knew the full story, that she had settled things with Bonnie and her husband Jake and that they could live with her in the house she and her wife had lived in. In exchange, they would help raise their grandchildren, but Abby would never give up custody of her children. When Jake had passed away, he had been one of the local deputies out of a neighboring town; Abby had arranged for the sub-station here in Northpoint to run out of her home. As she was already a deputy, she took over his work as well. Bonnie ran her office for her and watched the kids while she worked. The store had taken up some of each of their time, but it had been her wife's dream, not Abby's. Abby's grandparents had passed, knowing that it would be taken care of by this unorthodox family that their granddaughter had created; she had been happy, that was enough for them, and they accepted their great grandchildren without a qualm. It was her parents who refused to accept that Abby was gay, had a wife, and children via that wife. When her grandparents had died, especially when her wife died, they had expected her to sell up everything and come back to the mainland. Abby hadn't even considered it.

Remembering how the children had played with the pup at Christmas and how often Heather greeted the pup longingly as she stopped in at the store, she was certain that the dog would be well taken care of. She really didn't want him in the sterile atmosphere of the vets and in a cage. She shuddered at the thought. "If you are sure…" she began hesitantly.

"Of course I'm sure; if I asked the kids now, they'd jump out of their skins," Abby assured her. "What are the dates of your convention?" she asked.

Amy smiled; one problem solved as she discussed the particulars with her kind neighbor. She left Toby in her capable hands as she drove herself down The Thumb and to the airport in Green Bay, flying south to Chicago and then west to the convention where she looked for items that she could add to her store to make it authentic and add to its overall impression. She had a wonderful, if lonely, time. The lights of the big city didn't impress her, and she missed her little town. She found lots of things for the store and placed orders realizing she had needed the business cards and other paperwork she had ordered well in advance of the convention and gave them out willingly as she wrote up purchase orders with the various vendors. They all promised prompt delivery as she even wrote out a few checks to prepay her orders and get deals on free shipping or bulk orders. She congratulated herself on her business savvy and really looked forward to seeing the merchandise she had ordered in her store.

When she returned to Green Bay and recovered her SUV, she spent the rest of the day and the next day shopping around the town for her home and for the store. Deliveries weren't a problem, and she filled the back of her SUV once again before trekking back up The Thumb to home. She couldn't wait to get there; she loved living up in Northpoint. The people were friendly, her home was wonderful, she loved having Toby, and she felt like she had really made a place for herself. She'd made friends, and that was as good as having family.

She picked up Toby who seemed almost reluctant to leave the two children after a week with them, but then remembered who he loved the most and willingly got into the SUV with Amy. "I can't thank you all enough for your kindness," she told Abby and Bonnie as she gave them a few packages for them and the children.

"You didn't have to bring us presents," Abby protested, but she could see Bonnie was touched. Anything that made that woman happy was something, made things a little easier in her life; she was willing to let her have. Bonnie had always been a little unhappy at life, but the loss of her only daughter, first to lesbianism and then to life itself and followed by the loss of her husband, her only ally against Abby, had taken a lot from this prickly woman. Abby tried, she genuinely tried, but living with Bonnie was not easy. She helped a lot with the children, and since Abby worked a lot, it was convenient to have a second parent around. If she wasn't such a sour puss, it would make things a lot easier on everyone.

"Oh now, shush, everyone loves getting presents," Amy drawled graciously. "You enjoy them now, ya' hear?" she said with a smile and waved as she got in the SUV with Toby and drove off.

"She's a nice girl," Bonnie said magnanimously, and Abby was surprised she would compliment anyone after all this time.

Amy was pleased to see the little cabin, but not so pleased at the amount of snow in her driveway while she was away. She parked on the road and headed for the cabin, with the dog hopping from boot hole to boot hole in the deep snow. She knew it was going to be cold inside too as she and Toby slogged through the waist deep white stuff to the front door where she brushed them both off as best she could before unlocking the door. Going inside, she was pleased to see nothing seemed out of order, and her first chore was starting up a fire in the fireplace. When that was crackling merrily, she checked the rest of the house. Toby was snuffling in the kitchen, and she found a mess from where something had gotten into her cereal while she was away. She sighed as she let Toby clean up the mess, and she threw the now empty boxes into the fireplace shaking her head. She wondered if it was mice or heaven forbid a rat, and also wondered if it was a squirrel, but she thought they hibernated for winter? She and Toby, after their exertions, went back out to clear the driveway with the ATV before parking the SUV in the now cleared area and began to unpack the back of the SUV. Load after load she brought into the cabin and placed on her living room floor until she could sort it later. Toby had fun galloping in the snow, but she shut him inside when he started limping from snow between the pads of his feet; it was just too cold out for him for any length of time, and he didn't have the sense to stay out of the snow. It was fun, and he was still a puppy.

She was tired; it had been a long couple of days, and as she parked her suitcase and briefcase, her last trip from the SUV, she locked it up remotely with her keypad. She locked up the front door of the cabin, and she sat down with a sigh as she removed her outdoor garments. The cabin had warmed up considerably since she got there with the fire doing quick work. Whoever designed the cabin had known how to build a fireplace that warmed the entire building, and she was grateful for the thick logs. She hung up her outdoor clothes and lugged her suitcase into the bedroom, pulling out her bag of dirty clothes. She would have to go to the laundromat in the next town as Northpoint didn't have one that she had found. She could have gotten a washer and dryer for the cabin, but there was no room to put it in anywhere. She had plans for that, someday. She'd have to expand the little cabin, but that was in the future. Meanwhile, she would continue to take her clothes to the next town and spend an hour or two as the machines efficiently washed and then dried her clothes, which she folded into the baskets and lugged them out to her SUV.

She looked at the boxes and packages and considered leaving them until the next day, and then with a sigh, she got up and began to put things away. From bulk purchases of toilet paper to canned goods, she just kept putting things away until the pile in her living room was reduced to nothing. She opened her briefcase and looked at the many purchase orders and decided to work on that the following day in her spare bedroom that had been made into a small office. She had made it up with a day bed and a nice antique desk she had found on one of her many jaunts around The Thumb.

Amy's trip netted results and boxes, and deliveries began to arrive the next week. Terry groaned at some of her purchases as she began to put fixtures and other things into the store. His work was nearly finished, and he liked what he was seeing as she fussed and unpacked the many purchases. "Are you going to have a grand opening or something?" he asked as he watched her put things in the still covered windows.

"Oh, you haven't seen this," she said, as she reached for her briefcase and showed him the circular that was going into the newspapers throughout The Thumb and all the way down into Green Bay, inviting people to a Sunday 'social' at the store to celebrate its grand opening. It was set for February, the weekend of the snowmobile races that were such a big part of the social scene up there in Door County. People from all over, locals and tourists, would arrive to fill the Bed and Breakfasts as well as the few hotels that existed.

"You timed that right," he said knowingly. He hadn't thought her ideas for the store were sound, but seeing it come together with all the hard work he and his men had done he had to reevaluate; she had a nifty idea, and he was looking forward to the store opening himself.

She smiled at his gruff compliment, knowing he and his workers had thought she was nuts; her many suggestions and ideas caused them to roll their collective eyes, but their work had been very good, and she had appreciated it. She didn't begrudge writing the checks for it as it all was superior work, and the craftsmanship was superb.

CHAPTER TWELVE

"**W**here you going, Alex?" Abby called as she saw one of the numerous high school students she had observed heading for the store. He was just one of the many people she saw get in line in the cold January weather pummeling Door County. The snowdrifts were everywhere, and she had coordinated with the county to keep her roads clear.

"Oh, Miss Adams is hiring," he said, showing her the newspaper tucked under his arm.

"So that's it," she nodded; she hadn't read the paper today, so she hadn't known why swarms of people had been lining up to go into the store. She thought she had missed the opening or something, but she had heard the gossip that Amy was opening in February during the snowmobile derby out on the ice. A lot of people would be around that weekend, and she would have extra deputies up from the city doing overtime as they helped keep the crowds under control. Even Abby would have to wear her regular uniform instead of the relaxed clothes she normally wore with her badge only appearing when necessary. The locals knew who she was; it was the tourists who gave her any trouble as they figured she was just a hick sheriff's deputy in this one-horse village.

"Yeah, I hope I get it; it sounds fun," he said enthusiastically, his voice cracking in duress and his pimply face showing his excitement.

Abby smiled at him, wondering if she had been that way as a teen. There weren't a lot of jobs around this area, and Amy would have her pick of the kids, but she could see adults had come and gone from the store as well, and she wondered what jobs Amy was hiring for.

"I'm sure you'll do your best," she told him, and she was certain of that, knowing the kid since he was a baby. His parents would expect hard work out of him and his brothers, and she was sure if Amy hired him, he would do a great job.

"Gosh, you think she'll hire me?" he said with a gulp of his Adam's apple.

She smiled at the gawky teen, wanting to reach out and ruffle his hair, but he was long past that stage. Any chance to make money up here was sought after by the locals, from fishing to hunting guides, there wasn't a whole lot if you didn't have a business, but Amy was providing them with an opportunity they couldn't pass up. Abby understood the steady stream of people coming and going from the store now. "I'll put in a good word if you think that would help?" she asked the anxious teen.

"Gee thanks Chief, that'd be awesome," he said gratefully as he went up the stairs to the boardwalk and into the store. It was too cold to stay outside too long and chat.

Abby watched him go with a little smile and was determined she should check out the store anyway. She hadn't seen a lot of the remodel. Since Terry and his crew had finished, only Amy had been there for the many shipments, the UPS, the trucks, the many, many deliveries that people had gossiped about. People had noticed. She seemed determined, and no one had seen inside since she had the windows still covered with construction paper. Abby had to admit she was curious herself.

She waited until the sun was going down and the crowd of people had dwindled to almost nothing in the late afternoon before entering the store. She was surprised to see a set of curtains hiding the store from the view of anyone entering this section; poles held up the curtained sections and effectively hid the main store from their view. Amy had set up a couple of tables where applicants could fill out the stack of applications she had left there with pencils and pens available for their use. A desk was set up at the back of the curtained off area, and Amy sat there with an applicant she was interviewing. Abby could see he wouldn't be hired. He was too cocky and self-assured, and it was obvious he was annoying Amy who tried to ask him a series of set questions she had ready. His answers seemed to only aggravate her further. Finally, though, the brief interview came to a halt as she stood up and held her hand out which the belligerent teen limply shook. "I'll let you know if I decide to have a second interview with you Billy," Amy told him as she dismissed him.

The teen glanced at Abby as he went by giving her a saucy grin as he saluted and said, "Chief." Abby nodded at the teen, knowing what a troublemaker he had been over the years.

"Hi Abby, how are you today?" Amy said brightly, and Abby turned from where she had watched the teen thoughtfully leave the store.

"I'm good; I see you are interviewing applicants, did you get a good turn out?" Abby asked as she turned back.

"Oh, my goodness, I have a second day tomorrow for the applicants, but I don't know how I'll get through all these," she indicated the stack of papers she had already, containing her applications and the paper she filled out with her notes on them.

"Could you use an impartial, well slightly impartial, second set of eyes?" Abby asked.

Amy looked at her with interest.

"I probably know most of the applicants anyway; I've lived here forever and can probably give you some insight."

"That would be terrific; it wouldn't interfere with your work, would it?" she drawled.

Abby was enchanted at the accent as she always was. She hoped her friend would never lose it. She realized who Amy reminded her of now, a younger version of Reba McEntire, but with straighter and longer red hair. From the dimples to the heart shaped face, she was an attractive combination, and Abby had realized that from their first encounter.

"No, not at all; it's a fairly crime free day here in Northpoint," she grinned wryly. "It's a pretty easy appointment up here," she said fondly.

"You really love your job, don't you?" Amy asked as she gathered up the last of the papers and put them in the stack.

Abby sat down across from her and shrugged. "It's a no-brainer. I loved living here with my grandparents when I could. Then when they needed help and I met my wife, it all seemed to come together."

Amy desperately wanted to ask her about that, but she wasn't a gossiper. How could she ask without revealing that she had heard the gossip about the town's only police officer who happened to be a lesbian? Whose wife had died leaving her with two children to raise on her own with the help of hostile in-laws who had been determined to take the children away? Fortunately, Abby had gotten a good lawyer who had gone over her wife's will, which clearly left the children to her 'good friend' Abby, who could not under Wisconsin law be recognized as her 'wife.' "It's a great town from what I've seen," she said instead of the many questions she wanted to ask.

Abby nodded as she held out her hand for some of the applications. "It's good for the kids, and I benefited from visiting my grandparents; it was better here for me than with my parents."

Amy had already begun dividing up the applicants from her notes, making a pile of those 'possibles' to the 'probables' to the 'no ways.' She handed Abby the pile of probables as those were ones she was certain she wanted a second interview with.

"You know, I'm not going to do this for free, don't you?" Abby asked as she began to read Alex Martin's application. She was pleased he had interviewed well from the notes that Amy had written on her second sheet.

"What's it gonna cost me, officer?" Amy asked playfully as she filed the 'no ways' in a folder and put them away. She had to, by law, keep them on file for a set period of time before shredding them as they all contained personal information.

"Oh, just a personal tour of the store," Abby returned as she nodded at some of the questions Amy had asked and Alex had answered.

"You want to see it?" Amy asked, surprised.

Abby looked up to see if she was serious. "Of course I do; I've seen the things coming into this store from what Terry carted in here, and the many deliveries have left us all curious," she confessed.

"Now?" Amy asked with a slight hint of a grin, her dimples barely showing.

Abby smiled in return. "Let's finish these up," she indicated the small stack of applicants, the 'probables', and then the one of 'possibles.' "And then I want to see it *all*," she said forcefully, and they both shared a laugh.

Amy was grateful that her interviews had gone so well. She had been amazed at the amount of people who showed up, but then realized there wasn't a lot of opportunity up here, and people had to travel so far for the few jobs that were seasonally available. She intended to keep her store open year-round and would need trustworthy employees for that endeavor. She already had a few other ideas for other stores around town in the vacant buildings, but that would have to wait until she launched this one; hopefully, it would be a success and make her money back.

"Alex is a good kid," Abby commented as she showed the application she was looking at and then launched into everything she knew about the kid. She did the same with a few of the other applications as Amy took notes and marked them for second interviews. They got through the small stack quickly, and a few of those went into the 'probables' stack, and others got filed with the 'no-ways.' Abby, of course, didn't know each and every one of the applicants, but enough of them that she could offer an opinion on them. Amy was grateful that her own instincts on a few of them panned out, and she was determined to call a few of them this evening so she could set up interviews for the third day when applications would no longer be taken, and she could show them exactly what they would be doing in the store. In the meantime, she began to show Abby exactly what she had turned her grandparents store into.

Abby was amazed, the store had been transformed into an old-fashioned drug store with sections or various counters for the merchandise and services that Amy's 'general' store would be offering, from UPS and FedEx services to a mini-post office as well as payments for water, gas, and electric as well as phone including cell phones. She was well set up, and Abby could see the posters and products offered meant that locals and tourist alike would be well taken care of. She could see where Amy had moved back merchandise for her curtained off area that would be put back after her interviewing process was over. A postal annex stood in one area with the bars, keeping customers from the postmaster and the bank of postal boxes that were all shiny and waiting for the occupants to come in and collect their mail. They had to walk through the store and temptations of merchandise and food before gathering their mail, or they could unlock the side door and go straight to the boxes, a cage panel came down from the ceiling to block this off. That way, they could gather their mail anytime and not get into the actual store once the panel was down. The coup de grace though was an authentic soda fountain complete with an ice cream factory, homemade candy, and plenty of details such as a popcorn maker, a salt water taffy pull machine, and many other nifty little gadgets. The counter was smooth as silk with a wooden top and brass fittings. An old-fashioned juke box was in one corner where guests could sit and enjoy the music or dance on the polished wood floor in front of a large gas stove which stood in another corner. She could see it was an efficiency model that would and was already heating the whole store very well. It stood on Italian tiles and had a small gate around it to keep out the curious, but probably children most of all so they couldn't get burned. The booths all contained a mini-juke box on them to change the music and pay for it at their table.

"Wow, you really thought this out; I'm thrilled to see the changes," she said as she ran her fingers along one of the booths shaped like a

Cadillac back seat, right down to the big lights and tail fins that were standard on fifties style cars. "Where in the world did you get some of these things?" she asked as she looked at the neon and other touches.

"Some of these things were impossible to find, and I had to compromise," Amy admitted as she showed her the bank of lava lamps in three different sizes and colors on the various shelves behind the counter and in front of a mirrored wall, creating an illusion of an even bigger store.

"That's incredible," she said as she enjoyed the visual, even though they weren't turned on. "People are going to enjoy the nostalgia." She looked at the various vintage displays of touristy items from the fifties and up to the present, including postcards and signs of Door County that could be purchased. Some of the older scenes she had never seen before, some were from an era long gone. There were plenty of boxes waiting to be unpacked, but she could see why Amy had worked long hours in the store now as this came together. It had the feeling of a good old-fashioned drug store, somewhat fifties style, some even older, and yet enough modern stuff that the combination blended beautifully.

"What's this?" she indicated the computers by one of the shipping sections.

"Oh, people enter their own data in them and print out a shippin' label for either UPS or FedEx or even the post office, and then they pay over there," she pointed at the shipping counter. "That way it's up to them to get it right and the information correct. We won't, however, require it especially as I'm certain we will get a few technophobes who will be shy of the computers."

"Yeah, some of the older folks don't like computers," Abby agreed. This place was going to look incredible, she thought, as she looked at the neon around the edges of the café portion. It wasn't lit up yet, but she was looking forward to seeing it when it was. The candy counter and the soda counter looked just as inviting. "I didn't realize this place was so big," she commented absently as she looked around trying to visualize what she had and where it had all been placed all those months ago.

"It was huge, but we took advantage of the size, and some of it is an optical illusion," she pointed out to how the French doors leading outside to the deck were utilized and would bring in lots of light and 'space' to the café. "They will be able to eat out on the dock too when the weather is nice." She showed her how the mirrors gave the impression of so much more space too as they reflected off the walls, making it appear like a second store.

"Amazing," Abby enthused. "Too bad you can't rent out canoes as well as sell gas out there," she peeked through the window coverings at the snow-covered dock and the now winter-covered gas dispenser.

"Oh, I made a deal with Spencer's Canoe and Kayak rentals. They are going to 'store' quite a few of their rentals over here and use the docks; they ran out of room a long time ago at their place and were very interested in the deal when I brought it up to them," Amy told her modestly.

Abby looked at her in surprise. People would always underestimate this woman; she had such 'innocent' good looks, her southern drawl disarmed them, but wow, she had a head for business which was obvious from what she was seeing. "Good for you, any more surprises in store for us?" she asked with a grin.

Amy returned the grin. "I don't know anymore; I've just been trying to get everything organized and in place for the openin'."

"I saw the ads in the paper and the flyers," Abby commented, acknowledging her.

"Yes, the printers were very accommodatin'," she added, nodding. "They liked all the work I sent their way," she told her of the business cards, the various forms, and the brochures as well as the ads and menus she had sent their way. She handed Abby a menu.

"Can you make all of that in here?" she asked in surprise. It was then she spotted the small grill and the walk-up window to outside so that guests didn't have to come in the store from the boardwalk.

"Yes, I had to get the county to sign off on it of course, but I passed all my inspections with flyin' colors thanks to Terry and his crew. They did good work for me."

Abby shook her head; there's been so much work since last fall, and it was still going strong as she eyed the many unopened boxes around the store. "Wow, good luck!" she said encouragingly. "Did you manage a store like this before down south or something?" she asked, and then realized Amy immediately shut down at any mention of her past.

Amy tried not to let it show, but people were naturally curious about her and her past. She was very careful in her answers though. "My parents had a fishin' store, and I dreamed of places like this," she offered, more than many had gotten from her in a while. "I took business courses in college and thought this out as soon as I saw your store."

Abby nodded knowingly. She knew the redhead had to have had experience and some business sense. It was obvious she knew what she was doing, and this store would be a great success as a result. The various services she was offering would appeal to everyone.

"You let me know if my kids become a problem; they are going to want to live in here," she warned.

Amy laughed knowingly. "Heather comes by frequently to ask to see the store or to play with Toby, and I've let Bailey walk him as well."

Abby was surprised; she had never known.

"You know, I never knew you were the local Chief of Police. You don't dress in uniform," Amy finally felt bold enough to comment.

She shrugged. "I don't want to come on too strong, especially with tourists. Occasionally, I have to throw my weight around," she laughed as she made a muscle to stress her point; she was rewarded with Amy's tinkling laugh. "For the most part, I just wear the badge on my belt, and that's good enough for those around here."

"You don't act like a cop either," she observed cautiously, but she was still laughing at the flexed arm of the law.

"What do you know about cops and how they act?" Abby teased and saw something change in the redhead's eyes. It was infinitesimal but distinct. If she hadn't been standing right by her, she might have missed it.

"Oh, I don't know; I'm sure that you aren't typical," she said airily as she dismissed it. She looked away as she looked around the store. "I hope the locals like it as well as the tourists," she tried to change the subject.

"I can't wait to see it on opening day," Abby allowed her to get off the hook; there was something there though, and she wondered about it.

"Have you heard, Chief? I got the job!" an enthusiastic Alex told Abby when he saw her the following week.

"You did? That's great! Amy seems to be a nice woman to work for, and the store should do well," she told him. She hadn't told anyone that she had read the applications and given Amy inside information on them.

"It's going to be good," he said and then lost his smile. "Except...."

She waited and when he hesitated she asked, "Except what?"

"I just don't like being called a soda jerk," he complained good-naturedly.

SMALL TOWN ANGEL

Abby nearly laughed into his face. "You should be honored; a soda jerk was an important position back in the fifties. I bet if you Googled it and learned more about it, you'd have a lot of ammunition if anyone teases you about the title." She figured he would now that she mentioned it.

"She also wants us to wear these stupid hats," he showed her the little cap that was definitely from the 1950's and would look good on the kid with his height and narrow head.

Abby shrugged trying not to laugh at him. He was going to get a lot of razzings probably from other boys his age in town. "It's part of the job, is the pay worth the job?"

"Oh yeah, she pays more than minimum wage, and the job is really flexible. I'm gonna save up and buy a car," he told her as he headed to what was obviously his mother's station wagon.

Abby laughed inside; he had already bounced back and forth about the job, but it was obvious he was going to keep it just so he could get that car he wanted. Hat and title aside, the job would be good for him. It would show him responsibility. Others who had gotten jobs with Amy's 'Emporium' were just as pleased. A couple of them who had been displaced by her opening up the extensions for the phone, post, and electric had gotten first crack at the key positions and were grateful because Amy had managed to get them insurance too. Gossip had it that she was offering a good benefits deal, and people were delighted. Rumor also had it there was a scholarship opportunity for high school students, but Abby hadn't heard too many details on that—yet.

CHAPTER THIRTEEN

Amy had never experienced such cold weather. Throughout the month of January and February, she was out almost every other day with her ATV, plowing her driveway with Toby. She had gotten a coat for him so he could stay on the back and enjoy being with her in the outdoors. He still resented that she didn't take him when she went on the trails as it was too long for him to be out. She had tried to put booties on him too, but those didn't last long as he hilariously kicked them off and then chewed them up even though they kept the snow from between his pads.

The snow was bad enough, and she was grateful for the four-wheel drive on her SUV just to get to town, but the cold, it was *bitterly* cold. She worked hard in the store as she set it up, and even after hiring employees and teaching them the various positions and cross-training, some she could only hope that they would be reliable. During training, no one missed work, but that might be another thing come actual work time, and she couldn't do everything herself, although she alone knew each position fully.

As she inter-connected the computers and booted them up, she wondered if she should have had a pro in here to do some of that. The wires were strung by Terry and his crew with the internet and Ethernet as well as the intranet. She placed the computers one by one and connected them so that she could from her back office tell whatever was being sold at any given time. Discrete cameras around the store also could be shown on a bank in her office so she could view and record at any time.

Going over training time and again, they had so many dry runs as they unpacked the various products still coming in; they were almost ready. The back room was organized and now full of shelves and stock; the board still hung over the wall connecting her to the house next door, but a bank of shelves covered the board now too. The other backroom contained her small office and was pleasant and inviting. Her bathrooms were next to this office and were unisex, but there were two of them, and they were equipped for baby changing stations in both of them. They had a modern washer in both of them that rinsed the stalls down nightly, and it drained out the bottom of the floor so that employees only had to mop down the floor once in a while, but the bathrooms always smelled fresh and clean.

Amy stood at the windows of the darkened store, enjoying the quiet. All the employees were gone, she was alone except for Toby who had lain down on the floor with a sigh, and he was ready to go any time she was. With the lights off in the store, she could look out at the lake. All the boats were gone from the docks along with the anchorage in the bay itself. Instead the ice flowed out as far as the eye could see. Some of it was perfectly flat, but other parts reminded her of a glacier. The hues of the various whites to blues was breathtaking, and when the sun hit it, it was mind-blowing. She'd never seen something so pure and beautiful and dangerous. She'd not been brave enough to take her ATV out on the ice except for crossing creeks; she stayed away from water as a rule. Those who bravely went across the little ponds or lakes much less 'the lake' itself she worried about, what if they went in? The cold water could kill! Still, it was beautiful, and she admired it. She was amazed that it all wasn't perfectly flat, but Abby had explained that Lake Michigan was a large inland body of water. An inland sea actually, and the tides and waves meant that the ice would expand, contract, and be piled up by the winds. It was beautiful and it was dangerous if you turned your back to it or were foolish.

Amy smiled as she turned around and examined her old-time country store, The Emporium was exactly as she had dreamed it, and she looked forward to the opening. She checked that the doors were all locked one last time, grabbed her purse which seconded as a briefcase, and grabbed Toby's lead. He was there in a heartbeat, ready to go, and eager to please. She smiled down at the dog and snapped his leash on, heading for the front door so she could go home.

CHAPTER FOURTEEN

The day of the grand opening finally loomed. There had been some question of it as it snowed for days, and temperatures plunged to well below zero. People were surprised at this time of year that it was this cold, and Amy ordered extra hot chocolate in many different flavors for the derby in anticipation of lots of customers. She even had a couple of employees taking shifts in a booth down on the lake in a pop-up tent giving out free samples of cappuccino sized hot chocolate and salt water taffy to people from 'The Emporium.'

Amy gleefully pulled down the paper from the covered windows, letting in sunshine that hadn't been seen in months as the store was remodeled. Looking through the windows, they could see all the merchandise hanging in the windows' boxes as well as all the neon, the lava lamps, and the polished chrome and brass. It all intrigued and invited the viewer inside the store. The bell on the door began to ring early on that Thursday as the racers came into town and the townies and tourists began to swell the stands on the edge of the lake and on the lake itself where the derby would be held. Her employees were all neatly dressed in their outfits that Amy had ordered for them, taking pride in their clean and professional appearance. She wiped at an imaginary fingerprint on some of the glass displays showing off the candy and looked into the ice cream bins and hoped they had enough for the big weekend. Despite the cold, the ice cream should sell well, and they had plenty down stairs in the deep freeze.

Curious townies began to come in early and look around. Amy had warned everyone not to stare at the customers, as it was their first day open, and while everyone knew their jobs from her excellent training, they were all anxious to help and serve. She knew the feeling herself as she watched people coming in and looking over what she had done to the store and what she offered. She heard exclamations of delight and took pride in the selections offered. She was pleased to see her choice of employees was panning out too as they efficiently began to wait on people as needed. She walked around and helped where she could, but she didn't hover. As the day went on, she relieved employees to give them their well-deserved breaks as others came in for their shifts. They removed their outer clothes in the backroom and signed in on a computer before starting right to work, feeling the same awe that the other newbies had on this first day.

Today was going to be an extra-long day; they had opened at eight and would be open until ten tonight as the derby drew in people from all over, and they would want something to do in the small town. Some families didn't spend their time in the bars, and The Emporium would be a good alternative. It was about six o'clock when she saw one of her 'car hops', as she was calling the waiters and waitresses, taking an order for Abby and her family. Bonnie was with them, and she had a pleasant smile on her face for a change instead of the bitter one she normally wore. The kids looked thrilled and pleased as they looked around. The bubbles in the juke box along with some of the neon seemed to fascinate them, and then of course the banks of lava lamps, all of which were lit and bubbling after the long day looking terrific. She went over to say hello.

"Enjoying yourself?" Amy asked as she looked over the family.

"This is really something, Amy," Bonnie said appreciatively, and Amy was surprised; Bonnie rarely had something positive to say about anything. "Reminds me of something I grew up with!"

Amy smiled and thanked her and then glanced at the kids. "What do you guys think?"

"Wow," Heather breathed.

"It's okay," Bailey shrugged dismissively, and Abby poked him. He grinned and then said, "It's awesome."

Abby smiled at the boy as she put her arm around him to give him a one-armed hug. He blushed becomingly. "Really Amy, you put a lot of work into this place; it's fantastic!"

"I'm so glad to hear you say that," Amy drawled graciously. "Everyone has been so kind today."

"I'm sure you will have a lot of repeat customers tomorrow as well as all the newcomers," Abby assured her.

"Well, word of mouth is the best advertisin,' so I hope you enjoy your meal." Amy didn't want to impose further.

"Where is Toby?" Heather asked anxiously, looking around.

"He is sleepin' in the back, but after your dinner if you want to see him and it's okay with your mom and grandmother, you may come back and see him. He'd love to see you, I'm sure," she looked warmly at Bailey to include him in the invitation.

Heather nodded enthusiastically as Amy made her goodbyes and went on to greet other townies who had come to The Emporium to check it out. She received so many compliments on her hard work that she was flying high.

As she closed the doors firmly after ten and ushered out the last few stragglers, she thanked them for coming as she locked the doors behind them. The last two employees that came in from the lake where they had been handing out the hot chocolate from the clever dispensers strapped to their backs, which not only kept the chocolate warm but them as well, came in to wash the dispensers out for tomorrow. "Was it a success?" she asked them as they chatted with the others. There had been three shifts dispensing the chocolate and candy pieces. They had gone through a lot of both, but it was good advertising for the store.

"People loved it, and a few cheated," the teens reported.

She laughed; she knew some people when presented with 'free' took advantage, but most people were decent. She was certain she had more than made up for the freebies with what the store took in today. She watched as each 'department' cleaned up their area and some who finished their area early helped elsewhere. Everyone was scheduled through half past ten so that the store was ready for the next day. Normally, the store wouldn't be open this long or this late, but with the derby going on they would take advantage of the extra people in town to make some money.

One of the employees pulled the shades on each of the windows. Another employee counted down his till from the antique-looking registers that were computer operated and verified it off the computer read out. Each employee was responsible for his own till, and Amy had already done some of the preliminary totals. The day had been extraordinary and already very profitable. The whole weekend should be that way, and she looked forward to making her deposit at the bank on her way out of town; she already had a bank bag with lock waiting for the last of the tills. She recounted each of the tills with the employees to verify, and then they were let out of the store one by one. She counted out the bills she would keep on hand for change in the coming days and then made her deposit. Counting the credit cards, the various slips, balancing them against the register receipts, and she was done for the day.

Toby was very tired, but she was grateful how well behaved the pup had been. He hadn't been allowed into the store today, but Heather and Bailey took him for a walk, well supplied with bags to pick up any of his droppings. Amy was grateful as she had been too busy. It was well after eleven before she was done. She zipped the bank bag closed and stored it well under her clothing. She closed the safe for tomorrow and set the timer. She looked around the store one more time and checked all the doors a second time as well as the cage panel; her employees had been thorough. The lights were off all over the store; it was strangely quiet without the juke box going. The neon was all out, and the wax in the lava lights settled to the bottom of each of the globes. She smiled as she walked towards the shaded front doors, and looking out saw no one lurking about. She took Toby's leash and her car keys and headed outside after setting the alarm and locking the door behind her. She looked out at the night, the sky was so black, and the moon so full. She could hear and see people walking around town, quickly from bar to bar or back to one of the many bed and breakfasts.

"Walk you to your car, ma'am?" Abby's voice came from her house.

Amy jumped, startled. She had been so lost in her thoughts and laughed at herself. She had been more concerned about tourists than her friendly neighborhood cop.

"You okay?" Abby asked concerned as she walked up and tried to fend off an exuberant Toby.

Amy nodded. "I'm tired, pleasantly tired," she said with a smile of greeting.

They walked companionably along. Amy had her employee's park in the next block away from the store so that customers could park around the immediate area near the store; her own SUV was no exception, and she was grateful for the company as Abby walked with her in the cold winter night. Their shoes crunched on the icy snow, and their breath froze in the air as they exhaled.

"Was it a good day?" Abby asked, but she already knew. She couldn't help but see the crowds in and out of the store next door to her home. The little sips of hot chocolate and candy had garnered more 'friends' to the little southern belle than she knew. Not just among the tourists either. Her store had been mobbed and for good reason: it was an excellent location, its novelty was appreciated, and the food was good. Everyone said so. The only complaint she had heard was that it was too busy, but that would settle down in time. This weekend was an exception due to the influx of tourists. She wondered how summer would fare.

"It was terrific," Amy said without gushing. She ached in her whole body and knew she would sleep well tonight.

A cat darted out between two parked cars and zoomed for the fence around the sheriff's yard as they turned the corner and headed for Amy's SUV. Toby lunged but was pulled up short by Amy who had seen the cat before the pup.

"Dang cat," Abby muttered.

"You don't like cats?" Amy asked, surprised; she had seen how much Abby liked Toby.

"Just that one, it is determined to be adopted by my kids," she said disgustedly.

"You don't want a cat?" Amy was now amused at the disgruntlement of the woman.

"That one seems determined to annoy and irritate me," Abby complained. "It leaves footprints all over my patrol car, and I swear it's deliberate."

Amy laughed as they came up to her SUV, and she pushed the remote starter and door opener so she could put Toby in the passenger side. She had a towel on the seat for the lab. He had mastered leaping up into the SUV onto the floor and then the seat; soon he would be able to leap directly to the seat he was growing so fast. Already his gangly limbs were showing signs of filling out a little. "Well I sure could use a cat out at the cabin; I think I have mice," she informed Abby.

"Want me to catch Tabby and bring her out?" Abby offered half-heartedly with a charming little grin.

Amy shook her head. "Don't you dare, I don't want your kids hating me for taking their cat!" she teased.

Abby shook her head as she watched Amy get in the cold vehicle, and looking carefully, pull away with a friendly wave. She watched her drive down the street and head for the bank branch. She had guessed she would go straight there. She had been busy tonight and would want that cash put into the bank as soon as possible. Abby watched as she parked, left the SUV, and locked it with her remote but left it running. She pulled the deposit drawer and pulled something from under her clothes and quickly put it in the drawer, checking twice that it went in before she hurried back to her vehicle. Abby laughed, but it really wasn't funny as she looked around. One of her deputies had patrol tonight, and as she shivered in her own parka, she made a mental note to walk Amy to her vehicle every night when she worked this late and had a deposit. She didn't even think of it as favoritism or anything more, merely being a good officer and a friend.

CHAPTER FIFTEEN

Amy took her well-deserved day off on Tuesday. She was exhausted. The store, located near the waterfront as it was, was a hit to tourists and locals alike. She couldn't believe the amounts of food and merchandise she had gone through over the weekend alone. Monday, she had placed some rather large purchase orders with her various venders. She could fill the stock room as well as some extra space she had in the basement when it arrived, but she anticipated going through it all quickly enough as time went on. It wasn't every weekend that there was a derby full of snowmobilers and their families coming into town, but Door County was a tourist destination, and she had advertised heavily in newspapers, magazines, and circulars that attracted tourists to this area for future events and vacations.

Amy was sitting around doing absolutely nothing. Her household chores, except for the laundry, were finished early, and she was petting Toby and relaxing on the couch when a hesitant shuffle on the porch led to a knock on the front door. Toby, as the self-appointed guard dog, went off like a firecracker. "Shush," Amy told him as she got up to answer the door.

"Well, Bailey! What a surprise!" Amy said as she welcomed the pre-teen into her house. "Get in here, it's cold out there. Did you walk from town?" she asked as she looked out for the patrol car they normally drove in and saw nothing.

"Ohh, it's colder than I thought it would be when I set out!" he said as he stamped off the snow from his boots on the carpet put there for that very reason.

"I imagine so, what are you doing out here?" she asked in surprise. She helped him unwrap himself from the outdoor clothes he was wearing in layers. She was even more surprised when a cat dropped out of them.

"Oops," he said as he lunged for the startled cat, who upon seeing Toby spat at the surprised pup.

Amy grabbed at Toby, who lunged after the cat, who shot towards the doorway to the bedroom with Bailey in pursuit. "Let it go," she advised as she had her hands full with the excited pup.

Bailey looked up guiltily from where he had tracked snow across her pristine floor toward the doorway.

"Take those off," Amy directed him, pointing to his boots and the carpet by the front door. "There is a mop in the kitchen behind the door." She wrestled Toby back toward the couch and held onto the eager pup who was straining and was trying to keep an eye on the doorway in hopes of seeing the now absent cat. She watched Bailey pull off the snow boots, which still had plenty of slush and gunk on them, and put them carefully on the front hall carpet. Then in stocking feet, he went to find the mop and cleaned up the mess he had made. "So, what do I owe the pleasure of your company here, and why do I now have a cat in my house?" she asked conversationally. She could see him instantly squirm.

"My mom was going to get rid of that cat, take him to the shelter, and she said you needed a cat, so I thought I'd bring it and talk to you about it before she could..." he began, all in one breath. He quickly finished mopping up and then looked at the mop as though not knowing what to do with it.

"Put it in the sink," Amy advised as she looked at him thoughtfully.

He headed to the kitchen, and then he reluctantly joined her on the couch looking back at the doorway, as though the cat would reappear.

"It's not going to show up with Toby around, and it's probably scared," Amy informed him as she could see his interest in finding the cat.

"I'm sorry," he began.

"What am I going to do with a cat?" Amy wondered aloud, and the boy looked up hopefully.

"I just didn't want it to go to the pound; they put them in the gas chamber there!" he said earnestly.

"I understand, and I guess if Toby can learn to get along with it, it can stay," she said but really worried about what she was going to do with it. It was probably feral and wasn't an indoor cat.

"It's a really sweet cat," Bailey said as though reading her mind.

"Has it been indoors?" she asked, wondering at a cat pan.

The boy looked immediately guilty and nodded. "I let her into our house, that's how Mom found out," he told her reluctantly.

Amy almost laughed. Just the other night Abby had tried to talk her into having the cat, and now the boy had taken the situation out of her hands completely. "You walked here all that way from town with the cat in your jacket?"

The boy nodded, looking ashamed and yet hopeful. "You'll keep her, won't you? You won't let my mom take her to the pound?" he asked in a concerned voice.

Amy pretended to consider; she did need a cat to take care of whatever was in her kitchen. She didn't want the boy to think she was a soft touch though. "I don't know Bailey, with Toby to consider, I don't know if I'll have time to take care of a cat too," she began.

"I'll help," he offered, not thinking of what would be involved.

She smiled briefly before she continued, "Does your mother or grandmother know where you are?" she asked as Toby tried to get out from her hold on his collar. She glanced at the doorway herself that the dog was staring at in rapt fascination. She saw nothing, but it didn't mean there was nothing there. Cats were canny that way.

The boy squirmed. Not only had he let the cat in the house, but it had been so cold! But he hadn't told anyone where he was going either, and he knew that would get him in trouble.

Amy shook her head, and the boy took that to mean she wouldn't keep the cat. "Oh please, it's a really nice cat!" he pleaded.

"Well, let's get you dressed and home. I'm going to have to stop at the store and pick up some things," she told him non-committedly as she herself got up, holding Toby and pulling him over to the door, she grabbed his leash.

"You won't get rid of her, will you?" he pleaded as he went to put his boots back on.

"I have to think about it," she told him as she put on her own boots, and Toby made it difficult as he lunged with his leash on. "No boy, leave it alone," she said to the eager dog who wanted to go sniff out the intruder.

"It's a girl," the boy said as he looked down to tie the laces on his boots.

Great, Amy thought as she stamped into her boots and reached for her jacket. Another thing she had to take care of, and she had just opened her store, just another responsibility.

They were soon in the SUV with Toby and on their way back to town. "That's a long way to walk in the cold," she commented to the boy, noticing the footprints on the side of the road that led towards her cabin. Toby was relegated to the back seat with the addition of a passenger, and he let the boy know that he was in *his* spot by hanging his head over the seat and licking him when the boy wasn't shoving his snout away. "Back Toby," Amy told the dog who sat back for a moment before considering if he could get away with it again.

"Yeah, it was cold," the boy agreed. He still didn't know if she was going to keep the cat, but he hoped so.

"What's your Mom going to say about it?" she asked and glanced over to see him squirm a little.

"Can we not tell her?" the boy asked, looking up to plead. Today hadn't worked out at all like he had planned it to.

Amy glanced at him to see that he was serious. Abby could be a bit intimidating, she guessed. She knew how she had felt finding out that she was the local law.

They were soon in the little town, and she was pulling up outside of the house adjoining her store. She glanced at the store and saw a couple of people coming out of it and wondered briefly if she should go inside and then decided against it. It was her day off; she had to trust her employees.

"Are you going to keep the cat?" her thoughts were interrupted by Bailey.

She sighed deeply and then nodded. "I guess so but don't bring any others!" she teased.

He smiled brilliantly as he got out of the SUV with a wave and headed up the sidewalk. Amy watched as the door opened, and Bonnie stuck her head out. She waved at her before driving off. If she was going to have a cat in the house, she was going to have to get a few things for it, and Northpoint didn't have a large enough market for what she had in mind.

A bit poorer for her shopping expedition, she now had an adequate supply of wet and dry food for the cat, a litter box, and a few toys she hoped would entice the kitty, but she wondered if they were to entice the human buying them as well. She had felt guilty, and Toby now had a few new things that he didn't need as well.

Back at the cabin though, Toby went off in search of the newest member of their household and got his nose scratched for the effort.

"I'm not going to feel sorry for you," Amy told the pup; he had to learn, and she had told him repeatedly to leave the kitty alone.

She made the cat box up by the back door with Toby sniffing it intently, and her pushing him away. She put out a bowl of dry food that Toby was really interested in, but again she told him no and then reconsidered, she put it up on the counter only to yell at the exuberant pup who wanted to climb up and eat it. Shaking her head, she wondered about feeding times for felines.

She herself knew the cat was in her spare bedroom and was leaving it alone until it wanted to make an appearance. As she was having a lazy day, and half of it had already been taken up by the shopping expedition, she wanted to veg out on the couch with no more interruptions. She could tell when the cat tried to make an appearance by Toby lifting his head from his paws to stare at the doorway intently. She herself couldn't see it but knew it had to be curious.

It was only as she mindlessly began channel surfing through the limited stations offered without buying more cable service that she heard the distinct sound of a vehicle pulling into her driveway. The crunching of the frozen snow under its tires was rather distinct. A cutting of the engine and a few minutes later a knock on her door didn't surprise her; Toby had heard it all too but didn't explode into his exuberant barking until the actual knock. Amy didn't know if it was the knock itself or the dog's bark that had her jumping; she had been expecting both, so she didn't appreciate the heart palpitations that had her sitting up annoyed. Turning off the television, she got up from her convenient sprawl on the couch to answer the door.

"Down Toby," she told the master protector of the house. He sat expectantly, waiting for her to open the door. "Who is it?" she asked, it was dark after all.

"Abby," the muffled voice told her, and she wasn't surprised. "Hurry up, it's cold out here!"

Amy was laughing as she unlocked the door and opened it up to the cop who let the outer door slam behind her as she stepped into the warm cabin. "Well officer, this is an unexpected surprise," she drawled, even though she had a feeling it wasn't really unexpected or a surprise. She wondered if Bailey had told her, or Bonnie had questioned the boy.

"To us both," Abby mumbled through the scarf she was unwrapping.

Amy laughed at her as she went to help and ended up making it worse. Finally, hands raised she stepped back to let the woman get herself out of her winter apparel. She did take the pieces though and hung them up on the hooks by the door drilled into the wood. "To what do I owe the honor of your visit?" she asked once Abby was down to sweat shirt and jeans and her jacket hung up.

"Got any hot chocolate?" Abby pleaded, hoping she had some of the same delicious treats she had at the store. She was already addicted as were several of the people around town to the various flavors that were offered in the store; they were better than the expensive coffee offered at the Coffee Clutch. The only complaint anyone had about Amy's offerings at The Emporium was that she didn't have a drive-thru, a physical impossibility with the lake and docks.

"Why I sure do," Amy said as she headed for the kitchen with Abby following her. She felt immediately guilty seeing the bowl of cat food on the counter but ignored it hoping her guest wouldn't see it. That was the problem with having a cop as a friend, you always felt 'guilty' about certain 'things' in your life.

She turned on the stove and reached for the kettle to fill with water. She'd had hot chocolate herself earlier in the day after running around, so there was still water sloshing in the kettle. She couldn't help but feel a little self-conscious around the other woman and quickly put the kettle on the stove and reached for the cabinet door to open it and find the extra canisters of hot chocolate.

"Do you bring home work supplies?" Abby asked teasingly as she noticed Amy's flushed cheeks, almost as though she were guilty of something.

Amy laughed as she nodded. "Why yes, yes I do."

"Probably cheaper buying in bulk," Abby wryly noted as Amy indicated the different flavors she favored. "Oh, that one," she said pointing, glad to see they had similar tastes.

"That one is one of my favorites, too," Amy answered as she pulled down the inconveniently sized canister. It was made for a restaurant, not her small cabin kitchen.

"You could make a fortune selling these flavors that you offer in the restaurant," Abby commented as she anticipated the flavor.

It was like a light bulb went off for Amy, and Abby watched it happen before her. "That's a terrific idea, and I don't know why I hadn't thought of it before," she answered back thoughtfully.

"Probably because you had a million other things on your mind?"

They shared a laugh and then heard the sound of Toby's nails on the wood floor scrambling across it as he huffed out his breath chasing something. Amy looked up at an alarmed Abby guiltily as she called out, "TOBY!" in a warning voice.

"What's he after?" Abby asked.

Amy studied her for a moment and then decided honesty was the best policy. "Probably the cat," she said dryly.

"You got a cat?" Abby asked amused and then her eyes narrowed. "That tabby?" she asked, putting one and one together and coming up with two easily.

Amy nodded and waited.

"You stole my cat?" she asked alarmed and a little amused.

Amy shook her head. "No, I didn't steal your cat." She hesitated; she didn't want to get Bailey in trouble.

It was the hesitation though that allowed the facile mind of the brunette to put it together. "Bailey?" she asked.

Just then the water began to boil, and Amy turned to the whistling kettle, reaching to turn off the burner. At the same time, she reached for two coffee cups to fill them with the hot water. "He brought her to me," she answered and glanced at the cop.

"Well, I'll be," Abby answered with a grin. "He figured out a way to keep her and not keep her."

"You didn't want her, did you?" Amy asked, wondering if she had just spent money on the cat for nothing.

"I did, but I didn't; I threatened to take it to the pound when I found him sneaking her in through his bedroom window. That lets out a lot of heat, waiting for that cat to decide if she is going to come in or stay out. I guess…" here she hesitated. "I guess he believed me." She sounded contrite.

"Well, I hope this doesn't get him in any hotter water," she grinned as she spooned up some of the hot chocolate into the cups of hot water.

Abby grinned at the joke. This woman was funny. "How'd he get you to pick her up? Does he have your home number?"

Amy now felt uncomfortable. She wasn't sure of the rules around Abby's house, but she was pretty sure walking out of town on a freezing cold winter's day was probably one of the no-no's.

Abby saw her question had made her twitch. "Bonnie said she saw you drop Bailey off…" It was then her observation on the way out to ask about that paid off. "He walked out here?" she asked alarmed.

Amy looked up guiltily and nodded as she mixed the hot chocolate. "He brought me the cat under his coat."

"That little…" Abby was alarmed, but she also admired the little twerp. He must have known that Amy was a soft touch. She shook her head; he couldn't manipulate people this way though.

"I gave him hell," she drawled in her sexy southern way. "I also said he was going to have to 'pay me back,'" she used fingers to emphasize the quotation marks around her words. She picked up both mugs and handed the one mug to the brunette and took a cautious sip of her own. It was so good the smell made her want to gulp the concoction, but she was careful as it was still boiling hot. "Let's go sit in the living room by the fire," she offered hospitably.

Abby was still shaking her head at her son's audacity. Although she had teased Amy the weekend before about the cat, she hadn't really thought of imposing on her. She had said she was going to get rid of the cat in the heat of the moment; it made her want to bite her tongue now that he had called her on it. "If you want, I can take the cat back..." she began hesitantly as she took a sip of the heavenly hot chocolate.

"Nuh uh, nope, possession is nine tenths of law," she quipped in return and smiled showing off a slight hot chocolate mustache.

Abby found herself strangely aroused at the sight but resisted the urge to lick it off. She wanted to be friends with Amy and counted her as one in the months since she took over the store, but hitting on her friends was a sure-fire way to lose them. She laughed at the southerner's sally though. "Okay, okay, if you wanted a cat that bad, I know I could have found you a better one!" she returned.

"Why, what's wrong with this one?" she asked picking up the banter.

Abby shook her head. "Nothing that I know of, except she is a bit of a pest."

"Ah ha, see, I knew there was a catch here," she grinned.

The two of them found they were having fun teasing back in forth, and while Abby felt awkward about what her son had pulled, she also admired his spunk in taking care of it. It sounded like Amy didn't really mind, and they continued chatting as they got to know one another more.

"Well, you will have to give me one of the kittens or at least let me have first pick of the liter," Abby told her.

"Kittens?" Amy said weakly, realizing she was in for a lot more responsibility than she had intended when she agreed to this deal.

"He didn't tell you she was pregnant, did he?" she grinned admiringly at her son's trick.

"No, he didn't mention that little tidbit," she said back and caught the grin and twinkling brown eyes.

"I'm sorry; I can take her back if it's really a hassle," she offered contritely. It really wasn't fair to unload the pregnant cat on her like this.

"Nope, I've already bought a cat pan, she's mine now," she replied firmly, but she was taken aback a little at the news.

SMALL TOWN ANGEL

"Okay, okay, I won't argue with you," Abby replied, but she grinned to show she was still teasing. The conversation went on to other things, and Abby mentioned about how her wife had coped with her pregnancies.

"So how did your wife die?" Amy felt bold enough to ask after they had been chatting for quite a while.

"She died of a pulmonary embolism. That's a sudden blockage of a major blood vessel in the lungs. They are usually caused by a blood clot after giving birth," Abby told her sadly as she looked down into her now empty cup of hot chocolate.

"Oh, I'm so sorry I asked," Amy immediately felt contrite for asking too intimate a question. She had heard that Abby's wife had died in childbirth but didn't know the details. Their sharing tonight had opened them both up, and she suddenly felt awkward.

Abby shrugged. "I'm sure you've heard things around town."

"Yes, I have," she admitted. "But that doesn't give me the right to ask you so personal a thang." She was blushing, and Abby noticed it.

"Well, it was a long time ago. But now it gives me a chance to ask you questions," Abby said with a grin. Her eyes were sparkling in anticipation. This wasn't like a cop asking a suspect questions, but a friend being nosy. She noticed Amy immediately becoming tense. "If you don't want to answer, you don't have to," she added.

"Fair is fair," she drawled.

"So, what is your story?" she asked and watched her friend closely but could only see the shutters coming down on her eyes. "Have you ever had children?"

Amy was grateful for the second question. It allowed her not to answer the first. "No, I've never had children. Not that I didn't want them, but it just didn't happen for me." She didn't elaborate, but then she was becoming very adept at not answering direct questions from anyone who asked them. She was careful though, very careful, and very adroitly changed the conversation back to Abby. She learned how Abby had grown up in a fairly conservative household and how her grandparents had been so wonderful. She had met her wife who lived in the area and fallen in love with her. She told of their romance, their plans, and how they dealt with being the 'only' same sex couple around for a long time. But tourists and some others who moved in brought in a whole lot of gay and lesbian couples, so they didn't feel isolated forever. Her own grandparents had adored her, and despite her parent's misgivings, they had 'married,' or at least had a commitment ceremony, before giving each other legal paperwork that would bind them and keep others from making decisions for them. Even the children were legally adopted by Abby despite the fight with Bonnie and Jake over them. It had been Jake really who had kept it from becoming a nightmare as they worked out what to do over their shared grief over losing the woman they all loved.

It was a bonding of friends that they both enjoyed over the hot chocolate, and the tabby finally made a reluctant appearance, showing that the dog didn't faze her as she made her presence known in the cabin. She checked out the living room quite thoroughly as the two humans pretended to ignore her, and the alert pup watched her respectfully from his position next to *his* human.

"Well, I should be going," Abby finally said as she checked her watch. "The kids are probably in bed and Bonnie probably waiting up for me."

"That's nice that you have someone to worry about you," Amy said with a smile.

"Yes and no, sometimes she is worse than my own parents ever were. My grandparents allowed me more freedom than that woman does," she complained good-naturedly.

"Well, thank you for dropping by, please bring the children next time so that Bailey can begin his duties in takin' care of the cat. The cat pan is going to be pretty full by then," she teased.

Abby shared a grin at how they were going to slightly torment the kid at his audacity. "I'll be sure to tell him." She got into her outdoor gear-layers to protect against the intense cold that seemed to grip Wisconsin and especially this small peninsula of land almost surrounded by the big lake.

It was nice to make friends like this, no fuss, no muss, no expectations, but Abby sensed there was a lot about her new friend that she refused to talk about and wondered about it. The cop in her alone was curious, but the friend wanted to keep her nose out of her friend's business, unless she chose to share it. In a small town, that was sometimes harder to do than not.

"Did you find out why Bailey was with her today?" Bonnie asked as she came into the front room that was also the police substation. It was a large old living room that had been converted. It even had a small holding cell at the one end. It reminded most people of something out of Mayberry from the Andy Griffith show in its quaint, small town feel, but it saved the county from having to actually build a substation.

"Yes, the little squirt took that cat over to her; she's going to keep it," she assured her mother-in-law as she saw the alarm on the woman's face. She hung up her outer jacket and scarf, remembering how warm and homey the cabin had felt and how much she had enjoyed the conversation with a woman of her own age.

"Well, you did threaten to take her to the pound; you know she is due to have those kittens soon," Bonnie reminded her.

"Yes, but I didn't mean anything by it; now I feel bad that he took the matter into his own hands," Abby confessed as she sighed and looked on the fax machine for anything she had to check up on.

"The wanted posters came in, but I pinned them for you," Bonnie told her. After years of being married to Jake, she was a good receptionist for a cop.

"Thank you, I'll take a look at them later," Abby said wearily. Despite not having a lot of 'duties' in a small town, there was a lot of territory to cover and things to follow up upon; the county expected a lot out of her for her small territory, and it was only four times a month that she got someone rotated in that could relieve her for any length of time. God forbid if she wanted an actual vacation. It was a lax system, but this was not a high crime area, and most of her work involved tourists. In the summer, they would have three full time officers up here and the county would foot the bill, but that was to handle the increase in tourists that occurred every year. At special events, they brought in many more.

"One of them looked kind of familiar," Bonnie warned.

Abby smiled. Bonnie always thought one of the FBI's most wanted was going to hide out in the back of Wisconsin. What a perfect spot to hide in plain sight. She had said this often enough that Abby ignored her and proceeded to log in her daily activity, however slight. Maintaining good records at least kept her job consistent. Bonnie wandered away since she wasn't going to get any more conversation out of the brunette.

CHAPTER SIXTEEN

Spring breakup was a blast in The Thumb. Tourists came up in droves to take advantage of the spring-like weather, the blossoms on the fruit trees, and the flowers. The die-hard fishermen went out between the ice floes that still floated about on the lake but were rapidly melting in the huge inland sea known as Lake Michigan. The town was gearing up for the influx of tourists and the money that could be made from them. The Emporium was no exception, and the tourists were delighted to find the new store in a previously under-utilized space. The convenience, the variety, and the novelty soon made it a favorite. It helped that it had delicious food and treats as well as helpful people who seemed to enjoy their jobs.

"We need a bigger dance floor," one of the older employees complained as she came back from having to deliver burgers to a table and the crowded dance floor was jitterbugging.

Amy laughed delightedly. They were crowded most days, and she had hired a few extra people that she hadn't planned on originally to keep up with the influx. She wished she could expand the dance floor, as well as the whole store. She wanted to teach the newer generation the older dances that hadn't quite died out, but there was nowhere in town to do that, and she really didn't have the time. She was kept hopping to keep up on her escalating business which was an absolute success.

"You'd think these people hadn't ever heard of ice cream!" one of the other employees exclaimed good-naturedly as she went down to the basement to haul up a five-gallon container for the ice cream counter.

Overall, Amy was thrilled that her plans had panned out and everything was going well. She even got hit on regularly by tourists at least once a day. Some of the locals hit on her as well when she went to Chuckie's or one of the other places that the people who actually lived there congregated, but she was polite to all and refused each one of them gracefully. She wasn't interested in dating; she had her business, her dog, and now a very active cat.

"Tabby, where are you going?" she asked as she watched the cat sneak through her backyard past the spots where the long-gone woodpiles had stood.

She was thrilled actually, that Tabby had learned that this was home but didn't use the cat pan unless the weather was too bad to go outside. Where she went during the day she didn't know, but she knew any day now she was going to have those kittens, and she wanted her home for that, but short of locking her in the cabin, she wasn't going to keep the independent cat at home. The cat seemed to know it was home, maybe it was the delicious and always available food that Amy provided, or the petting, even the play that Toby learned *was* play and not chase-the-cat.

"I think you need a vacation from your store!" Thomas told her as she sipped a beer and ate her fish fry at Chuckie's the next Friday.

"I love the store, why would I take a vacation from it?" she asked once her mouth was empty of the delicious perch she had ordered that night.

"That's all you ever do, work, work, work, no one sees you anymore. You didn't go out on any of the mud runs this spring since you opened that place!" he complained good-naturedly as he ate his own fish at the bar. The place was packed with people eating the Friday night fish fry, a unique and quaint Midwestern event that Amy was told was common in Wisconsin, some of Minnesota, Iowa, Michigan and even into Illinois. She had never heard of it before, but found it amusing that it was originally for Catholics who couldn't have meat on Fridays. It was the only day of the week that they had it too. So, if she was hungry for fried fish during the week, she had to make her own, buy frozen from the grocery store, or just wait until Friday.

"I know; the store is doing really well, though," she conceded as she took another sip of her beer. It was common for people to drink beers made in Wisconsin, yet she preferred a lighter name brand but would never have told anyone here. It was hard enough to get in with her southern accent. They accepted her because she had hired so many of their friends and relatives, she was certain.

"Yes, but all work and no play makes Amy a dull girl," he teased.

"Leave the woman alone," his wife Carol admonished him as she took a sip of her beer, a dark ale that made Amy want to gag. She had tried it as Carol and Thomas assured her it was a good tasting beer, but it simply wasn't her type of beverage. Besides, she really preferred a nice wine, but in this crowd, that would be mutiny.

As always, when she met up with the other townies she was learning to befriend, their talk turned to some of their favorite hobbies. In Carol and Thomas' case, it was making beer in their basement. They made several different kinds and considered themselves experts in beer making. It was all 'in the water', and they had a fresh spring on their property that allowed them to have the freshest water for their brewing. It 'made the difference', according to them both, and Amy didn't argue with them since she knew nothing about it. She had tried some of their beers to be social, and one of them had knocked her on her ass with its alcohol content. It had also given her a helluva hangover the next morning, and that was after just one glass, albeit a large glass.

"You've got to watch that stuff; those home brews will kill you," Abby consoled her as she ate ibuprofen in quantity the next day and tried to work too.

"It was only one glass though," she complained as she hoped that the water wouldn't upset her stomach, which was doing a good imitation of a spin cycle on a washing machine.

"Yes, but it's quality stuff," Abby grinned as she sipped a sarsaparilla at the counter. She liked coming into The Emporium once a day, and their lunches were pretty damn good. Their clam chowder on Saturday night was killer too. The recipe that Amy used had crumbled bacon in it, and it was worth every penny. The thought of it just made Abby's mouth water waiting for Saturday night to come so she could have a bowl, never just a cup of the concoction. The diced potatoes and other additions were just a bonus to the rich broth the woman made, and you couldn't discount the tiny round crackers she offered with the soup or the homemade bread bowl she offered it in.

"Are you boring our local entrepreneur with beer talk again?" Abby asked as she came up to the bar to get more root beer for her and her family who could be found almost every Friday in their booth.

"She's not bored; she seems interested," Thomas defended himself, but he looked at Amy to be sure he hadn't bored her to death.

"I am interested," Amy assured him as she grinned unrepentantly at Abby who knew of these two's love of making the home brew.

"Just make sure you don't sell that stuff, or I'll have to get involved," Abby assured them.

"We should sell it the way the boys go through it," Carol complained.

Abby watched as a light went on in Amy's attractive green eyes. It was the same light she had seen go on when she had suggested she sell the hot chocolate in smaller packets. Within a few weeks, The Emporium's Hot Chocolate in various flavors was soon available to the general public and was very popular with both tourists and locals alike. Amy had given a gift basket to Abby of all her and her family's favorite flavors; it had been well received.

"Why don't you sell it?" Amy asked as she speared a forkful of fish and then put it in her mouth.

"Because it's illegal, silly," Carol said as she glanced at Abby. They didn't 'sell' their concoctions, but that didn't mean there wasn't a lot of barter going on.

"But what would it take to set up a micro-brewery?" Amy asked as she chewed the small bite of fish thoughtfully and gestured with her fork.

Abby rolled her eyes as she gathered the root beer bottles and headed back to her table. From the sound of it, she would have an ear full of beer talk with Carol and Thomas before the night was out. She had just lit a fuse.

Abby wasn't surprised that one of the vacant buildings in town became Northpoint Brew a few months later. They had taste testing and their own bottling and distillery. They'd applied for all their licenses and gotten certified by the state, and as long as they kept within those certifications, they could legally bottle and sell their brews. Carol and Thomas were over the moon at their new business venture. Thomas had been able to quit his day job as a custodian down at the local high school, and Carol was keeping her job as a cafeteria lunch lady until the place took off. Few if anyone knew that Amy had helped them and backed them in their endeavor. When Abby happened to find out, she wasn't surprised, but it made her wonder at the southerner more.

CHAPTER SEVENTEEN

"May I have an ice cream, Mom?" Heather asked as they came in from getting their boat ready for summer.

"Let's finish cleaning this up," Abby said as they stowed their gear. They had put the boat in the water for the first time this year and taken it out fishing. Bonnie had come along begrudgingly, but she seemed to have enjoyed herself. "How about you, Bailey, do you want an ice cream?" she asked as she ruffled his hair, something she couldn't do much anymore.

"Sounds good," he said in a happier voice. He seemed to have grown up a lot this spring. The kittens that had been born out at the cabin that Amy lived in meant he had to ride his bike out there at least once a day to check on them for Amy. She had told him he had misled her in this deal, and it was his responsibility to find homes for all four of the little mewlers as she called them.

Abby almost laughed aloud as she remembered Amy's frantic call about the kittens. "They're comin', they're comin'!" she said excitedly into the phone on a Wednesday night. She must have just gotten home from work. "Bring the kids over so they can watch, she's already had one. This is a good educational experience," she informed the cop. Abby had brought not only the kids, but her mother-in-law who seemed intrigued by the redhead. Abby knew it was because Amy had 'consulted' Bonnie on several things around the store, the dock, and the town. It had endeared her to the older woman who appreciated being valued.

"That's gross," the ten-year boy had said as he watched the tabby expel a kitten from beneath her tail.

"That's natural," Abby assured him as Heather scrunched up her nose in disgust at the slimy sack that was pushed out.

Amy stood back and watched as the two children, despite being grossed out, watched as each and every one of the kittens were born.

"You can't ask for birds and the bees like this," Bonnie murmured in Amy's ear as they looked on. Abby looked surprisingly young as she talked quietly with the two children, a softening to her tough cop demeanor that appeared now and then.

It had been actually a pleasant evening, and not until the fourth and final kitten had been born and a considerable amount of time went by did they even consider leaving. It took some convincing and promises from adults before the two children would go home. It was a school night, it was late, and the cat was proudly cleaning her offspring as she lay there purring contentedly. They could all hear Toby snuffling at the door in the master bedroom where he had been consigned.

"You won't let Toby get them, will you?" Heather worried.

"Tabby won't let him near them," Bailey answered her with a superior tone. He was proved wrong when Toby was found cuddled around the kittens while Tabby ate food in the kitchen a few days later. Toby seemed to think they were *his* charges. That Tabby, who he had accepted long ago, especially once he realized she had sharp claws, wasn't going to run from him, and treated him with disdain. He adored her and greeted her enthusiastically each time he saw her in the yard.

"Let's wash up before we go in The Emporium," Bonnie advised after a day on the water and fishing. They were all a little grimy. The boat had needed an outing, and now it would need to be washed down. They tied off at their dock next to the one for The Emporium, now lined on one side with canoes for rent and the gas pump on the other side waiting for boaters to 'fill up.'

"I'll water down the boat and cover it if you will all take the gear in," Abby offered. She rinsed the boat and pulled the drain plug so any water she sprayed over the deck would drain out as she sprayed it down. She used a scrub rag, and as she rubbed down the boat, she sensed rather than saw eyes on her. She looked up, not surprised to see Amy watching her from the store. She waved as she continued to wash down the boat. She was almost done, and she wanted to change before they went over for ice cream.

SMALL TOWN ANGEL

Amy watched her friend thoughtfully, wondering why she had parked so far in on her dock. She learned later that the second berth was for the sheriff's boat that was kept there, but it hadn't been put in the water yet. She was in her office for a few minutes and had watched the family dock at their private dock. She wondered at the odd family dynamics, but they seemed so natural, so right, she couldn't help but enjoy them.

"Did you catch anything?" she asked the family as she visited with them in one of the booths later.

The kids nearly let their ice cream melt as they told her about fishing and being out on the boat, going past the islands, and to one of *their* fishing spots.

"You should come with us sometime," Bailey offered as he licked at a drip on his cone.

"It sounds delightful. I'll let you all finish up now," she answered politely as she nodded to the adults who had barely spoken in the children's enthusiasm over the outing.

"You don't have to go, do you?" Heather mourned over her own ice cream which looked like she was wearing more of it than ingesting it.

"I do have work to do, but I'd like to ask you two to walk Toby if it's not too much," she looked at Abby and Bonnie apologetically for not asking them first instead of the children. The children quickly agreed, and Abby had no choice but to agree. She didn't mind, she really didn't. The kids enjoyed helping Amy like this, and Toby had become their dog, once removed.

Late in the spring after the breakup and for Memorial Day, the town hosted a festival with a parade, and plenty of people showed up for both. Amy saw that they took this seriously and made notes in her head to be better prepared for next year. As it was, any Veteran in uniform or who could show a Military I.D. got all the free ice cream they could eat. The Emporium was very popular for this gesture alone. It vied with the new Northpoint Micro-brewery that was giving samples to Vets in moderation.

"Wow, my feet are killing me," Thomas bitched good-naturedly the Monday after Memorial Day weekend. Their new store was a success, and he appreciated Amy's help, both financially and in marketing it. She had made both Carol and he go on a tour of micro-breweries in the state to see how they were doing things, and on a couple of occasions, she had joined them so that they could 'brew' ideas of their own, and the store would be a success.

"Just eat your cookies and cream," Carol teased him as she scooped up her own praline.

"We should work on a beer ice cream," he replied with a twinkle in his eye.

"Ahead of you there," Amy told him as she wiped the counter in front of him with a smile.

He shook his head; she really had been an angel to them, and the terms were generous. She had also put them in contact with a marketing genius who was worth every dime that they had spent to make the store a success. The huge cask that greeted customers as they walked through a plug hole to enter the store was genius. Terry had appreciated the work, and Lenora was thrilled to rent out another empty building in the small village. The work was first rate, and customers appreciated the brewery feel of their store. Many of the bars around town and the area were already carrying their different and distinctive brews. "I've got to enjoy this while I can; I have deliveries to make," he said importantly.

"And I have to get back to school," Carol said with a grin; she was going to put her resignation in at the end of summer and work at the brewery full time at this rate.

"Don't forget to talk to Terry about putting in that boardwalk if the city would allow it," Amy reminded them with a twinkle. She loved that she had helped them fulfill their dream. It had taken a lot of late nights to get it ready in time for this last weekend, but they looked pleased. Having outdoor drinking might be a problem on the lakefront, but it was still in the confines of the brewery. Patrons would be warned not to take it off the property. The views would mean the customers could enjoy their beer in the shade overlooking the boats.

Lavina Mason was surprised when Amy approached her about opening a small laundromat in the back of one of the stores. It was to be out of sight but would cater to anyone who had to haul their dirty laundry in the past to the next town. They had Terry build the platforms for the industrial machines and put up false walls so the machines could be easily serviced from behind.

"Why me?" she asked the redheaded owner of The Emporium.

"I've seen you many times at the same laundromat as I, and I saw you cleanin'. I want someone who will take care of the place and I can trust. I asked around," she confided, not telling her that Abby and some of the people at Chuckie's had vouched for her after some carefully placed questions were made. A widower who barely made ends meet, as a partner of Amy's, she would get a percentage of the sales to maintain the laundromat. The highest compliment that she received was from Bonnie, who assured Amy that the woman was the most honest she'd ever met. Amy had gone to her about the idea of opening the small business for their mutual benefit. It would certainly supplement her limited social security income.

"I'll make sure it's spic 'n span," she promised, and then proceeded to make it shine. People complimented that it never felt grungy as other laundromats did. It wasn't large; they didn't have a lot of machines, but what they did have was maintained and clean.

People around town wondered where Lavina had gotten the funds to rent the back of the market, much less to put in the machines, but rumor had it she had come into some money to start her business. No one, not Lavina, not Amy, and not the bank where they did business told anyone differently.

"I'd like to rent one of those canoes," one of the kids said enthusiastically as he bounced on the seat overlooking the dock as his mother tried to get him to eat the delicious meal they had ordered.

"Maybe, if you are good, you and your mother could check out Spencer's. Those are their canoes, and they have lots of interestin' things in their store," Amy told him as she delivered their sodas. She wondered if so hyper a child should really have a second helping of soda, but it was up to his mother. The mother looked at her gratefully at distracting the boy for a minute with the idea of looking through the other store.

"What else do they have?" he asked as he reached for the soda, but his mother adroitly pulled it out of his hands.

"Food first," she told him sternly.

"You will have to finish everythin' on your plate, and I'm sure you will see for yourself," Amy drawled with a conspiratorial wink at the mother who smiled back. Amy went to take care of other customers.

Spencer's frequently sent people over with one of their employees to take one of the canoes they kept on her dock. They also referred people to her for a free ice cream now and again. Amy referred people to them all the time, and they did the same, recommending her for gift items, ice cream, and her excellent food. People frequently stayed for the atmosphere or came in after a canoe rental. It had turned out to be a good relationship for both businesses.

Amy was taking a well-deserved break sitting on her own deck overlooking the water, listening to the ever-present gulls, and enjoying the late spring heat. They had said it could actually get up to high temperatures this summer, and she was looking forward to it. Having come from a warmer climate, humidity was actually something she missed.

"You look comfortable," Bonnie teased her, having seen her leaning back in one of the Adirondack chairs placed around the porch for customers. Amy had found someone locally who made these and made a deal that they could sell them from her porch in exchange for providing them to the store. Some of their creations were really extraordinary, and Amy had a beautiful rocker for her own porch at home. There were a few with designs so intrinsic that the viewer would breathe a sigh of appreciation at the beauty carved into the woods. Some, like the one she was leaning back in, were plain and functional.

Amy sighed as she lifted her face into the sun; it was so nice to just relax for a moment before her self-imposed duties once again intruded. The smell of the lake, the distinct musky scent of rotting plant life, a bit of fish, and the clear smell of the water wafted over her. "I am," she said reverently.

"Mind if I join you?" Bonnie asked as she prepared to sit down on an adjoining chair. She herself enjoyed the never-ending scenes over the water in the harbor.

"NO!" Amy said angrily as she leaped up from her chair.

"What?" Bonnie said offended and dismayed as she took a step back from the angry redhead.

Amy hurled herself down off the boardwalk around her store and onto the steps to the dock before running the length of her dock and diving off the end.

Bonnie followed her with her eyes, shocked and alarmed at her abrupt leave taking but watched open mouthed as she dove off the dock without a moment's hesitation; she looked out further to see a canoe in the water had capsized. A dark-haired woman was running down the dock and shouting something incoherent. Bonnie stepped back to her own house, and stepping inside, called to Abby who was in the front room that seconded as the police station.

"What? What's going on?" Abby came at a run at the commotion and the alarm in Bonnie's voice.

"Someone took a dip," Bonnie said as she turned so that Abby could follow her out the door.

They saw that Amy had reached the overturned canoe and had someone in a typical swimmer's lock, holding the torso in her strong arm as she swam one-handed back towards the docks.

"My baby, my baby," called the dark-haired woman, wringing her hands in uselessness.

"What happened?" Abby asked officiously as she walked up to the end of The Emporium's dock. A boat was on one side getting gas with one of the kids who worked at The Emporium in attendance. Several empty canoes bobbed in the water on the other side, tied up to the dock. People had started coming out of the store and along the boardwalk to stare as the redhead rescued the boy from the canoe.

"My son, *my baby*," the woman began, and seeing Amy was bringing him, she gulped. "He snuck off and got in one of those canoes," she pointed accusingly at the empty berth where they were tied. "Those should really be better monitored," she said importantly.

"You will be lucky if your son isn't charged for theft," Abby returned, seeing where this was going. The woman wanted to hold her son unaccountable for his actions.

"He can't swim," she said in defense, as though that excused his behavior.

"Well, the Y offers classes," Abby returned shortly as she leaned down to help Amy with the boy. Another set of hands was there to help her lift the rather plump little boy out of the water. Abby released him to the man who had appeared out of nowhere and helped Amy up on the dock. "You okay?" she asked the redhead as she could see the boy was fine, as well as being coddled by his mother already.

"I'm fine, that water is freezing though," Amy said as she began to rub her arms and shake a little.

"Here," Bonnie said as she handed her a big fluffy towel she had grabbed from their house and given another one to the little boy who was trying to say the canoe had gotten away from the dock, trying to be the hero. No one but his mother was buying it.

"Thank you," Amy said, genuinely grateful. It was a fluffy bath sheet and wrapped completely around her smaller frame.

"Let's get you indoors and out of here," Abby said as she urged Bonnie to take her, and with a nod, the older woman put her arm around the red head and led her off.

The mother didn't say anything as Amy passed, and Abby stared at her disgustedly. "Thank you," she told the man who had helped her get them both on the dock. She now recognized him from Spencer's.

"No problem," he said. Something in his tone told her that he too was annoyed with the little boy who had snuck one of their canoes out from the dock and without a paddle. His standing up in the canoe had capsized it out on the water, fortunately not too far out, and Amy had been able to save him. He went into another canoe with a paddle and went out to retrieve the capsized one.

Several hours later, some necessary paperwork had Abby annoyed at the tourist mom, who had indulged her son at every turn and gave him a sense of self-importance. After Abby got done with both of them, she was certain they would never again visit Northpoint, but she didn't care. Those headaches she didn't need. The threat of being charged with theft of the canoe hadn't fazed the kid, but the mother looked terrified. After paying a 'rental' fee to Spencer's who were satisfied with that and relieved that their insurance wouldn't be involved, the woman took her bratty son out of the station. Nearly stealing Abby's towel in the process, she came up with a plastic blanket the woman could use instead. Shaking her head at the different people she was forced to deal with, Abby let them go with a smile of good riddance.

"How's Amy?" Abby asked Bonnie when she saw her.

"She's fine," Bonnie returned, looking at Abby speculatively and wondering at her interest. Was it more than friendship? She tried not to judge, after all, her own daughter had been attracted to other women and had even 'married' this woman, but it didn't mean that every woman attracted them. "She went back to work."

"She didn't go home and change?" Abby asked surprised.

"She is down someone today and couldn't go. She just put on one of the costumes she makes those employees of her wear and went back to work; you should see her. She's playing up the role of a soda jerk to the hilt. I'd swear she was channeling those twenties soda jerks we see in the old movies," Bonnie said admirably.

The costumes were a bit of a cross of Americana. Where Amy had found her supplier, no one knew, but the uniforms her employees wore, from the thin Mrs. Oswald who looked like she had been an original patron of these kinds of stores, to the thick-set Johnny Meyers whose father was Johnathan Meyer, and supplied wood along with his brother

Jacob. They all looked 'dapper' in them, and Amy liked the authenticity of it as did the customers.

Abby strolled by The Emporium later and saw that Amy did indeed look good in her role as a soda jerk behind the counter. Her thick red hair was up and in an old time 'net' that made it look perfect for her role. She was talking animatedly with anyone who came to the counter and sat on its polished stools. She admonished any of the kids who tried to spin on the stools pointing out that they could be hurt. She'd just as quickly go back to the grill and flip a few burgers for customers who adored the flavor of the locally grown beef. Nothing like the best for her customers, she had been heard to say. She'd even made a deal with some of the local farmers to supply her with fresh vegetables when they were available, some of which she sold in old wooden crates on the boardwalk. Abby had heard a few stories about the redhead and marveled at how well she had fit into the community since her arrival last fall. Everyone adored her.

"Hey, whatcha doin'?" she called as she walked up.

"My nails," Amy answered, as she carefully trimmed another using cuticle scissors on her hand.

"Out here on the porch?" Abby asked amused, as she greeted Toby whose tail thumped on the wood in greeting.

"Well, it's better than having them fly everywhere in the house; I hate that in the bathroom. I can't get them all into the trash, and gawd forbid I do them in bed," she returned saucily.

"Well, I'm sure Toby doesn't mind," she said jokingly as she sat down next to the pup to pet him.

"I just did his nails; they were first. It was Tabby that would object, and she did when I cut her nails!" Amy showed her a scratch on her arm.

"You cut your cat's nails?" she laughed, imagining that.

Amy nodded. "She kept using them to climb on the bed instead of hopping up, which I know very well she is able to do!" She pulled up her bare foot and began to work on her toes, and then looking up embarrassed that she had company, quickly lowered it, making sure her pants' legs covered her ankles.

Abby saw her embarrassment and turned to hide her amusement. She shook her head as Amy had such old-fashioned manners on some things, and bare feet must be one of them, much less cutting her nails.

What, did she think that people didn't know she cut her nails? "Did you use the same clippers on your pets as you do on yourself?" she couldn't help teasing.

Abby heard the chuckle behind her as she petted the amiable dog who unashamedly rolled onto his back to present his tummy for rubbing. "I did not," was the response.

"I was wondering if you would like to join the kids and I for a picnic up on the island next weekend if you aren't too busy," Abby asked hesitantly. It was the real reason for her visit, and she knew that giving enough advance notice, Amy might be able to go, with her busy social schedule and the work that she did so much herself.

"That sounds wonderful, when were you thinking?"

Abby turned back to ask shyly, "Would Sunday be good? I've got the sheriff boat and have to cruise up anyway, and they won't mind if I take passengers, so I thought we'd take along a picnic basket and stop on one of the islands."

"Do you want me to bring anything?" she asked helpfully.

"Just this pup and yourself," she responded, giving Toby one more playful tweak before getting up off the porch and brushing off her pants.

They worked out the time, and Amy agreed to meet her in town on Sunday. Smiling as though she had really accomplished something, Abby headed off on patrol.

CHAPTER EIGHTEEN

"Look out there!" Abby warned as Bailey cast with his fishing pole.

Amy laughed as they had all thought she was too girly to bait her own hook. Not only could she bait it, she had expertly cast into the deep waters of Lake Michigan. She'd impressed them all by knowing how to do a double fisherman's knot, expertly. Later, she admitted to the amusement of her captive audience that she had YouTubed exactly how. Her giggles over how she had pulled that one over on them endeared her to Abby. "We should fry these up in a nice batter later," she said as she looked at the fish already on the line, holding their various catches. She had caught the biggest, and the children were in awe of their friend.

"That sounds delicious," Bonnie enthused. She had been surprised to be included in this outing. She had assumed it was Abby's way of dating the pert little redhead, but really, she saw nothing other than friendship in the two women. Although she hadn't approved of her daughter's relationship with Abby or even approved of Abby herself, she thought Abby was a good mother to her two grandchildren. Living in the same house had proven to be difficult at first, but her husband had smoothed the way as they all grieved over their mutual loss.

"Oh yes, I'll use my grandmother's secret sauce," Amy said before she could help herself and then quickly quieted as she realized she had spoken impulsively. She clammed up after that, but the adults pretended not to notice, and the children didn't notice at all.

"This is beautiful," Abby said as she lay back on the blanket they had spread on the island for their picnic. She had pulled the boat right up on the sand and tied a rope to a tree. They had all jumped over the side into the small surf against the beach and helped unload their picnic.

Abby was intrigued to see a perfect little angel tattoo on Amy's right leg; it was on the inside and barely noticeable, but she had noticed the trim little legs on the petite redhead as well as her tight little butt.

Amy laughed at the brunette who was dressed in a sleeveless blouse, revealing an intricate dragon tattoo on her upper arm. It showed off tanned muscular arms on the chief. Although she had used the Sheriff's boat and was still technically on duty, she wasn't wearing her officer's uniform at all. Except for the empty gun holster at her hip and the badge on her belt, she looked like a carefree woman on an outing with her children. Mischievously, Amy started pinching watermelon seeds with her fingertips at the officer. The children grinned and tried to duplicate Amy's technique of pinching them with moderate success.

"Okay you two, knock it off," Abby said as she got seeds all over her toned and tanned legs that were bare below the khaki shorts she was wearing.

Amy nearly giggled as she grinned in delighted evil glee, and the kids and her—even Bonnie, joined in, pelting the reclined brunette. Finally, feeling them coming from all angles, she opened her eyes and caught both Bonnie and Amy in mid-pinch. "Why, you two!" she exclaimed as she grabbed her soda and shook it up menacingly as she got up from her prone position.

"Now, now, Abby, what kind of example are you setting for the children?" Bonnie laughed as she held up her hands in supplication.

"What kind of example am I setting?" she returned as she shook the can.

Amy got up to run but was soon sprayed with the sticky concoction as the children roared and tried to duplicate the naughty adults. The dog barked and leapt up. They were all soon out of soda as they shook and sprayed each other. Their picnic was a mess, but they all trooped down to the cold water to wash up and giggle over their antics.

"You know, paybacks are a bitch," Amy threatened the officer of the law.

"What, you started it!" Abby returned with a grin at the idle threat.

"Prove it!" Amy said tauntingly and splashed water at the crouching cop.

All too soon a new fight began with sprays and handfuls of water, and everyone joined in over the cold lake water. When they were all dripping, the dog included, hair hanging down limply, and everyone wearing grins in the hot air, they trooped back to their picnic site to clean up the mess they had made there.

"This is going to require washing," Bonnie said practically.

"We can dunk it and you in the lake," Amy teased with a glimmer in her eye.

"Nuh uh, I'm never going to trust you near water or soda again!" Bonnie laughed.

They soon had it all cleaned up, the wet sticky mess tucked in the blanket and back on the boat as they decided to go for a wet walk and dry off as they explored the little island set aside in the lake as a natural preserve. As no one lived there, it was left in its wild state with no natural pathways or even man-made ones to direct them, so it was pretty much where the children wanted to go as the adults followed them. It was pretty but overgrown with brush and trees. They had to be careful as rocks turned up in the most inopportune places. Since they were all still barefoot, it was a little dicey now and then as they explored.

"Careful there," Abby cautioned as Amy nearly fell trying to maneuver around a large sharp rock that jutted out of the turf. She effortlessly lifted the much smaller woman by her arm and held her steady until her feet were back under her. For a second, they exchanged looks, and Abby saw fear in Amy's eyes, if only for that moment. In Abby's eyes, Amy saw polite concern and something more, something subtle that her subconscious responded to—if only for that second after she let the surprise of being grabbed by her arm like that pass. Her heart beating hard, she could shrug off to her surprise and momentary fear of falling.

"I think there are plenty of stickers on this rock," Amy said to cover up her clumsiness.

"You mean those," Bailey asked pointing to the weeds with sharp pointy things jutting out from the stems, waiting to catch their clothes and scratch their exposed skin.

"Yes, those thangs are dangerous!" she said, avoiding another batch as they climbed through a particularly dense section.

By the time they climbed all over the island and back to the boat, they were bug bitten, scratched, and dry from their earlier soaking. All of them walked into the cold lake water to wash up a bit and watched each other warily in case anyone started the water fight from earlier again. The adults were vigilant at keeping the kids from starting it again as they all felt the coolness on their scratchy skin.

"I hear the radio," Abby said as she finished first from washing her cuts and scrapes and letting her feet soak in the cooling water. They all headed back to the boat so she could answer it. Abby effortlessly climbed on board using her hands to springboard herself over the side.

Amy had been surprised at the toned and tanned muscles on the cop, as she normally wore full covering clothes, she had never suspected that the brunette was this muscular.

"Hey, we got to go check out a couple of fisherman southwest of here," Abby soon shouted after answering the call on the radio. She should have taken a hand-held radio; they had been trying to reach her for a while from base where another officer was on duty while she went out on the lake.

Abby helped them over the side. Amy was particularly ungraceful as she climbed over the side like a seal on land. She ended up tumbling to the bottom of the boat, looking particularly abashed as her skin blushed under the other woman's scrutiny.

"Are you okay?" Abby asked, trying not to laugh at the smaller woman.

"Yeah, just a bit clumsy today," she said as she looked down and got herself up. Abby leaned in at the same time to help her up, and their faces came close enough that Abby's breath fanned across Amy's cheek. They both stopped, shocked for a moment before Amy was steady on her feet.

"Wanna help an old woman here," Bonnie interrupted them as she tried to get over the edge.

Both women turned to help the older woman over the side.

They were soon heading out back into the lake and towards the coordinates that Abby had been given. They had to give a little gas to the fishermen who hadn't realized how little had been in their tank, and they followed them back into the protective harbor as the sheriff's boat parked in its usual berth, and the men parked by The Emporium, and an employee ran out to help them gas up.

"I'll take these home, and you all come over in an hour or so and help me clean and fry them up," Amy said as she lifted the string of fish up.

"I can't let you do all that," Bonnie complained as she lifted a cooler to the dock.

"Oh no, I need to make the secret sauce," she teased as she helped with the sticky blanket.

They soon had the boat cleaned out, and after the fishermen left the dock, the chief drove the Sheriff's boat over to the dock to gas up as she watched her children go in the house with her mother-in-law and Amy and Toby head for her SUV. She didn't realize the officer's eyes watched her every step.

Later as they ate out on the picnic table under the towering trees of Amy's yard, they all appreciated the sun staying out later, the frogs croaking, and the crickets making their chirping noises. It was a beautiful late spring evening surrounded by family and friends. The children chased Toby around, and even Tabby made a reluctant appearance, followed by her kittens which hadn't been large enough to give away quite yet. Toby was giving Amy the stink eye since she refused to allow him to have more than one marshmallow as the kids made s'mores over the open fire.

"Where exactly do you come from?" Bonnie asked Amy, and Abby perked up to listen to that answer from her seat by the fire. They were all seated around the fire, the children poking sticks in the flames as the adults sipped on beers. Gently, they slapped at the occasional mosquito, but most of them stayed away since Amy had put four large citronella torches around the burning pit.

"Well, I told ya'll that I came from down south," Amy hedged, and her eyes flicked towards Abby almost guiltily.

"Yeah, but you never actually said where," Bonnie persisted.

"No, no I never did," she returned uncomfortably. She was obviously delaying the answering of that question, and Abby could see it. She also saw when she decided to answer as she took a deep breath and opened her mouth to speak.

"Bark, bark, bark," Toby exploded at that very moment.

Amy sprung up out of her seat, an overly large log, and rushed after the pup who was heading for the edge of the clearing around the house. "C'mon and help me get'em," she called to the now tired children, who sprung up after her.

"Careful, I think I smell…" she barely had the words out of her mouth when the pungent odor assailed all their nostrils. "…skunk," she finished mournfully, covering her mouth.

The yells of the adults and the children were something to behold. Abby herded the children back to the car along with Bonnie as Amy encouraged them to leave. She was holding a struggling pup by his collar as he tried to go back after the little animal that had sprayed him with the disgusting odor.

"I hate to leave you with that; I'll bring back some tomato juice," Abby told her as she held her shirt over her mouth and nose.

"Sure you will," Amy teased as her eyes watered from the odor, and she pulled the pup to the faucet on the side of the cabin.

"I swear, I'll be back," she promised and got everyone in her car. She watched as Amy began to wet down the soaked pup, who struggled more at the cold water she was spraying on him. She laughed, but knew it was no laughing matter.

"Is Toby going to be hurt?" Heather asked concerned.

"Toby will be fine; we will get you home and to bed, and I'll take back some tomato juice to wash that dog," Abby promised as she looked in the rear-view mirror at her daughter. "You sit down and buckle up," she said sternly as Heather craned to look back at the cabin.

"That skunk got Toby good," Bailey said with a grin as he held his own shirt over his nose and mouth and talked through it. His cheekbones rose, and Abby could see the grin despite the shirt. She smiled in return.

"Yeah, he's going to be ripe for quite a while," she agreed.

"You think tomato juice will be enough?" Bonnie asked, concerned. They had rushed away so quickly they hadn't taken the extra fish that Amy had fried up for them for leftovers.

"I don't know, too many cures other than time for that smell," Abby pointed behind them with her thumb and grinned at the pup's antics. That smell could linger for weeks.

They discussed the fine and long day, and the children were definitely crabby when she helped Bonnie get them in the house, showered, and tucked into bed. She gathered the tomato juice she had in the house and then stopped by one of the bars for any extra they had.

"Why so much?" Pete asked as she placed her order.

Explaining, he exchanged a grin with her. "That poor dog," he laughed and gave her several large cans of the stuff. "This is when we need a convenience store," he mentioned as she gathered in the cans in her arms.

"Yeah, twenty-four hours of problems," she countered. They had a nice, quaint, little fishing village that the tourists adored. A small market that sufficed for most of their grocery needs. The year-round residents didn't need a convenience store. It was then she remembered that Pete only lived here part of the year.

Pete helped her by opening the doors for her and then slipping the keys from her belt so she could put the cans in the trunk of her cruiser.

"That it?" he asked helpfully as he returned her keys to the palm of her hand.

"Yep, and thanks," she said as she got behind the wheel and drove out to Amy's cabin. The odor assailed her nostrils as soon as she got out of her cruiser. A disheartened-looking pup was tied to the corner of the cabin.

"I didn't think I'd see you back here," Amy said as she came down off the porch where she had been sitting.

"I thought this might help," Abby returned as she popped open the trunk.

"Whatcha got there?" she drawled as she walked up.

"Bug juice," Abby teased as she held up the overly large can from the bar. "Got a can opener?"

Amy grinned in delight and grabbed a couple of the cans to take them inside and open them. Toby started whining and crying outside, with an occasional bark as though they had forgotten him. When Amy returned, Abby had all the cans from her house and the bar on the edge of the porch.

"Wanna help me wash 'im?" she asked with a grin.

"Sure," Abby returned and reached for the can.

Not expecting the actual help, Amy was surprised, and the can swiped out of her hand caused her to spill some on Abby's shirt. "Oh dear, I am sorry," she said but didn't look quite contrite enough.

"Oh, you are, are you?" asked Abby with a gleam in her eye.

"I really am," she drawled, but then couldn't help it, and a snort of laughter followed it.

"Uh huh, you know paybacks are a bitch?" Abby asked.

Amy stopped laughing and continued on towards the poor wet pup who eagerly greeted them hopefully. "And revenge is a mother…" she mumbled under her breath, but Abby heard her and wondered grinning.

Between them, they washed the poor pup with the tomato juice, saving the rest for another bath as the dog would still stink. They both got wet in the process as Toby was cold and not happy about the outdoor process.

"The poor guy," Amy consoled him. "Can you hold him while I get a towel for him?" she asked as she handed Abby his leash.

"I got him," Abby said, just before Toby knocked her off her feet now that he knew they were done.

"Are you okay?" Amy asked, trying to help the cop to her feet.

"Jeez, this has been one cluster…" she started to say, and then realizing where her language was going, she stopped herself. She grinned at the redhead, right into those amazing green eyes that she could barely see in the darkness, and said, "I guess Toby is paying us back too."

Amy grinned. She had been sure Abby would be furious at the pup. She'd braced herself for it, especially with the tone of what Abby had been about to say. In the light coming through the living room window, she saw the softness of Abby's eyes and took an involuntarily step forward. She hesitated a moment and then caught herself. Turning, she quickly headed towards the house for that towel for the dog and ones for the adults.

"I don't want him in the cabin with that smell," Amy said emphatically as they all stood on the porch and tried to dry off in the cool of the evening.

"We are all wet," Abby emphasized what she was saying by wringing out the ends of her hair. "I'm cold; I'm sure you're cold, and look at Toby," she gestured.

Toby looked up at the two women as sorrowfully as he could. He knew he'd done something bad that they got him soaking wet with the hose, and the red stuff stank and wasn't even good to eat, he knew, he'd tried! He was contrite though, and willing to make amends as his tail thumped from where it was tucked between his legs, and he looked up at them.

"Aww," Amy said under her breath; she knew she was a sucker for letting the stinky pup in the house, but it was Abby's eyes that were really getting to her. She didn't know why, but they were making something twist in her stomach. Maybe one of the fish she had eaten was bad. "Okay, let's let him in," she said after rubbing him one more time with the towel to remove most of the wetness.

Toby seemed to know he was forgiven and ran with enthusiasm into the cabin once the door was open. He tried to chase Tabby, who was with her kittens and spat at him in alarm, the kittens copying their mother's anger with arched backs, and small noises of protest. Both Abby and Amy laughed at the scene.

"Down Toby," Amy told the enthusiastic dog. He wanted to run around and play, he felt good, he was wet and wild and... "Toby, DOWN!" Amy commanded him in a tone that brooked no nonsense.

Toby thought he had done something wrong again and immediately went to the floor in obedience.

"Good boy," she praised him, but when he would have gotten up, she commanded him to, "Stay."

"Wow, maybe I should have you teach my kids to obey," Abby marveled.

Amy laughed. "Why don't you take the first shower," she said pointing to the bathroom. "I have some extra towels, and I think I have some sweats that might fit you," she instructed.

"Giving me commands, too?" Abby's eyebrow raised questioningly.

"Or you could drive home in the wet," she pointed to the jeans that Abby was sporting that were quite wet from the help she had rendered washing the pup.

"I'll take you up on those towels and sweats," Abby grinned sheepishly.

Before long, both of them had showered and were sharing hot-toddy's on the couch. The now nearly dry pup was sleeping in front of the fireplace. Amy had gone outside and made sure the fire in the fire pit was out while Abby showered. Amy asked that Abby start the fire in the fireplace to take the chill out of the air. The cabin was soon warm and toasty, and when Amy came out of the shower, rubbing her hair to dry it, she offered the hot-toddy's to warm their insides.

"Well, you certainly have made a home here," Abby commented as they companionably watched the cat and her kittens play together on the floor. They were endlessly amusing and much better than television.

"My family keeps growing," Amy said cheerfully, but there was an underlying worry there that Abby's trained ear heard.

"Is family bad?" she asked; she knew her bio-family wasn't much, but the family she had made with her wife was better than anything she could imagine. She had a good job, a great group of friends, and a life she enjoyed.

"Oh no, family is forever," she said, with a sad note.

"Who are you, Amy Adams?" Abby said with a smile to soften the question. She knew that Amy was skittish about that question or any question regarding her past.

Amy looked at her. "Does it matter?"

Abby shook her head. "Not really, I just…wondered," she finished with a hopeful note. She wanted to know this friend of hers better. She had been a good friend, a good addition to their community. She wished that she…

"What's it like being gay?" Amy surprised both of them to ask.

Abby laughed at the question. "What's it like having green eyes?" she countered.

Amy shared in the laughter, realizing what a stupid question it was.

"Haven't you ever met a lesbian before you moved here?"

Amy shrugged. "If I did, she hid it well; it probably wasn't allowed down south," she drawled, sounding very southern.

Abby was intrigued. She wanted answers, but only if Amy wanted to share with her. She sensed there was a lot about this woman that she hadn't shared with any of them. She was intrigued, she was annoyed, and there was so much she wanted from her if she was willing… "What about you? Have you ever been attracted to a woman?"

"Oh no," she said quickly, much too quickly, not realizing she was insulting the brunette sitting on the couch with her. "It wouldn't have been allowed."

"Allowed?" Abby cocked her head in question, wondering at the wording.

"Well, the way we all were raised, you simply didn't think like that. Boys went with girls, not with other boys, and girls were friends, not girl*friends*," she emphasized, although she was slow in how she said it; there was *something* else there.

"That's the way it is everywhere, but it's changing. *Thank God*," she mumbled the last part of that.

"It must be hard," she stated softly. At Abby's glance, she continued, "People not accepting of you, making judgements…" she left off as she realized what she was actually saying.

Abby was picking up nuances; Amy was talking from her own point of view but with a tone that told the experienced cop that she had experienced such things herself. "Have you ever wanted to kiss a woman?" she teased hopefully.

Amy looked at the muscular cop in surprise. "Is it different?" she asked naïvely.

Abby almost laughed but caught herself in time. Nodding, she answered, "The lips are softer, and the taste is…."

"What?" the redhead asked, wide-eyed and curious.

Abby shrugged intriguingly. "You'll have to find out yourself."

Amy bit her lip worriedly, an endearing habit of hers when she was upset or thinking. Abby watched fascinated, her eyes glittering with suppressed humor, but it was immediately extinguished when Amy asked, "Would you show me?"

As much as she was tempted, she refused. Shaking her head, she replied just as softly as Amy's question, "No, I'm not anyone's science experiment."

"I'm sorry," she apologized emphatically. "I didn't mean it like that," she twanged.

"I know you didn't. But I won't let you experiment on me," she calmed her voice from the anger she was beginning to feel.

"I didn't mean…" she began again, but Abby got up off the couch and put the cup she had been holding down.

"I should get going," she said abruptly. Toby lifted his head from the floor where he was laying, eyeing her warily to see if she was going to command him to do anything; he was exhausted.

"You don't have to leave," Amy protested, feeling she had insulted her friend, even unintentionally.

"Yes, it's late. I should be going. Thank you for today," she said as she smiled and headed for the door. "I'll get these back to you," she indicated the sweats that showed off her legs; her being taller than the petite redhead, her midriff showed when she reached for the wet clothes that were hanging on the hooks. "If you need more help with him," she indicated Toby, still eyeing her warily. "Let me know," she smiled as she quickly opened the door, then the screen door, and pulled the door shut behind her.

Amy was alarmed at how quickly Abby had left. She knew she had insulted her. Damned curiosity! She spread out her wet clothes, locked the doors, and turned off the lights. A tired puppy followed her to the bedroom, but when he tried to get on the bed, she pushed him to the floor, he still stank.

CHAPTER NINETEEN

Amy had a problem the next day. She had to call her manager into work for her. Toby still stank, and she washed him again, this time in the bathtub with the tomato juice, giving him a good soak. He wasn't happy. All these baths and while he didn't mind being wet, he wanted it on his terms. Plus, his human didn't seem to like it when he played enthusiastically afterwards…but he loved how it felt, and rolling in…another bath, blah!

Amy washed Toby twice that day. Once to help get rid of the skunk smell, and once because he rolled in the mud in the yard. She couldn't win, and the house stank of the dog. The smell of skunk at least had dissipated in the yard, but she thought perhaps the rain they got took it away. Once she went back inside though, the smell hit her like a wall. Toby seemed to realize the smell when she took him in too, he looked about guiltily; she took him right to the tub for another tomato juice bath along with a shower to get rid of all the mud he had on his coat. She shook her head; he was worse than taking care of a child.

Abby watched for Amy and even went over to The Emporium for a sandwich. That's when she found out that Amy had taken a personal day. She wondered if Amy was avoiding her, but then remembering Toby, she figured out that she had stayed home to deal with a stinky dog. She'd thought a lot about the previous night, wondering if she should have let the curious redhead kiss her and find out it was no different than kissing a man, that kissing a woman, as with a man, depended on the person. She knew that if Amy kissed her though, she might reveal her growing feelings for the straight woman. She'd tried not to, there was someone she had dated further south in Sturgeon Bay but realized it just wasn't worth it. Lesbians were few and far between living up here on the Thumb. She did better with casual dates of the ones who traveled here for their getaways. No real relationships though. She knew she was probably just lonely. She should plan a trip up to Washington Island with the kids, maybe a camping trip. Give Bonnie a few days away from them. She had friends elsewhere she could visit. Still, she worried about her friendship with Amy, and if perhaps somehow, they had ruined it.

Amy was determined to get back to work the next day; Toby may still stink a little, but she had aired out the cabin. With the nice rain they were getting, it was a bit cold, but she had the fire in the fireplace. She realized if she was going to live here another winter that she was going to have to buy the place; her lease option was nearly up, and put in regular heat. Heating it with logs was romantic but not very practical for an even, steady heat. She looked around at the cozy little cottage and wondered if she should buy it.

Gathering up her laundry, she firmly shut the pup in the house, determined to leave him alone at home for a change. Toby went with her everywhere, but she had to teach him to be alone for periods of time. She had left him from time to time but usually with Abby's kids or someone at work for that time. Not too often had she left him alone. He had to learn. She hoped her cabin would be in one piece when she got back as she carried her small basket out to the car. Driving through Northpoint, she quickly headed to the back of the market to do her laundry. She considered buying a washing machine and hanging her clothes to dry, but she knew if she bought that, she'd want a dryer too. Sighing, she also knew she had spent too much money in this small town already. If she bought the cabin, she'd buy the washer and dryer then, and not until then.

As she sat waiting for her clothes to wash, she read all the magazines people had left there. After the load was done, she stuck it in the dryer, except for her jeans that she laid out to be dried at home in the bathroom. She hated how jeans felt after they'd been in a dryer, and they wouldn't shrink if she laid them out. She eyed the pay phone at the laundromat and considered. Over the months she had lived up there, she had made a phone call from one at least once a month. She had considered making this phone call from The Emporium, but paranoid that they would somehow trace it, she had resisted. Maybe she should let it go this time, but something compelled her to pick up the phone and put in her change and make the call. The news this time though had her heart thumping. She panicked for a moment and then hung up. Thinking about it some more, she idly watched her laundry spin around in the drier. She could go…she should stay…but, but, but…her lip got chewed on as she worried and considered.

As she folded her now dry clothes, placing her wet jeans over the top, she considered. As she drove distractedly home, she considered. As she turned from town towards the cabin…she considered.

"Hello?" Abby answered her private cell, pleased to hear it was Amy.

"Hi, could I ask a favor?" Amy asked breathlessly.

"Sure, anything wrong?" she asked concerned. She was sure Amy wasn't asking for the same favor from the previous night.

"Could you watch Toby for a couple of days while I go out of town?" she asked in that peculiar breathy voice she was now sporting.

"Can't stand the smell anymore?" she laughed at her own joke.

"No, that's not it…actually he is getting better. But somethin' came up, and I need to go out of town. I've got my staff coverin' for me; I should only be gone a few days, but I don't want to take Toby to the vets…."

"Sure, sure. We'll take him, but what about Tabby?" she asked concerned. She wanted to know what it was that had Amy acting so out of character and going away for a few days.

"Ohh shoot, I forgot her…" she left off distractedly as she looked around the cabin for things she wanted to take with her in her carry on. She refused to take the big suitcase she owned.

"How about you leave me a key, and Bailey and I will check on her once a day. You can leave Toby with us…" she began.

"Oh, that would be wonderful! Thank you!" Amy gushed. "I'll be right over," she promised and hung up the phone before Abby could say anything.

Abby stared at her cell phone in consternation. She wondered what in the world would have Amy behaving in this manner. She knew it wasn't over the kiss question. She would have to wait and see.

Amy dropped off a happy Toby to Bonnie and the kids; she didn't even see Abby who had been called out on a call. She began to drive quickly south. It took longer than she thought it would, and she nearly missed her flight from Green Bay. It connected in Chicago, and from there, she got really nervous.

Abby was disappointed to have missed Amy. She had hoped by being there that she could compel Amy to give her some information. But Toby and his bag of dog food were there for a couple of days, and the kids couldn't be happier. Amy had also left a small travel bag for the dog which contained the rest of the tomato juice and some toys. Abby laughed at it, packing a bag for a dog! She would just have to be patient and wait to hear what Amy had to say when she got back.

Abby didn't hear from Amy, but then no one else did either. Carol and Thomas mentioned that they hadn't seen her. People at Chuckie's mentioned it as well. None of her employees at The Emporium knew where their boss had gone. Abby thought about doing a little police work but didn't want to go too far. She did find where a one A. Adams had taken a plane out of Green Bay to Chicago, but after that she let her need to know go. She didn't want to invade Amy's privacy. She didn't do that to her friends.

There was no clue in the cabin, and she idly looked as Bailey cleaned the cat litter box and fed Tabby. The kittens vying for attention and now solid foods was hilarious to watch, and they spent a good hour over at the cabin. It provided her with plenty of opportunity to do a thorough search if she wanted, but other than cursory glance, she wouldn't be pawing through Amy's things.

The first Abby knew of Amy being home was two dejected children when she came in from patrol about a week later. Amy had come and picked up Toby and his suitcase and took him home. She had left presents for all of them. Abby didn't even look at hers as she felt hurt for having missed Amy.

"We weren't sure how long you'd be, and she went to check on the store first before she came over to visit with us. She's looking pretty run down," Bonnie told her.

"Did she say where she had to go?"

Bonnie shook her head. "I thought she'd tell us when she felt better. I'd guess someone died."

"Why do you say that?" Abby's police training began to kick in, and her questions were becoming pointed.

Shrugging, she answered, "Because she looked so down."

That didn't tell Abby anything she wanted to know. Going back into the office, she looked at the day's correspondence, including reports from up and down the Thumb that the other precincts shared. As a county sheriff, she had to know what was going on. She wrote plenty of her own that got put into the system for others to read as well. Nothing was going on, just the usual tourist stuff. She got antsy though, and after an hour of paperwork, she got up and pretended she had a call; she headed out to her cruiser and headed over to Amy's.

CHAPTER TWENTY

Toby greeted her profusely through the screen door of the cabin. "Hello there boy, where's your human?" she asked him with smile. He looked over his shoulder as though in answer to her query. Seeing that Amy hadn't answered the door, despite Toby's bark, Abby knocked. Toby wagged harder as though to tell her something. "Amy?" she called through the screen, looking about curiously at the lit room. When there was no answer, she hesitantly tried the door. Loath to invade her friend's space, she remembered she had a key and should be returning it. She used that as an excuse to go in. Petting Toby, she saw nothing was out of place. Then she heard something, Toby heard it too and led her towards the master bedroom. "Amy?" she asked, seeing her friend sobbing on the bed.

"What? What are you doing here?" Amy asked through her tears as she sat up, rubbing her eyes like a child.

"Are you okay?" Abby asked concerned, she went to the bed to take her friend in her arms.

"I'm fine," she lied unconvincingly.

"Yeah, cause everyone who is fine cries like their heart is breaking," Abby returned sarcastically. She liked the feel of Amy in her arms; she'd thought of her a lot lately, more than she was comfortable with.

Amy laughed as she was meant to. "I mean, I will be fine," she corrected with a hiccup.

"Care to share?" Abby offered, but Amy shook her head against her shoulder.

Amy wasn't sure why, but she felt wonderful in the strong cop's arms. She could feel the muscles under her shirt and for some reason she felt safe...something she hadn't felt in a very long time. She wanted to confide in her friend; she knew she could trust her, but she also knew that Abby was a very moral person and might not understand.

"C'mon, you can trust me," she cajoled her, pulling back slightly to look the redhead in her face. The darkness of her beautiful hair and the tears beading up on her eyelashes made her look so tragic in the fading evening light from the window.

"I know I can, but I just...I just...can't," she finished with another hiccup as she shook her mane of hair.

"Sometimes it helps to get it off your chest," Abby said quietly. She glanced over at Toby who was sitting on the side of the bed looking worried. His human was obviously upset, and he wanted to help too. "Look, you even got Toby upset," she pointed out.

Amy looked over at the dog and saw his hopeful expression. He was concerned, that was apparent. She smiled down at the silly dog, no longer a pup, but still with pup-like tendencies. He had been so overjoyed to welcome her home. He saw her looking at him, smiling, and wagged his tail optimistically. "It's okay, boy, I'll be fine," she told him, praising him for his affection. He leaned over to smell her leg and to give her a slight poke with his nose. She smiled again at him and reached to pat him. It was as she was leaning over that she really became aware of the woman holding her. Looking up again at Abby, so close to her, holding her, she felt her nipples harden and realized the hours on the plane hadn't been wasted. Her thoughts while she flew to and from her destinations had been spent thinking about her new life here in Northpoint and this woman. She realized now she was attracted to the brunette, had been attracted for quite some time. Her breath caught as it all came crashing into her psyche.

"What, what's wrong now?" Abby asked hearing the catch.

"You're beautiful," she said softly, wonderingly.

Abby blushed immediately at the compliment. "Thank you," she said equally as soft. It was as she was looking deep into the bright green eyes of Amy, she saw the look that told her the woman was attracted. Her heart leapt at this information, and when Amy leaned in to kiss her, she accepted the kiss but didn't return it.

Amy explored the contours of the unresisting officer. The lips did feel softer; her breath was minty fresh, as though she had just spit out her gum. She tasted good too. Not the mint of a piece of gum…but different than she would have expected. She smelled appealing too when she used her nose to breathe in, and Amy enjoyed all the sensations simultaneously. She tried to deepen the kiss, to get a response out of Abby; hesitantly her tongue peeked out and licked at the lips of the brunette. Abby's mouth didn't open from where it sat naturally. Finally, Amy ceased kissing her and pulled back questioningly.

Abby's eyes darted between Amy's, equally questioning and searching.

"You don't like me?" Amy asked, a little hurt, beginning to withdraw from their embrace.

Abby's hands tightened from where she was holding the smaller redhead. "Of course I like you," she responded immediately, automatically.

"But you don't want me?" she drawled, feeling she should pull away but was stopped by the superior strength of the woman.

"I do want you," she parroted back. "But I want you to know what you are getting into…"

"I'm not using you as a science experiment," she assured her. "I've thought about you a lot while I was gone," she confessed.

"You have?" she asked surprised.

Amy smiled a little at the tone of the question. "Of course I have. I've never been with a woman," Amy said as she blushed a deep red.

Smirking a little and trying to hold back her laugh, she pushed some of the red hair back from Amy's shoulder as she answered, "I guessed that."

Looking at velvety soft brown eyes that held a sparkle in them, Amy felt like stomping her foot in outrage. "Don't you dare laugh at me," her southern accent was never more apparent.

"I'm not laughing at you; we all have first times. It's a matter of choosing the when, the how, or the who."

"Would you do me the honor of being my first?" she asked naïvely.

Abby felt this was the strangest conversation she had ever had. The idea of being Amy's first appealed to her on so many levels, but all the signs pointed to Amy being straight. She was the one that was going to be hurt here, her emotions were involved, not Amy's. "I'd like to," she admitted honestly. She could feel herself becoming aroused…and strangely protective as she held the woman in her arms. "But I don't think you are ready," she finished, just as honestly.

"How will we know when I am ready?" her voice almost had the marbles in it, it sounded so southern at this point.

'ANNE MEINEL

"We'll know," Abby smiled as she played a little more with Amy's hair. It smelled of...gardenias, something inherently south in her mind.

Amy looked deep into the soft velvety eyes that held her captured. She leaned in again to kiss Abby and this time was thrilled to feel her respond.

Abby kissed her back for all she was worth, putting so much pent up emotion and passion into that one kiss that Amy was overwhelmed for a moment and then, her own emotions chaotic, returned it just as hard. Her arms wrapped around Abby and held her fast, drawing her closer if she could. Pulling at her, her body surging against her in her joy to find her kiss returned. Abby slowly lowered her to the bed, covering her with her body, pressing her into the mattress.

It was the feel of the badge against her belly where Abby's belt dug into her that had Amy coming to her senses. For a moment, she had been overwhelmed by her passions. Her body throbbed between her legs where she desperately wanted to feel the pressure of Abby's body; the thought of her touching there made her mind go weak. The badge all brought that to a halt as she realized what it was. She pulled back, almost violently.

Abby sensed her withdrawal and immediately pulled back. For a minute there, her mind had gone and her body had reacted automatically, almost without her consent. She ached to continue where they had left off, the kisses had been so sweet, Amy's tongue so velvety soft and delicious... She stopped herself at Amy's confusion and pulled up. Looking down, she saw the redhead's alarm and shock. "You see, you aren't quite ready," she said kindly, through her own hurt as she caressed Amy's face with her hand. For a second, she thought Amy was going to flinch from the caress, and she wondered if she had been hurt at one time. She wondered so much about this woman and needed to know before they went any further. She sat up with a little smile, showing none of what she was thinking, trying to calm the redhead's obvious distress. "We can take this slow," she assured her.

"I'm sorry...I want...you. But I just don't..." Amy faded off looking up at the brunette worriedly. She was sure she had offended her with her high school behavior. Hot one minute, cold the next.

"It's new. It will happen if we just take it slow. You have to be sure though..."

"Thank you," she drawled, realizing this wonderful woman was a lot wiser than she was in the ways of love and lust.

Abby smiled again, hiding her own needs and desires. She didn't want to frighten Amy off. It had been too long since she was this attracted to a woman. Since her wife, she realized. "So, would you mind telling me where you had to run off to so quickly this last week? This guy," she said rubbing Toby's head that had poked between them affectionately. "Worried about you," she finished, never mind that she had worried about her too.

Amy slowly sat up again. She had to tell Abby something. She decided on telling her the truth. "My grandmother died," she confessed.

Abby's head swiveled up as though on a fulcrum. She had wondered, but the obvious anguish in Amy's voice had her hurting for her. "I'm sorry," she said automatically. "Were you close?"

Amy nodded but didn't add to it. She didn't tell her that she couldn't go to the actual funeral. She couldn't tell her why. She couldn't tell her that she had instead gone to the attorney's office. "She helped to raise me after my parents died," she added. She'd been an adult, and Grams had made sure she wasn't neglected, wasn't totally left destitute. She'd outlasted them all.

"Didn't you say you had a brother?" Abby recalled. "Did you see him?"

Amy shook her head to the negative.

"Why not?" she asked curious. Her own family she didn't see by choice, but she couldn't imagine this kind and generous woman not having a loving family that would want to see her.

She shrugged trying to avoid the questions.

Abby tried to see under the swath of hair that fell forward, hiding Amy's face. "Is there something you don't want to tell me?" she asked softly. She wanted to learn everything she could about this woman; she wanted a relationship with her, but she didn't like how little she did know, how little Amy shared with her friends.

Amy hesitated. It wasn't that she didn't want to confide in Abby, it was just…she would be obligated to…she didn't finish the thought as she shook her head in answer to the question. "He would have made things difficult for me," she confessed instead.

"Is he domineering?" Abby smiled, trying to make a joke and lighten things up.

Amy glanced up, and Abby nearly sucked in her breath at the look in her eyes. She couldn't put her finger on it, but there was something…Amy swallowed and looked down at her hands, she was wringing them. "He would make decisions for me that I don't want," she confessed.

"Is that what he did before?" she asked gently, not joking anymore.

Amy nodded. She glanced up again, whatever was there before was under control again. "He's a bit…" She bit her lip again, hesitating for the word. "…chauvinistic," she finished but knew that was a weak word for what he was.

Abby laughed slightly, relieved that it wasn't more. "Ah, we get those a lot anywhere. You don't have them exclusively in the south," she consoled.

Amy smiled tremulously, glad that Abby hadn't probed further. "It's a bit sexist too," she shared but knew that wasn't an adequate description either. He would control her life, her destiny if he could have.

"And your grandmother kept him from behaving that way around you?"

Amy wanted to share with her everything, but something held her back, and she found herself staring at the badge on Abby's belt. She knew now what it was and nodded as she got up off the bed, pushing Toby aside so she could move. She sighed gustily as she stood with her back to Abby. "I am going to miss that old bird," she said with her twang.

"I miss my grandparents too," Abby confessed as she too got up. She was thrilled to have this in common with Amy and to have her confiding in her, finally. She didn't know, she couldn't know, that this was just such a tiny part of the woman that was Amy.

Amy escorted Abby out of the cabin and to the front porch.

"Hey, don't worry about this. We'll take it slow and figure out where it's going, okay?" Abby assured her as she gently brushed back the red tresses hanging over her shoulder, brushing her neck deliberately as she did.

Amy loved the tender touch and wanted to explore it more. This wasn't the right time though for that. She almost hated that she had started anything with this kind woman. Her damned curiosity was getting the best of her.

"Oh look, there's fireflies out tonight," Abby pointed out in order to change the tense subject. It was all too much, too soon at this moment. She thought perhaps Amy was feeling vulnerable about her grandmother's death.

"Them ain't fireflies," Amy protested with a laugh. "They is lightnin' bugs," she corrected.

Abby laughed at the different words for the same thing. "Whatever they are, they are pretty," she countered.

"They shore are," Amy had to agree. She reached out and took Abby's hand and squeezed it. "Thank you for being my friend....and thank you for not pushin'," she added.

"You're welcome. Someday though, we need to have a long talk okay? I want to know you, all of you."

Amy nodded and with a kiss on her cheek, Abby left her standing and watching as she got back in her patrol car and drove away. The last thing Abby saw as she left was Amy waving madly.

Amy turned and went back inside before the mosquitos could eat her alive. She was sad, not only about her grandmother's death, but she was scared. The money she had used to start her new life had dried up rather suddenly with that death. She didn't dare take anymore out as her brother would be alerted, and if he knew where the money had gone, he would be sure to tell...she left off thinking about the consequences before fate or karma or something in the universe made it a fact. The lawyer had been straight with her, until Gram's estate was settled, any further draws on her inheritance, and they would have to notify the other heir, her brother. She knew what that meant and the warning behind it.

K'ANNE MEINEL

CHAPTER TWENTY-ONE

Amy returned to work the next day with a chipper attitude. You would never have known that she was gone for a week as she quickly got down to work, greeting customers, new and old alike, playing the consummate hostess to her many visitors at the store. It wasn't until noon that she realized how many people from town had stopped in and told her how sorry they were for her grandmother's death. She rolled her eyes knowing that the only person she had told was Abby, and she could bet Abby had told Bonnie. From there, it got all over the small town. She appreciated it and realized how many friends she had made. It was nice to be 'home.'

The Fourth of July celebration was spectacular. The town swelled up with visitors from Chicago, Milwaukee, and elsewhere. Many were on boats so they could watch the fireworks out over the water. Some would leave to go down south to Green Bay and watch the celebrations there too. The Emporium was very busy all the time with people discovering it. Amy was excited at the success and carefully watched her expenses so she could tuck the profits away in an interest-bearing account.

She was also excited because she had been invited to spend the evening with Abby's family; Bonnie had invited her, and she had offered to bring her grandmother's secret fried chicken recipe. The chicken tasted good hot or cold. They closed The Emporium at a reasonable hour so that all the employees could go home and enjoy time with their own families. Amy had considered leaving it open to take advantage of the crowds, but selling ice cream when her employees couldn't enjoy their own families seemed wrong. It was then that Gladys Winters suggested she ask who might want to work for overtime pay. She had enough single people who would rather earn money than go to the celebrations to keep the store open and supply the crowds with ice cream and other treats.

She roped off a spot on her own boardwalk from the surging crowd gathered by the marina to watch the fireworks. She had chairs set up for Abby and her family. Abby was out in the crowd keeping the peace along with the volunteer officers who came up every year in order to earn some extra money. She saw her long enough for her to grab some cold chicken and other goodies that Bonnie had laid out for the family. Amy gazed at the muscular officer and wondered what it was about this woman that had her dreaming about making love to her. Abby caught her watching her and smiled up at her in return. They hadn't had any time to be alone again, but they both thought about it.

July was such a perfect time of year for the town that it was a couple of weeks after the Fourth that the two of them were able to find some time alone together. Abby, under the pretense of heading south for dinner, actually arrived on Amy's doorstep for the promised biscuits and gravy that the redhead had made.

"This is good," she said around a mouthful. It really was delicious. She had always thought that biscuits and gravy would be something sloppy, but whatever was in this gravy was almost sinful.

"Grams woulda been proud," she drawled and smiled. "Would you like some more sweet tea?" she asked generously.

Not really a tea drinker, she declined. She wasn't used to these southern ways, but this southern belle sure intrigued her. She watched her many times over the past few months, and the past few weeks alone, she found reasons to hang out near The Emporium. She handled the most fractious customers, the drunks, and the various personalities with charm and wit. Few if any weren't endeared by her accent and treated her like a lady. She demanded it without saying more than a few words. There was a steely grit under the petite exterior.

"Then how about a beer?" she offered, being the consummate hostess.

"That sounds good," Abby agreed and watched as Amy got up from the dining room table to make her way into the kitchen. She unashamedly watched as the jean clad body swayed slightly within them. They looked painted on they were so tight, and her buttocks were molded beautifully. She wasn't embarrassed when Amy looked back for a moment and caught her admiring glance.

"Like what you see?" she asked as she returned with a bottle of the local brew.

"I do," she smiled as she took the beer. Glancing at it, she raised an eyebrow. "This is new; I don't think I've seen this bottle of theirs before."

"Thomas only makes a small amount of this for their special friends," she explained as she smiled.

"Rumor has it that they had an anonymous investor to start their microbrewery?" she asked, wondering if Amy would fess up or not that she was the reason they had gone ahead with the idea.

"I've heard that rumor too," she admitted as she took a drink of her sweet tea, and her eyes twinkled over the glass.

Abby smiled, this woman could teach evasion to people. She was really good at it. "Come on now, I've known you how long? What's your story?" she asked in a kidding manner, hoping that Amy would confide in her, finally.

"There's not too much to tell. I grew up down south; I got sick of it and wanted to start over. I told you about my parent's place. It's how I learned to run a store." She tucked into the rest of her meal, hoping to evade the rest of the questions.

"Did you go to school for business? You seem to know a lot about how to run things? Have you ever had a boyfriend? Come on Amy, I won't bite," she smiled to show she was friendly.

Amy stopped eating to fix the cop with a stare. "Is this an interrogation?" she asked kiddingly. "I thought it was two friends having a meal together."

"You never tell me anything," Abby pointed out, using her fork to emphasize what she was saying as she gestured with it.

Amy shrugged. "You know enough. How about you?"

"Nuh uh, you know more about me than I know about you!"

"I know you had a wife; you have two children and a mother-in-law. That all is common knowledge."

"See, you know more about me…" she argued.

"You know that I own a business in town and that I love my dog. Is there any more than that?" she said it with a smile, still joking, but trying desperately to turn the conversation away from herself again. Something she had become very adept at for a long time.

"You really don't want to talk about your past, do you?" Abby suddenly got serious.

Amy shrugged. "It's in the past. I'm making a future here. That's all that matters."

Abby had to be accepting of that. "I hope someday to find out the mystery that is Amy Adams," she teased to lighten the mood again.

Amy just grinned and said, "I made cherry pie for desert. Do you want yours with or without ice cream?"

CHAPTER TWENTY-TWO

They played cards after dinner, a light and friendly game of Rummy but found that each had their own set of rules.

"I think you should tell me which Rummy game we are playing before springing those on me," Abby complained good-naturedly.

"I think there are too many kinds of Rummy not to discuss which one we are playing when the cards are dealt," she agreed.

They found each was competitive in her own way, and they had a nice time. Despite the heat of the summer evening, Abby started a fire in the fireplace, and they ended up drinking a local wine in front of it as they discussed non-confrontational things such as people in town and things that went on around The Thumb. They were planning on going to some of those things together, including a fair, a carnival, and a few of the festivals that took place in the various towns. Some of them with Abby's kids, some of them by themselves.

"This is nice," Amy commented as they wound down and relaxed together.

"It is," Abby agreed. She'd learned quickly not to ask any personal questions, but she was enjoying spending time with the redhead.

"Are you dating me?" Amy suddenly asked out of the blue.

Abby started in surprise. She looked over at the redhead over the brim of her wine glass. "I guess I am," she answered.

"You don't want to?" Amy asked, misinterpreting the brunette's surprise.

"Of course I do. I just..." she almost said what she was thinking and stopped in time.

"Just what?" she asked with a hint of humor. It wasn't often the cop was unnerved or stuttering.

"I'd like you to trust me," she finished lamely, not quite what she wanted to say.

"I trust you," she protested.

"Not with the stories of your life," she said quietly, suddenly serious again. She looked into her wine, knowing it was a mistake, but she wanted to know. She knew Amy was hiding something from her.

"Someday, maybe," she promised but didn't sound too confident in that promise.

"But not now?" she glanced up again.

Amy shook her head. "Please don't push," she requested.

Abby let it drop again.

"I do trust you," she repeated softly and moved in to kiss her gently on her cheek.

Abby felt warmed from the wine and the nice little kiss. She looked deeply into the green eyes and smiled, feeling captured by them.

Amy loved the browns in Abby's eyes. They were flecked with various shades. You couldn't see them though until you were closer. Otherwise, they just looked brown, but even then, they were so soft; she thought of them as velvety and very expressive too. Right now, she could see the attraction in Abby's eyes, and with that in mind, she set her wine glass down on the coffee table. Carefully, she took the brunette's face in both her hands and leaned her head sideways so they wouldn't mash noses as she leaned in for a gentle kiss on her lips.

Abby was touched by the gesture. She leaned up so she could put her wine glass down too, and she turned to take Amy in her arms, tucking her in rather nicely. She fit beautifully into the embrace, and she leaned down to kiss her, opening her lips slightly to taste the wine on her tongue. It tasted better this way.

Gently they shared kisses until it got heated, and Abby determined her resistance was waning. She didn't want to tempt fate, she didn't want to push it, she didn't want... "Why don't you tell me about your tattoo?" she asked, continuing on their conversation from earlier.

Amy, bemused by their kissing and its sudden halt, had to blink for a moment to make sense of the question. "Don't you want to..." she began, and seeing Abby's determined look and slight shake of her head, realized this must be part of the 'dating.' She sighed gustily, putting all her frustration into it. "It's a reflection of my name," she told her honestly. She figured she could hide within the truth. "Grams used to call me her 'little angel.' I guess it stuck." She turned her foot so they were both looking at the beautiful Seraphim angel. It was tall and thin and beautiful in appearance.

"So why this angel? Why not a cherub?" Abby asked, trying not to notice Amy's legs. She wanted to take her hand down them and back up, perhaps stopping to—she concentrated on Amy's answer.

She shrugged slightly. "I guess because this," she gestured at the tattoo, "...embodies an angel, it's what people expect to see." There was a world of meaning behind that statement, and Abby wondered at it as Amy continued on. "If you see a cherub you think cute and sweet. An angel is supposed to be tall and idyllic and almost holy," she laughed at it. "I just wanted an angel to show off to Grams; she hated that I punctured my God-given body." She turned the smile on Abby to show her joy over upsetting her grandmother, her rebellion.

Abby smiled in return. This was the kind of story she wanted from Amy, the little things, so she could get to know her better. "Did you ever think of it as a guardian angel?" Abby asked to keep the conversation going. She was still holding Amy, just not as heatedly as a few moments before.

Amy considered for a moment. "I don't know, I never thought of it that way. I mean, I know I've been lucky. I've thought before I might have a guardian angel or two watching out for me. I always assumed that was my parents."

"Do you want to talk about your parents?" Abby asked, she was cringing inside as she saw Amy close it down immediately.

Shaking her head, her answer was one syllable, "No."

Abby sighed inwardly. Here they had finally shared a story, and she'd gone and ruined it. She pulled from where they were sitting companionably on the couch in preparation for getting up.

"You aren't leaving, are you?" Amy pouted prettily, almost mournfully. She knew that Abby was exasperated with her inability to share her life from before. She knew someday that would come between them.

"It's getting late. I should go," she said automatically as she got up off the couch.

"Don't go. I'm sorry," she apologized as she too got up to face Abby, her height never bothering her before. At this moment though, what she wouldn't give for a few more inches so she could face Abby.

"Sorry? For what?" she feigned

Amy sighed, aloud. "I'm sorry I can't share what you want to know."

"And why can't you?" she ventured to ask.

"It's complicated. It's..." she hesitated, and seeing that Abby was so willing to leave, she almost desperately added, "it's dangerous."

"Dangerous?" Abby cocked her head sideways as though to hear the word better.

"Look, it's just in the past. It's better that it remains there. Don't you have secrets or things you'd rather have left...buried?" She had hesitated over that last word, infinitesimally, and Abby had caught it.

"No, my life is an open book. You get what you see. I'm not hiding anything," she said it almost bitterly. She was angry. She wanted this woman. She was frustrated. Getting to know her though was like pulling teeth.

"Well, bless your heart," Amy replied caustically. "I guess your life has just been charmed," she added meanly, knowing full well that it hadn't been charmed, or easy. "I'm sorry that you need to know every livin' thing about me."

"I'm not asking for everything about you, but when you shut yourself off like that, it hurts. It shows you don't trust me. I feel like you are hiding things from me." Abby nearly shouted in return. At the hurt look in Amy's eyes, she knew she was on to something, and she turned to leave.

Amy was frightened. She hadn't gotten angry like that in a long time. Afraid yes, but angry, no. She wouldn't let Abby badger her into saying something she didn't want to share though. She watched as the tall cop left, banging the screen door behind her. She sat down on the couch with a thump, angry at the brunette, at the fates...at herself.

CHAPTER TWENTY-THREE

"Still mad at me?" Abby asked as she came up beside the chair that Amy was reclining in on the boardwalk outside her store.

"Was I mad at you?" Amy sat up slightly in order to shade her eyes from the sun.

Abby grinned as she sat down on an adjoining chair, admiring the redhead's ability to sit in the sun and not worry about it. Most redheads burned in her experience, but this one tanned nicely and had the figure that…she stopped her inappropriate thoughts. "Coulda sworn you were," she commented idly.

"Nope," she drawled succinctly.

"Well, that's good," she answered, dropping the sore subject. She'd been sure she blew it with this little spitfire. She knew what 'bless your heart' from a southern gal meant.

"You going to the bonfire?" Amy asked. The Emporium had a booth at the park to give patrons a treat. During the day, it was Art in the Park, and at night, there would be the bonfire.

"Yep, but not on duty. I got the night off, and the kids and I are going. Bonnie didn't want to go, and I have all those extra officers. Might as well use them. You going?"

Amy nodded. "I'll be manning a booth for part of the day, but a few of the others will come on board later, so I should have some free time to enjoy it all."

"Want to join us?" she offered generously.

"I don't want to impose," she quickly said. She didn't want Abby to feel she had been hinting. She was just curious if she was going to be there and in what capacity.

"You won't be imposing. The kids were complaining the other day they don't see enough of Toby," she lied.

Amy cocked an eyebrow at that one. She knew a whopper when she heard one. The kids came over to The Emporium at least once a day, specifically to *see* Toby and to take him for well-needed walks.

"You're bringing him, right?" she finished lamely, knowing she was caught out.

Amy smirked and nodded. "He'll be there, where else would he be?"

"Well, you might have gotten rid of him like you did those kittens. Bailey isn't happy with you by the way," she smiled to take the sting off her words.

"Well, they had to go. That was too many kittens, and you wouldn't take one!" she pointed accusingly at the officer of the law.

Abby shook her head at how neatly Amy had turned that around on her. "I was never asked," she said slyly.

"Well, no one told me that the cat was pregnant when I took her in," she pointed out.

They bantered back and forth for a while, each enjoying it immensely. Each knowing that the underlying hurt from their fight was at least salved. "So, I'll see you Friday at the park?" Abby finished with; she had to get back to patrolling the streets of their little town. She was dressed in khaki shorts with plenty of pockets, her badge on her belt, her gun in the holster, and she wore a dark blue polo shirt that had the sheriff's department embroidered over where a pocket would normally go. She looked fit.

"I'll see you then," Amy agreed. She was glad that Abby didn't hold grudges.

CHAPTER TWENTY-FOUR

The night of the bonfire was perfect. It was a hot August night with plenty of people, both locals and tourists alike. It was an annual event with booths for arts and crafts and people from all over. The local fire department was there. They had their hoses in the lake so they could pump the water through their apparatus and have water fights with the various local townships who participated. The object was to shoot a barrel, your opponent, along a suspended cable; the opposing fire department was shooting at it too with their high-pressured hose. Both teams were bound to get soaked from the deluge as they waged their war. Watching children frequently fell in love with the idea of being a firefighter from this event alone.

"Ma'am, I asked for a chocolate cherry ice cream. This is not a chocolate cherry. This is a chocolate with a cherry," a man got in Amy's face.

Amy was tired. One of her reliefs hadn't shown up, and dealing with hot and cranky customers all afternoon hadn't been fun. Plus, one of the generators had quit working, and they nearly had a literal melt down of ice cream in the portable freezer until Thomas fixed it for her. She was eternally grateful and gave him and Carol credit for the beer ice cream she had created, adults only.

"Well sir, I'm sorry, but we don't have chocolate cherry ice cream, and as you've eaten over half of that portion, *I can't* refund you the money," she told him sadly.

"I need to talk to the owner," he nearly shouted.

"I *am* the owner," she said quietly.

"You should keep your customers happy!" he informed her as if she didn't know this. He made a gesture, and she involuntarily flinched.

"Look sir, I'd have been happy to refund you the money you spent on that ice cream, but you ate most of it. It is not my fault you didn't understand what you got there," she pointed out, angry at her previous reaction. She wasn't going to back down now, though.

He looked her up and down as though seeing her for the first time, and it wasn't to his taste. Lacking something to say, he said, "I shoulda figured." He then turned and walked away, still eating his chocolate ice cream with cherries.

"What was that about?" Abby asked as she came up. Toby rose from where he was cowering from the angry man. Abby had seen the man and his anger and hurried over to diffuse the situation, but now saw that Amy had it well in hand. She had seen her flinch though and wondered if the man had tried to hit her.

Amy was all smiles as she hid her thumping heart. "Oh, just an unhappy customer," she said and then glanced beyond Abby to see her replacement coming up. "Oh, hello Brandon. Ready to work?' she asked the young man as she reached behind her to untie her apron that read The Emporium in cute embroidered letters.

"Yes ma'am." He looked around. "Where's Lydia?"

"She didn't show. Do you think you can handle it by yourself?" she asked worriedly as she got ready to leave.

"I got this," he assured her. "You go have fun." He looked at the chief standing there and wondered, as had several others who noted their friendship, if they were dating.

"We will," she said as she took Toby's lead. She knew there was speculation around town. Who could help it? It was a small town.

"You okay?" Abby asked concerned as she fell into line walking with Amy.

"I'm great!" she assured her friend. Peering around she asked, "So, where are Bailey and Heather?"

"Well, Bailey is trying to act all cool with his friends over there," she pointed. "And here is Heather," she sing-songed.

"Hello," Heather cooed but not to her mother or her friend, but rather the dog who enthusiastically wagged his tail in greeting to one of his favorite people.

"Heather, don't you think you should say hello to Amy?" her mother asked exasperatedly.

"Oh, hi Amy," the child said as though she was unimportant.

"Hi Heather," Amy greeted the child with a laugh. The children really amused her, and she enjoyed their enthusiasm. They and their friends in The Emporium almost daily really made her day. Toby's too, she noted, as he wagged his tail exuberantly.

They all enjoyed the bonfire. The fire department, on hand for their annual contests, were also on hand to make sure the fire didn't get out of control. It was still overly large, and people had sparklers besides. A few kids had firecrackers, but Abby's officers soon confiscated those and issued citations. Any child who was caught with those illegal things was given detention at the local school; they had to help clean it in preparation for school in September. It was a fate almost worse than death.

Amy loved the sense of community. Even the tourists brought that. They came here year after year, and she was looking forward to being a part of it in the coming years. The Emporium was a real success. The micro-brewery catered to a great following, and they were growing. Thomas already had inquiries about opening other micro-breweries elsewhere. She was happy for him and Carol, they were happy with their success.

"I'll walk you to your car," Abby promised much later as she watched Amy quickly help Brandon and one other employee pack the ice cream back into The Emporium from the mobile refrigerator. Amy had pulled it behind her SUV, and in quick order, they were unpacked and the refrigerator washed out and stored.

"I'll see you both tomorrow," Amy called to the two young men who had helped tonight at the bonfire. She got a friendly wave in return. Amy was known as a generous and sweet boss. She had lost very few employees, only a couple, and that was due to them leaving for college or elsewhere. Everyone enjoyed working at The Emporium and for Amy Adams.

"Do you want to come over to the cabin?" Amy asked shyly up at the brunette who was escorting her back to where she had parked the SUV. What she was really asking was, was it time yet to consummate their relationship? They'd been dating awhile. They both knew it had been long enough. It was time to take the next step.

Abby looked down at Amy, wondering if she was really too tired. She had a spring in her step that belied the fatigue she had to be experiencing from the full and busy day. She stopped a moment, waiting for Amy to look up, and when she did, she smiled down into the green eyes. "I'd like that," she said quietly.

Under the pretense of making one last check around with all the revelers, Abby followed Amy home to the cabin. Amy jumped in the shower before she got there, a five-minute lead, and Abby used her key to let herself into the cabin. Toby greeted her, and then Tabby came over to give her a thorough sniff. She swallowed frequently, nervously. She wiped her hands on her jeans. She didn't know why she was so nervous, but she was.

"Hi there," Amy said quietly as she looked out from the bathroom. She was dressed in a merlot colored satin robe that covered her from head to toe. By the way it hugged her warm and damp body, she had nothing beneath it.

Abby's mouth went suddenly dry at the sight. Amy's red hair was plastered to her head, but it was obvious she had run her fingers through it, it was very untidy. It suited her perfectly though. The site of her lush body in that robe had Abby trying to swallow once again. "H...hi..." she said in return as she got up off the couch to confront her. The few feet separating them seemed to be a chasm.

"Are you nervous?" Amy asked, her drawl never more apparent than at this moment.

Abby nodded. "You?" she asked in return. She hoped Amy was as she couldn't handle that much confidence.

Amy nodded in return, relieved. "I shouldn't be, should I?"

Abby shook her head and took a hesitant step forward. "We can do this another time if you want?" she offered tremulously.

The redhead shook her head to the negative. She wanted this. She had instigated this. Yes, she was curious. She had pursued this. But she wanted this woman. She knew she did. She wouldn't let anyone stop her if she could prevent it. She was her own woman, and she was determined to find out what this was all about. Lord knew she had played with herself often enough imagining what it would be like to be with a woman, but not just any woman, this woman. "Have you changed your mind?" she asked fearfully, she didn't know what she would do if Abby rejected her now.

Abby shook her head. "There's no going back," she warned with a smile.

"I don't want to go back," she said cryptically. "I want to go forward," she smiled. "With you."

Abby loved the sound of that and the promises it implied. She took another step forward, Amy took one towards her as well. Then, noticing that both of them weren't being very brave, she took another and then another until she stood in front of the tall officer of the law. Reaching up, Amy drew the brunette's head down for a kiss.

Abby wasn't feeling shy anymore. She knew what she wanted, but she had also wanted to give Amy a way out. She didn't want to play games; they had courted for a while. It hadn't been a typical courtship, but they were ready for this next step, and she hoped Amy wouldn't regret it. She hoped she wasn't the science experiment in this redhead's schooling. She didn't care, as she kissed her deeply.

Amy had always thought that kissing someone straight down to their toes was just a saying. The kiss that Abby bestowed upon her had her standing on her toes, reaching for more as Abby slid her hands around the petite woman. It was made easy by the satin, it felt smooth, it felt sexy, and Abby appreciated that it hid nothing from her.

"You smell wonderful," she commented as she came up for air, the inadequate amount she was getting from her nostrils causing her to take in great gulps of it through her mouth.

"Apple shampoo," Amy teased as she smiled up at the taller woman. "I remember you telling me once you liked apples so much that you'd wear their blossoms as a child."

Abby was surprised; she had told Amy a story about visiting her grandparents with her parents and going through the apple orchards that abounded on the Thumb. She smiled down at the woman, leaning her forehead against Amy's in delight.

"Would you like to take this someplace more appropriate?" she drawled her question in a prissy fashion.

Abby loved the manners on this woman. She was oh so polite. "Lead on," she whispered.

Amy was happy to take Abby's hand and lead her the few steps into the bedroom. When they got next to the bed, she felt awkward and shy. "Why don't we make you a little more comfortable?" she asked, making a broad hint as she reached for the buttons on Abby's blouse.

Abby watched her fumble with them for a moment before she grabbed both of Amy's hands and said, "Why don't you pull down the blankets and I'll undress myself."

Amy turned gratefully away; she knew she was blushing ferociously from her embarrassment.

Abby easily unlatched the buttons and shimmied out of the blouse, underneath she was wearing a lacy bra, her one nod to frivolity. She quickly unbuttoned the jeans and pulled them down, using her shoes to step on the hem and pull. She quickly kicked off her shoes, and then using her feet, pulled off one sock and then the other. By the time Amy had the covers turned back, she was shocked to see the taller woman standing there in her very feminine underwear.

"Are you okay?" Abby asked concerned and then looked down at herself to be sure.

"I guess I just assumed you'd be wearing," she gestured at the underwear frillies. "Something more…" she couldn't finish and started blushing, realizing that she just might be insulting her intended lover.

Abby pulled her head up and smiled, seeing the blush just added to it. She took a step forward so she could take Amy in her arms. "Well, what did you expect?" she asked.

"Well, you know…" she squirmed a bit, to the unintentional delight of both of them.

"No," she shook her head. "I don't know."

"I thought that women who liked women wore…" she looked down, ashamed at her own assumptions.

Abby pulled Amy's chin up so she could look at her and still the redhead looked away. "Hey, look at me," she commanded and when Amy looked past her shoulder, she commanded again. "Look at me!"

Amy was startled to hear the tone and bravely looked at Abby in the eye. She saw laughter and concern in the brown flecks, and a little of something else…something intense that her heart leapt at.

"No preconceived notions here, okay? I may be a dyke, but I like nice underwear. It makes me feel girly. I also like it when my partner likes it on me," she confided.

Amy nodded mutely and looked down again. She was embarrassed, and that wasn't conducive to the plans they both had. It was at that moment that she realized that Abby was holding her. She was in just a flimsy robe, and Abby was standing there in her underwear, unashamed.

"Are you still up for this?" Abby asked, bending slightly so she could look into the redhead's face.

Amy looked up surprised at the question. "I'm sorry, I'm just nervous," she said, feeling foolish.

Abby smiled sweetly. "We'll take it slow," she promised, her hands beginning to caress Amy's body through the satin, trying to calm her and more.

Amy smiled and asked, "May I touch you?"

"I'll die if you don't," Abby breathed as she leaned in for a kiss, pulling the redhead against her body. The feel of the satin against her own underwear clad body was delightful. The fresh smell of her hair, the natural body odors that were only now beginning to make themselves known, and then, only slightly. She was enjoying this.

Amy hesitantly started to touch Abby's body. The skin felt so very soft, so very warm. At first, only her fingertips began their careful exploration. Then slowly she relaxed them into feeling the skin with the palms of her hands. She could feel the corresponding reactions of Abby's body under them.

"Mmmm, that feels nice," Abby whispered around the kisses. Her tongue was making inroads into Amy's mouth, delicately fencing with Amy's. Her own hands were caressing along the satin, wondering when she could finally slip inside. She knew nothing, but the robe was between her and Amy's skin. She wanted to touch her so badly. Gently, she cupped the side of Amy's head, using her fingertips to tickle along her neck and ear, easing them along to her neck as she explored.

Amy loved the kisses. It amazed her that a woman could feel so…different than a man; the kisses were completely different. They felt so…right. This was what she had been wondering. This was the right place to be. This was what she wanted; she tried to kiss deeper, almost harder, to show her lover that she wanted more of this.

Abby sensed the change in Amy and responded. Her fingers gently tickled their way along the edge of the robe, following down to where it v'd in front of Amy, across her breasts. She played with the skin, teasing it, touching it, lightly, so lightly.

Amy arched slightly in response, but Abby's other hand was holding her firmly against her, warmly against her back, pulling her close. Her breath began to come harder; she used her nose to inadequately bring in the oxygen, and then she realized Abby was the oxygen she needed. She relaxed a little, and let it all happen.

Abby slipped inside the robe, hesitantly, almost shyly. She palmed the right breast, it's pert little tip fitting perfectly in her hand. The tip grazing her skin, sitting up and speaking to her, 'pick me, pick me.' She removed her lips from Amy's and kissed along her jawline, listening to the gasps coming from Amy as she sucked in air through her mouth. She moved the lips to the soft skin under Amy's ear, relishing the gasp as she tongued her delicate diminutive lobe and along its rim.

Amy grasped at Abby's body, squeezing her ass at the sensation caused by her tongue in her ear. It made tingles shoot down her spine, deliciously enticing her. "I want you," she managed to get out, telling Abby honestly how she was feeling.

Abby smiled as she kissed along Amy's shoulder and nuzzled aside the robe, loosening the tie and opening it. She gasped at the perfection of Amy's petite body. Her breasts were even more beautiful to see than to feel. The curves led down to the red v between her legs, proving she was a real redhead. The trimmed hairs begged to be nuzzled; they didn't have to beg loudly as Abby began kissing her way down Amy's body.

Amy wasn't sure what she should be doing. She had never made love to a woman, any woman. She'd realized after analyzing her feelings and attraction for Abby so many times that there had been other attractions to women. Some were a bit inappropriate. She wouldn't think of that now as Abby's tongue encircled her nipple.

"Oh," she breathed, surprised at the sensation, and when Abby sucked, a corresponding tug hit her between her legs. "Ohhhh," she moaned this time, throwing her head back slightly, her hands coming to hold Abby, to hold herself up.

Abby looked up from where she had her mouth plastered to Amy's nipple, tugging on it with her lips, tonguing it gently as she explored the flavor of Amy's body. Seeing her throw her head back and moan was a sweet sound and sight to behold. She began to kneel as she kissed her way further down Amy's body, parting the robe that kept wanting to close. Her hand came up to massage Amy's breast as she kissed across the smooth expanse of Amy's stomach; her nose nuzzled briefly inside the redhead's belly button, and she licked her way across Amy's stretch marks. Stretch marks? She filed that away for a question later as she kneeled further down and caught the scent of Amy's arousal. Her finger gently inserted between the folds, encouraging Amy to part her legs.

Amy felt a whirlwind of emotions. No man had ever made her feel this way. The tingles were unsettling, and trying to maintain her balance, she clutched, first at Abby's muscular shoulders and then at her head. She was certain she was going to fall. The bed was there to catch her, but she had never made love standing up before. The touch of another woman on her body was intoxicating, and she nearly fell when Abby touched her...there. *'Oh God,'* her mind screamed. Her legs felt wobbly, and she began to fall, only to be caught by Abby, who removed her robe, trapping her arms for an instant, and then smiling down on her.

Abby felt or rather sensed Amy's uneasiness. She could feel her wobble and caught her in time to keep her from falling ingloriously onto the bed. She knew she could take her now, and they would both cum and have a good time, but she wanted to cherish this, to enjoy it. She wanted Amy to enjoy this and cherish her. She wanted her to love her. She had found this admirable woman had somehow captured her heart.

"I need…" Amy tried to get out, standing there naked and proud and wanting… "I need…" she got out as she started kissing any of the skin she could reach. The broad expanse of Abby's chest was before her, and she wrapped her arms around her to reach the catch on her bra. She quickly discarded it and found herself staring at two heavy breasts. Never in her wildest imaginings of Abby's body had she thought that her clothes contained these. She was in awe; her hands came up of their own accord to weigh them in their palms. Hefting them to her face, she buried her nose between them.

Abby looked down at the red head in between her breasts and smiled. She wanted an orgasm, and she wanted it quickly, but she cautioned herself as this was Amy's first time. She relished the idea that she would be Amy's first. She wanted to be Amy's last. Slowly, she pushed Amy onto the bed and covered her with her body, pushing her breasts into Amy's face. She nearly smothered her with them. Amy didn't seem to mind.

Amy couldn't imagine the feeling of having Abby's nearly naked body on hers. The skin on skin contact was incredible, the heat was rising. She craved…more. She ground up slightly as she kissed first one rosy peaked tip and then the other. Remembering the delightful sensations that Abby had given her, she slipped a nipple into her mouth and sucked.

"Ahhhh," Abby exhaled in delight. She pressed her pelvis down on Amy's and saw the delight on her face at the pressure. Slowly, her hands came down the sides of Amy's body, and she slipped a hand between the two of them. Using the heel of her hand, she applied pressure between Amy's legs.

"OH," she squealed, surprised.

"You like?" Abby asked with a smile, knowing the answer already.

"Oh God yes, please don't stop," she begged in and around the nipple she was tonguing.

Abby was using her body against Amy, grinding slightly, surreptitiously, pleasuring them both. She used her finger to slip between the folds, feeling the moist slickness already awaiting her. She nearly groaned at it. Leaning down, she began to kiss along Amy's shoulder, nibbling, and then licking at the pleasure-pain.

Amy was busy trying not to suffocate at the twin orbs that were presented to her. They were a lot larger than she had thought, and she was loving it. Her own were much smaller, and while at one point in her life she would have been jealous, instead she was now thrilled to be playing with Abby's. The fact that it gave Abby pleasure too was just a bonus.

Abby's finger slipped between Amy's legs at the same time she insinuated a leg between them, widening them, nudging them apart and providing her with access. Her hand followed the finger, and she caught her breath at the gush of fluid between them. Her finger slipped inside, seeking, probing, and Amy fell back in pleasure at the sensation. When Abby added a second finger and then a third, she arched, but the third finger was too much, and she cringed slightly. Abby, watching closely, quickly pulled the extra appendage out and continued thrusting inside with the two. She then curled them, and Amy nearly came off the mattress at the sensation.

"What the hell was that?" she asked surprised. She had never felt it before and couldn't believe how terrific it felt.

"Shhh, I'll explain later, just enjoy it…feel," Abby said with a smile at her lover. She kissed her on the lips to shush her and to show her the affection she felt for her. Her leg she threw across Amy's to hold her captive to her hand as she thrust, her thumb 'happening' across the raised clit now and again.

"Oh, oh, Ohhhh," Amy was soon panting as the crescendo rose within her. A tingling began at the apex of her legs. It spread down her legs to her toes, causing them to curl. As it spread up her back, she arched into Abby's body, desiring the skin on skin contact as she began her climax. All the blood drained from her lips as she clenched her fists into Abby's hair and pulled her hard against her at the peak. She turned her head aside to gasp lungs full of oxygen into her. Her teeth grazed along Abby's shoulder at the body clenching spasms she was experiencing. "Oh, my Gawd, oh my Gawd, oh my GAWD," she drawled out endearingly.

Abby watched amazed. She'd made love to a few women in her life and was endlessly fascinated by their reactions. Seeing Amy respond to her lovemaking was the embodiment of her love for the smaller woman. She wanted to see how far she could push her, as Amy bit into her shoulder; she felt a familiar surge in her own body and tamped it down. It would be better if she could hold off, make her rise higher for the sensations she craved. She concentrated on Amy and this first time together. She knew not to keep it going too long though or the edge could be painful; she began to pull back and let her return to earth, slowing things down as she played with the wetness. Finally, she removed her fingers and gently wiped the wetness off on her own hip, on the underwear that she still wore.

Amy lay there limp and lifeless as she licked at her lips, feeling the delightful sensation of the blood returning to them. It had all focused at her middle, and she couldn't describe the feeling to her befuddled mind. All she knew was that this wonderful woman had made her feel incredible, and as her brain function returned, she smiled dreamily at the brunette watching her, her arm supporting her head as she grinned down in pleased pride, caressing her gently. "That was wonderful," she tried to say, but her voice was raspy. She swallowed, or tried to, but her mouth was really dry. It took a couple of tries until she could swallow normally, and she was able to repeat what she wanted to say.

Abby was pleased beyond measure and wanted to make love to Amy again but knew she might be too tender. She didn't know the last time she had made love before, but it was apparent she had at least once in her life by the pucker marks on her abdomen. Those were only caused by one of two things, extreme weight, and there were no other signs of Amy ever being overweight, or she had been pregnant at least once. She brought her hand up to her nose to smell the scent of Amy; the odor caused her to send a jolt of desire through her own throbbing body. For good measure, she licked at the moisture still between her fingers.

"Do I taste good?" Amy asked bemused. Her voice was still raspy, and that puzzled her until she remembered how fantastic her orgasm had been. She now remembered crying out in pleasure, which must have strained her vocal chords.

"Delicious," her lover told her, absolutely convinced as she smiled down with a gleam in her eye.

Amy blushed and hid her face in Abby's shoulder. It was then that she saw the teeth marks. "Oh no, does that hurt?" she asked, bringing her hand up to touch gently at the red marks.

"Not at all," Abby told her with a smile, she was totally pleased with what she had caused in this woman.

Amy glanced up at her to see if she was laughing at her and caught her breath at the naked desire in the brunette's face. Her eyes no longer contained the beautiful flecks of brown that she so loved. They were so dark a brown that they appeared almost black. It was beautiful, it was primitive, it was...what she wanted, and she reached up to kiss Abby. Vaguely she realized the taste on Abby's tongue was her own essence, but it didn't stop her from deepening the kiss and enjoying it. Slowly, she pushed Abby onto her back and climbed on her body, feeling her own wetness trickle down from between her legs. She would have normally been embarrassed, but at the moment, she wanted Abby to feel what she had felt.

Abby was enjoying the fact that Amy wasn't being shy. Her aggressiveness was a helluva turn on. Her little Valkyrie, the redheaded spitfire that she loved. Loved? The thought was confirmed as Amy began to kiss her way down Abby's long body, taking time to kiss and lave attention on each rosy peaked breast. Learning Abby's likes by the way she responded, Abby encouraged her by holding her head to first one and the other, her hand buried in the deep red tresses. When the sensations began to mount, she subtly pushed on Amy's shoulder.

Amy looked up to see what her lover wanted of her as she pushed away, and then she realized what Abby wanted and took a deep breath. If she was going to make love to a woman, what was the most intimate thing she could do for her? She knew as she began to kiss her way south towards Abby's center. She scented Abby's arousal long before she got there.

Abby easily slid her legs apart in anticipation of what she wanted from Amy. Her hand continued to encourage her as she leaned back to enjoy what Amy would do to her.

Amy wasn't sure at first, what if she was bad at this? Glancing up at the supine woman and remembering how wonderful Abby had made her feel, could she do any less for her? Slowly, she peeled Abby's panties from her long body. She took a deep breath and leaned in for a taste. Although foreign on her tongue, it really wasn't bad. A bit smoky in flavor, even salty it began to taste good. The odor wasn't unpleasant, it actually was exciting her. She knew she hit the right spot when Abby's hand on her head pushed harder as her pelvis rose to greet her. She smiled, even though she didn't know what she was doing; Abby obviously was enjoying it.

She didn't know if she was just too aroused or what, but with any little touch, and she would go over the edge. Amy's hesitant tongue was driving her insane. She arched up as she pressed down on the back of Amy's skull; the sensation was worth the effort, and she gasped.

Amy brought up both her hands, her shoulders spreading Abby's legs further. She spread the folds of the bald mons and took a proper taste of the juices contained between. Her nose began to dip into them as her lips and tongue sought out further south and inside. She stuck her tongue out as far as she could inside of her lover.

Abby couldn't believe that this was Amy's first time; she was a natural, and the sensations were out of this world. She didn't realize how hard her handhold was on Amy's head as she rose up and ground her center into Amy's face.

Amy was smothering and thought, *'What a way to go.'* It wasn't uncomfortable, just intense, and she held on as Abby bucked and twisted below her onslaught from Amy's tongue and lips. Even her nose, running up the slit to Abby's clit came into play as she bucked. If

Amy wasn't an active participant to the extra gush of fluids between Abby's legs, she would have thought Abby was faking it; she was so quiet as she silently orgasmed. Her only real noise, a series of gasps, as she intensely held Amy in place.

Abby had learned to be quiet in all her lovemaking over the years. Getting caught would have resulted in embarrassment and humiliation. Later, it was just a habit, especially with small children who heard everything. She loved the sensations that Amy was causing, and before she realized her near strangle hold on the poor woman, she ground out the series of orgasms that rocked through her straining body. Finally, she released Amy and fell back to the bed, disentangling her hand and wondering if she had pulled out any of the fine red hairs she so admired. She petted the head in contrition and waited for Amy to look up at her from between her legs.

Amy smiled, knowing what she had caused. Her hair was nearly yanked from its follicles, and she still managed to continue on until she wrung every last drop of moisture she could from her lover; the taste was incredible, and it changed slightly in the middle of it all. She began to kiss her way north, wiping her cheeks on Abby's skin until they met up for a deep kiss between them. Both could taste the other on their tongues, but neither minded as they shared their passions, hands still caressing each other, calming each other.

Abby finally pulled away, sorry to be the one to stop it, but she had to admit she was exhausted. Cuddling Amy in beside her, no longer on her long body with her much shorter one, she fit just right next to her. She pulled the blanket from under them, noting the wet spot, and pulled it over them. Their bodies had cooled considerably, and neither had noticed until that moment.

"Are you okay?" Abby asked. Amy hadn't said a word.

"I'm wonderful. And you?" she said in her familiar slow drawl.

Abby smiled at that response. "I'm wonderful too," she admitted.

They stayed in quiet reflective splendor, enjoying the feel of each other's body against them, sharing body heat as it warmed up under the blanket. When Abby began to doze off, she shook herself awake.

"I need to go," she said quietly.

"Do you?" was the mournful question in reply.

Abby smiled, wishing she could stay. But there would be questions, and she didn't want them, not yet, not now. It was far too soon for them. "I'd love to stay, but..."

"You have the children," Amy sighed out the answer. Her arms tightened reflexively. "I still would like for you to stay."

"And I'd love to, but…" she repeated as she began to slip out from under the warm blanket, making sure that Amy and the heat remained behind. She could feel the cool air hit her naked skin immediately.

"Aww," she complained.

Abby quickly dressed, but she could tell that Amy was nearly asleep by her breathing. The thought of staying the night and saying she had a call was tempting, but she would have to write a report, and with Bonnie as her clerk, that wasn't a good idea. It had taken a long time for the two of them to work out an agreeable relationship between them. Bonnie hadn't liked that Abby had loved her daughter and never forgave her for the fact that she didn't die instead of her only daughter. There were times that Abby would have gladly switched places with her wife; the survivor's guilt alone had nearly devastated her. If not for the fight with her parents over custody of the children, or her own family over things, she might have succumbed to the depression. Those two harmless little children were her reason for survival though. She didn't want to rock the boat. "I'm leaving babe," she breathed as she leaned over for a kiss. She hadn't been able to find her underwear in the dark but didn't want to wake up Amy in her search. She finally just pulled on her jeans and went commando.

"Good night, Abby," Amy wearily whispered. Her day had been just as full as the brunettes. She was exhausted.

Abby let herself out the front door, nearly tripping over Toby who was lying across the entranceway. She supposed he hadn't understood what his two humans were doing back in the bedroom and had retreated into the living room to escape their weird antics. She smiled as she scooted him away and petted him to show there were no hard feelings. She locked the door behind her with the spare key she still had and headed home.

CHAPTER TWENTY-FIVE

"I enjoyed last night," she said shyly as she looked down on the redhead.

Amy looked up, equally shy and smiled in return. "I did too," she whispered so only Abby could hear.

"Would you like to go out tonight somewhere?" Abby asked hopefully.

Amy looked around her office where they were having this quiet conversation, past Abby into the store to see if they might be interrupted. "Do you think anyone will notice?" she asked.

"You don't want to be seen with me?" she fretted. She had known Amy was straight when she got into this and now…

"It's not that. I'm proud to be with you," she hurriedly assured her. "I just don't want to create problems for you."

"Problems for me?" she asked astounded.

"Your standing in the community," she pointed out, rising from her desk chair to shut the door.

"You are worried about my standing in the community? What about yours?" Abby felt like laughing at this conversation.

"What about mine?" Amy frowned, her back against the door she had just shut.

"Well, people know that I'm gay, how about you?"

Amy hadn't really thought about that. Her damned curiosity! The attraction she felt for this tall brunette had been undeniable. She had woken with a smile on her face and a longing for more of what she had experienced the night before. It hadn't been like being with a guy, oh no, it was so much…more. So, sensual…so...she was distracted for a moment and returned to the conversation at hand. "You think they will mind?"

"Do you care?" Abby sounded worried. She didn't want to ruin this when it had only just begun. She'd thought about Amy until she drifted restlessly off to sleep, wondering what it would be like to hold her in her arms, all night long. Wake up with her, if she had a raspy voice, if she woke with bed-head. She wanted to know it all.

"I don't, but you have to think of your standing in this community," she pointed out seriously.

"My standing? They will probably think I corrupted you?" she laughed.

Amy laughed with her, relieved that Abby wasn't worried about it. If they ever came out publicly, people would talk, but then, they would talk anyway. "I have something for you," she admitted shyly and dug deep in her slacks.

Abby's eyes nearly popped out of her head as Amy pulled her bikini underwear out of her pocket. "Oh," she said embarrassed.

"Did you deliberately leave them so I'd have to see you to return them?" Amy teased, she was blushing furiously anyway.

Abby, equally embarrassed, shook her head as she nearly snatched the offending underwear out of Amy's hand. "No, I didn't, I just couldn't…what happened to them?" she asked as she realized they were now crotchless.

"I'm sorry, Toby actually found them first," she apologized, blushing more if that was possible.

Abby started sniggering at the mental picture, and then Amy joined in. They were both laughing hilariously and finally were able to meet each other's eyes over it. As the laughter subsided, they exchanged a warm and loving look.

Amy was sitting on her porch, absently slapping away mosquitos. They weren't too bad as she leaned back her chair, enjoying her evening. She was pleasantly surprised as she saw the familiar patrol car come down the road and watched it pull into her driveway. Abby pulled it around the back by the garage so it would be less noticeable. Amy leaned down and had a bottle of Northpoint's Best ready and waiting when she walked up.

"Hi there," Abby smiled as she accepted the dark bottle. Easily, she twisted the top off.

"I didn't think I'd see you tonight," Amy commented as she took a sip of her own beer. Thomas had really outdone himself with this brew.

"Yeah, me either, but I got lucky and Russell wanted to work," she shrugged, looking up under her lashes. "So, I magnanimously let him take my shift." She grinned.

"Yay for Russell," Amy smiled at the grin and lifted her bottle to clink them together.

Abby obliged her and asked, "May I sit down?"

"Hmmm, yep, okay," Amy pretended to consider. She watched as the woman sat down in one of the Adirondack chairs, and Toby came over to greet her now that she was 'helpless.'

"You don't mind that I came by?"

"No, not at all," she teased back at Abby's tone.

"Well, I could have called…"

"Yes, you could have. But then I would have had to get up and answer the phone. Or, I could have let it go to the machine…" she pointed out.

"Then that would have defeated the purpose of my calling."

"Yes, I believe it would have."

They shared a smile at their lighthearted teasing.

"So how was your day?" Abby took a hearty slug of her beer. She looked at the label, barely able to make it out in the fading light of day. "Thomas really is out-doing himself," she commented.

"Yes, he is," Amy agreed. "My day was productive. It amazes me how many people come through this little town."

"Yes, the tourists really make our town this time of year. They are trying to get in their last hurrah before fall sets in and school starts. Makes my job pretty busy too."

"Yeah, I saw those kids you nabbed. Must have really been fun to arrest them," she teased with a grin.

"They were so sick, all over the cell," Abby remembered ruefully with a grin. "They sure pissed off Bonnie! She gave them such an earful. All over homemade wine."

They laughed over the foibles of tourists, and even some of the locals. "I saw Lenora with all her feathers ruffled over that developer arguing for condos."

"Some of the locals want to keep the quaint old world feel of the village. They don't want modern development."

"I'd have to agree," Amy hoisted her beer for another salute.

"You run an emporium that caters to people's love of nostalgia, of course you would agree," she answered wryly. She looked up and asked, "How do you do what you do? How do you know exactly what people want or need?"

"I've observed people for a long time. My Grams taught me exactly how to cater to them without giving too much away. People will pay for what they want. Who woulda thunk I could get four dollars for a hotdog much less seven for a hamburger?"

Abby laughed, but she had to agree. Some of the prices on food in the places that catered to the tourists were exorbitant. Some of the locals didn't even bother to eat in town. The Emporium was actually one of the more reasonable places to eat, with her variety of sodas and ice creams, much less the candies and the services, she really had a good thing.

They chatted some more about the town as they watched clouds rolling in, listening to the crickets on the late summer's night.

"Here it comes," Abby said and barely got the sound of it out of her mouth before a ting ting noise began around the quiet of the cabin. The crickets stopped chirping as the water began to come down, harder and harder. A clap of thunder was followed almost on top of a big flash of lightening.

"We better go inside," Amy said as she got up from her chair to scoop up the bottles and calm her cowering dog.

"It's going to be a doozy," Abby said as she watched out the front window.

"Sounds like it." They both listened to it pour down on the roof and watched through the flashes of light as it lit up the front yard, and they could see the buckets of water coming down.

"Would you like me to start a fire?" Abby asked as she gestured to the fireplace.

Amy sighed. She was running out of wood…and time. She was going to have to make some decisions soon. It was a good thing that The Emporium was doing so well, or she wouldn't have the money to continue. With the death of her grandmother, she no longer had a fall back.

"You don't want a fire?" she misinterpreted Amy's silence.

"No, of course I do," she hurriedly said, coming back from her thoughts.

"Anything wrong?" she asked from where she was about to strike a match at the laid logs and kindling; something she admired about Amy: she seemed to always be prepared.

"I was just thinking, not too long now and I will have lived here a year," she noted.

Abby lit the match and applied it to the newspaper; there, there, and there. When the flame was eating up the paper and begun on the wood, she threw the nearly burnt match into the flames. She stood up and clapped her hands together. It didn't matter what time of year it was, a fire was always a nice thing. With the rain coming down, it was romantic as hell, and she was delighted to spend time with Amy. "I'm glad you moved here," she said giving her a smile.

Amy put down the empty bottles of beer on the table and went to take the taller woman in her arms. "I am so glad I met you," she said sincerely.

They exchanged a kiss and then just held each other, each lost in her own thoughts.

"Let's sit on the couch for a while and enjoy the storm," Amy offered. The lightning and thunder were pretty consistent...and loud.

"So, what are you going to do?" Abby asked after they were cuddled on the couch together, Abby's arm around Amy's smaller frame.

"Do?" she asked puzzled.

"Your lease to own is almost up on both the cabin and then the store. You've made the store a success, so you've proven that." She was proud for her; everyone seemed to like her.

"Yeah, I've thought of that," she said sadly.

"What, you don't want to stay?" she joked, inside though she was starting to quiver in fear.

"It's not that, it's just that I'm...scared," she admitted honestly.

"Scared? Of what?

"Of actually buying these places. I mean, this place could use a makeover. It's definitely in need of a heating system," she gestured to the fireplace. "I'm going to have to buy some more wood. I saw Jacob Meyers in town the other day, and it reminded me."

"Well, we can extend your lease on the store if you aren't sure," she said. She was disappointed though. If Amy bought the store, that meant she would stay.

"Oh no, it's more practical for me to buy," she assured her and looked up to see the worry on Abby's face. She reached out and cupped her face, loving it when Abby leaned into her hand with her cheek. She settled back down on the couch, her head in Abby's lap. "I guess I should go to the bank next week," she commented idly.

Abby was relieved. She had fallen in love with this woman, and despite knowing nothing of her past, the future looked pretty good. She looked down at the woman in her lap and leaned down for a kiss.

Abby's arms wrapped around her, feeling the nipples harden against her hands. Amy quickly wiped the drool with the back of her hand from her lax mouth where she had been breathing so hard.

"Don't look at me," she told Abby.

"What do you mean? You don't want me to make you feel like this?" she asked as her hand caressed from shoulder to waist. The warmth of her hand giving them both pleasure.

Amy shuddered in response, enjoying the feel of the skin being touched so intimately. "It's a sin," she said prudishly.

"How can loving someone be a sin?" she asked simply, earnestly.

Amy twisted slightly in her arms to look over her shoulder at Abby. "You love me?"

Abby nodded and kissed her shoulder, the sensation causing a tingle in her lips. Amy got a corresponding tingle in her own body. "Yes," she breathed as she continued kissing her way down Amy's bare back, using the suction of her lips to raise the skin along her spine.

"Ohhh," Amy moaned in delight at the sensation. She waited until Abby finished at the base of her spine to roll over and take the brunette in her arms. "I want you," she stated unequivocally, pulling Abby down on top of her.

Abby smiled in delight, not disappointed that Amy hadn't told her that she loved her too, merely satisfied that they were together and enjoying each other. She reached between Amy's legs as the redhead reached between Abby's. Together, straining against one another, they pleasured each other until the late hours of the night.

"I wish you could stay," Amy said sadly as Abby got up to get home before the kids got up.

"I wish I could stay too," Abby told her as she leaned in for a kiss, shrugging into her bra. She turned, and Amy fastened it for her, caressing down her long back and watching as the goose bumps rose on her skin.

"I guess, eventually we will have to work out something, an arrangement?" Amy hesitated to ask.

"What do you mean?" she asked as she reached for her shirt to button it up.

"Eventually we are going to have to let people know we are a couple."

Abby smiled at the thought. This sneaking around they had been doing for months was fun at first, but now she wanted to declare that this was her woman, and she loved her. "I'd like that," she admitted honestly. She had waited patiently for Amy, and this declaration made her over the moon. She reached for her panties.

"No leaving any of that here," Amy teased pointing to the panties. It had become a joke between them that Abby had 'deliberately' left her panties that first time.

"Like I do that deliberately," she protested with a grin.

"Uh huh, you think I keep those under my pillow? Smell them later for your essence?"

"Would you?" she asked surprised. Her redheaded lover was really inventive.

"Now would I do that?" she asked innocently, laying out on the bed temptingly.

Abby froze in the act of pulling her pants on, staring at the lovely woman on her bed. She wanted to crawl back into bed with her, but discipline kept her pulling the pants back on. "You are a hard woman to leave," she said instead as she sat on the edge of the bed to pull her socks on, not bothering to button or zipper the pants.

Amy crawled down the bed to be behind Abby, to take her in her arms. She kissed her on the back of the neck, nuzzling, causing shivers down the officer's spine. Her hands began to wander across her front, finding the bountiful breasts she had come to adore. "Are you sure you have to leave now?" she whispered huskily as her hands creeped towards the open front of the trousers.

"You are bad," Abby assured her, leaning into her. "If I could stay, I would," she told her emphatically and quickly finished pulling on her socks before the redhead could do any more damage to her. She was already seething with desire for her again.

"I can be," she teased as her hands wandered.

Abby turned with lightning swiftness and pinned the naked redhead on the bed. She used her legs to spread Amy's and hold her captive beneath her. "Don't tempt me," she ordered before she leaned down to ravage Amy's mouth with her own, punishing her for teasing her.

Amy gave as good as she got, and while she was helpless beneath Abby, she loved every minute of it. She trusted her implicitly and allowed her to have her way with her naked body. She was left wanting…very wanting. "I'm going to pay you back for that," she promised when Abby finally arose from her.

"Only as much as I'm hurting," she was assured as Abby leaned over from the pains in her own body that were unfulfilled.

"Then why did you do that?"

"Because we both will be having pleasant thoughts today when we get to work and anticipate tonight," she promised.

Abby left Amy with a big smile of anticipation as she went back to sleep for a few hours.

CHAPTER TWENTY-SIX

"**G**ood afternoon, may I have a cherry coke?" Abby asked formally and then smiled when Amy turned in surprise.

"I thought you were going out to check boats or something and the islands?" She hadn't anticipated seeing her until tonight.

"I got back early," she told her with delight, checking out her ass in the mirror.

Amy saw her look and turned to see what she was looking at, realizing she was checking her out. Her eyebrow went up as she shared an anticipatory grin with the officer. They frequently flirted and actually hoped no one noticed. Several of the locals had noticed, and they couldn't find any objections to the two women enjoying each other. Except for a select few that felt two women loving each other was wrong, they were getting approval on all sides. People were being kind about waiting on the two women to announce they were in a relationship. They were fooling no one, but they were at least getting the space they needed to cultivate the connection as they needed.

"Are you almost off work?" Abby asked, almost innocently, drawing circles with her finger on the wood surface. It wasn't as though Amy didn't catch the gleam in her eye.

"Actually, I am almost off," she assured her as she spotted one of her relief workers coming in. She didn't have to close the store tonight, and she was relieved since the two of them had a date. "What about the kids?" she whispered worriedly.

Abby loved that about Amy; she was always worried that she wasn't spending enough time with her kids and balancing her time with the redhead. "Today was a school holiday, didn't you realize the amount of kids in here?" she pointed at the full seats in the eating area, all the kids seemed to be eating ice cream.

"I did notice, but I didn't *notice*," she said as she shook her head.

Abby laughed at the redhead's distraction. Ever since she had gone to the bank and gotten the papers for her loans on the store and the cabin, she had been a bit distracted, almost as though she were jumpy. "I took the kids with me around the islands. I think we have had enough quality time. I apparently cramp Bailey's style," she finished with a typical parent's moue.

"Is he hitting the teen years? Already?"

Abby shook her head. "That boy is growing up too fast; he isn't a teen...yet!"

"Yeah, but you're just his *mom*; you don't know what you are talking about," she teased.

"Ain't that the truth," she replied with a full dose of sarcasm.

"How long until you can leave?"

"Give me five minutes, and you can walk me to my car," she promised as she sauntered away, putting a little extra swing in her hips, knowing Abby was watching...and she was.

"We should head down The Thumb and look at all the trees turning. The leaves are going to be particularly gorgeous this weekend," Abby said idly as they walked along towards Amy's car. "There is the Apple Harvest Festival..." she droned on, offering places they could go together as a family or as a couple.

Amy wasn't paying attention though anymore. She had looked up at the taller woman and then beyond her, frowning. "Do you smell something?" she asked concerned.

Abby smelled and then shrugged. "Someone burning leaves?" she asked if that was what Amy meant.

"No, it's something else...it almost smells like gas or oil burnin'," she answered knowledgeably, looking around.

"I don't smell...."

"Abby, LOOK! Your house is on fire!" she yelled, making fire sound like far.

They both turned and began running towards the house which was indeed on fire. Amy dropped Toby's lead as she ran. Just before they got to the front door, it exploded outwards in flames. They both fell back from the explosion.

"Oh my god, the kids are in there with Bonnie!" Abby exclaimed.

"You see if you can get them out the back, I'm gonna empty The Emporium," Amy called and gave Abby a shove to the right as she went to the left.

Amy calmly yelled to everyone to drop everything and leave the store. There was a fire next door, she told them coolly, not mentioning that the next door was attached to this building. She saw Abby on the dock behind the building and ran through her store to open the door. "Anything?" she called.

"I can't see them; all the windows and doors have flames," she called frantically.

"Did someone call the fire department?" Amy asked calmly.

Abby held up her cell phone where she had made the call.

"You go out front and direct them, tell them," she ordered, noticing that Abby was looking panicked, something she had never seen her do before. She had handled drunks and other altercations in their small town effortlessly, but since her children were involved, she was going to pieces. Amy remembered something. "I'll be right there," she called as she rushed back into her store. No smoke was in there, and she hoped that the fire department would come and put the fire out before it spread. This was her life, and she'd put so much into this that she couldn't lose it! She wouldn't! She glanced up at the modern sprinkler system and wondered what a mess it would make if it went off. She hurried to her stock room and began to pull aside the shelving that blocked the hole between the Sheriff's home and her own store.

She soon had the shelves aside, and then she pulled the sheet of wood she had put there nearly a year ago to block the kids from coming into her store. She pushed at the panel that blocked it the rest of the way from Abby's home; it slid aside. She crawled through and called, "Bailey!" she waited a second or two for an answer and then, "Heather?" Again, she waited and repeated the call. Then she called, "Bonnie?" She began to walk through the small back room and along the hall. She had never gone through this hall; they had kept it locked, and really, she hadn't seen the inside of their house before as she had been relegated to the kitchen for a couple of meals that they shared. She kept calling when she thought she heard something, almost a whimper. As she tried the door, she found it locked. She lunged against it, hurting her shoulder. It opened from the other side; the lock seemed sturdy too. She kicked at the lock repeatedly, lunging at the door, and amazingly it finally came loose. She opened the door; she didn't think to put her hand against it, and as she opened it, the smoke began to pour out from behind it, she saw flames and found one of the children as she stumbled over them. She quickly regained her balance and tried to see through the smoke which one it was. Whoever it was whimpered, and she began to pull them along the hall, back to the hole. The smoke was filling the hall, causing her eyes to smart, and she began to cough. It was only when she got to the hole that she realized she had Heather. "Heather! Heather," she shook the small girl who was coming to. There wasn't much time. "Heather, I need you to go through the hole. Do you know where Bailey is? Do you know where your grandmother Bonnie is?" she asked the barely conscious child.

Heather looked up at her with incomprehension. She shook her head. She started sucking on her thumb.

"Heather! You need to get through the hole, can you crawl?" she asked. At the child's nod, she pushed her towards the hole and then ran back along the hall to look for the others. She found Bailey in the kitchen, coughing and crying out, crawling along the floor. He too was trying to find his sister, his grandmother, his mother.

"Bailey, you need to come with me," Amy told him as she grabbed him. Her eyes were smarting. She was coughing at all the smoke.

Bailey turned towards the back door that led to the dock, but the flames were too fierce.

"No, this way," Amy directed him, trying to remember where the hallway was from the kitchen.

"I have to find Heather!" he said frantically. "Mom will be mad if I don't," he reasoned.

"Heather's safe, she went through the hole," Amy told him.

"The hole?" he asked dumbly, not comprehending and coughing horribly.

"The hole between my store and your hallway," she prompted. "Do you remember she was going through there to check out my store last year?" she reminded him further. He nodded. "Let's get you out there," she hoped he knew the way, between the unfamiliar house, the smoke, and her frantic worry over finding the children, she was beginning to panic.

Bailey led the way directly to the back hall. It was full of smoke now, and she could see the walls were about to go up in flames; they were beginning to have a different tinge to them, and she saw peeling wallpaper through the smoke. The last few feet they had to crawl in order to get enough oxygen.

"Go through," she ordered him.

"What about Grandma?" he asked.

"Where was she?" she asked in return as she urged him through the hole. She could see clearly into the back room, and Heather hadn't moved.

"She was in the jail area; she was doing some paperwork for Mom," he told her.

"How do I get there from this back hall?" she asked coughing; the smoke was becoming worse. She thought she could hear the sirens outside.

He told her quickly, and she hoped she had enough time; it was as she saw him through the hole and turned back towards the end of the hall that she saw the flames coming down the hall. She didn't have time, and she ducked down for oxygen to hurry. She didn't make it halfway down the hall when a second explosion rocked the building. She fell to her feet and looked up at the flames at the end of the hall; it was engulfed. She quickly turned around, her eyes were tearing so bad she was nearly blind, but she made it to the end of the hall and pulled herself through the hole. She quickly put back the board.

"Wait, what about Grandma?" Bailey shouted as he fought her for the board.

"I can't," Amy cried, the tears were already there, but more began to fall as she struggled with the boy. "I'm sorry Bailey, get Heather out," she knew it was only a matter of time before the flames she had seen began to burn this side of the building. She leaned her weight against the board for a moment until the sense of what she was saying got through to the boy. He turned and pulled at his sister's hand. Amy leaned some supplies quickly against the board and followed him. She looked back at the board for a moment; already she could imagine the flames coming through that tiny gap between the two places. She hurried to catch up with the children and caught them at the door.

As they came out she saw it was chaos. Two people were trying to hold Abby back, one of them was Thomas and the other the bartender from Chuckie's. "My children are in there," she kept screaming like a crazy woman. She was irrational and stronger than they thought; she lunged against one and then the other in her desire to escape them and get to her children inside the burning building.

It took a while until Amy's yells in return to get her attention penetrated her frantic mind. The sense of what Amy was saying finally began to seep in, and then she saw them; she saw Amy's arms around each of them, and she fell to her knees. Both men let her sag down as the children ran to their mother and wrapped their arms around her. The three of them held on for dear life as Amy and the others who had come to watch gazed on. Abby finally looked up from where she was hugging and kissing and petting her children to see Amy's sooty and tear soaked face. She held out her arms wider to include the redhead in their embrace, and Amy kneeled down to join the three of them. Finally, Abby pulled back and asked, "What about Bonnie?"

Amy shook her head and looked down. Abby understood and began to cry some more, joined by the two children who had such a narrow escape.

CHAPTER TWENTY-SEVEN

Inside the front offices of the jail, Bonnie had been alone, working on paperwork when a strange man came in. He looked around oddly, and she asked, "May I help you?" watching as he seemed to inspect the room.

"Hello," he drawled. "I'm with the county commissioner's office, and we are inspecting the various sheriff's branches," he told her as he continued to look around, as though he were looking for something as he poked and prodded.

"I'm the one who would handle such a thing here, do you have any paperwork on that?" she asked, watching him suspiciously. She hoped one of the deputies would be in shortly; this man was acting odd. She didn't believe his story for a minute. Furthermore, she knew the guys at the commissioner's office, and none of them had a southern accent like that. The only person she knew with a southern accent around here was Amy. She idly wondered when Amy and Abby would admit they were seeing each other.

"Don't interfere," he warned as he pulled out a gun, quickly and effortlessly.

Bonnie was startled. They weren't some big town with any high falutin' need for extra security. Except for unruly tourists and an occasional local with too much to drink, they led a fairly quiet life up here. She put her hands out to show she meant no harm.

The man quickly and easily cuffed Bonnie to her chair. "Don't make a move," he warned as he headed for the back door that led to their small holding cell and then to another door that led to their home.

"My grandchildren are in there," Bonnie pleaded, wondering what the man had in mind. Maybe Abby had arrested him once, and he was out for revenge.

"That's too bad," he said angrily and went through the door. He was back within ten minutes, and in that time Bonnie had worked her way around the edge of the desk and towards one of the dispatch radios. "Nuh, uh, uh," he said as he back handed her hard enough that she rose in the chair, and then she fell backwards against the wall. As she fell down the wall, the chair came with her, and together they took down the bulletin boards on the wall, including the wanted posters and all the town bulletins. The man quickly opened and shut the door behind him as he went outside.

It was then that Bonnie smelled the smoke coming from the kitchen through the holding cell. She could hear slight popping sounds from the office, and she stared in amazement as little flames burst out all over the office. The drapes caught fire immediately from the front windows, and the papers along the bulletin boards. Bonnie began to yell to get the children's attention; she thought she heard them come downstairs into the kitchen, but she couldn't be sure. It was as she saw the wanted posters had caught fire that she saw one she had pinned there nearly a year ago with a reasonable likeness of Amy Adams. She watched absently as the edges of it curled and burned, the flames spreading across the heart shaped face. It was then that she heard an explosion of sorts; she didn't hear anything after that.

The four of them held each other, people coming by now and then to put their arms around them and give them hugs. Everyone realized that Bonnie hadn't been able to escape the odd fire. Someone had caught Toby and brought him to Amy to hold; he was very agitated at all the excitement and the smell of the fire. He was further confused by the smell of smoke on his person.

The fire department was able to put out the fire before it did too much damage to The Emporium.

"Oh, your store," Abby said consolingly to Amy.

"It doesn't matter," she dismissed. She looked deeply into Abby's sad brown eyes and glanced at the children.

"How were you able to get them out?" Abby finally realized they had come to her with Amy. She couldn't get in the doors or the windows of the house, all of them had been too hot with flames.

"Through the hole in the storeroom," she explained.

"I thought that was closed off?"

"All I did was put a sheet of plywood over it," she confessed.

Abby nodded. She had meant to close it off from her end as well but had forgotten it. She was grateful now that she hadn't. Maybe it was meant to be.

Someone took the children home for Abby after the paramedics checked them and Amy out. Except for a little smoke inhalation that was quickly taken care of with some oxygen, they were all fine, lucky, but fine.

Amy and Abby waited, watching as the fire department not only put out the fire, but began to sort through it to determine the cause. Many people stayed to watch and console their friend and chief. Abby received many hugs as they waited. Bonnie was finally brought out, and Abby made a sound as though a sob. Amy put her arm around her despite their audience as the black bagged body was put into an ambulance.

"Chief, you should leave. We'll have a report in a few days for you," the fire chief told her.

Abby nodded, and they looked around wondering what to do next.

"You all are just coming with me," Amy assured her taking command. "We'll find you something to wear, and I have that extra bedroom," she said loud enough for those listening in. She turned to the fire chief and said, "My store is unlocked for you all, please lock up when you are finished?" At his nod, she began to lead Abby away.

Abby nodded at the other chief and allowed Amy to lead her to her SUV, Toby on his leash following along. Amy even went so far as to put her in the passenger seat and strap her in. Abby stopped her and looked at her sorrowfully. "Bonnie," she sobbed.

Amy gathered her into her arms, noting that a few people were still watching them. She hoped it only looked like she was consoling her friend. They didn't need the gossip, not now. "I know Abby, I know," she said patting her on her back. She finally managed to disentangle herself and close the door before going around to her side and getting in. She knew her store was unlocked, but with the firefighters there, and in and out, it was probably for the best. She trusted them anyway, and they had saved her store, although she was certain it was a mess. She'd worry about that in the morning as well as the money in the various tills and the ice cream melting from the power being out. She had to get Abby home.

Amy stopped in her driveway and just sat for a moment, taking in everything that had happened that day. She had been looking forward to a date night with Abby, and while she had her here, this was not how she wanted it. Not over the death of Bonnie. It had been so close with the children too. She had to wonder at all that smoke and how quick it had all been. She hoped the fire chief would have some answers, and she had to call her insurance company. She'd had to change the insurance from the rental to an owner's policy with her loan at the bank, and thank goodness she had. She'd worry about that tomorrow too. She glanced over at Abby, she seemed to be in shock, and Toby put his head between them, waiting for his humans to do something, like get out of the vehicle. Amy slowly opened the door, and he hopped onto her seat right behind her. She removed his leash and let him jump down while she closed the door and went around to open Abby's. She was staring straight ahead. Amy leaned across her to let her out of the seat belt. "C'mon baby, I gotch you," she drawled as she pulled the brunette from the vehicle.

Abby allowed herself to be led from the SUV and onto the porch and into Amy's place. She knew superficially where she was, that her children were safe and with friends, but Bonnie was dead. Her home was gone. The home that had been her grandparents, and then her first real home with her wife, the house her children had been born into...was gone.

Amy led her to the bedroom and undressed her, then took her to the shower and put her under the spray, adjusting the heat for her to take a warm one. She then left her to return to the bedroom and shake out Abby's clothes. They smelled of the fire. She looked down at her own clothes; they were filthy as well, but then she had actually been in the fire. She could only imagine how she looked. She quickly stripped and joined Abby in the shower; she hadn't moved. Amy washed them both, including their hair, and Abby just allowed her to do so. Amy admired the muscles on her girlfriend's body but didn't wash them down with the intention of arousing her; instead, she simply cleaned them both, to get the smell of smoke and ash out of their hair and off their skin. She finished with a perfuming body wash that they both enjoyed. She pulled Abby from the shower after turning it off and rubbed her down with a big fluffy white towel. She used one on herself and ran her fingers through her hair. Leading Abby to the bedroom, she considered dinner but knew that neither of them were really hungry. Remembering that she had left Toby outside, she quickly tucked Abby into bed and then put on her robe and called to him; she found him lying patiently on the porch after giving the entire yard a thorough sniff. There were some interesting smells on the property these days, besides the normal animals that lived there.

Locking up, she turned out the lights and returned to the bedroom. Abby was just sitting there, silent tears running down her face. Amy climbed into bed with her, shedding the robe, and took her in her arms. She wouldn't ask anything, Abby wouldn't say anything, and she just held her until she fell asleep, exhausted.

Amy watched Abby from time to time throughout the night. She could tell she was having nightmares, but her exhaustion was mental, and she didn't wake from them. She herself dozed from time to time but never really got a good night's sleep. When she finally got up in the morning, Abby was still restlessly sleeping in her bed, and she left her to it. It was not how she wanted to wake up next to Abby, or how she had dreamed it. Both of them had fantasized about sleeping an entire night together, but this was not the way to do it. She climbed out of bed and gathered her robe to go to the bathroom to pee. She looked in the mirror and saw the circles in her eyes from the restless night. Everything about the day before was fresh in her mind, and she had gone over it time and time again, all night long. She saw her hair was a right mess from not combing it the night before when it was wet; she could only imagine what Abby's would look like when she finally got up. She wet her own again and quickly brushed it into submission before brushing her teeth and going quietly back into the bedroom. She watched Abby sleep, thrilled to have her in her bed all night long, but not for this reason, not this tragedy.

Amy quickly pulled sweats from her drawers to leave for Abby to change into when she was ready. They would be a bit small on the taller and more muscular woman, but it was all Amy had. She was too petite in comparison, and Abby had never left a change of clothing there. They would have to go buy her new clothes later. She went into the kitchen to put on the cocoa, feed the cat, and let Toby out into the yard. He ran to the back of the lot, and she worried once again about him finding a skunk, but instead he seemed to be on the trail of something else. She watched him for a moment before Tabby pulled her attention back to her. She usually spent evenings petting her pets or with Abby these last few months, and she was content with this life. She wondered how things would change now with Abby, and she worried about her. She glanced once more outside to see Toby lifting his leg at various favorite spots, marking his territory, and she went back to the bedroom to get dressed herself.

"Is that coffee I smell?" Abby asked sleepily from the bed as Amy pulled a shirt over her bra and panties.

"No, I have cocoa. Would you like me to bring a cup to you?" Amy offered. She was pleased to see that Abby no longer had that vacant look about her.

"Sounds wonderful," she said politely and then noticed the sweats. "Are those for me?" she asked.

"Yes. I have an extra toothbrush you can use, and you might want to run my brush through your hair," she pointed out as Abby sat up in the bed, naked to the waist, her beautiful breasts hanging down slightly from their weight, her hair all over the place from going to bed with it wet.

Abby raised her hand to hair and grinned sheepishly. "I bet I look a sight," she said ruefully.

"You look beautiful," Amy assured her with a laugh at the vanity.

Abby smiled at her. "It all happened, didn't it?" she confirmed.

"Yes darlin' it did," she didn't lie.

Abby sighed and got out of the bed, the coolness of the cabin never more apparent than when she was naked. "We better get going and find out what the chief has for me. I'm sure he's called in an arson investigator," she said as she pulled on the sweat pants, hopping to pull them up, and even then, they looked like below-the-knee shorts in length.

Amy was trying not to laugh at the outfit as Abby struggled into the too small sweat shirt. She turned to finish dressing herself and grabbed two pairs of socks and threw one to the now dressed brunette.

"Are you hungry?" she gently asked, knowing that neither of them had eaten the night before.

"I need coffee," she grunted and that was all. Her mind was already on the case. "And the bathroom," she added as she walked in sock clad feet to the bathroom.

Amy watched her and wondered what she was thinking, but she wouldn't snoop; she would wait patiently for Abby to share with her. She absentmindedly looked at her angel tattoo before covering it up with her sock. She put her feet into her shoes and headed for the kitchen to let Toby in.

"That smells good," Abby commented as Amy poured two hot cups of cocoa for them both. Toby greeted 'his' other human good morning, and Abby absentmindedly petted him.

"I can whip up some eggs and bacon," Amy offered, but Abby was shaking her head. "You've got to eat," she insisted, and Abby shrugged and went to sit down. Amy shrugged herself and started to pull out the eggs from the refrigerator along with bacon and bread, butter, and some local jam.

After forcing breakfast on her, Amy could see that Abby was fidgeting to get going. She quickly washed the dishes and put everything away. She gathered their smoke-filled, and in her case grimy clothes, and put them in a laundry bag. She'd wash them later after she found out what she could and what they would be doing. Gathering the bag and her keys, they left with Toby in her SUV.

"Let's go to the store and see if the investigators are there," Abby ordered in a no-nonsense voice once they were going.

"Why do you think they would send investigators?" Amy asked surprised, trying not to take offense at Abby's tone.

"One, someone died," Abby held up her index finger. "Two, I heard an explosion. I'm almost certain that someone used an incendiary device to start that fire, that means arson." She held up her second finger and then her third. "Three, I'm the Chief of Police up here, a deputy sheriff, and they may have been targeting me personally or the police in general, that is terrorism." She would have gone on, but they were already pulling into town, and she was anxiously looking for her first glimpse of the scene of the fire and its aftermath. The reality in the light of day was sobering.

There were investigators there combing the site and sifting through the ashes. Amy didn't bother parking on the side street but pulled right up to the police tape. Someone went to wave her vehicle aside, but then the Chief of Police got out of it, and he stopped to stare at the outfit.

"Something amusing?" Abby braved it out. She knew she looked awful.

"Not at all ma'am," he said respectfully. "Chief Skinner is looking for you," he mentioned to take the heat off of himself.

Abby nodded and ducked under the tape that cordoned off the site. Amy followed, leaving Toby in the SUV. He stood between the seats with his front paws on the console, panting happily. He knew where they were, could see them clearly, and normally he would be going into work with Amy. There were so many people, and he was anxious to greet them all. Amy didn't look back as she walked away and towards the store.

"Chief," the Chief of the fire department greeted Abby.

"Chief," Abby nodded back. "What have you found so far?" she asked officially.

He glanced at her outfit but didn't say a word, never batted an eyelash as he became all business. "Well, it's definitely arson," he began, but Abby interrupted.

"Well, duh," she said succinctly.

He grinned, knowing she didn't suffer fools gladly. "We've got a team in there, and it appears that someone lit a few firecrackers up on you," he answered.

"Firecrackers?" she asked incredulous.

"It's a term they used. Apparently, it's some sort of time activated thing that starts fires. I've never heard of that type of thing in all my years here," he spread his hands helplessly. He was a simple fire chief in a small town in Wisconsin. They didn't handle something like this. It was why these investigators from Green Bay were here. Someone was saying they would be sending some things to Madison, the state capital, for analyzing. It was well beyond his scope of knowledge.

"Chief, may I go into my store? Is it clear yet?" Amy asked when she had a chance.

"Well Ms. Adams, it's safe. I'd prefer you to wait until those folks clear out though," he nodded towards the teams of people going over things at Abby's house.

"Did they save anything?" Abby asked sadly.

"Oh, this and that, I had them stack them in that truck over there," he pointed to a pick-up truck with the bed full.

"You were able to save that much?" she asked surprised.

"Yes, the upstairs and some other things that we found in the debris," he confirmed.

They began to talk about technical things that Amy had no interest in. She wandered towards her store but didn't go in. Instead, she pulled out her cell phone and called her insurance agent. He already knew about the fire and would be coming down to ascertain the damage. He was also Abby's agent and would write up the report for both properties. Since they had shared an adjoining set of walls, there would be overlapping on the policies, but he assured her that everything would be taken care of.

Someone found a decent outfit for the Chief to put on, and Amy let Abby into the store so she could change in the restroom. She looked much better in the uniform of a cop than in the small sweats of Amy's. She looked...normal. It also must have helped with her self-esteem as she became much more self-assured and took control of the scene. She began having her people fill out reports and demand information from the investigators as they had it.

SMALL TOWN ANGEL

Amy met up with the insurance agent, Tom Grieves, and they walked around her property which had very little damage except where it met up with the town jail and the house that had been Abby's grandparents. That was a total write off. There was some damage to Amy's roof, but the fire department had arrived in time to put that out before it became too much of a problem. "We can get people in to fix this," he pointed at some of the damage on the walls as they viewed the situation from inside. "Probably the same people who remodeled?" he offered and Amy nodded. As it was, she would probably be closed for a week or more, and she wondered what Abby would want to do. Tom was very generous in his reports and promised to file them immediately so they would get their claims in and a check out to each of them. "Sad thing this," he nodded towards the people poking and prodding through the ashes. "That might affect both your claims," he noted.

"Why? My store has nothing to do with the town jail," she pointed out.

He nodded but kept the rest of his thoughts to himself. He would have to find out if it was arson, and if it was, that would hold up the claims as the insurance companies wouldn't want to pay out on arson. Especially if the Chief or her children had caused it. Right now, it didn't sound like they had, but that would have to be investigated. Also, with the death, there would be further investigations from the insurance companies, further holding up of the beneficiaries check. He remembered that Abby had a life insurance policy on herself and her children, not a lot on the children, just enough to bury them, and had Abby died, enough to support them for a while. He made a note to check if Bonnie had one too.

Amy left after Tom did to check on the children. They had been taken to friends of Abby's, and they were a little skittish when she found them.

"Is Mom okay?" they asked worriedly.

"She's already working to find out what happened. I thought I'd come and get you. I have a few things to do, and I could use your help," she told them to distract them and calm them.

"What do you have to do?" they asked.

"Let's get in the car and talk about it on the way." She thanked the friends of Abby's who had taken them in and left with the kids.

"What is this?" Bailey asked as he sniffed in the back seat. The bag was beginning to stink from the clothes inside it.

"Some laundry I need to do. That leads me to my errands. I need to order a washer and dryer and shop for them. We need to pick up a couple of outfits for you and your mom too. Where do you think we should do that?" she asked him as though it were important.

They discussed the various stores in the smaller communities in the Thumb while she threw the clothes in a large washer. She washed them twice to get the smoke and grime out before throwing them in the dryer. There were quite a few she could shop at, but really she wanted to keep them busy and off the subject of Bonnie's death or to worry about their mom who was busy getting to the bottom of this investigation. She couldn't go into work anyway, so she may as well help with Abby's kids.

"Grandma's dead, isn't she?" Heather asked as she watched Amy try to teach Bailey how to fold their few clothes.

"Yes darlin', she is," Amy drawled. She didn't believe in sugar coating anything.

The child stood there; she'd cried last night when she realized the truth of things, but now hearing it, she started crying again.

Amy went to her to pull her in her arms.

"Why?" the little girl kept sobbing.

Amy didn't have the answers, and when she looked up and saw Bailey crying too, she held out her arm for him to join them and was surprised when he did. Both of them wet her shirt with their tears. Other patrons of the laundromat looked on curiously but didn't interfere. When first Bailey and then finally Heather were all cried out, she pulled them back to look at them both. "I don't know what to say. I know you loved your grandma, but your mama is hurtin', and you're gonna have to be patient with her."

They both nodded sagely even if they didn't really understand why they would have to be patient. Their grandmother, their second parent after losing their birth mom, and then their grandfather, was gone. She had been the second most importing person in their world, and they didn't understand that either.

Amy finished folding up the clothes, pleased with how much had come out in the wash. She put them in the now laundered and clean bag and put that in the back of the SUV. "Let's go to Green Bay; I know it's a little far, but we are going to find the best prices down there, and it's a nice day for a drive." It was a nice day too, bright and sunny and a bit on the cool side as fall came to The Thumb. The drive was over in just under an hour, and Amy let the kids determine if they would talk, if at all.

"Do you think Grandma is in heaven?" Heather asked.

"Yes, I do. I believe that with all my heart," she assured her.

"Didn't your grandma die?" Bailey asked from the back seat.

"Yes, she did. I was sad too," she confided. She didn't tell them she couldn't go to the funeral though.

They talked of this and that and then talked about what kind of appliances she would be looking for.

"After we get those, we need to get you some new clothes," she told them.

"Why?" Heather asked, concerned.

"Because all our stuff burned down, stupid," Bailey said nastily.

"Now Bailey, that isn't nice. There is no such thing as a stupid question, just stupid answers, and yours was not only stupid, but it was mean. You apologize to your little sister," she ordered and waited for him to say a very contrite apology and almost whispered *'sorry'* before she continued. "I think we'll get you each a couple of pairs of jeans and shirts. You're gonna have to help me choose some clothes for your mama too," she informed them. They seemed to look forward to that idea.

It didn't take too long to find and order a washer and dryer set for the cabin. Now all she had to do was worry about getting the higher voltage put into the cabin and where to put it exactly. There wasn't a whole lot of space anywhere in the place. She expected that Abby and the children would be staying with her indefinitely. She liked that idea but wasn't making that plan without Abby's input. It was solely up to their mother now, and she'd respect Abby's wishes, even if she did begin to cotton to the idea of them all living together.

They had fun picking out jeans and shirts for both of the children as well as a couple of outfits for Abby. Amy resisted Heather's suggestion of a t-shirt with some cartoon character called Sponge Bob on the front of it as well as the one that Bailey suggested with a picture of a pig. Instead, she got Abby some nice button-down blouses in her size and hoped she came close on the jean sizes based on the pants she had just washed earlier.

After a good lunch at a fast food place, they headed back up The Thumb. Abby had called to see where Amy was, pleased that the children were with her. "Do you want to meet me at the cabin?" Amy asked to make sure they were coming there.

"I'll be there. I hope you don't mind me using your phone there?"

"Not at all, it doesn't get much use," Amy assured her. She wondered if they were being so formal for the children's sake, or Abby was upset about something.

"Do you mind if we stay with you for a while? Lenora said she'd take me around to look at rentals tomorrow. If it's a problem, we have offers to stay with the Katzenbergers or others."

Amy was hurt. She'd made assumptions, and although she'd logically known they were Abby's decisions, she'd hoped they were on the same wave length. "You're welcome to stay as long as you want. I thought we'd put the kids in the spare bedroom; maybe Bailey would enjoy using my old blow up mattress and the sleeping bag?" she glanced over at the listening boy and found him delighted at the idea. "We'll figure it out. I should be there in about half an hour or so."

"Okay, see you there," Abby returned distractedly.

"Can Tabby sleep with me?" Bailey asked when she got off the phone.

"She might pop the bed," Amy pointed out, and they shared a laugh.

"If he gets Tabby in his bed, I should get Toby," Heather said from the back seat.

"I don't know if I want my fur-kids in your beds," Amy drawled.

"Fur-kids?" Bailey laughed at the word.

"Well, I don't have any real kids. So, these beggars are my fur-kids," she said, squeezing Toby's snout from where it popped up out of the back seat. He had known she was talking about him somehow. The kids shared a laugh with Amy.

They returned to the cabin to find a patrol car in the driveway. Amy and the kids unpacked the SUV with Toby running around sniffing the yard thoroughly. Amy frowned as she glanced at him. He seemed awfully concerned about something these days. Some animal must sure be making tracks through the yard the way the dog was sniffing about. She was distracted when Abby came out of the cabin.

"So, where'd you all go?" she smiled but was soon engulfed by both of her children. They hugged her, relieved to see that she was okay and alive. "Wait, wait, wait, what is all this?" she asked as both children burst into tears in relief.

Through the tears and the hiccups, the children expressed their worries to their mom. Amy left them, discretely taking in their purchases and laying them out on the beds. After due consideration, she put Abby's in her bedroom. She hauled her old blow up mattress out of the closet and set it up in her spare bedroom where she had the daybed set up. Both beds needed sheets, and she put clean ones on each one. By the time both spare beds were made, the family had caught up and made up.

"Would you like me to start a fire?" Abby asked, gesturing to the fireplace; it was becoming a bit chilly.

They all shared a look at the word 'fire' and laughed uneasily as Amy nodded.

"I put your clothes on each of your beds in the spare bedroom," Amy told the children and then watched as the children ran off to check the clothes out.

"I hear you got me a couple of outfits?" Abby asked with a smile.

"Yes, I put them in our bedroom," Amy informed her.

"Our bedroom?" she raised an eyebrow at that.

Amy shrugged. "I thought it best that you stay with me instead of out here on the couch."

Abby grinned. "Do you want me to have a conversation with my kids?"

"About what?" she asked confused.

"About our living arrangements."

Amy looked at her to see if she was being teased, but unsure, she said, "Well, that's up to you."

Abby stood up after lighting the fire and took Amy in her arms. "Thank you for buying us some clothes. I think they saved some of those in the truck load they will be bringing by. They are going to need to be washed, but I hear you bought a washer and dryer."

"Are your children going to be okay with you living here with me?"

"Do you want us to live here with you?"

"It's going to be cramped with the living space, but if this works out, maybe we should add on?" she asked with a grin.

"I love you, Amy," Abby said simply.

"I love you too, Abby," Amy responded.

"You do?"

"Of course I do, how could you not know?"

"You've never said it before."

"I thought I showed it instead," she replied indignantly.

"You do, babe; you do in so many ways," she calmed her, caressing her as she leaned down for a kiss. It was as they shared that kiss that Bailey walked into the living room from the spare bedroom.

"Oh, yuck," he said succinctly.

The two of them nearly sprang apart but stopped in time. "Bailey, I want you to be the first to know that I love Amy, and she loves me," Abby told him with a grin.

"I knew that," he said with a wrinkled nose.

"You knew?" his mother asked surprised.

He shrugged. "Everyone knows."

"What does everyone know?" Heather asked as she came into the living, surprised to see her mother holding Amy.

"That Mom loves Amy, and that Amy loves Mom," he told his little sister.

Heather turned to the two women, nodding. "Yeah, everyone knows that," she said prissily.

Abby turned to Amy. "And we thought we were being so discrete."

Amy laughed nervously. "So much for that."

"Do you mind much?" she asked worriedly. It was all so new now, even though they had been seeing each other for months.

Amy shook her head and reached up for another kiss. They heard groans of childlike revulsion behind them. Amy turned to the kids, "Get used to it!"

Later, after a supper that Amy cooked for them all, commenting that she was going to have to go shopping more often with a family to cook for, she heard Abby ask the children how everyone knew and when they knew about the two of them.

"Grandma told us," Bailey confessed around a mouthful of Jell-O.

"What did Grandma tell you?"

"That you were seeing Amy. That's why you went on so many night patrols," Heather told her importantly. She too was sucking down her Jell-O, a treat they only had occasionally in their own home.

"And she didn't seem to mind?" she queried further.

"Nope, Grandma liked Amy," Heather told her with all the innocence of youth.

Abby exchanged a meaningful look with Amy.

"Do we have to go back to school tomorrow?" Bailey asked. He had liked playing hooky today with Amy, especially knowing all his friends were being tortured by having to go.

"Yes, and we are going to have to arrange for you two to ride the bus," Abby informed them.

"We get to ride the bus?" Heather asked excitedly, nearly bouncing in her chair.

Toby was watching hopefully that she might drop something on the floor for him to clean up. Tabby was pretending that she wasn't interested in the food on the table, and failing; it was a cat thing.

"You like that idea, do you?" Abby asked with a smile, their interests were so simple at this age.

Heather nodded and so did Bailey. Living in town, they had walked to school frequently with Bonnie in attendance. She had called it her morning absolutions.

"Well, the bus can pick you up in the morning and drop you off here in the afternoons."

"Until The Emporium is back up and running," Amy interjected.

"The Emporium?" Abby asked confused.

"Then they can come to the store to do their homework, and we will figure out other things. We are going to have to figure out a schedule once the station is back up and running and your schedule as well."

It was at that moment that Abby really realized how much she had relied on Bonnie for parental duties. That Amy would volunteer like this pleased her no end.

"Are they going to build us a new house?" Bailey asked.

"I don't know yet," Abby answered as she finished up her own portion of Jell-O.

"I talked to the insurance agent," Amy informed her.

"When?" she looked puzzled as to when Amy had time to do that.

"While you were talking to the fire chief," she pointed out. She was done with her Jello and sat there talking with 'her' new family. She was happy but sad too at their loss. Hearing that Bonnie had not only liked her but approved of her relationship with her daughter in law, thrilled her to the core. Such acceptance from not only the children but now a dead woman made her happy.

"Don't I need to go see him?"

"Probably, he said there might be a delay if they call it arson," she said meaningfully. She hadn't been totally oblivious to what it might mean if the police sub-station had been deliberately burned down.

"What's arson?" Heather asked as she played with her Jello on her spoon and her tongue.

"It means someone deliberately set the fire. Watch what you are doing young lady, and that's not how you eat," Abby admonished her.

Heather guiltily started eating properly.

"Do you think someone started the fire, Mom?" Bailey asked as he finished sucking down his Jello.

She weighed the pros and cons of telling her son the truth versus the rumors he would unintentionally spread at school tomorrow. "I don't know son; that's up to the fire department and the investigators to decide," she compromised.

"You'll arrest the bad guy if someone did burn it down?"

She smiled at his faith in her. "I would if I knew they had," she confirmed.

"Bailey, you and I are going to do the dishes and Heather, you clear the table and bring us the dirty ones, okay?" Amy put in as she rose to take her dishes with her.

"Why do I have to wash dishes?" he asked indignantly.

"Because tomorrow, Heather will help me," she told him firmly.

"No," Abby interjected, shocking them all into immobility. "I'll do the dishes with Bailey." She looked meaningfully at her son. "It's time you learned how, and tomorrow Heather will do the dishes with me and learn how. Amy made the dinner, so she's done." Abby rose and took the dishes from Amy's hands and smiled at her. "Thank you for dinner, babe," and with that she gave her a peck on the mouth as she stood there in shocked silence.

The kids looked on, giggled, and hurried to do what their mom asked.

"You think it will work out, them sharing a room?" Abby asked as they got ready for bed. She was using an overly large t-shirt that Amy had as a nightshirt. She'd already tried on and hung up or folded the clothes that Amy had bought for her, thanking her with a hug and a kiss. She'd even had the foresight to buy her socks and underwear, very nice underwear at that.

"Until I expand the cabin," Amy said as she slipped beneath the covers. It was cold, and the fireplace hadn't given out as much heat tonight as she felt they needed. She felt cold and shivered until Abby cuddled up next to her.

"You're going to expand the cabin?" Abby asked surprised.

"Well, you and I should discuss it, but if you all are going to be living here, I think we should, don't you?"

"Looks like we have a lot to talk about," Abby said as she leaned in with her nose, snuggling into Amy's neck.

"Your nose is cold," she complained good-naturedly.

"Well, that makes up for your feet," she responded. "What do you do, put them on ice before you get under the covers?"

Amy giggled in reply as she put her arms around Abby. "This is nice," she sighed.

"Can you believe those kids? Here I was worrying about how to break it to them, and they already knew. Bless you Bonnie," she said the prayer aloud and sent it up to heaven.

"Poor Bonnie," Amy said sadly.

Sighing loudly, Abby repeated it back to her, "Yeah, poor Bonnie. I'm going to have to make arrangements for her funeral tomorrow."

"I'm going to have to meet with Terry about the remodel here on the cabin and then the touch ups on the store," she reminded her.

"I'm going to want to talk to him about maybe rebuilding my grandparents' house," Abby mused.

"Do you think the state will pay to have another sub-station put in?"

"I don't know. There are a lot of things up in the air. This is going to take a lot of time. With winter coming on, I don't relish the thought of dealing with it all. That reminds me, call Jacob Myers and ask him to put in a few chords?"

SMALL TOWN ANGEL

They talked back and forth about common, everyday things until they both drifted off. Neither realized that this was the real romance of their relationship. Being able to sleep together, wake up together, be together…and accepted by two of the most important people in their lives who slept in the room next door.

CHAPTER TWENTY-EIGHT

"**D**o you think Mom will marry Amy?" Heather whispered to Bailey.

He turned on the blow-up bed, making a horrible noise against the plastic; he froze in case they had awoken Mom. She wouldn't be pleased that they hadn't gone to sleep. "I don't know. I don't think it's legal anyway."

"What's legal?"

"Marrying another woman," he told her importantly.

"But Mom married our birth mom," she told him. It had been explained to her; it was natural to her.

"That was done with lawyers for us. It's why Grandma and Grandpa fought with Mom until they worked out a compromise. Our birth mom was Grandma and Grandpa's daughter. Mom isn't. But they went to a lawyer and got it all worked out." He was older, and Bonnie had explained as best she could, so had Abby when he asked.

"Maybe Mom and Amy will do that," she stated hopefully.

"You want Amy to be our Mom too?" he was curious.

"Don't you? She's nice." She had a nice store, too.

"Yeah, she is nice," he said as he lay back and made the horrible sound again. He froze, listening to see if someone would come in their room from hearing them or their whispering.

"But if it isn't legal, does that mean they can't get married in a church?"

"Nope," he told her as though he knew it all.

"Well, we're living here now. Maybe we can call Amy Mom."

"Don't you be calling Amy Mom without Mom's permission. You'll hurt her feelings."

Heather nodded, but he couldn't see in the dark. "What do you think they will do with Grandma?"

He shrugged, his arms were behind his head now, and he was looking up at the ceiling in the dark. "Bury her I guess."

"Yeah, bury her," she parroted. They both lay there until sleep claimed them. They didn't have the worries that adults did.

It was nice to wake up in each other's arms and exchange a kiss. They were both saddened by the events of the other day, but they were alive, the kids were alive, and despite the tragedy of Bonnie's death, they would survive and move on. They had a lot to do, not only today, but in their future together.

Amy slipped out of bed first, after a good morning kiss, grope, and hug. She smiled at that and quickly got in the shower, making it short, and thinking that in a remodel they were going to need a bigger hot water tank with this many people living here.

While Abby got up and got showered, Amy quickly put on her makeup and got dressed. She let Toby out as he was practically dancing in the kitchen with his need to pee. Making hot chocolate for all of them and setting out cereal, bowls, and milk, she was supervised by Tabby who yawned at her efforts. She poured the last of her orange juice and parroted in her mind the idea of shopping more often with this many people living here. She didn't mind.

Amy went and knocked respectfully on the children's bedroom door. When no one answered, she looked in to see that both of them were sprawled across their beds.

"Hey you two, up and at 'em. You've got school today," she told them loud enough to wake them both. When that didn't work, she turned and walked across the cabin to the back door to let Toby in. "Go get them up, boy," she told the overgrown pup. He didn't know what that meant exactly, but he went, and discovering the children's door open, went inside. Amy soon heard squeals of childish laughter coming from the room and knew they were up. She heard the shower turn off.

While Abby got dressed, Amy cleaned out the fireplace. She kept checking for any hot coals but hadn't banked the fire the night before to keep it burning. In winter, that was a must, and she didn't clean it for months on end. While she had the opportunity, she kept it fairly clean. She laid new wood and kindling for a quick start later that day. She heard Abby go into the other bedroom and get the children rolling. She heard the bathroom door slam as one of them raced inside.

When she got up to wash her hands, she saw Heather shuffling into the living room, still looking half asleep, her hair all askew.

"Good Morning, would you like some breakfast?" Amy asked cheerfully.

She got a grunt, and she helped the girl to a chair, handed her the orange juice, and then got a glare for her offerings of cereal.

"Don't you have fruit loops or sugar cin-a-min?" she lisped.

Amy had to remember that Heather was still a very little girl, and those sugary cereals were probably a mainstay for the kids, an easy morning meal for her mom and grandmother. But she only ate fairly healthy things and had oat circles and corn squares for breakfast. "You might like these," she tried to cajole the grumpy girl. She finally convinced her to try the oat circles.

By the time she got Heather eating some cereal and drinking some orange juice, Abby came out of the bedroom.

"Good Morning," she greeted her and handed her a hot cup of chocolate.

"We are going to have to get a small coffee maker for me," Abby confessed.

"You don't like my hot chocolate?" Amy pretended to be devastated by the news.

"I do!" Heather said supportively.

"See, that's one vote," Abby smiled. "I love your hot chocolate, but it doesn't have the caffeine I need to exist."

Amy laughed. "Okay, today when I'm out shopping, I'll pick up a small coffee maker."

"Something that makes more than two cups of coffee?" Abby begged sweetly and leaned over for a chocolate flavored kiss.

"Don't you guys do that enough?" Bailey asked from the doorway where he stood, dripping on the floor in a fluffy white towel.

"Don't you dry off before you leave the bathroom?" Abby asked him pointedly, glancing at the floor where a puddle was forming.

"Oh, sorry," he said, not sounding sorry at all. "We're out of hot water," he announced.

Amy rolled her eyes at this news. She had known that was going to happen.

"How am I going to take a bath?" asked Heather around a mouth of oat circles.

"Finish your breakfast, and some of the water will heat up again," Abby assured her and then spun to look at Bailey. "And you, go get dried off and dressed for school, then come out here and clean that up," she said, pointing at Bailey's feet. The boy hurried off to the spare bedroom, slamming the door behind him. "And quit slamming doors," she yelled after him. She hadn't missed the bathroom door slam.

"My, you do have a way with words, Ms. Shipman," Amy smiled at her. "Here, sit down and eat," she said, pointing at the set table.

"Do we have the time?" Abby checked her watch, then realizing she wasn't wearing one; she pulled out her cell phone to check the time. "I'm going to need another charger for this," she commented, holding up the phone.

"Well, you are going to have to take the kids to school and arrange the bus for them from now on. We need to know what time they have to be waiting outside on the drive," Amy informed her as she sat down to eat a bowl of corn squares. She poured them from the box into her bowl and added a sprinkling of sugar over them before she poured the milk.

"Can't you…" Abby began and then realized that no, Amy couldn't. She wasn't their legal guardian. She smiled wryly. Her plans for the day would have to wait until she took care of her parental duties. "I'm going to put you down as their emergency contact and have the school made aware that you can pick them up?" she asked to confirm with Amy who nodded. Abby poured herself some oat circles and added milk to her bowl before she sprinkled some sugar over the top. "Do you have one of the chargers for this in your store?"

"Probably," Amy answered dryly and then grinned. "We have that one that is a combination wall and car charger that will probably work."

That morning set a routine for them that would last weeks. The two adults had many responsibilities to take care of, but that morning was reminiscent of many mornings to come.

Abby took the kids to school and made the arrangements for the bus and for Amy to be their emergency contact as well as being able to pick them up. She then went to the funeral home to make arrangements for Bonnie's funeral the following Sunday, after regular church services. Then, she went to the newspaper office and arranged an obituary for her mother-in-law. She had never thought writing an obituary would be hard until she tried it, and then she was horrified with how expensive it was, especially when she had it placed in the local paper and then again across on the mainland. Next, she met with law enforcement officials about the fire and the new sub-station they would need.

"We're pretty certain it was arson. Someone was seen leaving the sub-station before the fire," one official confirmed from their investigation.

"We don't think locating the sub-station in your former home was a great idea, but that was the last administration; we're going to build you a small office," another promised her.

"I've heard that before," she pointed out.

"Well, we'd delayed because the situation was working, why fix it?" he grinned ruefully. "Now we are forced not only to get the new building but pay you for the old one."

"Pay me for the old?" she asked confused.

"It was because of our police sub-station that you were targeted. Your grandparent's home was torched. You lost your mother-in-law. We will be compensating you for the loss of your home."

Abby was tempted to ask if they would be compensating her for the loss of her mother-in-law but held off as they went over many things they would be doing in the interim.

Amy quickly did the shopping, stocking up on nearly three times the amount of things she normally bought for food. She found a small four cup coffee maker, and after inhaling the wonderful aromas down the coffee aisle at the supermarket, she bought a nice French Vanilla blend for Abby.

Putting away their groceries, including food for the pets, she set the coffee maker time and then the timer, carefully reading the directions as she set it up to make the coffee automatically for Abby the next morning.

She sat down then and made her calls, arranging for wood from Jacob and Johnathan Meyers, buying an extra cord as she now had a family that would burn more wood, or so she reasoned. Next, she called Terri about looking at the work that needed doing at the store and then coming out to the cabin the following day, after she and Abby had time to plan what they might need. She also talked to him about bringing the two-twenty volt into the house for the dryer she was expecting.

She spoke to several of her employees, assuring them that The Emporium would re-open shortly and that they still had jobs.

She worked on what she could from home, but as her store had all her purchase orders, inventory sheets, and such, she knew she would have to go in eventually. She glanced at the clock, determined to be home when the children got off the bus. She had no idea what time they would be home.

She chanced it and drove into town. Unlocking the door to her store, she hated the peace and quiet inside. None of the fancy machines she had bought were working, and the electricity was off. Even the phones were quiet until that was all hooked back up. She took the numbers for each of the services she provided and called them with her cell, explained what had happened, and assured them she would be up and running in a few days. She crossed her fingers at that.

"Hello?" someone called, and she walked out of her office to see the postman delivering the tote of mail for her mail box holders.

"Hello," she said in reply, pleased to see a familiar face.

"I wasn't sure you would be open," he said surprised.

"Well, neither sleet, nor snow, nor fire," she paraphrased and shared a laugh with him.

"I'm glad you're still here. This town needs a store like this," he ascertained.

"Well, thank you. I'm glad you like it."

"Yep, me and the wife have been here many times; it's nostalgic."

"I'm glad to hear that, too."

"It's kind of eerie to hear no music in this place," he glanced over at the darkened juke box.

"Yes, it is, but we will be back up and running in no time," she assured him.

"That's good to hear. Well, I better make my deliveries," he said. "Oh wait, do you have any outgoing?" he asked.

Amy checked and there were a few letters in the outbox, and she handed them to him with a smile. "See you tomorrow," she said cheerfully.

As he left, in walked Alex Meyers. "Hi Ms. Adams," he said cheerfully.

Amy started in surprise. He had been one of the few she couldn't get a hold of today since he went to school, and no cell phones were allowed outside of their lockers. She thought she'd left him a message though.

"I know we aren't open, but I got to thinking about those," he pointed back with his thumb at the ice cream freezers. "I bet that's all melted and a mess," he explained.

"I bet it is, too," she agreed. If they didn't clean them soon, it would stink.

"I'll get to pouring them out one by one," he assured her.

"I hadn't planned on anyone working…" she began. She was a little depressed from the events of the past few days, and being in here alone had allowed her to lick her wounds in private, be alone with her thoughts of what might have happened with the fire.

"Oh, you don't have to pay me," he assured her. "I just want to do a good job."

She smiled at his exuberance. "I'll pay you," she assured him. "And thanks."

He smiled, showing the potential man inside the boy as he put his book bag down in the back room and pulled on an apron to work in to protect his school clothes. Amy was pleasantly surprised to see two others of her students come into work to clean as well. She turned to put the mail in the appropriate slots for her mail box holders and then headed back to her paperwork. Having to do things by hand without the aid of the computers was a difficult task, but she managed.

"Um, Ms. Adams?" Alex knocked on the office door.

"Yes Alex, what can I do for you?" she asked.

"We're done with the first freezer and halfway through the second. Do you want us to go in the basement and empty those?"

"I don't know how dark it's going to be down there, and without any lights, it might be too difficult. Do what you can and then go through the refrigerators and throw out everythan'."

"Everything?" he asked, bewildered.

"Yes, we can't take the chance that anythin' has spoiled. Put it all out for the garbage collectors." She checked the map on the wall for collection days. "The garbage picks up tomorrow."

He nodded and gave her a mock salute, but before he could leave the office, another head popped in. "Mr. Lenoir to see you Ms. Adams!"

Not used to hearing Terry called by his last name, it took her a moment to place him, but she got up and went to see who was there for her and was delighted to see the contractor.

"Boy, you were lucky here, Amy," he greeted her with a hug. "Abby got the worst of it," he assured her, but then she already knew that.

They discussed what needed to be done to clean up the side of the building, the roof, and the make of the outside a full wall now. They would have to discuss it with Abby since they didn't know if she would be rebuilding. According to the purchase of the store, their buildings could butt up.

"Make sure you put in for a fire wall, then," Terry advised succinctly, and Amy had to agree. It only made sense.

Amy had a full day, and Terry agreed to meet her at the cabin in the morning. Her electricity was going to be turned back on tomorrow, and he was pretty certain that there was nothing he couldn't fix in a short period of time for her at the store. The roof would take the longest, but he assured even that wouldn't take long.

.

Terry did have the store back in tip-top shape in a matter of days. With the electricity back on, they were able to clean up inside, although there was still the faint odor of smoke that would linger for a long time. Terry put siding on the now exposed side of the building, and then Amy hired some local high school artists to re-create some 'nostalgic' originals from the fifties and earlier to advertise the store. Having a wall that was forty feet long and being paid for their artistry inspired the kids, and she gave each of them a bonus in the form of a five-hundred-dollar scholarship for their work. The town was thrilled that she turned the charred eyesore into something useable. The town wasn't as thrilled at seeing the charred ruin of the house still sitting there after a while, though. The investigation had been taken over by the feds, and that meant it was taking time. Whoever had set the blaze had used very unique incendiary devices, and they wanted to catch him or her. Every bit of evidence they could find was being taken and scrutinized before they would allow the site to be bulldozed.

"So, I want a sun room, but I also want a bigger kitchen, a bigger basement, and another bedroom," Amy was expounding out at the cabin, and Abby looked on in amusement. She was so feisty, and it was a helluva turn-on to the brunette.

"I can build you anything you want, but we are going to have to take out a tree or two," he warned.

"Oh no, can't you build around them?" she asked naively. She loved her lot with its shaded trees, but she supposed if she wanted a 'sun' room, it would make sense to actually have some sun.

"Not unless you want a tree in the middle of your new bedroom?" he teased as he looked at the sketches she had scratched out for him.

She laughed as Abby did. "What about an extra bathroom?" Abby pointed out as it was glaringly obvious it was missing from the plans.

"Oh, that's a good idea," Amy enthused and looked at Terry hopefully.

"Why don't we add the bedroom here," he pointed at the sketch. "Make that the master bedroom, and let it have its own bathroom?" He was also thinking how nice it would be to utilize the existing pipes from the old bathroom and not to have to run the lines to it all too far.

"That could work," she agreed, biting her lip. Abby watched, fascinated.

"What about digging the basement? We should get on to that before the ground freezes," he suggested practically.

Abby nodded, and Amy after a thought nodded too. "I bet it will be easier to work then after you get the framing done, and you can work indoors."

"Well, the weather is always a consideration, and the sooner we start on this project, the better. Your police department is going to be mostly cinder block and stucco, and I'll be busy with that too," he said, including Abby in the discussion.

"They finalized that then?" she confirmed.

He nodded. "Yeah, they bought that lot further down; it's smaller than where your house was, and we can get the concrete in and up in no time. It's the detail work inside that will take a little longer," he explained.

"Good, because that mobile unit they brought in sucks," she said succinctly, and they all shared a laugh.

It was nice how friendly and companionable they all were. He said he'd get the plans and the cost estimates finalized for her within a week, and Amy was pleased.

"I should buy the rest of your lot from you," Amy said after he had left the two of them.

"Well, I got paid twice," Abby considered.

"Twice?" Amy asked, confused.

"Yeah, the sheriff's department was paying to use my home as its sub-station. It got bombed because of that, or at least that's the official determination. Then the insurance company paid me as well. So, I checked before I cashed either check that it was legit and lo and behold, I'm rich now," she teased.

"Well, you can't get compensated for all the stuff you lost," Amy pointed out, knowing how hard it had been for Abby to go through the stuff in their garage. They had to wash all the clothes they found, but a lot had to be replaced. A few pictures made it through the fire, and one really precious one of Abby's former wife, but that was all.

"Are you okay with this?" Abby asked, seeing Amy looking sad for a moment.

"I love that I have a family and we are expanding," Amy said taking Abby into her arms. She loved putting her arms around the taller woman and looking up into her velvety soft eyes. People knew they were living together now and didn't really care. Some convinced themselves that Amy was merely helping out her 'friend,' while others knew the truth; the two women loved each other.

"Expanding?" Abby teased, pretending to look down at her petite girlfriend's frame. "Lucy, you've got some 'splainin to do," she mimicked with a smile.

Amy smiled too, but it didn't reach her eyes, not quite.

"What, what did I say?" Abby asked, knowing she'd pushed a button, however unintentionally.

"I lost a baby once," she shared quietly, knowing she had to share some of her past, however painful it was.

Abby nodded. She had known that Amy was pregnant before. She'd seen the stretch marks and never asked about them. She'd wanted to ask; she'd been on the verge many times. She also knew if she pushed that, Amy would stubbornly have clammed up. She waited now, but the redhead didn't elaborate. She sighed and leaned her forehead in to touch Amy's.

"When you're ready to tell me, I'm here," she said softly, leaving it at that, although she was curious. Being pregnant meant she must have been with a guy.

"Thank you," Amy told her. It was obviously still painful for her to talk about.

Abby had noticed that Amy had let her in a bit more, but still there were huge gaps in her past that she refused to talk about or disclose. Sometimes it was so frustrating as they would be in the middle of a conversation and the redhead would simply close down or refuse to continue. She wanted to shake her, but at the same time, she didn't want to fight with her about something she didn't know. She didn't know if it was merely painful or something more.

CHAPTER TWENTY-NINE

Abby talked Amy into letting her 'invest' by 'selling' her the lot where her house had stood. Amy in turn was going to turn it into a dance hall with large porches along the lake side front, lattice work all over to make it look pretty, and big enough that wedding receptions could be held. The windows alone were going to cost them a fortune, but her partner in this endeavor, Abby, loved the ideas that flowed out of this redhead.

"Amy, I'd love to accommodate you, but you are getting a bit over-extended, and I can't see the bank lending you anymore against the cabin or the store, I'm sorry," the bank manager told her.

Amy was disappointed as she had counted on further expanding the store with the dance hall. They could even subdivide it into smaller halls so that three venues could be going on at the same time, and they could use the first venue from the store itself as she had always hoped to. She wasn't used to having to take loans out, but she didn't dare contact her grandmother's lawyer for the estate. "What about my percentage in the brewery?" she asked, knowing that the laundromat wasn't worth a lot.

"They too are maximizing their loans, as they want to expand," he informed her. "Didn't they tell you?"

It was obvious they hadn't as Amy had no idea of their plans. After leaving the bank, she went to see Thomas.

"Hello Thomas," she said as she entered the micro-brewery. It was a pleasant place to get a hamburger or sandwich and to try the various micro-brews that Thomas and his wife had created.

"Well, hello there, stranger. You've been so busy lately with The Emporium we thought we'd never see you in here," he responded with a smile of greeting.

Carol waved from where she was taking an order from a couple of tourists who were seated at the now closed windows. It was late fall and too cold for them to be open or the guests to be on the landing outside.

"Hey, what's this I hear you're expanding?" she asked to open the ball.

Thomas looked immediately uncomfortable. "We meant to discuss that with you, but you've been so busy," he began lamely.

"Look, *Partner*," she stressed. "We went into this with barely more than a handshake. I'd make time to discuss finances with you," she pointed out.

"How did you find out?" he asked worriedly. They wanted to open some more breweries further down The Thumb and then on the main land, but they were still so new that he hadn't been able to get the loan. He had then intended to ask Amy to invest more; she seemed to be doing well, and she had come into town only a year ago with plenty of money, it seemed.

"The bank, when I went to apply for a loan myself," she told him. She wasn't happy. She owned most of this brewery but was a hands-off owner. This was how they paid her back?

"Oh, you need a loan?" he asked, curious.

She nodded. "Even I need to expand," she told him, not really explaining how maxed out she was.

He nodded as though that explained things but didn't apologize for not keeping her in the loop.

"Are you two ready to buy me out from this?" she gestured at the busy micro-brewery they were running.

He laughed as though she had said something genuinely funny.

"No, we just thought we could make more money if we expanded and opened a couple of more sites," he explained.

"You do realize that you couldn't have done that anyway without my permission?" she pointed out.

"Why do we need your permission?" he asked a little testily.

"Because I'm the majority investor here, Thomas. I haven't asked for a dime of the profits. You have left me out of the runnin' of it, and that is fine," she quickly put in before he could argue, putting up her hand to halt him from speaking. "I need to be kept in the loop as a silent partner if we decide to expand. Make sure you read the contract," she advised.

"But the other sites would be ours," he protested, getting a bit louder.

Carol came walking up to put the order in for their guests. "What's going on here?" she said, putting her arm around Amy and giving her a sideways hug. "I can hear you over there," she said admonishingly to her husband.

"She says we have to get her permission to open any of the other sites," he said hotly, lowering his voice ominously.

"Did you go to her when I told you we needed to figure out costs and stuff?" Carol asked him incredulously.

"It's our beer, we should decide where we sell it!" he argued.

"Did you go to her with the costs?" she shortened the question.

"No, I went to the bank so we could expand without her," he said, pointing at Amy as though she wasn't there.

"You dumb dork," Carol said succinctly. "She invested in this place so you could start your dream. I told you we had to get those costs together before we proceeded. Then I was going to run them by her. You went to the bank with what you had? You're an idiot," she told him and stared him down.

"But it's my recipe," he said weakly.

Amy watched the two fight back and forth for a while before she put in, "Thomas, I own this establishment. You agreed for me to invest in you and your ideas; you would give me that right. I own your recipes as without them, this place isn't anythin'. So technically, you work for me. I don't come in here and tell you how to run it, but I don't like you going behind my back to open other places usin' my recipes that you willingly signed over in exchange for my investment." She couldn't think of how to get through otherwise to the hot-headed blockhead.

"They're my recipes!" he gasped angrily.

"That you signed over to her," Carol countered.

"You're my wife; you're supposed to support me! You're not on my side?" he was getting louder again.

"Not when you could cost us all our hard work. I put as much into this business as you did. Did you realize that she could shut us down for what you pulled, you dumb dork!?"

They stared angrily at each other for a while, and Amy had enough. "Well, you know where to find me when you need me," she dismissed. She was very disappointed, but she was glad the contract she had with them was iron-clad. She had agreed to be the silent partner, but she owned most of the place and the recipes that Thomas or Carol would come up with during the course of the business, so she knew she had the upper hand. She hadn't liked pointing that out, but he'd been foolish and greedy. She left shortly afterwards with a look at Carol who understood and nodded.

Amy was disappointed as she looked out at the empty space where Abby's home had once stood, now bulldozed flat. She had wanted to start building on the dance hall, which she thought would be an excellent use of the space. She simply didn't have the money with the expansion at the cabin and the work on The Emporium. While insurance had paid for the damage, it was still money she simply didn't have. She hadn't received any money from her investment with the brewery, and while The Emporium was going well, she was feeling a tiny kernel of fear. Even the laundromat, which was mostly a cash business, was still not making so much that she could start on the dance hall. She wished she could contact her grandmother's estate attorney, but she simply couldn't take the chance of anyone finding out where she was…her worry began to tell.

Abby knew something was bothering Amy because while she was normally an exuberant bundle of energy, she seemed distracted. She didn't take an interest when they began to dig the cellar on the cabin once the building permits came through. They lined the edges with a special building block to give it better definition, and on the outside was black tar to seal it from the elements; then they back-filled it with gravel to keep the water out. Amy simply smiled, a fake smile, and nodded as Terry showed her the logs he was going to use to make the addition natural and conform with the log cabin look of the original structure.

"What's wrong with you, baby?" Abby asked her. She was worrying that perhaps having the three of them living there with her was asking too much of Amy. Between the dog, the cat, and the kids, it was one endless parade of cleaning and feeding. They didn't have as much time alone as they thought they would. Hell, when they had dated they had more time alone together.

"Wrong?" she feigned surprise. "Nothin's wrong. I think the addition is coming along beautifully," she said to distract the cop in her girlfriend.

Abby wasn't fooled. She might not know everything about this intriguing woman, but she knew something was bothering her. She caught her idly sketching plans for the dance hall that she hadn't even approached Terry about building. She knew Amy hadn't approached him because she asked him.

"A dance hall? Nope, this is the first I've heard of it," he said in surprise.

Abby had seen the sketches. They included a glass cupola on one end, a round pagoda on the other end, and stained-glass windows along the walls. Rich wood floors and a wide balcony on the front and back of the building completed the beautiful concept. She'd lose over half the mural that the students had drawn on the side of her building. The media coverage she had gotten from the original design had more than paid for the outlay in costs. The scholarship idea had endeared her to everyone who heard about it. When Abby asked about the loss for the dance hall, Amy shrugged and said, "Then we will have to have another contest for the new side, don't you think?" Abby knew that the local artists would go wild with that idea.

"And what about at the store, everything going okay there?" she probed to try to find out what was bugging Amy.

"Oh, it's wonderful; we came up with another flavor of ice cream," she confided.

"Don't tell Heather, she'll be in to try it!" Abby warned.

"She's in there each afternoon anyway," Amy laughed. She was uneasy though. She wasn't exactly lying to Abby, but she wasn't telling her the whole truth. It wasn't just the money that was making her uneasy. Toby had been acting funny here at home and something, some intuition, was telling her there was something wrong.

CHAPTER THIRTY

"So, I'm in the local Piggly Wiggly, and I couldn't get the buggies apart, and this boy is laughing at me instead of helpin'," Amy was complaining.

"A buggy?" Heather asked concerned, picturing a baby buggy.

"Yeah, you know a buggy?" she gestured, indicating her holding one with her hands out before her in fists. "A shopping buggy?" she asked to clarify.

"You mean a grocery cart or basket?" someone who was listening put in.

Amy looked up and smiled at her contributor as she nodded.

Heather nodded, relieved to know what the southerner was talking about and then waited anxiously for her to finish the story.

"So, this boy keeps laughin', and I yelled at him to come on over and help me with this buggy," she pointed at Heather. "He too didn't know what I was talkin' 'bout, and I musta garbled it or somethin'," she explained. "But finally, some lady helped me separate them there contraptions," she finished, shaking her head. "Why they gotta make it so complicated?" she asked the little girl who shrugged.

"I think it's a test," the listener put in. The child hadn't been a good audience.

"A test?" she asked, confused.

"Yeah, they see if you want to shop there bad enough, and then they jam the carts together to see how badly," he laughed.

Amy laughed with him. "Can I get you somethin' sir?" she indicated the ice cream in the freezer or one of the soda machines.

"Are you Angel Sleuter?" he asked with a sudden alertness.

Amy froze from making her gestures to the machines and turned slowly looking at the man. "Who?" she faked.

"Angel Sleuter?" he repeated, watching her carefully.

She shook her head as though trying to clear her ears. "I don't recall hearin' that name before around here," she said honestly.

He caught on before she could blink. "But you have been called that before?"

By then, her heart was pounding in her chest. "I don't believe I know you, sir?"

"No, no you wouldn't," he told her with a smug smile. "But I believe I know you," he said, and with a gesture of a salute, he got up from the stool and walked out of the store.

Amy watched him go. She clung tightly to the edge of the counter, her heart beating a mile a minute. How in the world had they found her? She knew she couldn't panic; she knew she had to leave. She had to do it methodically and organized or...it was then that she was aware of the child she had been trying to share her story with—Heather was watching her raptly.

"Are you okay?" the little girl asked, concerned.

"Of course I am honey; why do you ask?" she faked a smile.

"You look like you're gonna be sick," she said with the innocence of youth.

"I'm fine," she assured her, hoping to distract her. "Did you want an ice cream or somethin'?"

The little girl shook her head. "Mom doesn't like it when we have that every day," she confided.

Amy knew that and had been careful not to give the children free ice cream or candy.

"Well honey, we have other things," she said distractedly as her mind raced. She could run; she could sell The Emporium; she could have her grandmother's lawyers handle it all for her. She didn't have to go back; she couldn't go back. She glanced at the child, began thinking about Abby, and realized she couldn't go, not yet, not now; she had some time. She glanced to where the man had left her store and considered, biting her lip absentmindedly.

SMALL TOWN ANGEL

Abby was thrilled with the new police sub-station. They'd done it out of concrete blocks, and she thought it was going to be ugly, but they really had done a good job covering up the blocks. It now looked like a stucco building, in white, that was all clean and new and modern. The two cells they now had for drunks or disorderliness were clean and could be washed down with a hose so they wouldn't smell like pee when someone missed the toilet. They were just now moving in the various legal books and policies and procedures onto the new shelves in the admin area. They were going to have a full wall for their pin board of notices and wanted posters, and she had just put up some really interesting facts and figures for the public to read. As she was putting up the duplicates made available from other precincts, she realized one of the wanted posters from the past year made a striking resemblance to her current girlfriend. The hair was quite a bit longer from the picture, and the description was dead on. The name, however, was Angel Sleuter, not Amy Adams. She was puzzled as she gazed at the poster for a long while, wondering why this wanted woman looked like her lover. She put it aside as she continued pinning the posts, but her eyes kept wandering back to it, over and over. She took it home with her that night.

Amy was busy getting dinner just right. She enjoyed the idea of cooking for 'her' family. Terry promised to finish the addition before snow flew, but she knew that was an impossibility as it snowed around here in time for Halloween. She was a little depressed that they couldn't have the dance hall; they could have had a Halloween celebration there, and with the store attached, it would have been fun for both adults and children. They had something at the grade school, but according to both Bailey and Heather, it was 'lame.' She wasn't sure what 'lame' constituted, but she was disappointed she couldn't offer an alternative. Maybe next year would be different for the kids.

She was trying to forget the man from the store that day but knew that she would have to leave because of him; she'd have to explain to Abby why she had to go, and none of that was setting well with her. She was cooking stuffed pork chops, big baked potatoes, and even had a big bowl of warmed applesauce sprinkled with cinnamon from one of the local orchards. All of it was to butter Abby up as she knew leaving her was going to be a wrench. She looked around the cabin at the home she had made. From the polished logs, to the pictures she had hung. She gazed for a moment at the one of the two labs in the canoe with paddles in their mouths. It saddened her that all this hard work was going to be for naught. She'd have to start over somewhere else. They'd found her. She had to wonder when though. That man hadn't been an accident, and she had to wonder about the fire months ago. Was that a warning? Was it supposed to engulf her store too? She wondered at Toby's strange behavior; were they watching the cabin? They had to know that Abby and the kids were living with her. Were they watching through the windows? She glanced through them but couldn't see into the darkness. She'd looked at the work on the addition, and it was coming right along. Maybe she could sell the cabin to Abby and the kids? Her heart was breaking at the thought of leaving Abby, of leaving them all. She'd made so many friends in this small town. Loving Abby was the hardest part of it all. She'd found such happiness with her.

"I'm home," Abby called as she came in the front door. Toby was the first to greet her, and after a bit of rubbing, petting, and rough housing, he was content. Heather got a hug and Bailey a cuff on the head to mess up his hair as they worked on their homework at the table. Most of it was done anyway since they went to the store daily, and Amy made them do it there before letting them play with other kids, but tonight they had more for some special projects.

"Hi there, ready for dinner?" Amy asked, not quite meeting Abby's intense look.

"Whatcha making?" she asked heartily, feigning a happiness she wasn't feeling. She had read the little poster over and over. There were too many similarities to Angel Sleuter. She was convinced the wanted woman was standing in the kitchen.

"Taters, chops, and applesauce," she said in her pleasing southern way.

"What, no okra or grits or something?" she tried to tease. Amy had tried to introduce their palettes to other southern foods, but the kids weren't that open to trying new things.

"Nope, not a sign of them. And I tucked away the chocolate covered crickets for another time," she teased in return, but again, didn't look Abby in the eye.

"Chocolate covered crickets?" Bailey said in surprise. "Gross!"

"Naw, they ain't too bad. It's just when you get the legs between your teeth," Amy told him. "That's a little rough."

"Are they alive when they cover them in chocolate?" Heather wanted to know.

"I don't think so," Amy answered her with a genuine smile. Yes, she would miss this. *Her* family, the one she acquired when she fell in love with Abby.

"C'mon, let's clean this off and set the table for dinner," she encouraged the kids.

They quickly got their things off the table and put them in their backpacks. She handed Bailey the plates, and he handed them to Heather who put them on the table. He came behind her with the cups and silverware. Amy put down the napkins and even put candles on the table to be a little fancy. While they did that, Abby changed from her uniform and put a couple more logs on the fire to heat the place. Terry promised central air but not until spring since they couldn't get under the main cabin to install it until then. Meanwhile, the addition was being put together and just waiting to have it hooked up.

Dinner was a success, but Abby looked at Amy suspiciously. She loved pork chops, and the stuffing Amy used inside it was a blend of finely chopped nuts and bread that was delicious. In fact, the potatoes or 'taters' as she called them and the applesauce were among her favorites as well. It was almost the same meal they had shared the first time they ate together. She bided her time, just relating her day in innocent terms that wouldn't arouse anyone's suspicions.

"Well, Amy had that weird guy in the store," Heather innocently told her.

"What weird guy?" Abby queried her daughter.

"Oh, just some odd man that came into the store. It happens now and then," Amy answered with a fake laugh. "Do you want some more taters?" she asked helpfully.

"I'm good. What did he do that was weird?" she asked to continue the conversation that Amy was obviously avoiding.

"Just asked after some woman we never heard of, right Heather?" Amy asked to confirm her side of the story and to keep it light.

"Yeah, someone named…HEY!" she began, but Amy accidentally spilled some of the applesauce she had picked up from the bowl.

"Oh, I'm so sorry gurl," she quickly grabbed her napkin to help mop up the mess on the girl's blouse.

"That's my favorite shirt," the girl complained, near tears over the mess.

"Well, let's get it soaking in cold water to keep it from staining. Here, let's get you another shirt," she said helpfully, pulling the little girl from the table.

Abby watched and wondered if everything Amy was doing was suspicious, or was she seeing too much into the woman now. She knew in her line of work that people lied, sometimes innocently, sometimes with much bigger consequences. She hoped there was some reasonable explanation for the wanted poster.

Later, much later after the dishes were done and the blouse was already in a load of laundry in the new washer and dryer that were temporarily in the corner of the kitchen until the addition was finished, they relaxed in front of the fire. Amy was obviously agitated as she wasn't relaxed; she kept fidgeting.

"What is wrong with you tonight?" Abby finally ventured. The kids were in bed, whispering, and she'd already shushed them through the door twice. A third time and threats would begin. They were quiet now.

"I have something I need to tell you," she began and then thought she should have packed first. She could have had it all packed and in the SUV. She could leave Tabby and Toby with Abby since they had bonded so well with the children. Surely Abby would let them keep the pets?

Abby waited. It wasn't often that Amy volunteered anything. She wanted to know about the wanted poster, but she also wanted the truth. Accusing Amy of anything would only make her defensive.

"I have to leave," she began again.

"You have a business trip?" Abby asked. That wouldn't make Amy this restless though.

Amy desperately wanted to say 'yes', but she didn't want to lie to this wonderful woman she had found. She wanted to be brave. But she had to let her go. It was breaking her heart. She shook her head. "No. Not on a business trip. I have to go. I have to disappear," she confessed.

"Like when you disappeared from wherever you came from?" Abby asked quietly. She was trying to remain calm, but she didn't know if she was going to have to arrest her girlfriend before the night was through. She couldn't let her leave if she was this Angel Sleuter. It was her duty to hold her even on suspicion.

Amy nodded. "I left Louisiana over a year ago," she confessed. "I had to go. I couldn't stay."

"Why'd you have to go?" she asked. The wanted poster hadn't said *why* she was wanted, and that aroused Abby's suspicions. Was the crime so bad that Amy had to disappear?

"My husband wanted me to go," she confessed, looking down at her wringing hands. She bit her lip endearingly, but Abby wasn't seeing that.

"You're *married*?" she involuntarily ground out, her tone changing.

Amy nodded sadly and looked up in time to see the rage on Abby's face at what she had just revealed. She unconsciously cringed away from her on the couch.

"Stop that, I'm not going to do anything," Abby said abruptly as she digested this information. She had been sleeping with, having sex with, making love to a married woman! She didn't *do* things like that!

"It's not like that," Amy tried explaining, knowing she was really screwing this up. It was worse than she had expected. She shouldn't have said anything. She should have just left. She glanced at the brunette, and the attraction was still there; the love she felt for this woman was still there. She couldn't do that, not again.

"What was it like then?" she asked bitterly, feeling betrayed. Amy had lied by omission. She hated liars. She looked at her intently, waiting for her explanation.

Amy licked her lips, unconsciously looking cute and vulnerable, but she knew how angry Abby was. She could sense it. It rolled off her in waves.

"I met my husband when I was sixteen," she began. She might as well start at the beginning, tell her everything. She was going to judge her. She had already.

"What, you married this back-woods redneck at sixteen?" she scoffed derogatorily. "What's his name, Billy Bob or something? Does he have all his teeth?"

"Do you want to hear this or not?" she asked, taking offense at the stereotypes that Abby had just uttered and implied.

Abby calmed herself. It wasn't often that Amy volunteered anything about her past, and she wanted to hear this. She *needed* to hear it. She needed explanations. Demanding them wouldn't work. It had to come from Amy and in her own way. She nodded once, one short bob of her head, as she looked into the flames of the fire, anything to not look at the redheaded liar.

"I didn't want to meet Landon. He was nice enough, but it was his sister Lori I was actually interested in. I didn't know it then, but I was attracted to her." Abby's head swiveled at this bit of information, and Amy quickly added, "Oh no, nothing happened, but I can look back now and realize it for what it was, attraction." Abby's head went back so she could watch the fire and listen.

"Landon was nice, but his brother Noah was pure mean. He didn't like me at all. When my brother Bobby Ray—" she paused as Abby's mouth twitched at the redneck name. "Introduced us, all he was concerned with was matchin' us up. Bobby Ray is considerably older than me, and he thinks he knows better. He said I was gettin' to be a looker, and I better have a good protector. He thought Landon a fine and upstandin' young man. At the time, I thought he was right. Landon though, after we got married on my eighteenth birthday, ignored me. Especially once he got me pregnant. I realized later; it's probably because he likes other boys," she explained, and Abby looked at her again, not saying a word as she listened to her story.

"Noah now, he's a man's man. He don't like no 'sissy boys', as he calls them. Landon shorely couldn't tell his brother what he liked, and he had proven his manhood by gettin' me pregnant."

Abby noticed that Amy's accent was becoming thicker as she told her story.

"I didn't realize that Noah wanted me for himself. He started watchin' me, wantin' what his brother shore done had. It scared me. I didn't realize that there was money in the marriage. Landon handled that for me and Bobby Ray before that. My Grams warned me about making the marriage, but I didn't listen to her, and I regret that to this day. She looked out for me as much as she could. But when Noah got all heated up and slammed that door into my belly, causing me to lose my baby, she told me I should get out. When Noah got to be sheriff, he couldn't help hisself, and he started throwin' his weight around. He's nothin' but a big *bully*," she sneered that last word as she remembered.

"Gram's, she told me, she said 'Angel,'" she smiled in remembrance. "She always called me her angel," she gestured at the tattoo. "'You gotta save yourself from yourself,' she told me. She arranged to have a second set of identification made for me, all legal like and such."

"Is that where Amy Adams came into play?" Abby asked astutely, speaking up for the first time.

Amy nodded. "My real name is Angel, and my grandmother's maiden name is Adams. We figured no one would figure that out. When the accident happened to Landon and Noah began talkin' all biblical about 'a man marryin' his brother's widow', I got scared. Landon said I needed to be goin'. There weren't no reason for me to be stayin' and watchin' him die. I was a good wife to him. I couldn't see him sufferin'. I signed the papers that gave them all permission to pull the plug, no extraordinary measures. Landon thanked me and told me to go."

"What was the accident?" Abby asked for clarification, trying to make sense of it all.

"Noah done found out that Landon was a man lover. He didn't take it too well, and while Landon said it was an accident, I don' believe it none. He's goin' to die of his injuries someday. He told me to go, to run. He put money in Gram's name; she had money comin' from Gramp's estate too, and she was goin' to leave me."

"Is that how you were able to rent the house and buy your SUV?" Abby asked.

Amy nodded as her eyes glazed over in remembrance. "The night I left, Noah done come by and tole me that when Landon was gone, I was his and not to forget that. He frightened me. He was so certain I would go along with whatever he planned. I went to visit Grams, and she gave me the new identification. She tole me, 'you get gone girl. You don' look back, and you don' worry about me none. I love you too much gurl to have to worry about that bad seed. That family made a lot of money off of your joinin''. She told me how that marriage had been a joinin' of money, not of hearts. That Bobby Ray had practically sold me to them Sleuters. He was willin' to sell me again to Noah. He could make me too."

"How could he make you marry again?" Abby asked, incredulous at the tale. "No one can force you to marry!"

"Bobby Ray can. He'd have made my life so miserable, he…" she couldn't finish.

"Did he hit you?" Abby asked astutely, remembering how some things made Amy flinch.

She nodded. "He liked the money that Noah gave him, and I didn't know about that, I swear."

"How do you think they found you?"

"I think when I went for Gram's funeral they follered me. I was so careful too. I didn't go to the funeral. I went to the lawyer's office. The money had to dry up until it was all settled, and they weren't sure that Bobby Ray didn't have some spy in the office. They just wanted me where they wanted me."

"What about Landon? Is he still alive?"

Amy hesitated for only a fraction as she nodded. "He is shorely poorly though. He don't look good at all. Rumor has it he's got the aids, but I know that man; he don' have aids. Somehow Noah's got him looking like that so when he dies, it looks all natural and like. He just didn't realize that Landon would hang on so long. I think he recognized me when I visited him, but he was worried and kept tellin' me to go, so I did. Maybe Noah heard I'd been there," she worried.

"What made you decide you needed to leave today?" Abby asked now that she understood better.

"Today in the store, that man that Heather mentioned, he called me by name. I think he's a private investigator or somethin'," she was still thick in her southern accent.

Abby's heart went out to her. Now that she understood, she realized Amy had broken no law. Living under an assumed name was no crime. She hadn't taken it with the intention of committing one either. Her grandmother must have really done well with the name, as she commanded the money she did to not only buy this cabin, but the store that had been Abby's grandparents'. She'd even invested in that silly brewery that no one was to know about, but Abby did.

"You can't leave," she said sadly as she reached in her back pocket for the wanted poster. Unfolding it, she showed it to Amy who read it.

"Why, that liar!" she exclaimed, making it long and drawn out and sounding like 'laar.' "I didn't do nuthin' to warrant this," she slapped at the paper. "How can he put out a wanted poster on me when I didn't do nuthin'?"

Abby wanted to laugh at Amy's indignation; here was the redheaded spitfire she knew and loved. Her story pulled at her heartstrings.

"Well, obviously he has powerful friends, or he made it up and made it look all official, but I don't think so. That was sent out all over the United States, so he can get in a lot of trouble for doing that."

"I have to leave though, if I stay, Bobby Ray or Noah is gonna show up next," she told her girlfriend, looking genuinely frightened. "If they haven't already," she added as she thought about things. Toby's actions of constantly checking the yard as though someone had been there, the fire….

"Do you think they have been here watching you?" the investigator in Abby was coming out as she weighed the facts. She didn't want Amy to run. The wanted poster was a real threat too; someone else might not listen to her story and arrest her because of it. Then Bobby Ray or probably Noah could pick her up, and there was nothing she could do.

She slowly nodded and bit her lip again. "They're both sneaky that way. They're like two peas in a pod. Toby's been acting squirrely lately, and I thought it was just a phase or somethin', but now I don' think so."

Abby proved they were on the same wave length with her next question.

"Do you think they had anything to do with the fire?" She remembered the report of a man leaving the station right before it burst into flames.

Amy thought for a moment. She didn't want to make false accusations. Then it struck her! "Noah was in the military at one time!" she gasped.

"I need to make a call," Abby said suddenly as she stood up from the couch.

"Are you going to turn me in?" Amy gasped again, suddenly feeling very vulnerable and betrayed.

"No, but I am going to have Noah looked into," Abby said authoritatively.

K'ANNE MEINEL

CHAPTER THIRTY-ONE

Amy was shocked that within two hours federal agents, not just police, but *federal* agents were at her cabin asking questions.

"Can y'all keep it down?" she kept warning as the children were in the bedroom.

"Ms. Sleuter…" one of the investigators began.

"Adams," she corrected automatically.

He nodded and glanced at Abby who was standing there in a relaxed pose, legs and arms crossed, leaning against the doorway. She was dressed casually in a button-down flannel shirt with a white muscle shirt beneath it, jeans, with her badge prominently displayed on her belt. She wore no gun holster.

"Ms. Adams," he started again, and she had to repeat what she knew of Noah, her brother Bobby Ray, and what she knew of them. Being a part of the family, she knew quite a lot. Abby heard how Landon made her continue in school although Noah thought it was foolish to educate a woman; it was how she earned her business degree. They heard how her grandparents had a place in Morgan City, Louisiana where tourists came, and that was how she learned to deal with customers.

"Now this doesn't mean we aren't going to have to arrest you," one of the officers said about two hours later. It was late, about four a.m., and it was obvious they were all tired; the officers from the long drive up The Thumb and the two women from the night of being interviewed.

Arson was bad enough, and they knew incendiary bombs had been used, but fraud and possible attempted murder were a lot to prove. Having Angel Sleuter in the wanted data base confused and complicated things. He saw out of the corner of his eye as the Chief of Police, the small-town cop, made a move. Everyone knew this was her girlfriend, and while they were trying to accord her special consideration, they might have no choice but to arrest her, for her own good.

"For now, though, we are going to ask that you don't go anywhere. I understand you thought you had to leave?" he confirmed.

"We've been over that already," she pointed out. She'd been asked each question five different ways. "You'd think you all were lawyers or somethin'," she said with a grin to show she was kidding. "But I thought I had to leave to protect my family," she said quietly. She was speaking, not in a whisper, but in a sotto-voice so that the children wouldn't wake up. They had taken their cue from her although they had offered to take her to the new police station for questioning. She'd panicked at that, sure she wouldn't see Abby again, and to calm her, agreed to talk to her at the cabin.

"We want you to go on with your life as though nothing is out of the ordinary. From what you have said, it is possible that one or both of those men are in the area to keep an eye on you. We are going to create a ping on your wanted poster but in the Green Bay area as though you've been sighted. From that, we may get them to 'hurry' up with their plans."

"And what exactly do you intend to do to protect her from those plans?" Abby asked ominously.

"Mom? What's going on?" Bailey asked as he opened the door to his room. He could see there were people in the living room.

"Go back to bed, Bailey," she ordered in a no-nonsense voice. When he hesitated, she repeated herself a little louder and more ominously. He closed the door, but she knew he didn't get back in bed.

"We're going to have to wrap this up," she announced into the living room, a little louder than before as they had all tried to keep it down and obviously failed.

"And what will you be doing for us, *Chief?*" one of the investigators challenged. He was a cocky son-of-a-bitch, and Abby had disliked him from the moment she met him. If it was up to him, and thank goodness it wasn't, Amy would have been handcuffed and taken to Green Bay before being turned over eventually to other federal officers. Meanwhile, she would be in the system, and Noah could access that system, and who knew what contacts he had.

"I'll be keeping Ms. Adams protected. In my *personal* protection," she said snidely and gave the jerk a little smile.

"I think we can be sure that the Chief will keep us in the loop. Don't forget she's a member of law enforcement, and she did call us," another of the investigators warned the younger detective. He turned to Abby. "You have my cell number," he stated.

She nodded, and they both exchanged a look that spoke volumes. Abby saw them out and asked a few more questions before they drove away. She turned back to see Amy looking worried on the front porch, rubbing the chill of the fall morning from her arms. She looked small and fragile and pale, very, very pale from the interrogation.

Walking up the steps, Abby gently put her hands on her shoulders, "It's going to be okay," she promised.

"You don't know that. You don't know Noah or Bobby Ray like I do. They get what they want," she started to work herself up.

"Let's go in the cabin and go to bed. It's late, and you aren't going to get much sleep if you want to have a normal day tomorrow," Abby pointed out, trying to console her.

"I have tomorrow off," Amy reminded her.

Abby gently steered Amy into the cabin and locked the door behind her. The cabin seemed warmer for some reason with all those people in it, and now it was cold. She put a couple of logs on the fire to hold them over until they got up and returned to walk Amy back into their bedroom.

"So, Angel huh?" she asked gently. She liked the name. She didn't like the name Sleuter though, not one bit, and perhaps it was because of the stories that Amy had told about Noah. Landon sounded nice though, and she could tell Amy loved him. That bothered her.

"Yep, but I haven't really gone by that except for Grams in a while. I was always 'Hey You' to Noah and even Bobby Ray."

"What did Landon call you?" she asked curious, as she began to get ready for bed. A few hours of sleep would be helpful at least for her.

"Landon," she smiled fondly at the memories of her husband. "He called me 'Sweetie.'"

Abby wasn't certain, but Amy's voice had changed as she remembered him. She couldn't help it, but she was jealous of this unknown husband. She hesitated for a moment as she changed, maybe she shouldn't be sleeping with a married woman.

"Did you love him?" she couldn't help asking, feeling insecure.

Amy immediately nodded. "He saved me. He made me go to school, he was patient with me, and he kept Bobby Ray away. He couldn't keep Noah away though, and I avoided him as much as I could. I think Noah got impatient, which was why he got meaner." She paused for a long moment. "He was my *best* friend," she said softly.

Abby nodded. She respected this unknown Landon for the admiration and obvious loyalty he engendered in Amy, but she had to wonder, now what?

"You'd like him," Amy continued, unaware of the thoughts swirling in Abby's head. "He is sweet, kind, and he's very wise and tender. Even when I lost the baby, he said it didn't matter. He didn't need no son. He was just happy if we remained married and friends."

Abby swallowed and watched Amy get into bed. She sat there reminiscing about her husband. He wasn't even her ex-husband. He was still alive. That meant she was legally married to him. She looked across the room at Amy.

"What happened to Lori?" she asked, wondering at the first woman her girlfriend was attracted to.

"Now that there was a real accident, and I think what really unhinged Noah. She was the little princess in that house. Everyone adored her. She was hit walkin' home one night by a drunk driver, and everyone seemed to go crazy," she remembered. "My in-laws died a year later, each within a month or so of each other...from grief," she said sadly. "I think that's when Noah began to realize he was the head of the family and the power that came with that position." She got really quiet after that for a while as she remembered how scary it had become.

"Are you coming to bed?" Amy asked, looking suddenly worried as she realized Abby was too quiet.

"I don't know if I should," she confessed. "You're married," she pointed out.

Amy smiled sadly. "It weren't like that," she told her. "Landon didn't even like doing the deed. He weren't good at it from what I can tell, and once I was pregnant, he never touched me like that again."

"How long have you been married?"

"Twelve yars now," she answered reminiscently. "I lost my baby six yars ago. That is probably why Noah were gettin' impatient."

"How long has Landon been incapacitated?" she tried to sound professional, but it was for herself. She'd heard some of this when the two investigators arrived, two others came along, but she wasn't quite sure of their function.

"Two yars before I left. He done told me to clear out. Noah was acting mighty peculiar, and I think that's when I knew that Noah had something to do with Landon's injury."

"Did he tell you how he got injured?"

Amy shook her head. "I got a call one night from the police in a neighboring town. They said they had found someone with the identification of Landon Sleuter on them, but he was beaten so bad they couldn't identify him from his license." She started to cry. "They beat him so bad. He was so beautiful, and he looked like Frankenstein then with all them stitches. He'll never walk much less be a whole man again," she said as she emphasized what she meant, gesturing downwards.

Abby hurried to get into bed with the redhead so she could wrap her arms around her. "I'm sorry, you don't have to talk about it if you don't want to," she comforted, rubbing Amy's back consolingly.

"I have to talk about it. I never could. Grams didn't understand. She just thought them Sleuters were no good. I couldn't tell her everythin'; she wouldn't understand. She wouldn't understand about Landon lovin' other men. She just knew I needed to be gone, and she and Landon made sure I had an out. One day, I just up and left. I packed my suitcase, my backpack, my new life, and left. I meandered for a while. But someone left a tourist book on a bus bench in Fort Wayne, Indiana, and I began to read about Wisconsin. Livin' on the water again appealed to me, so I took the bus up the east coast of Wisconsin, and you know the rest," she said sobbingly.

"You know you can tell me anything, don't you?" Abby said earnestly. She couldn't imagine not being able to share the burden of the things Amy had been through.

"I almost stayed in Port, Washington. It shore was purty, but I got curious about what else was up here," she said with a little smile. She inhaled, but it was unsteady as she still tried to stop her tears.

"I'm glad you did," Abby said as she looked down into the face she so adored. She sent up a silent prayer of thank you to whomever left the tourist book on the bench and set Amy on this path.

"I'm sorry I couldn't tell you anything sooner. I was too scared," she admitted.

"I suppose me being a cop didn't help things either," she guessed ruefully.

"Nope, nor with you being a woman," she added with a grin. "Landon would understand though. He wanted me just to be happy. Noah wants to own me," she added bitterly.

"I'll do my best to make sure he doesn't come near you," she promised.

"There might not be much you can do," Amy pointed out.

"We'll see about that!"

They continued on for a while until Amy drifted off to sleep in Abby's arms. Abby too drifted in and out, but any little noise had her coming awake, and by the time the kids got up for school, she slipped out of bed to leave Amy sleeping, carefully closing the bedroom door behind her.

"Isn't Amy getting up to make us breakfast?" Heather asked surprised.

"What? You can't handle me making cereal for you?" Abby teased as she let Toby out the back door. She watched interested as he sprinted for a corner back by the garage. She made a mental note to check that out later. There was nothing there now, and he snuffled at the fallen leaves.

"Can you do that without spilling the milk?" Bailey teased back as he slung his backpack on an empty chair.

Abby laughed with the kids as she distracted them from why Amy wasn't there to see them off. She quickly had three bowls of cereal and let them pour their own milk on it. She'd knocked a full gallon of milk off the table once in clumsiness, and they all hadn't let her forget it for an instant. She watched as they got on the bus to take them to school, and then she called in her deputy to take her morning shift so she could climb back into bed with Amy for some cuddling time.

CHAPTER THIRTY-TWO

Amy woke up a few days later with a gasp and tried to get her breath back. It was morning, and while they had gone with their lives, trying to remain normal, she had begun to have nightmares.

"What, what is it?" Abby asked as she too got up quickly in case she had missed some noise. She'd been sleeping light these days, especially after finding men's booted foot prints behind the garage. Someone had been there...often. He smoked Marlboro unfiltered cigarettes too from what she could see. These had been turned over to the Feds for their lab and possible DNA.

"Nightmare," she admitted as she rubbed her face. Since making a clean breast of it, they had returned. She frequently worried that Noah grabbed her, or that Bobby Ray was yelling at her, telling her she had to return to the bosom of her family. It was her obligation to give the Sleuters a child. If Landon wasn't up to the job, he was sure that Noah would do fine. Besides, Noah cared for her. She knew every argument he would use before he even uttered it. In her nightmares, they went through all of them. How dare she thwart their plans?

"We'll find them," Abby tried to reassure her, rubbing her back. The extra feds were stationed around town as locals, but the locals were uneasy, reporting these 'watchers' frequently for loitering. They stuck out like a sore thumb, and it was obvious they weren't tourists. Abby had her hands full with her regular duties much less as liaison between the feds and her citizens as well as watching out for Amy.

"If they don't want to be found, they won't be found," Amy assured her. "You don't know those backwoods like they do." No one could find either her brother or her brother-in-law who had taken a leave of absence from his job. Supposedly, the last anyone heard was they had gone hunting.

"I'm sure they can't hide out on an island the rest of their lives. What was it called, Baseman?" she tried to console her.

"Bateman Island. With all that water around it too, they can be in and out before anyone knows they are there. You got the Atchafalaya River and Sweetbay Lake as well as Bayou Schaffer and Halfway Bayou…thars plenty of places for them to hide and disappear."

Abby loved how those names rolled off Amy's tongue effortlessly. She wished she could take her worries away. The dark circles under the redhead's eyes weren't becoming to her pale white face. Her summer tan was long gone from her skin. It seemed paler these days, and with her dark red head, it made it almost glow in the pre-dawn light.

"Let's try to sleep," Abby offered as she rubbed Amy's back. She leaned over to kiss her, not trying to push it, but letting her know she was loved.

Amy hadn't felt like making love since she confessed who she really was. She enjoyed the closeness they now shared, and being held was a comfort, but the constant worry of how and when they would strike was wearing on her. To her, it wasn't a matter of *if*, but *when*. She cuddled into the closeness of Abby's long and muscled body. She felt safer with her, but what Abby didn't know is that Amy worried Noah would go after her because he was jealous. She tried not to think too much of what he could do to her. What he had done to Landon. Landon hadn't said it was Noah, but she knew, deep down she knew. What he would do if he got a hold of Abby made her daydreams a horror she wouldn't share.

Amy knew as soon as Abby entered The Emporium a couple of days later that something had happened. She had kept a cheerful face up to her customers, answering questions, but only a few knew something was going on. There was something in the air.

Abby nodded her head towards the back office.

Amy dreaded what she had to say but was relieved to see her alive and well. She excused herself and sent an employee over to help the customer as she followed the brunette to the back of the store and her office. "What's up?" she asked.

Abby looked at her sadly; she hated that she had to be the one to tell her. One of the Feds had offered, but Abby knew it was her place. "Landon is dead," she told her without any preamble.

Amy had known it wouldn't be good news, but she hadn't expected…this. She'd known he could die at any time, and then she wondered… "Was it natural or…?" she asked bravely, trying not to let Abby see how much it hurt inside. Her best friend was dead!

"We don't know yet, but there will be an autopsy," she informed her, watching her carefully.

Amy closed her eyes and shook her head. "No, there won't. The Sleuter's won't allow it. It's against their religion or somethin'," she informed her.

"Because it might be murder, there will be an autopsy," the Chief of Police informed her knowingly.

"You don't realize the power this family wields. It's why they were able to buy me to marry their queer son," she explained, trying to emphasize certain things. "I been tellin' you all, but you don't hear me!" She was exasperated. "These people don't think the laws of this ole United States apply to them!"

Abby was beginning to understand. She had a much broader view of things as Amy had repeated them and little tidbits were explained. She couldn't fathom that Amy had basically been sold for her child-bearing abilities to hide their son's queerness. That the other brother had lusted after his sister-in-law, and failing to get what he wanted and desired had possibly killed his own brother to get it. The Feds weren't too convinced of Amy's story, but they were checking into it.

"Now Noah will think the way is clear," Amy said mournfully, knowing he was coming now.

"Then we'll get him," Abby answered, convinced.

"It won't be like that. He won't do it all legal," she tried to explain.

"You are never alone. We have people watching the store; I'm home when you are home…"

"You don't think he knows all that? That's why he sent that private investigator. He probably had him tip me off to make me run so they could catch me easier. I wouldn't be surprised to find they got some trackin' device on my SUV!"

Abby didn't tell Amy that they had indeed found a tracking device on the vehicle. They also found one on Toby's collar, how they had put one on there no one would ever know, but they'd accidentally found it when they were checking out the SUV with a handheld scanner, and the curious dog came over to see what they were doing. She didn't want to frighten her, so she hadn't told her.

"Would you like to go into protective custody?" she asked, knowing she might not see her again for a long time. She'd be magnanimous about it, if it meant keeping Amy safe.

"No, I ain't gonna let them run me off again. With Landon gone, they are gonna come for me. Let 'em come!" she said defiantly.

Abby couldn't tell Amy now, but every time she displayed the little redheaded spitfire she was, she fell more in love with her. Then, thinking it was never too late to tell someone something of such importance, she pulled her into her arms. "I love you," she said simply.

"You don't want me to leave, do you?" a muffled Amy asked against her shoulder.

Abby pulled back to look down in horror at Amy. "Leave me? Hell no!" she answered vehemently. "Don't you ever leave me!" she said almost frantically as she pulled her close again. She'd lost one woman in her life, she wasn't losing another!

"I thought maybe you might want to leave 'cause I lied to you," she said, again muffled as Abby was holding her tight against her, almost too tight; it was getting hard to breathe.

Abby loosened her hold so she could look down into the redhead's face. "You lied because you had to. Just don't ever do that again, okay?" she said affectionately as she leaned her head down so they could touch foreheads.

Amy took advantage of her proximity to kiss her, hard. "I love you, do you know that?" she emphasized.

"I think I'm going to need more convincing," Abby teased. Just then, her radio went off.

"Chief?" came through the static filled device.

"Go ahead for Chief," she pushed the button, letting Amy go reluctantly.

"We got a situation down at the Brewery we need you here for," the voice came through crackly.

"Roger that, I'll be right there," Abby turned the radio down since it was so static filled. She looked at Amy, reluctant to leave her. "Are you going to be okay about Landon?" she asked, concerned.

Amy nodded. "It's not unexpected," she drawled. "I'll miss him, and I'll try to remember the good times."

Abby nodded as she leaned over for another kiss and then took her leave.

SMALL TOWN ANGEL

CHAPTER THIRTY-THREE

It did indeed snow again before Halloween. Amy stared in wonder. She loved how it coated everything, the trees, the plants, and still the dark greens peeked through against the white. It was beautiful; it was dangerous for anyone out in it. She listened as the workers finished the addition despite the winter wonderland.

The kids were helping her bake cookies in the kitchen as she wanted to gift the hard workers with freshly baked and hot cookies from her ovens. They were nearly done putting in her new kitchen, and the old one would be turned into a mud room. They had put in the new steps to the now much larger basement, and she was looking forward to exploring this extra space. Terry had promised now that the police station was finished, that his whole crew would be working on her addition shortly. The windows were in the sun room, and the new master bedroom and bathroom were almost done. She was excited to have them move into these extra spaces when they were finished.

Abby had gone into the station for work, knowing that Amy was surrounded by Terri and his additional workers. The children and she should be well-protected until she could get back. Amy was watching the workers work. It was fascinating as they put up some of the finishing touches; she hadn't realized that there were so many details that went into building. She admired their skills as they used saws, hammers, and other machinery to get the finishing touches.

"Sorry we didn't get it done in time for the first snow," Terry smiled as he adjusted his tool belt. His jeans were filled with sawdust and other things that Amy couldn't identify.

"Oh, shouldn't be much longer now?" she asked hopefully. They had plastic up to keep the dust, debris, and cold from the rest of the house; she wasn't sure the heat from the fireplace could reach this far.

"Well, I'll be jury riggin' something for the heat since the central air and that setup can't be done until next spring," he explained, reading her mind. "That's gonna take some time."

Amy nodded, everything took some time.

"Oh, and I got those sketches for the hall for you," he added.

"The hall?" she asked confused.

"Yeah, Abby said you were building a dance hall next to The Emporium and wanted me to put up some estimates. She gave me your sketches, and I made some mock ups of what I could do. That's okay, isn't it?" he frowned a little at her puzzlement.

"Oh yeah, that's perfectly fine," she stuttered as she realized what Abby had done. It had been a while since she swallowed her disappointment over expansion. Abby had promised that she would be her silent partner on the deal if she got the loan, but since she hadn't gotten the loan, Amy had dismissed the idea. It hadn't stopped her from gathering magazine pictures of details she wanted, the cupola, the pagoda, the porches, and the lattice work. The windows alone would cost an absolute fortune.

"I'll go get them," he said as he headed through the patio doors that now led out to the back yard where his truck was.

Amy looked at the sun room, anticipating many hours of sitting in the room and enjoying herself. She could well imagine reading books or the newspaper in here with Abby. She with a hot chocolate, Abby with her coffee, maybe curling up on a sofa together. She'd found a place in Sister's Bay with Abby that had some beautiful wicker furniture that would be perfect for this room.

"Ms. Adams, we're leaving for the day," one of the workers announced. "They'll be finishing that up over there," he indicated something in the new bathroom. "And Terry said he'd be right back; he forgot some papers for you."

"That's fine," she smiled. "You all do such fine work," she praised as she handed him a gaily wrapped parcel of cookies.

"Thank you. We aim to please ma'am," he said modestly as he gathered the last of his tools, and with a salute, he left; a couple of the other workers were cleaning up before they too left with parcels of cookies. The remaining two were fitting something in the bathroom, but she couldn't see what. She turned to return to the main cabin, going through the plastic that separated the two sides; it was thick plastic that hung down in layers so the cold from the addition didn't enter the warm area. At night, they could close the two French doors that led to sun room. She glanced back at the space lights that lit up the addition and saw them reflected in the windows; she also saw one of the men from the bathroom walking towards her, she gasped and twirled.

"What are you doin' here?" she asked fearfully.

"You knew I'd be comin' for you," he said. "It's time you come home with me," he said menacingly.

"Nope, I ain't gonna come with you," she said as she began to back away, but he had anticipated that and cut her off from the exit.

Amy looked fearfully through the plastic, hoping the kids, who were now watching a television program, would stay there and not come looking for her. She backed away from him, nearly tripping over a hose one of the workers had left there.

"No Noah, I ain't a goin'," she said vehemently. "I have a new life here," she said confidently. Her heart was hammering as the much bigger man came towards her, tracking her, almost like a hunter.

"Yeah, I saw the life you have here," he sneered. "You're livin' with a woman! That's immoral!" he twanged.

"What I do with my life is my business," she argued, knowing it was futile, and hoping that Terry or Abby would return soon.

"Nuh uh, the bible says it's a sin what you're doin'. As your brother in law, it's my duty to see you stay on the straight and narrow. Now with Landon gone, you're to be my wife," he bragged. She could see the bluster in him as he hitched up his belt.

"I ain't gonna be your wife," she insisted. They'd had this very same argument before. He wouldn't listen then, he wasn't listening now. "Besides, you can't marry me without my permission."

"He can, and you will," another voice was heard, and Amy turned slightly to see Bobby Ray standing there. Both were dressed as construction workers, which was how they had gotten into her home, by working for Terry. She swallowed her fear.

"No, I won't," she repeated, knowing it was futile, and feeling her fear rising, blinding her.

"You will do what you are told!" Bobby Ray insisted angrily. "Women are to cleave to their husbands," he said piously.

"My husband is dead," she insisted. "I don't have to answer to no man."

"He weren't no man," Noah said with a sneer. "And he is dead; I saw to that," he bragged.

"What did you do to him?" she asked to make conversation, afraid of the answer. She was watching both of them and saw they were trying to corner her by the stairway to the new basement, the gaping hole looming ominously behind her. She looked frantically about the room for some sort of escape. Short of screaming which would involve the children, she saw no options. They could and would take her out of here through the patio doors, and without anyone aware of where she had gone.

"Just helped him on his way and out of his pain," he said with a leer. "You shore look purty *Angel*," he said, almost drooling.

"I no longer go by that name," she informed him frostily.

"I heard," he answered, proving he had information on her.

"You shouldn't have involved Grams in that," Bobby Ray put in.

"She volunteered. She never did want me to marry into the Sleuter family," she informed him.

"What, we weren't good enough for the Adams?" Noah asked indignantly. "Always too good for us." He turned to Bobby Ray to brag, "I'll whip that outta her."

"She might need more than that!" Bobby Ray agreed wholeheartedly. He stood to make more off this marriage than he had brokering the first one. Noah had promised to match the funds that Grams had left Angel.

"I'm not goin' with either of you," she said, trying to make it clear and to delay the inevitable.

"Listen to her tryin' to talk all proper and like these northerners," Noah sneered. "You'll always be from Morgan City, Louisiana darlin' and don't you forget it!"

"I won't forget it, but I started over," she insisted. She was getting frightened; the terror was building inside. Any moment, and either of the children could walk in here to see where she was. Where was Terry? Where was Abby?

"You'll start over all right, with me," Noah promised her.

It was then that Bobby Ray lunged at her. Amy flinched away, catching the movement out of the corner of her eye. Nimbly she danced out of his reach, but he was too confident, and he flew past her into the hole that was the stairwell to the new basement. There was no railing. He tried to catch himself, but he'd been too confident and too assured of catching her; he hadn't thought of where they'd end up. He fell headlong into the basement, a slight yell that was cut off abruptly.

SMALL TOWN ANGEL

Amy used the momentary commotion to sweep up a nail gun that was lying on a step ladder near the hole in preparation for them nailing down the railing that lay in sections against the wall. She looked at the side to see the safety was on and slipped it off. "Now you stay away, Noah," she warned.

Noah, shocked at the disappearance of Bobby Ray, looked up to see the redhead pointing the nail gun at him. "Now darlin', you don't want to be doin' that, put it down," he ordered, he was certain she would listen. Women obeyed when he spoke, or they learned the consequences.

"I am not kidding," she said clearly and distinctly, concentrating on her words and not allowing her accent to come out.

"Oh, aren't we high falutin' talking like your betters," he sneered. "Now you put that down and come with me. No more of that nonsense!" He was getting angry and flushed. He took another step toward her, trying to intimidate her.

"You take one more step, and I promise you Noah, I am gonna shoot you dead," she asserted. She'd never felt such fear or anger before. She held the gun out in front of her as though it would save her.

"You don' even know if that there nail gun is loaded or on," he assured her to undermine her self-confidence. She shore looked purty with her angry green eyes; they were the deepest blue-green of the ocean. In contrast, her dark red hair made him want to run his fingers through it. He wanted her, he wanted her bad. She'd make good children with him.

"You want to take the chance? You want to find out?" She was willing to chance it, and she kept a firm hand on the trigger and her eyes on him, not taking them off for an instant or he would strike, like a snake.

"Why don't you think you are good enough for the Sleuters?" he asked suddenly, changing tactics.

For a moment Amy was surprised at the question. "You Sleuters are the ones that thought I wasn't good enough. Between your Mama and you, you treated me like dirt beneath your feet. Landon was the only one decent in that whole family!"

"But I wanted you!" he insisted, as though that explained years of abuse, the years of condescension, and sexism.

"But I didn't want you!" she returned, and that was when she heard the dog barking at something in the front of the cabin. Her momentary distraction was all he needed and he lunged. Amy's finger pulled on the trigger and shot out a five-inch nail. Her shock over actually doing it and his falling towards her caused her to pull the trigger again, and then again. That was how Noah ended up with three fatal shots of five inch nails in his chest.

Noah was shocked, and he looked down incredulously to see the three nails protruding from his chest. His hand came up to grasp at one, but it was firmly embedded in his breast plate. He had enough time to see that the last two had hit where his heart would be before the darkness began to over shadow him. He felt himself falling but was dead before he hit the floor.

Amy stood there with the nail gun in her hand. She looked at it and then at Noah in shock.

"Let me take that," Abby said gently as she took the gun from Amy's cold and limp fingers, easily setting the safety back on before releasing the air hose from the gun and putting it all on the floor. They both jumped a little as the air made a slight hissing sound as the air hose was released. She had come in the front door, and the kids told her Amy was in the addition with Terry. Not having seen Terry's truck in the driveway, she came back to see if he had shown her the plans for the hall. She'd been paid enough for the house that she wanted to make this idea of Amy's come true; she hoped she wouldn't be mad at her for giving him the sketches. Seeing the man lunging at Amy, she was just as shocked as they as the redhead shot him three times in quick order. She watched him fall to the floor, and then Amy just stand there staring down at what she had done. "Are you okay?" she asked next.

Amy looked up at her and shook her head before bursting into tears.

Abby gathered the smaller woman into her arms and held her; she was shaking uncontrollably. "Shhh, shhh," she said consolingly.

"Mom?" Bailey asked from the plastic partition. He stared, horrified at the man on the floor; the blood seeping around his body in a large pool.

"Bailey, go and dial 911. Tell them I'm on the scene, and I need an ambulance and my deputies immediately," she ordered over Amy's shoulder. She held the redhead to her chest tightly so she wouldn't look at the body. She was slowly walking Amy backwards away from the scene.

The boy nodded and turned, grabbing his sister on the way as she came to see what was going on.

"Hey," she protested angrily.

"C'mon," he insisted and forced her back into the front room.

"I don't have to," she said snottily.

"Do too," he returned quickly as he grabbed Amy's cell phone and dialed 911.

"What are you doing?" she asked; he wasn't supposed to touch the cells.

"I'm calling," he began, but someone answered, and he repeated what his mother had said.

"And who is your mother?" the operator asked.

"Chief of Police Abby Shipman," he said importantly.

In no time at all, they assured him that an ambulance was on the way. By then, Abby had Amy back in the front room and on the couch, a blanket wrapped around her as she started to shake.

"What's wrong with Amy?" Heather asked curiously.

"Shock," her mother Abby told her, not hiding anything from the young girl.

"Why does she have shock?"

"Because she had to shoot a bad man." Abby pulled the blanket tighter around the redhead.

"Why did …" Heather began, but Abby sent her a look that quelled her constant questions. Abby realized the girl was looking behind her, horrified. She turned to see a redheaded man staggering into the room, blood dripping down his head. Abby stood up to protect Amy from his view, but she saw him too when she looked up to see what caught the brunette's attention.

"Bobby Ray," she breathed as she stood up.

"You're comin' with me," he slurred out.

"No, I am not," she said very clearly and distinctly.

"No, I am not," he mimicked with a sneer and pulled out a gun and shot Abby who didn't have time to draw her own weapon. She fell to the floor at Amy's feet.

"Oh my God, look what you've done!" Amy screamed horrified.

"You're comin' with me," he slurred out again and took another step into the room; Amy can see the blood running down into his shirt.

"You're hurt, you're not thinking…"

"You're comin' with me or…" he starts to point the gun to where the children stood frozen by the table.

Amy gets the implication, loud and clear.

"Okay, okay…I'll go with you," she agrees to distract him from them. *Anything,* anything to get him out of the cabin and away from the children. She glanced down at Abby, who seems to be breathing, but she can't be certain. She looked up quickly at Bobby Ray.

He waved his gun at the front door, and she turned to head for it, dropping her blanket on Abby to keep her from his view. Perhaps he would forget about her. "Yourn gonna marry Noah Sleuter ifn it's the last thin' you do," he told her, the odd slur finally penetrating her consciousness.

Amy realized that he hadn't seen Noah on the floor in his condition. The blood streaming down his head must have kept him from noticing. He had been determined to get to her. Subliminally, she realized that Bailey had called 911. She saw the phone in his hands and wondered if they were still on the line. Heather made a move as though to go to her mother, and Amy made slicing sideways signals with her hand to stop her. Then she put up her hand in front of her to keep Bobby Ray from seeing it and made a halting gesture.

Reaching the door, she asked, "May I put on my coat?"

"Yeah, hurry up," he said trying to wipe the blood from his eyes with the back of his hand. It was stinging and making it hard to see.

Amy quickly put on her jacket, trying to stall for time. Surely the deputies would be here shortly? The Feds would have heard the call and would come running too. She wanted to stay in the cabin, but Bobby Ray thwarted that plan.

"Outside," he ordered ominously, waving the gun.

Amy couldn't take the chance, not with the children there. With one last look at the two of them, a glance for their now covered mother, she turned and opened the door. She saw a grinning and happy lab wagging its tail behind the storm door. She opened it to slip outside before the dog could come in; she didn't need Toby getting shot by her deranged brother. He'd do it too, just out of spite.

Bobby Ray had closed the space between them so she couldn't slip outside without him and was right behind her. He didn't see the lab and found himself tripping over the beast. His balance wasn't good from the blow to his head, and he found himself trying to regain it against steps that went downward. He didn't dance that well and was flung to the hard, snow filling ground. He was out cold, and the gun was flung from his senseless hand.

Amy was startled as this all occurred in an instant, and she had the sense to go down the steps and retrieve the gun so Bobby Ray couldn't have it again. She slipped the safety on and quickly ran up the steps towards Toby who was looking guilty over his imagined crime. She patted him idly as she held the door, and the two of them rushed into the cabin. Amy found both children already on the floor trying to revive their mother.

"Mom, Mommy," Bailey cried desperately as he rocked her now exposed head in his arms.

"Mommy," cried Heather pitifully.

"Let me see?" Amy asked quietly, slipping the gun into her jeans pocket discretely so the children wouldn't see it.

"No, you left her to die!" Bailey accused, trying to ward her off.

"I had no choice," she told him calmly as she pulled the rest of the blanket aside to see the wound. It looked nasty and was bleeding profusely dark blood, that meant something major. Using the corner of the blanket, she pressed it to the wound to hold in the blood that wanted to leak out.

"He made me," she explained as she tried something, anything to save Abby's life. They needed her, they all needed her.

The children stared as the life of their mother began to fade away. They all heard the sirens.

"Heather, get Toby on a leash and keep him away," Amy ordered before turning on Bailey. "Lead them in here and tell them to hurry!"

The children, feeling useless, scattered to obey her. Amy looked down at the pale face of her girlfriend. The woman who had taught her what love was all about. Not the love of a friend, like she had for Landon. Not the love of a parent like she had with her children or Amy had with Grams. But real love, between two people, regardless of their gender, the kind that she'd never experienced before. The kind of love that loves regardless of the secrets one keeps, regardless of who you are or were.

"Ma'am, we got this," someone tried to pull her away from where she was holding the blanket against Abby's midriff.

"She'll bleed out," she argued, but she was finally pulled away while the first responders did their thing.

In no time at all, the cabin was full of not only the deputies from town and the Federal Agents who had stayed to protect them, but soon others began appearing. Abby was hustled away in an ambulance, but they refused to allow Amy or the children to go.

"Did someone arrest Bobby Ray?" Amy thought to ask when they kept questioning her. They had found Noah in a pool of blood in the addition, tracks as Bobby Ray slogged through it, unknowingly creating a path to the main room of the house.

"The man on the ground outside?" someone asked her, she didn't know who, she hadn't gotten names.

"Yes, did you arrest him?" she asked, concerned that he had gotten away.

"He's dead," he stated for affect, to see her reaction. They were disappointed as she sat down on the couch in relief. Both children put their arms around her; their earlier fear that she didn't care if Abby lived or died was gone. She was the only adult that cared about them at the moment, and she put her arms around them as well and hugged them close. She was furious that these law enforcement officials wouldn't let her go with Abby to the hospital. She had to know if Abby would make it.

"What's going on here?" Terry asked from the door, holding rolled up copies of paper. He looked about curiously.

"And who are you, sir?" someone asked him officiously.

"I'm Terry Lenoir; I'm the contractor here," he offered quickly. He looked around and saw not only the bloody tracks leading into the main room, but a shaken-up Amy and the kids.

"Are you okay?" he asked her, concerned.

Amy had an idea, and she stood up giving both kids an equal squeeze on their shoulders.

"Terry, did you have two employees recently join your crew?"

He nodded. "Yeah, a redheaded guy by the name of Bill and another guy by the name of Noah, has something happened to them?" He glanced about concerned at all the officious looking people.

This confirmed the story that Amy had been trying to get across to the law enforcement officials. She'd told them what she suspected, but they still wanted to grill her five different ways to find a hole in her story, a lie. As she had lied about her past before, they were suspicious.

The questions came fast and furious from three different mouths.

"Do you have their employment applications on file?"

"Did they tell you where they were from?"

"How long have they been working for you?"

"Whoa, whoa, whoa, hang on there," Terry tried to back up, but they were on to him wanting information.

"Why don't we take this up at the police station while you wait here forensics," one of the Federal Officers stated to his partner, indicating the bloody footprints and the room at the back of the cabin.

"I am not going to the police station. I am going to the hospital. And if you don't want to arrest me and Abby Shipman's children, I suggest you get the hell outta my way," Amy told them in no uncertain terms.

"Hospital? Abby? What the hell happened here?" Terry asked wonderingly as he looked around the room.

"Those two men you hired were my brother and brother in law. They tried to kidnap me tonight, and I fought back. Abby tried to defend me, and Noah shot her. She was alive when she left here a little while ago, but these…*gentlemen*," she sneered at the term. "Wouldn't let me leave without a full questioning." She said it all clear and succinctly, barely a trace of her accent. She wouldn't let them interrupt, not this time. "You can arrest me if you want, but wait until the children have seen their mother?" she asked sarcastically as she urged the children towards the front door. Grabbing the children's jackets, she ordered, "Put these on," to the children and dared any of the officers to stop her.

"We can take a formal statement from you Ms. Sleuter..." began one of the Federal officers.

"Adams, my name is Amy Adams," she told him angrily. "When will you get that through your thick skull?" The accent was back, and he nearly winced at his mistake.

"Can I drive you, Amy?" Terry offered chivalrously.

"No thanks Terry, there is no room in your truck. I think these gentlemen will want your employment records," she finished with a hint of derision over something so trivial holding them up.

Terry acknowledged the incongruity of the request to see their employment applications, but he also knew if they were asking him questions, they wouldn't be bothering Amy, and she needed to get to the hospital. He didn't know how bad Abby was, but he was certain Amy needed to be there and not here. He nodded to her as he mentally wished her well.

"Don't let the dog or cat get out," she said as she pulled the storm door shut behind her. She ushered the children to the SUV and told them, "Get in your seat belts," before she herself got behind the wheel.

Driving erratically, she worried that the snow would impede her somehow. When she felt herself slipping on the road, she slowed down. At the next stop sign, she put the vehicle in 4-wheel drive. She didn't need an accident on top of the events of the evening. Slowing down though meant that it would take longer to get there, and she felt in her gut she didn't have the time.

The hospital was busy with other people who didn't know how to drive in this first snowfall of the season. Abby had explained it to her once; they needed one or two snowfalls before the residents were seasoned enough to drive on it and less accidents occurred. The ambulance had just pulled in again when Amy and the kids parked and hurried into the Emergency Room. The area was in chaos, from people who brought themselves in with imagined injuries, to family and friends trying to find out about those in accidents.

Amy made her way to the counter, holding tightly to Heather's hand so she wouldn't be lost in the crowd. "Abby Shipman? I'm here for Chief of Police Abby Shipman?" she asked.

"Are you family?" she was asked automatically.

Amy never hesitated, nodding she answered, trying to cover her distinctive twang, "Yes, I'm her sister, and these are her children."

"I'll see what I can find out," she was told.

Amy hadn't realized that her voice would carry as she began to recognize people from town.

"Did you say Chief was brought in? What happened to Abby? Was she in an accident?" was asked of her before she could fully turn around.

"Abby was shot," Amy told them, not telling them that the Chief had taken the bullet for her. That her own brother had shot her so that Amy would go with him willingly. Everyone in town knew something was up; the Feds weren't as discrete or unnoticeable as they thought. Everyone had known the strangers. Amy was no longer a stranger after living there a year. She could see she was, if not among friends, at least concerned citizens that knew not only Amy but certainly knew the Chief of Police, Abby Shipman. Anything she said would be texted, phoned, or otherwise spoken about. The whole town would know in a matter of hours what had happened. Abby explained about the two who had lied to Terry Lenoir on their employment applications; she figured that way Terry wouldn't lose any business or prestige from being duped. She explained that her brother and brother-in-law had come to fetch her home, that she didn't want to go, and they had gotten ornery. She didn't tell them that she had shot her brother in law or that her own brother died tripping down stairs. She left that for the rumor mill that was sure to follow.

"Ms. Shipman?" the nurse called, and Amy turned at Abby's last name. Realizing the nurse assumed she had the same last name as Abby, she went forward, both children glued to her side.

"Come with me. The Doctor will see you now," the nurse told her and opened a door that was normally kept locked between the reception area and the treatment rooms.

Amy held both children's hands now, hoping the news was good. They wouldn't want to talk to her if Abby wasn't alive, now would they? They showed her into a small waiting area, and a doctor was already there.

"Ms. Shipman?" he asked, holding out his hand.

"Adams actually," she corrected, trying not to sound so southern. "I'm Abby's sister," she repeated for the third time that evening. She knew no other person would get to see the Chief otherwise. The state wouldn't recognize a same sex partner, and they hadn't been far enough along in their relationship to have medical powers drawn up. "These are Abby's children," she said to play further on his sympathies.

"Ah, Ms. Adams, my apologies," he began, and Amy's heart sank at his tone. But he went on, "The Chief was shot, and we've had to remove part of her liver. She's bled a lot, but we think she will make a full recovery."

"You can live without part of your liver?" Amy asked, unsure.

He nodded and added, "Yes actually, you can. She was very lucky. We've removed the bullet, but as I said, she lost a lot of blood, and it will take time for her to recover from that. You can see her if you wish, but only a moment." He glanced at the children, so she understood why it was only a moment.

"That's fine," she said and nodded that she understood.

They were shown to an ICU bed where Abby lay. She was hooked up to many machines and for once looked small in a bed. She was very pale. She did not wake up from their visit, even when Heather tried to crawl up on the bed to give her a kiss.

"Easy there darlin', let's not jar the bed," Amy warned her as she looked on in horror at her girlfriend's pallor. If the doctor hadn't told her she should recover, she wouldn't have believed him. She knew they had just let the three of them see her for their own well-being. Abby was still unconscious not only from the loss of blood, but from the emergency surgery they had to perform to remove the bullet.

"We can visit your mom when she's feeling better and awake," she promised.

"She's gonna die, isn't she?" Bailey asked on the ride home. It took much longer as the roads were heavier with snow, and there didn't seem to be any snow trucks on the road plowing it away. Heather had fallen asleep already in the back seat.

"No, the doctor said she should recover," Amy responded, surprised; the boy had been right there when the doctor spoke to them.

"He didn't give you any signal or anything?" the boy asked.

"You watch too much television," she told him with a laugh. "Your mama is gonna be just fine," she hoped her words were true. There might be a host of things that could still happen to her. She crossed her mental fingers as she concentrated on the road.

"You love her, don't you?" he asked next.

Amy was feeling uncomfortable. She wasn't raised in a family that said, 'I love you,' too often. You just knew it. You didn't speak it. She knew that only the truth would satisfy the boy this time.

"Yes, I do love your mama, very much."

That calmed him somewhat, and he was silent the rest of the trip back to the cabin.

When they arrived there, all the official vehicles were gone except for one.

Amy used her key to get into the cabin where all the lights were on. It was cold inside, and she carried Heather to her bed, to put her down for the night.

"You wash up and go to bed too," she ordered Bailey who wanted to find out what they were doing in the addition.

"Can I help you?" a voice confronted her officiously from the plastic separating the addition from the rest of the cabin.

"I live here," she asserted.

"Oh, we didn't think you'd be back here tonight," he said conciliatorily.

Amy walked into the room through the plastic, shocked at the mess in the room. Not that it had been clean before with saw dust and building debris, but they'd removed the body of her brother and were now dusting everywhere for prints and still taking pictures. "Can't you finish this up? You've had hours," she complained.

"It takes as long as it takes," one of the others stated.

Amy rolled her eyes. She was tired, it was late, and she was worried about Abby. She intended to go back to the hospital as soon as she got the children off to school. They'd tried to argue they should go with her in the morning, but she told them they could go after school. Turning from the distasteful scene and the blood still staining the wood floor, she slipped through the plastic again and headed to the old master bedroom to change for bed.

The kids tried to argue again the next morning that Abby would want to see them; Amy argued that their Mom would want them to go to school and see them after school. It went back and forth, but she won as she bundled them in the SUV and headed them off to school. There was a team still investigating she could see, so she didn't bother locking the house up.

"Hey, do you think we can get back to work soon?" Terry stopped her on the road, glancing at the vehicles in her driveway.

His beat-up construction truck was belching noise, and she had to shout over it to be heard.

"Your guess is as good as mine," she rolled her eyes. "Did they question you some more?"

He nodded but glanced at the children who were avidly listening and leaning forward to see him through the driver's side window.

"Well, call me if you hear anything?" he said meaningfully and then thought to add, "How's Abby?"

"They had to remove part of her liver; did you know you can live without part of that?" she asked trying to make it sound light for the children's sake. "I'll let you know," she dismissed as she waved back towards the cabin and drove on. She arrived at the school just as the bell was ringing, and she went in with the kids so that the school would know what was going on with their Mom. They already knew, but then, that was what small towns were about.

"Oh, you are such a saint for taking care of these wee ones," the school secretary intoned, sounding slightly Irish.

"Of course, I'd take care of them," Amy assured her stoutly, curious as to what they thought but then realized she didn't really care.

Amy hurried back to the hospital, noting that the odd and freak snowstorm had finally stopped but saw several instances of where cars had to be hauled out of the ditches. She drove carefully and steadily until she was pulling into the hospital. Anxious to see if Abby was awake and begrudging the need that sent her home to sleep, she'd have stayed all night but for the children; she took the stairs instead of the elevator. Arriving slightly breathless at the room that Abby was in, she was alarmed to hear raised voices. She hesitated to enter.

"We should have been informed instead of finding out about it on the police computer," a male voice was saying accusingly.

"If I had wanted you to know, I would have had you on my list of contacts," Abby said, she sounded weak.

"But we are your family!" an exasperated woman's voice said.

"Really, and how often have you come to visit me and my kids?"

"Well, there was that unfortunate matter..." began the woman's voice.

Amy had to wonder if this was Abby's parents and figured this was her cue to make her presence known. She walked into the room and made for Abby's bed, but a man immediately grabbed her arm, halting her progression.

"This is for family only," he told her in a firm voice.

"Dad, this is my partner," Abby protested weakly from her bed.

"Oh God, not another one," he turned on the prone woman in an exasperated voice, dropping his hold on Amy's arm.

Abby didn't look put out by this at all; in fact, she smiled at Amy, pleased to see her. Amy, however, was startled at the man having laid hands on her.

"Yes, another one," Amy said in a chirpy voice. "I'm Amy Adams, and you are?"

"We are Abigail's parents," was the tight-lipped response from the woman.

"I figured," she answered in a tone that would have melted butter, only Abby saw the glint in the southern belle's eye. "Well, bless your heart," she smiled disarmingly; only Abby knew what was meant by that little phrase.

"Adams, Adams," her father stated musingly. "Aren't you the reason my daughter is here?"

Amy glanced at Abby and saw she didn't hold it against her. So, she turned to the father.

"Yes sir, and lucky for me that Abby came in when she did. I'd have been killed for shore," she drawled. "Your daughter is not only brave but a hero."

He wasn't sure how to take that. He had expected excuses or hostility, not compliments. He looked at her suspiciously as she spoke.

"How are you darlin'?" she asked Abby concernedly.

"I hurt," she grinned to show she didn't mind. She was just so grateful to see Amy alive and well, if taking a bullet for her was what it took, that was the least she could do, but it did hurt like a son of a bitch.

"I imagine so," she smiled in return, leaning down to kiss Abby on the lips. They were cold and dry. Amy pulled a tube of lip balm from her purse. "May I?" she asked before applying.

Abby enjoyed the pampering, but she could see her parents were uncomfortable by these signs of affection. She was often puzzled that she was the product of these two who never showed any fondness towards each other over the years. Then she remembered her grandparents had enjoyed each other until the end. It was something else that she and Amy had in common: grandparents who had loved them unconditionally.

"How are the kids?" she asked to make conversation, not that she didn't worry how this was affecting them. Losing one parent was bad enough...

"They are doing well. Had a fight to get them off to school, but I promised I'd bring 'em back this afternoon," she explained.

"That's good; everything work out okay? No one will tell me what happened after I passed out."

"Now, you don't worry a thing about it. Except for the mess at the cabin, I'm certain they would have told you if it was something you needed to know."

"Not you too," Abby protested weakly. She wanted details.

"I think we'll take the children with us this afternoon when we leave," Abby's mother spoke up.

"What?" Abby protested, trying to get up out of the bed angrily.

Amy stood up from where she was bending over Abby and firmly shoved her back to the bed. Much smaller than her partner, she was amazingly strong, and Abby didn't call her a spitfire for nothing. She turned to face Abby's parents.

"I think the children are fine under my care until their mother," she gestured at Abby, "can return home to care for them herself."

"Well, family should…" she tried again.

"Yes, family *should*," Amy emphasized. "Since the children don't know you, and you haven't bothered to visit them, at least in the time I have been here, they should stay in the family they *know*."

Abby's mother flushed unbecomingly. She didn't have Abby's looks, but there was something about her eyes that reminded Amy of Abby. Abby was dark like her father.

"Look Mom, I appreciate the gesture," Abby sounded almost as though she meant it. "But the kids don't know you. They are better with Amy."

"Well, if you're sure," she said, unsure herself. The children should be with family, but she never considered them her grandchildren since they weren't born to Abby. The right thing to do though…after all, Abby *had* adopted them….

"Just leave them alone, they are probably upset enough by this," Abby pointed out and glanced at Amy who was looking at her intently. "How are you holding out?"

"I'm fine," Amy responded automatically, withdrawing into the same quiet woman who didn't talk about herself, especially among strangers.

Abby understood, but it hurt a bit to see it again. She glanced at her parents, wondering why they had even come. Then she realized how it would look to others if they hadn't. She also wondered how long they would stay around since it was obvious they were both uncomfortable.

Amy turned and looked at Abby's parents. Without thinking twice, she opened her mouth, "Why don't you all come by the store later and meet the children before I bring them here to visit their Mom?"

"The store?" Mr. Shipman asked.

Amy narrowed her eyes slightly. She knew he had to have known about the store, the fire, everything by now if he was keeping an eye on his daughter. She didn't let on though. "Oh yes, I own The Emporium in Northpoint. Come on in and see what we did to your parent's store," she offered sweetly. "The children will come there after school. It will give you a chance to meet them. Perhaps another time, you can come out to the cabin, and we can all have dinner together."

Abby nearly choked at the saccharine sweetness of Amy, but at least *someone* was trying in this awkward situation.

"That would be…nice," Mrs. Shipman answered weakly, clearly put out by the genuine sound of Amy's offer.

"Well, that's settled. Y'all stop by The Emporium before you leave?" Amy asked, a genuine request for *them to* leave.

"That sounds nice," Mrs. Shipman answered, again sounding as though she wasn't sure what had just happened.

"We'll be there," Mr. Shipman answered abruptly. He realized they had been out-maneuvered by someone with much better manners than them.

Amy smiled as they made their awkward goodbyes to their daughter and left the room.

"That was very clever of you," Abby said with a grin from her hospital bed.

"*What?*" Amy asked with every bit of innocence in her tone. Then she laughed to show that she knew very well what she had done.

"How are you? Really?" Abby asked, reaching for her hand.

Amy was just thrilled that Abby was okay and going to recover. That she didn't hold any ill will over the troubles she had brought into her life was just a bonus.

"I'm fine," she repeated her earlier statement, then seeing Abby was going to be stubborn about this, she started to explain. "They wouldn't let me go with you when they took you away in the ambulance." She brushed back a stray hair on Abby's forehead affectionately. "You looked so pale. The kids were upset, and they questioned me for too long," she complained. "I didn't know much except for what had happened. They were looking for something more than I could give them."

"That's because we had to make sure you were telling the truth," a voice said from the doorway, and Federal Agent Brad Pine came into the room.

"Great, now I get to be grilled by you?" Abby complained. She hoped they would get done soon; she was exhausted by her parent's visit.

"Just a few questions, if you two don't mind?" he asked, but it sounded rhetorical.

They both shrugged as he began to verify the facts of the previous evening, from Amy being left with the 'workmen' who turned out to be her brother and brother-in-law, how her brother lunged at her and fell down the hole, and how she shot her brother-in-law with the nail gun.

"Good shot by the way," the agent said off the record before continuing. "Did you think your brother was dead in the basement?" he asked as he consulted his notes.

"I just heard the sound of him landing. I didn't look," she told him; her hand was grasping Abby's almost painfully going over this again. She'd done it several times in her mind over the time since then. She hated reliving it.

He consulted his notes again. "They think he broke his neck with the fall," he commented idly to see her reaction.

"Then how was he able to climb the steps and shoot Abby?" she asked, feeling like they were trying to trip her up.

"It was a crack; tripping over the dog and down the front steps finished him," he informed her and looked up to see her anguish over it. She seemed genuinely upset, and that told him far more than her statements the night before. She wasn't a killer; they weren't going to charge her for killing anyone, not even with a nail gun. It had clearly been self-defense, and they would tell a judge this so no charges would be brought against her. He went on to apologize for the mess at the cabin and informed her a cleaning crew would be brought in before they would allow Terry back in to finish up the work on the addition. By the time he left, Abby and Amy both were exhausted.

"I'm going to let you get some sleep," Amy excused herself soon afterwards.

"I don't want you to go," Abby said selfishly. She knew how exhausted she was though and yawned mightily. "I'm sorry this happened," she said as she began to drift off.

"I'm grateful you were there and are here," Amy said gently.

CHAPTER THIRTY-FOUR

The whole town practically visited Abby during the length of her stay. The Shipmans stayed overnight at Sarah Katzenburger's inn, The Duck and Swan. Apparently, almost losing their own daughter had awoken some parental feelings, and they did want to know their adopted grandchildren better. Abby was certain it was the guilt trips that Amy heaped on them under the guise of being sweet and innocent.

Abby was at first resentful of the intrusion of her parents in her life, but as Amy pulled a guilt-trip on her too, she realized that they were her only parents and wouldn't be around forever. Besides, they lived far enough away that they would never be intrusive. Her father even seemed to resign himself that she would always love women, and Amy wasn't too bad a choice in that.

Abby wasn't too thrilled that the town, her parents, and especially Amy were firm about her recovery. She wasn't allowed to do anything and was on leave from the police force, small as it was. Amy made her sit on the porch outside the store, wrapped up in blankets when it got cold, and then made her sit inside near the fire when she felt she got enough fresh air. The pampering was sweet and genuine. Abby marveled at how much she was willing to put up with from this little redhead who bossed her and others around her so effortlessly.

Amy was not happy to have the lawyer from Louisiana show up on her doorstep, but as the sole heir to both the Adams and Sleuter fortunes, he had a mound of paperwork to go through. At first, she was tempted to donate it all, but cooler heads, including Amy's own, prevailed. She realized what she could do with the money.

"You know I wanted to help pay for the building of the dance hall," Abby admonished her after she saw Terry starting to lay out the concrete base. It was too shallow to dig a basement in this area of the point, and they were lucky to even have a small basement for The Emporium.

"I know, but I have this need to prove myself," she explained, hoping she hadn't hurt Abby's feelings.

"You realize people will think I made you pay for it yourself?"

"Not at all, I'm hoping they will see my vision, and besides, you are my partner in this since you wouldn't take any money for the lot," she pointed out.

"Partner, eh?" Abby asked; they had both thrown that word out a few times, testing it out.

Amy turned from watching out the window of The Emporium where Terry and his crew were laying out lines for a concrete pour. It was too cold really, but they would have a break before winter poured down the tons of snow and cold that the Farmer's Almanac predicted this year.

"Yes, you are my partner and someday, when it's legal here, maybe my wife?" she asked softly.

"Are you sure?" Abby asked incredulously.

Amy moved into her arms. "I was sure when you didn't leave me for lying by omission. I was sure when you took a bullet for me. I was sure when I realized you loved me as much as I love you."

Holding her tightly, despite the possible audience in The Emporium, pleased with what she had just heard, Abby smiled down at her and said, "We can make it legal without the state approving."

Amy smiled but shook her head. "I'm in no hurry; I'm not going anywhere."

"No, no you're not. You're mine," Abby said, her arms convulsing to hold her tighter.

"Yours eh?" Amy smiled up at the taller woman.

"You're my Angel."

~FINISH~

∽ About the Author ∾

K'Anne Meinel is the BEST-SELLING author of LAWYERED, REPRESENTED, SAPPHIC SURFER, DOCTORED, VEIL OF SILENCE, and VETTED as well as several other books including her first, SHIPS which was written in 2003 over the course of two weeks. A gypsy at heart, she has lived in many locations and plans to continue roaming. Videos of several of her books are available on YouTube outlining some of the locations of her books and telling a little bit more...giving the readers insight into her mind as she created these wonderful stories. As of this date she has more than 88 published works including shorts, novellas, and novels. She is an American author born in Milwaukee, Wisconsin and raised in Oconomowoc. Upon early graduation from high school she went to a private college in Milwaukee and then moved to California for seventeen years before returning to the state. Many of her stories have Wisconsin in them as settings for her wonderful, realistic, and detailed backgrounds. Named the lesbian Danielle Steel of her time, K'Anne continues to write interesting stories in a variety of genres in both the lesbian and mainstream fiction categories. Her website is www.kannemeinel.com.

If you have enjoyed *SMALL TOWN ANGEL* you'll look forward to a sample of K'Anne Meinels splendid and unforgettable novel:

In print and E-book and available at fine retailers.
Two different covers, same GREAT story!

Don't judge a book by its cover! Nothing, and no one, is EVER what they seem.

Ellen Christenson escapes from an abusive life, but does one ever escape the scars that are left on their soul? One must move on, one must try. But life has a tendency to circle back to what one once knew and one finds that her life choices bring her back to the scenes of her abuse to deal with it finally and fully, in ways she had never thought she would. It is then that the healing can begin, as she repairs her soul and the people she has devastated along the way.

Ellen hadn't intended to end up in Silicon Valley and its high-tech

world, but due to life and its circumstances she finds herself the head of a startup tech company. Cool, calculating, efficient – she shows the world a side of her that she doesn't have, and few if any know the real Ellen. Nearby San Francisco provides her with plenty of girlfriends. That elusive one, that soul mate, she has a hard time recognizing due to the scars within.

For years, she has lived with her decision of letting someone die for their sins, and Ellen is blown away by the feelings and emotions she has bottled up for so long....

❧ CHAPTER ONE ❧

REMEMBRANCES

She stared at the ruins of a once beautiful farm house. Memories came, flashing back in an instant yet spanning years. There once stood a beautiful pair of oak trees with a swing between them for her to play on. She could still hear the echoes of her mother telling her to be careful as she climbed them. Skinned knees and scraped palms; she never complained about the slivers her mother had to remove because of her tomboyish activities. The shade of those oak trees provided her with endless hours of escape from the relentless sun but still she would burn from it. The wind would part the leaves and beams of sunlight would beat down between them, making her red hair shimmer. Her imagination could play for hours as she gazed up through them, envisioning them as towering giants and she a mere mortal. She loved those trees.

"I can't believe you climb like a monkey, and in a dress, too!" her mother would scold. She remembered that fondly – the inflections – the lilt in her mother's voice was still in her consciousness despite the span of years.

The house still tilted haphazardly. Weather and time hadn't pulled it to the ground and for this she was surprised as she stared at its sturdy build. Her great-grandparents had been among the first to build in this area and had used good wood and stone to construct their sturdy home. Their son and granddaughter had both raised families in this house. She scowled as she remembered she had been the last raised in this house.

It looked well picked over. The weeds around the place were elbow high and although she hadn't seen it in over twenty years, she couldn't help but wonder why it hadn't yet been torn down, which was why she was now there.

"Ms. Avril?" a voice asked her respectfully. She started in surprise as she hadn't heard anyone approach. The man who had spoken began to apologize. "Oh, I'm sorry miss, I was expecting…."

"It's okay, you just startled me," she said in precise and clear tones without a hint of the accent that was unique to this part of the country and that was so apparent in his voice. That accent brought back other memories, ones she had tried to quash and couldn't. Ones that she'd known needed exorcising, which could only be done by coming here. It was why she had come. She needed to stop the dreams that had returned. Her feeling was that they were in the past and they should remain there. Her psyche, though, was haunting her and she had to face it one last time.

"I was expecting Ms. Avril," he began again, peering at her intently and wondering who she was. He was shorter than she, his skin brown from the winds that blew there, and he was stooped from a lifetime of work.

She smiled, not realizing the beauty that was apparent in her face. Her pale white skin hid the freckles that came out in the sun, but no tan touched her creamy milk-white skin anymore. "I'm A…Avril," she answered, hesitating over the name for only a millisecond. '*Or, I was,*' she mentally corrected herself, but not aloud, as he wouldn't understand.

"You're Ms. Avril?" he asked, puzzled. He peered at her for a long time while shaking his head, trying to see some semblance of the youth he had known. As her smile faded, he saw a glimmer of recognition. Not of her but of her mother and that was when he took on a relieved look. His hat came off his head in an instant and his weathered face wreathed a smile showing several missing teeth. "Why, Ms. Avril, you've all growed up!" he drawled, pleased at his discovery.

"How are you, Mr. Davidson?" she asked pleasantly. The smile didn't quite reach her eyes, though. Not with the memories pushing at

her temples begging her to remember, to relive them, and she tried hard once again to suppress them.

"Poorly," he said honestly. "Right poorly, but I aim to do the job you is needing done. I shorely do. Just like I promised." He gestured to the truck that was parked at the end of the drive. On the trailer attached to it sat a front-end loader, securely chained to its bed.

She glanced at it, then back at the house he had come to demolish. It was the town's attempt at getting rid of an 'eyesore' that had sat there empty for over two decades. Why they had decided that it needed to be done now, she didn't know. But she was there, as requested, to get it done. Mr. Davidson had answered her call and was surprised that she remembered him. He was eager to earn the money she had promised him for the job.

"Do you want to go through the house to look for anything?" he asked, as he noticed her silently staring at it.

She shook her head. She had done her picking long ago, her few belongings in some measly boxes and trunks. There had been a storage unit she had gone through as well with a lifetime of memories and knickknacks that meant nothing to anyone but herself. "Just bulldoze it," she said shortly. She wanted it taken care of so she could leave.

"You'll have to move your car," he mentioned as they turned to head back down the driveway.

She glanced at her Maserati and nearly laughed aloud at the contrast between it and his old rusted out Chevy. She hadn't thought of that when she decided to drive back here. If she hadn't before, she would surely stick out like a sore thumb now. Another reason to get the job finished and get out, get gone. Something she had done years ago and not looked back. She glanced over at the barns and silos. They still looked as solid as the day her great-grandparents and grandparents had built them. Nothing had touched them, not time, nor weather, and they seemed to be as strong and steady as the day they were built. They could use a little paint, but with the weather that came through this part of the country it was amazing they were still standing. She could see they were used well by the tracks that led from the path up to them and down the driveway, but that was all. Everything else – the chicken coop and a few other outbuildings – was abandoned. The grass was overgrown and obviously untrodden with no animals or people to grind it under their heels.

"Can you tear down those, too?" she asked as she gestured to the outbuildings.

"Ahyup," he grunted as they reached her car. She automatically pressed the button on her keychain to open the door and let her in. He glanced at the car as the door opened quietly on its own for her. It was expensive enough to pay a couple of years' salary for someone like him and for most folks around here. It was none of his business, though, so he hurried over to the trailer where another man stood, awaiting orders. "Let's get her down," he gestured, and they immediately began removing the chains holding the machine to the bed of the trailer.

The younger man kept watch out of the corner of his eye as the redhead steered the expensive sports car onto the road. She parked it opposite the driveway so they could drive the front-end loader onto the property. She was definitely worth a second *and* third look and he wondered if she remembered him as she watched his uncle maneuver the heavy machine off the trailer. She caught him staring as she got out of the car and he felt his cheeks redden. He hurried after his uncle to collect any boards worth salvaging and hoped she hadn't noticed. She had said they could take whatever they wanted.

She followed along slowly and looked down at her Prada shoes knowing she should have dressed down for the farm, but after twenty years she had nothing appropriate to wear in such a place. She hadn't thought about it as the miles passed and she had headed for this part of Oklahoma.

❖ CHAPTER TWO ❖

THE ESCAPE

She remembered the reverse trip vividly. She had run away as fast as the bus could take her. Was she running away from her past or running to her future? She didn't know, but to her, getting away from South Oklahoma had seemed like the best thing to do. Her bags were packed and Mrs. Davidson had agreed to send on the few boxes and trunks when she was settled.

"All set?" Sheriff Worley asked as he gave her a lift to the bus stop.

"Yep," she answered. She was frightened out of her mind but she knew she had no choice but to go. She had to leave it all behind her. Leave the memories, the only home she'd ever known, the problems, and let time fade it all.

He glanced at the young girl; he could see how scared she was. He knew he would be at her age. She was just a week over eighteen and had signed all the papers renting out the farm to the co-op. It would be used as they saw fit by farmers who wanted to use the land and the sturdy barns and silos that still stood on the property. He didn't blame her for leaving, as there was nothing left. It wasn't a good time to sell. It never was, not in this economy. Farming was a gamble at the best of times, and this wasn't the best of them. She had lost in so many ways and leaving was about the only option. Maybe some time away would do her good. Some of the boys who went off to school returned a little wiser, some didn't last, and few stayed away for good. He was sure he'd see her back. Small town girls were worse than small town boys for wanting to return to what was familiar, what they knew. There were a few boys around her age and a little older who would gladly marry her. She might be scrawny but she had the farm and that would draw them like bees to honey.

He didn't know her, though. Avril Christenson might have died that day a couple of weeks back, instead of her father. At least in her own mind she had. Not that day, but the week before. They said lightning couldn't strike twice in the same place. They were wrong. Tornadoes did it, and lightening did it too. This time, though, the tornado had taken her life in this world and left her with the shell of the person that was escaping on a bus. Everyone thought her grief was over her father, but it wasn't. It was for the young woman who had been caught in her Chevy truck the week before. The woman had been her best friend and allowed Avril to be brave in the face of a dismal future. She was the one who had given Avril hope. She tried not to remember how much she had loved her best friend, how much they had planned, how much she had wanted to....

"Here we are, now you want some help buying your ticket?" the sheriff offered helpfully, as he would have any young woman.

"No thank you, Sheriff Worley, I've got it," she said in a flippant, teenage way. She threw her red hair back over her shoulder, her freckles standing out in relief against her tanned face with the sun making them seem unending. "Thank you for the ride," she remembered to say politely, as her mother would have wanted her to.

"No problem. Now you take care, ya' hear?" he spoke in return and watched as she gathered her backpack and two duffels before heading into the office that doubled as a bus stop and cafe. He watched through the door and looked around to see if any undesirables were loafing about. He didn't want this young girl hassled. He would have treated her as a daughter, as any young thing in this area would be treated. Poor young thing to lose her best friend and father within a week of each other, and have to graduate high school all alone with no relatives or close friends to see her off. Mrs. Davidson had been kind enough to take her in these last few weeks until she graduated, but other than that,

Avril Christenson was on her own. Maybe she was better off. That best friend of hers had been nothing but a troublemaker since she was born, with unnatural leanings from what he had observed. He had never caught her at anything, but a person knew about such things. He thought her interest in the young Avril a tragedy in the making. It had only been a matter of time until she corrupted that innocent child. Maybe God had taken her for that reason, to prevent it. That poor child, with a father like Owen Christenson to have been left with nothing like that. It was best that she leave, at least for now.

Avril knew the Sheriff was watching her. He couldn't help himself, nosy bugger that he was. She bought a one-way ticket to California, and when the clerk asked if she wanted the return ticket, she declined. The clerk had graduated from the same high school the year before and couldn't blame her for leaving and not coming back; she wished she could do it. She knew who Avril Christenson was. Everyone knew. The tragedy had been all over Oakley. Losing her father like that, the poor child, and right before graduation and her eighteenth birthday was such a loss. The clerk watched her as she sat down on one of the benches for the bus that was due at any time. Avril looked out and saw the sheriff's car was still there, waiting to see if she got on the bus so that his 'obligation' to the citizens of this small town was discharged. She suspected he was afraid she would stay and expose him for the lecherous fool he was, a drinking buddy of her fathers, who hadn't protected her from his abuse. The many scars on her soul she laid firmly at her father's feet, but that man outside waiting in the sheriff's car could have prevented some of them after her mother's death.

It wasn't her fault that her mother had been 'poorly' after giving birth to a 'girl child' instead of the much-anticipated son and heir. She couldn't have any more children and the blame had been placed solely on Avril, as she had been told over and over throughout her life. Her mother tried to make up for it by shielding her from her father's abuse while she was alive, but he wore her down. He killed her slowly and surely until the shell of the woman blew away in the Oklahoma winds. Her death had been laid firmly at the young Avril's feet, and she was made to feel the abuse that her mother had shielded her from for so long. She was to take over all the duties of running a household. At ten, this was too much for any child. Farm work is tough on a woman at any given time but as a child with no one to teach her, she faltered at every turn. Only her friendship with Ellie had given her hope. Ellie implanted a fierce courage that gave her a will and strength to survive to escape her father's tyranny.

She learned to do her chores quickly and if not perfectly, to hide the flaws so that she would have time to meet Ellie out on the prairie and escape her father's notice for a few minutes every day. She shared all her girlhood dreams with the older girl. With four years separating them, Ellie seemed worldly and wise. She understood what was happening to the smaller, younger girl without being told. She saw the bruises and scratches from the belt she had been given for not finishing her 'work' in a timely manner or not meeting her father's expectations. Many times, his rage was fueled by liquor and he had no idea of his strength as he yelled at the youngster.

Avril put aside her memories for a moment as she watched the bus come in and one person get off. It looked bigger than the school bus she had ridden for nine years. She bravely got up from the bench and gathered her things, her most cherished possessions, in two bags and a backpack. The rest lay in storage at the Davidsons'. For how long she didn't know, but it couldn't be long as they were charging her for keeping it there. It was their way of profiting from having to 'keep' the minor and not getting enough out of the deal as she had turned eighteen this past week. Had she not been so close to turning eighteen, they would have been appointed her guardians and stolen every dime from her parent's small estate. She slowly approached the bus with her ticket in hand and the driver leapt off to assist her.

"Two bags, miss?" he asked respectfully as he opened the massive storage container underneath the bus. She nodded as he took one bag and gently put it inside the bin before reaching for her second one. He closed the doors behind them. She must have looked worried since he said, "They'll be safe in there." She nodded with a tremulous smile.

"Ticket please?" he asked, and she hesitated to head for the door of the bus. She handed it to him as she adjusted her overly full backpack on her shoulder. He looked it over, surprised to see the destination, and handed it back to her. "You first," he said politely while indicating towards the stairwell. With a last look over her shoulder at the station and the sheriff car sitting there, she went up the stairs and looked for an empty seat, one where she could watch the container if it were opened up again. All her things were in those bags and she couldn't afford to have them stolen. Sitting down, she put her backpack on the empty seat beside her to discourage anyone from sitting there. She glanced

around, taking care not to make eye contact with anyone, and noticed the bus was almost empty. A few people in the back seemed to be traveling together, but most were sitting by themselves like she was. She was close enough to the front to watch for her stuff, and close enough to the driver in case anyone wanted to start something. She watched as he closed the door, sat down, and strapped himself in. She looked for seat belts, but there were none, just like on the school bus. She had often wondered at that. The bus driver had once explained that in the event of an accident, it was so the driver could get the kids out easier. She hoped a bus this large didn't get into accidents. As it pulled away from the depot, she saw the sheriff's car pulling away in the opposite direction with a small cloud of dust blowing up from the tires. She guessed she was no longer Sheriff Worley's concern.

At first, she watched the familiar landscape go by as the bus picked up speed and headed for the interstate. It would take a while as there were several small towns such as hers where it would have to stop. Sometimes, someone would get on, but not always. Sometimes it was a total waste of time. They had to stop, though, from what she could see. The landscape gradually began to change, and once they were on the interstate it went by rapidly. She gulped. She had never been this far from home and she knew she had to be brave. A lot would change and there was no going back. The hands of fate had been turning for weeks now and she would be brave. She was going on. Ellie would have wanted her to for both of them.

That was the day Avril began to go by her middle name Ellen. To honor her mother who had also been named Ellen, and it was close enough to "Ellie" that it would honor her as well. She gulped, remembering Ellie's sweet face and the plans they had made together. They had just been waiting for her to graduate high school and turn eighteen. They had *so many* plans. Ellie had saved up enough for both of them to start over somewhere else by working at the gas station. The two of them against the world. They had been ready; they were just waiting for the right time.

Her father must have sensed she was getting ready to leave. His drinking had never been worse and his abuse had only increased. He felt he owned her. She was *his* child and she had to do what *he* said. His sense of ownership was truly distorted. Though her eighteenth birthday must have bothered him as it came closer, and he started getting meaner, if that were possible. He didn't approve of Ellie May

Fredericks or her family – those 'white trash' Fredericks that lived in the mobile home trailer park. They were *better* than anyone living in a trailer park. He had told Ellen often enough to stay away from *her*. The rumors about that girl were positively unnatural. He had laughed when he heard that the tornado had ripped through the trailer park where the Fredericks lived and killed not only Ellie, but many other 'white trash' families. He thought he was better than anyone living in "tornado magnets" as he called mobile homes. He owned a home, he had a farm, and according to himself he was better than anyone in that part of their small town.

Avril had been the one to identify Ellie when the body was found along with her truck. Only her short yet beautiful honey blonde hair with its shaved sides and the designs scored in them gave her away. Avril had run her fingers through it just the night before. Ellie had been caught in the tornado, pulling into the park just as the storm hit. She never had a chance to run to the bunker for residents that was in the center of the park. The terror that she must have felt when the twister sucked up her Chevy must have been horrifying, and her face, now at peace, still had remnants of the dirt and debris that had embedded itself under her skin. The rescue workers that had found her hadn't bothered to clean her up, and Avril had been hard pressed not to throw up at the sight of her beloved best friend mangled by what nature had done to her. She left the 'temporary' morgue after identifying Ellie and headed right for the mobile home park. The mobile home that Ellie had lived in was off its blocks and on its side, but she crawled in anyway, taking one look around to check if anyone had seen her. She knew scavengers would be arrested, but the cleanup crew would be through if she didn't get to Ellie's things first.

She crawled through the debris to find the 'safe place' that Ellie used to hide her money and most treasured things. She found the box after a long search through all the jumble. She was relieved to find the rolls of bills and the various trinkets in the box, and she cried when she found the engagement ring she had known Ellie wanted to give her, but was waiting until she was 'legal.' She looked around the room and took a sweatshirt she found, but other than that she left everything as it was and crawled out of the trailer. She was just in time, and she took off when she noticed the other scavengers coming into the park who would be looking for anything they could find and sell. Though they were supposedly looking for bodies, any money or jewelry 'found'

would disappear. She hid the box among her own things, hoping to keep it from being discovered by her father.

Owen Christenson didn't care about anything but what he could find in the bottom of a gin bottle. If his friends distilled something a little more than one hundred percent proof, well, that was fine by him, too. When he saw her after the death of her best friend, he laughed and told her she was better off without that 'trailer trash' and now she could go find a 'real man.' He even offered to find her one. She shuddered in distaste, but knew better than to answer. Around her father she was shy, quiet, and respectful, and she attempted to remain as invisible as possible. She kept his house as much as she could and waited for the day when she could leave. She had promised her mother that she would graduate high school, something her mother herself hadn't had the advantage of and regretted her whole life. She wanted to keep from his notice, and the idea of his 'friends,' who looked at her with barely disguised lust, made her disgusted. For years, lecherous hands had reached out to her as she fetched beer for them. He never stopped them and never defended her. She had learned to avoid them, for if she ever complained or spilled the beer, her father would berate her. Words were almost worse than the physical beatings, as he harangued her for 'fun' in front of those friends, much to their mutual amusement. Egged on by their silent appreciation of his abuse, he continued his particular style of child rearing.

She watched the telephone poles loop up and down as the sun went down and she headed into it. She was heading west – far, far away from the devastation of the two tornadoes that had hit this section of Oklahoma in one week's time. Ellen couldn't help but wonder if her father would still be alive if she had woken him when she heard the tornado sirens go off. They had been loud and clear across the prairie, miles from her bedroom. They woke her and she headed to the stairs for shelter. He had been asleep on the couch wearing his wife beater shirt, appropriately named since he had always worn such disgusting things while beating not only his wife, but his daughter as well. He was snoring loudly and she briefly debated waking him, knowing she would be backhanded for bothering him, but also knowing that the sirens were going loud and clear and that they should head for the shelter her grandparents had built. He drooled in his sleep, and his hand came up to rub his crotch before traveling up to rub his nose. She shuddered in disgust at the sight. The sirens grew louder and then fainter, and she realized that they must be spinning around. It was their next circuit that decided it for her, and she headed to the shelter, alone.

It was difficult for her small frame to open the heavy steel door. The wind was blowing so hard she nearly lost her footing as she struggled. She could see the vent spinning around on top of the storm shelter to let in some air to the close quarters. The door was built tough, but she managed to pry it open. The wind caught at it, before she was pulling it shut behind her and bolted it. She was in absolute darkness and she reached for the flashlight kept on the shelf. Something soft brushed against her hand and she didn't know if was a spider web, a mouse, or something more sinister. She squealed in fright at the sensation but determinedly felt for the flashlight through the eternal blackness surrounding her. She wouldn't go down the steps without seeing where she was going. It was a black pit, a void, an absence of any light, and she was frightened. The steel door had shut out the roar of the wind, but the absence of any sound frightened her further. Finally, she found the flashlight. She quickly pulled it to herself and flicked it on. The batteries were old and unused and the beam was feeble. She cursed in her head but stayed silent in case someone could hear her and berate her for her naughty mouth. She shone the flickering beam around and saw another flashlight on the shelf. This one was also weak and unused, but between the two flashlights she felt better. She saw a lantern deeper in the shelter and headed carefully down a set of stairs. The sound of debris hitting the door frightened her and she wondered how long she would have to stay down there. She toyed with the idea of going back up to get her father. Remembering how he had laughed at Ellie's death and taken pleasure in devastation on his young daughter's face, she firmly decided that he was on his own. He would punish her in countless ways later, but it was a price she knew she had to pay.

She retrieved the lantern and lit it, noticing that it provided much more light than the weak flashlights. The wind could be heard around the steel door and a little gray through the small window in the door, but nothing she could see beyond an absence of black through it. She looked around the storm cellar. Her grandparents and even her mother had stored things in here, but her father never did. He didn't even use it, only swore that he had to cut around it in the backyard with the lawn mower.

Occasionally she jumped as something fell against the door; she could sense the power of the wind. Suddenly, she remembered she had forgotten Ellie's box in her hiding place. It was all she had, but she'd carelessly left it back in the house. She got up for a moment with the intention of heading back to retrieve it, but a loud crash outside made her halt in her tracks.

~End Sample Chapter of BLOWN AWAY~
For more go to www.Shadoepublishing.com to purchase
the complete book or for many other delightful offerings.

 ~ *Because a publisher should stand behind their authors*~

 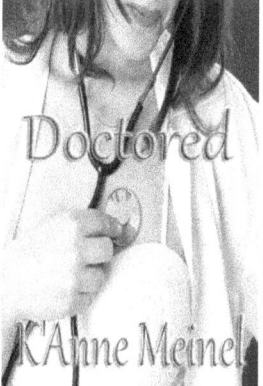 

www.shadoepublishing.com

~ Because a publisher should stand behind their authors~

What do you do when you meet someone who changes everything you know about love and passion?

Paige Harlow is a good girl. She's always known where she was going in life: top grades, an ivy league school, a medical degree, regular church attendance, and a happy marriage to a man. Falling in love with her gorgeous roommate and best friend Alyssa Torres is no small crisis. Alyssa is chasing demons of her own, a medical condition that makes her an outcast and a family dysfunctional to the point of disintegration make her a questionable choice for any stable relationship. But Paige's heart is no longer her own. She must now battle the prejudices of her family, friends, and church and come to peace with her new sexuality before she can hope to win the affections of the woman of her dreams. But will love be enough?

www.shadoepublishing.com

As I watch the wormhole start to close, I make one last desperate plea..."Please? Please don't make me do this?" I whisper.
"You're almost out of time, Lily. Please, just let go?"
I look down at the control panel. I know what I have to do.

Lilith Madison is captain of the Phoenix, a spaceship filled with an elite crew and travelling through the Delta Gamma Quadrant. Their mission is mankind's last hope for survival.

But there is a killer on board. One who kills without leaving a trace and seems intent on making sure their mission fails. With the ship falling apart and her crew being ruthlessly picked off one by one, Lilith must choose who to trust while tracking down the killer before it's too late.

"A suspenseful...exciting...thrilling whodunit adventure in space...discover the shocking truth about what's really happening on the Phoenix" (Clarion)

~ Because a publisher should stand behind their authors~

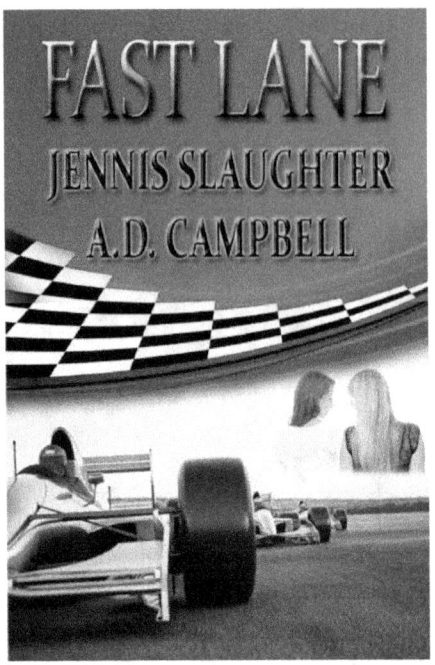

 In the male dominated sport of Formula 1 racing, Samantha 'Sam' Dupree is struggling to make her mark against the boys. She hears about a driver who is making a name for herself in NASCAR and goes to check her out. Little does she know that she's in for the race of her heart.

 Addison McCloud wants nothing more than to drive. She doesn't care about fame or fortune; she just wants to be fast enough to get herself and her family away from her abusive father. Meeting Sam, changes her world and revs her life into overdrive.

 When the two women meet, sparks flies like the race cars that they drive. Will they be able to steer their relationship into something more and win the race, or will their families make them crash and burn. The boys of Formula 1 are going to learn that Southern girls are a force to be reckoned with.

www.shadoepublishing.com

Carrie flees from the demons of her present, trying to protect the ones she loves.

Frankie hides from the demons of her past, and the memory of loved ones she failed to protect.

A modern day princess thrown to the wolves, Carrie's only hope is the rancher who had spent the better part of a decade in self imposed, near total, isolation. Frankie's history of losing those she tries to save haunts her, but this madman threatens her home, her livestock, her sanctuary. She knows she can't do it alone, has she still got enough support from her oldest friends?

www.shadoepublishing.com

~ Because a publisher should stand behind their authors~

Amelia Gittens had the credit of being the first and only woman thus far in the United States military of being a sniper in combat, made possible by being in the Military Police unit of the crack 10th Mountain Infantry Division. After retirement she joins the City of New York Police Department, and suddenly finds herself involved in a suspect shooting incident which soon encroaches upon her entire life. In order to protect her therapist who has been targeted as a revenge killing, Amelia takes on the responsibility as if she was still in the Army, treating it as a tactical maneuver.

~ Because a publisher should stand behind their authors~

When U.S. Marine Dakota McKnight returned home from her third tour in Operation Iraqi Freedom, she carried more baggage than the gear and dress blues she had deployed with. A vicious rocket-propelled grenade attack on her base left her best friend dead and Dakota physically and emotionally wounded. The marine who once carried herself with purpose and confidence, has returned broken and haunted by the horrors of war. When she returns to the civilian world, life is not easy, but with the help of her therapist, Janie, she is barely managing to hold her life together...then she meets Beth.

Beth Kendrick is an American history college professor. She is as straight-laced as they come, until Dakota enters her life, that is. Will her children understand what she is going through? Will she take a chance on the broken marine or decide to wait for the perfect someone to come along?

Time is on your side, they say, unless there is a dark, sinister evil at work. Is their love strong enough to hold these two people together? Will the love of a good woman help Dakota find the path to recovery? Or is she doomed to a life of inner turmoil and destruction that knows no end?

If you have enjoyed this book and the others listed here Shadoe Publishing is always looking for first, second, or third time authors. Please check out our website @
www.shadoepublishing.com
For information or to contact us @
shadoepublishing@gmail.com.

We may be able to help you bring your dreams of becoming a published author to life.